Praise for *New York Times* bestselling author Diana Palmer

"Palmer proves that love and passion can be found even in the most dangerous situations."
—*Publishers Weekly* on *Untamed*

"You just can't do better than a Diana Palmer story to make your heart lighter and smile brighter."
—*Fresh Fiction* on *Wyoming Rugged*

"Diana Palmer is a mesmerizing storyteller who captures the essence of what a romance should be."
—*Affaire de Coeur*

"The popular Palmer has penned another winning novel, a perfect blend of romance and suspense."
—*Booklist* on *Lawman*

"Diana Palmer's characters leap off the page. She captures their emotions and scars beautifully and makes them come alive for readers."
—*RT Book Reviews* on *Lawless*

Dear Reader,

I can't believe that it has been thirty years since my first Long, Tall Texan book, *Calhoun*, debuted! The series was suggested by my former editor, Tara Gavin, who asked if I might like to set stories in a fictional town of my own design. Would I! And the rest is history.

As the years went by, I found more and more sexy ranchers and cowboys to add to the collection. My readers (especially Amy!) found time to gift me with a notebook listing every single one of them, wives and kids and connections to other families in my own Texas town of Jacobsville. Eventually the town got a little too big for me, so I added another smaller town called Comanche Wells and began to fill it up, too.

You can't imagine how much pleasure this series has given me. I continue to add to the population of Jacobs County, Texas, and I have no plans to stop. Ever.

I hope all of you enjoy reading the Long, Tall Texans as much as I enjoy writing them. Thank you all for your kindness and loyalty and friendship. I am your biggest fan!

Love,

Diana Palmer

DIANA PALMER

TEXAS TOUGH

2 Heartfelt Stories
Connal and *Harden*

⬡HARLEQUIN SPECIAL RELEASE

 **HARLEQUIN**® SPECIAL RELEASE

ISBN-13: 978-1-335-14684-7

Recycling programs
for this product may
not exist in your area.

Texas Tough

Copyright © 2023 by Harlequin Enterprises ULC

Connal
First published in 1990. This edition published in 2023.
Copyright © 1990 by Diana Palmer

Harden
First published in 1991. This edition published in 2023.
Copyright © 1991 by Diana Palmer

For questions and comments about the quality of this book, please contact us at CustomerService@Harlequin.com.

Harlequin Enterprises ULC
22 Adelaide St. West, 41st Floor
Toronto, Ontario M5H 4E3, Canada
www.Harlequin.com

Printed in U.S.A.

CONTENTS

A prolific author of more than one hundred books, **Diana Palmer** got her start as a newspaper reporter. A *New York Times* bestselling author and voted one of the top ten romance writers in America, she has a gift for telling the most sensual tales with charm and humor. Diana lives with her family in Cornelia, Georgia. Visit her website at dianapalmer.com.

Books by Diana Palmer

Long, Tall Texans

Fearless
Heartless
Dangerous
Merciless
Courageous
Protector
Invincible
Untamed
Defender
Undaunted

The Wyoming Men

Wyoming Tough
Wyoming Fierce
Wyoming Bold
Wyoming Strong
Wyoming Rugged
Wyoming Brave

Morcai Battalion

The Morcai Battalion
The Morcai Battalion: The Recruit
The Morcai Battalion: Invictus
The Morcai Battalion: The Rescue

Visit the Author Profile page
at Harlequin.com for more titles.

CONNAL

CHAPTER ONE

BECAUSE OF THE DATE, Penelope knew she wouldn't find him at the barn. That was where he usually was at this hour of the day. Any other time, C.C. Tremayne was always two steps ahead of his men in feeding the animals, especially with the drought that had turned the grass brown and brittle these past few weeks. The drought had been a bad break for her father. Even with the Rio Grande only a few miles away, water was a precious commodity and wells kept going dry, leaving the tanks they filled empty.

West Texas was usually hot in mid-September, but the wind was up and it was unseasonably cold this evening. Penelope had worn a jacket outside, and now she was glad she had. She shivered a little in the late afternoon chill.

It was just beginning to get dark, and Penelope knew that if she didn't get to C.C. before her father did, it was going to mean another nasty quarrel. Ben Mathews and his foreman had been at each other's throats enough in recent weeks and Penelope didn't want any more arguments. Her father always got bad-tempered when money was tight. Things couldn't be much worse right now.

C.C. was drinking. She knew it; it was that time of year again. Only Penelope knew the importance of that day in September in C.C.'s life. She'd once nursed him through a flu and a raging delirium and he'd told her everything. She didn't let on that she knew, of course. C.C.—he was called that, although nobody knew what the initials stood for—didn't like anyone knowing private things about him. Not even the girl who loved him more than life.

He didn't love Penelope. He never had, although she'd worshiped him since she was nineteen and he'd been hired as foreman when her father's oldest hand retired. It had only taken one long look at the lithe, lean, dark-eyed man with the hawkish features and unsmiling face for her to fall madly in love with him. It was three years later, and her emotions hadn't undergone any changes. Probably they never would. Penelope Mathews was pretty stubborn. Even her dad said so.

She grimaced when she saw the light on in the bunkhouse, and it was not even dark. The other men were out riding herd, because calving was in full swing and everybody was in a mean temper during calving. It meant long hours and little sleep, and it wasn't normal for any of the men to be in the bunkhouse at this hour of the day. That meant it had to be C.C., and he had to be drinking. And liquor was one thing Ben Mathews wasn't about to tolerate on his ranch, not even when it was being abused by a man he liked and respected.

She brushed back her light reddish-brown hair and nibbled on her full lower lip. She had her long, wavy hair in a ponytail and it was tied with a velvet ribbon that just matched her pale brown eyes. She wasn't a pretty girl, but he thought she had a nice figure that filled out her jeans nicely. Her hair was almost red-gold when the sun hit it, and she had a line of freckles over her straight nose. With a little work, she could have been lovely. But she was a tomboy. She could ride anything and shoot as well as her father. Sometimes she wished she looked like Edie, the wealthy divorcée C.C. dated frequently. Edie was a dish, all blonde and blue-eyed and bristling with sophistication. She seemed an odd choice for a ranch foreman, but Penelope tried not to think about it. In her mind, she knew the reason C.C. dated Edie and it hurt.

She paused at the door of the bunkhouse and rubbed nervously at her jeans, tugging her nylon jacket closer against the cold wind. She knocked.

There was a hard thud. "Go away."

She knew the curt, uncompromising tone and sighed. It was going to be a long day.

Her gloved hand pushed open the door and she stepped into the warmth of the big common room where bunks lined the wall. At the far end was a kitchen arrangement where the men could have meals cooked. Nobody stayed here much. Most of the men were married and had homes on the ranch, except C.C. But during roundup and calving, the new men who were hired on temporarily stayed here. This year there were six, and they filled the building to capacity. But they'd be gone within a week, and C.C. would have the bunkhouse to himself again.

C.C. was leaning back in a chair, his mud-caked boots crossed on the table, his hat cocked over one dark eye, hiding most of his dust-streaked dark hair, his lean hands wrapped around a whiskey glass. He tilted the hat up, peered at Penelope with mocking derision and jerked it down again.

"What the hell do you want?" he asked in his curt drawl.

"To save your miserable skin, if I can," she returned in equally cutting tones. She slammed the door, skinned off her coat to reveal the fluffy white sweater underneath, and went straight to the kitchen to make a pot of coffee.

He watched her with disinterested eyes. "Saving me again, Pepi?" he laughed mockingly, using the nickname that everyone called her. "What for?"

"I'm dying of love for you," she muttered as she filled the coffeepot. It was the truth, but she made it sound like an outrageous lie.

He took it that way, too, laughing even louder. "Sure you are," he said. He threw down the rest of the contents of his glass and reached for the whiskey bottle.

Pepi was faster. She grabbed it away, something she'd never have managed if he'd been sober, and drained it into the sink before he could stagger to his feet.

"Damn you, girl!" he said harshly, staring at the empty bottle. "That was the last I had!"

"Good. I won't have to tear the place apart looking for the rest. Sit down and I'll make you some coffee. It will get you on your feet before Dad finds you," she mumbled. She plugged in the pot. "Oh, C.C.," she moaned, "he's combing the hills for you right now! You know what he'll do if he finds you like this!"

"But he won't, will he, honey?" he chided, coming up all too close behind her to take her shoulders and draw her back against the warm strength of his lean body. "You'll protect me, like always."

"Someday I won't be in time," she sighed. "And then what will become of you?"

He tilted her worried face up to his, and little shudders ran through her body. He'd never touched her except in amusement or at a dance. Her heart had fed just on the sight of him, from a distance. He was very potent this close, and she had to drop her eyes to his lean cheeks to keep him from knowing that.

"Nobody ever gave a damn except you," he murmured. "I don't know that I like being mothered by a girl half my age."

"I'm not half your age. Where are the cups?" she asked quietly, trying to divert him.

He wasn't buying it. His lean fingers brushed back loose strands of her hair, making her nerves sit up and scream. "How old are you now?"

"You know very well I'm twenty-two," she said. She had to keep her voice steady. She looked up deliberately to show him that he wasn't affecting her, but the smoldering expression in those black eyes caught her off guard.

"Twenty-two to my thirty. And a damned young twenty-two," he said slowly. "Why do you bother with me?"

"You're an asset around here. Surely you know how close we were to bankruptcy when you got hired?" she asked on a laugh. "Dad owes a lot to your business sense. But he still hates liquor."

"Why?"

"My mother died in an automobile accident the year before you came here," she said. "My father had been drinking and he was behind the wheel at the time." She tugged against his disturbing hands and he let her go.

She looked through the cabinets and found a white mug that wasn't broken or chipped. She put it down by the coffeepot and filled it, and then she took it to C.C., who had sat down and was rubbing his head with his lean hands at the table.

"Head hurt?" she asked.

"Not nearly enough," he said enigmatically. He took the mug and sipped the thick black liquid. He glared at it. "What in hell did you put in here, an old boot?"

"Twice the usual measure, that's all," she assured him as she sat down beside him. "It will sober you up quicker."

"I don't want to be sober," he said shortly.

"I know that. But I don't want you to get fired," she returned, smiling pertly when he glared at her. "You're the only person on the place except Dad who doesn't treat me like a lost cause."

He studied her smooth features, her soft dark eyes. "Well, I guess that makes us two of a kind, then. Because you're the first person in years who gave a damn about me."

"Not the only one," she corrected, smiling in spite of her feelings as she added, "Edie cares, too."

He shrugged and smiled faintly. "I guess she does. We understand each other, Edie and I," he murmured quietly, his eyes with a faraway look. "She's one of a kind."

In bed, she probably was, Pepi thought, but she couldn't

give herself away by saying so. She got up and brought the coffeepot to refill his cup.

"Drink up, pal," she said gently. "The vigilantes aren't far away."

"I feel more steady now," he said after he'd finished the second cup. "On the outside, anyway." He lit a cigarette and blew out a thick cloud of smoke, leaning back wearily in the chair. "God, I hate days like this."

She couldn't admit that she knew why without incriminating herself. But she remembered well enough what he'd said, and the way he'd screamed when the memory came back in a nightmare delirium. Poor man. Poor, tortured man. He'd lost his wife and his unborn child on a white-water rafting trip that he'd had the misfortune to survive. As near as she could tell, he'd blamed himself for that ever since. For living, when they hadn't.

"I guess we all have good ones and bad ones," she said noncommittally. "If you're okay, I'll get back to my cooking. Dad's reminded me that he's due an apple pie. I've been baking half the afternoon."

"You're a domestic little thing, aren't you?" he asked strangely, searching her eyes. "Is Brandon coming to see you tonight?"

She blushed without knowing why. "Brandon is the vet," she said shortly. "Not my boyfriend."

"You could use a boyfriend, tidbit," he said unexpectedly, his eyes narrowing, his frown deepening as he fingered the empty mug. "You're a woman now. You need more than companionship from a man."

"I know what I need, thanks," she replied, rising. "You'd better stick your head in a bucket or something and see if you can get that bloodshot look out of your eyes. And for heaven's sake, swallow some minty mouthwash."

He sighed. "Anything else, Mother Mathews?" he asked sarcastically.

"Yes. Stop getting drunk. It only makes things worse."

He stared at her curiously. "You're so wise, aren't you, Pepi?" he asked cuttingly. "You haven't lived long enough to know why people drink."

"I've lived long enough to know that nobody ever solved a problem by running away from it," she returned, glaring back when his eyes started flashing black fire at her. "And don't start growling, either, because it's the truth and you know it. You've spent years living in the past, letting it haunt you. Oh, I don't pretend to know why," she said quickly when he began to eye her suspiciously, "but I know a haunted man when I see one. You might try living in the present, C.C. It's not so bad. Even at calving time. And just think, you have roundup to look forward to," she added with a wicked grin. "See you."

She started out the door without her jacket, so nervous that she'd given herself away that she hardly missed it until the wind hit her.

"Here, you'll freeze," he said suddenly, and came toward her with the jacket in his hand. "Put this on."

Unexpectedly he held it for her and didn't let go even when she was encased in it. He held her back against his chest, both lean hands burning through the sleeves of the coat, his chin on the top of her head.

"Don't bruise your heart on me, Pepi," he said quietly, with such tenderness in his deep voice that her eyes closed instinctively at the tone. "I don't have anything left to give you."

"You're my friend, C.C.," she said through her teeth. "I hope I'm yours. That's all."

His hands contracted for a minute. His chest rose and fell heavily. "Good," he said then, and let her go. "Good. I'm glad that's all there is to it. I wouldn't want to hurt you."

She opened the door and glanced back, forcing a smile to her lips even though he'd just destroyed all her dreams. "Try some of Charlie's chili peppers next time you feel like a binge," she advised. "The top of your head will come off just as fast, but you won't have a hangover from it."

"Get out of here!" he grumbled, glaring at her.

"If I see Dad, I'll tell him you're getting a snack, before you feed the livestock," she returned, grinning. She closed the door quickly and she heard him curse.

Her father was already home when she got there. He glared at her from the living room, her mirror image except for his masculinity and white hair.

"Where have you been?" he demanded.

"Out counting sheep," she said innocently.

"Sheep or one black one named C.C.?"

She pursed her lips. "Well…"

He shook his head. "Pepi, if I ever catch him with a bottle, he's through here, no matter how good a foreman he is," he said firmly. "He knows the rules."

"He was making himself a snack in the bunkhouse,"

she said. "I just poked my head in to ask if he'd like some of my…excuse me, *your*…apple pie."

He scowled fiercely. "It's my pie. I'm not sharing it!"

"I made two," she said quickly. "You old reprobate, you'd never fire C.C. You'd shoot yourself first and we both know it, but save your pride and say you'd fire him if it makes you feel better," she told him as she stripped off her jacket.

He finished lighting his pipe and glanced at her. "You'll wear your heart out on him, you know," he said after a minute.

Her back stiffened. "Yes. I know."

"He's not what he seems," he continued.

She turned, eyeing him warily. "What do you mean?"

"You tell me." He stared at the window, where snow was touching the pane under the outside lights. "He drove in here without a past at all. No references. No papers. I gave him a job on the strength of my instinct and his very evident ability with animals and figures. But he's no more a line-riding cowboy than I am a banker. He's elegant, C.C. is. And he knows business in an uncommon way for a poor man. You mark my words, girl, there's more to him than what shows."

"He does seem out of place at times," she had to admit. She couldn't tell him the rest—that she knew why C.C. was out here on a ranch in the middle of nowhere. But even she hadn't learned from her involuntary eavesdropping during his delirium why he'd left that shadowy past. He'd come from money and he'd suffered a tragic loss, she knew that, and he was afraid to risk his heart again. That didn't stop Pepi from risking hers, though. It was far too late for any warning.

"He could be anything, you know," he said quietly, "even an escaped convict."

"I doubt that." She grinned. "He's too honest. Remember when you lost that hundred-dollar bill out in the barn, and C.C. brought it to you? I've seen him go out of his way to help other cowboys who were down on their luck. He's got a temper, but he isn't cruel with it. He growls and curses and the men get a little amused, but it's only when he's fighting mad that they run for the hills. And even then, he's in complete control. He never seems to lose it."

"I've noticed that. But a man in that kind of control, all the time, may have a reason," he reminded her. "There are other men. Don't take chances."

"You old faker," she muttered. "You're always pushing me at him."

He threw up his hands. "I like him. But I can afford to. You understand what I mean?"

She grimaced. "I guess so. Okay. I'll let Brandon take me to the movies, how about that?"

He made a face. "What a consolation prize," he grumbled. "The poor man's a clown. How he ever got through veterinary school is beyond me, with his sense of humor! He's the kind of man who would show a stuffed cow at a championship cattle show."

"My kind of man, all right," she said fervently, smiling. "He's uncomplicated."

"He's a wild man," he countered.

"I'll tame him," she promised. "Now let me get those apple pies finished, okay?"

"Okay. But I'll take C.C.'s to him," he added gently. "I want to see for myself if he's eating."

She stuck her tongue out at him and went to the kitchen, sighing her relief once she was out of sight.

CHAPTER TWO

BRANDON HALE WAS a carrot-topped maniac, and in his spare time, he was a veterinarian. Pepi adored him. Probably if her heart hadn't been appropriated by C.C., she might have married Brandon one day.

He came by just as Pepi and her father were sitting down to the supper table.

"Oh, boy, apple pie." Brandon grinned, staring at the luscious treat Pepi had made. "Hello, Mr. Mathews, how are you?"

"Hungry," Ben said shortly. "And don't eye my apple pie. I'm not sharing it."

"But you will, won't you?" Brandon leaned down. "I mean, considering that you need your new calves inspected and that sick bull treated, and those inoculations given, with roundup on the way…"

"Damn, boy, that's hitting below the belt," Ben groaned.

"Just one little slice," Brandon said, "the size of a knife blade…"

"Oh, all right, sit down." The older man sighed. "But I hope you know I wouldn't share it with just anybody. And if you don't stop coming over here at night without a reason, you'll have to marry Pepi."

"I'd be delighted," Brandon said, winking at Pepi from his pale blue eyes. "Name the day, honey."

"The sixth of July, twenty years from now," she promised, passing the corn. "I expect to live a little before I settle down."

"You've already lived twenty-two years," her father remarked. "I want grandchildren."

"You have them yourself," Pepi invited. "I've been thinking about joining the Peace Corps."

Ben almost dropped his coffee cup. "You've what?"

"It would be something to broaden my horizons," she said. Not to mention getting her away from C.C. before she slipped up and bared her aching heart to him. Today had been a close call. He seemed to be suspicious of all the attention she gave him, and worried that he couldn't return her affections. It was getting too much for her. A year away might ease the pain.

"You could get killed in one of those foreign places," her father said shortly. "I won't let you."

"I'm twenty-two," she reminded him with a grin. "You can't stop me."

He sighed angrily. "Who'll cook and keep house and—"

"You can hire somebody."

"Sure." Her father laughed.

That brought home the true situation, and she felt instantly regretful that she'd brought it up. "I won't go right away," she promised. "And don't worry, things will get better."

"Pray for rain," Brandon suggested between bites.

"Everybody else is. I've never seen so many ranchers in church."

"I've seen prayers work miracles," Ben remarked, and launched into some tales that kept Pepi's mind off C.C.

After they'd finished off half of Pepi's apple pie, Brandon went out with her father to check the sick bull. "I don't usually do night work when I can get out of it," Brandon told Pepi. "But for an apple pie like that, I'd come out to deliver a calf at three in the morning."

"I'll remember that," she said pertly, grinning.

"You're cute," he said. "I mean that. You're really cute, and if you ever want to propose matrimony, just go ahead. I won't even play hard to get."

"Thanks. I'll keep you in mind, along with my other dozen suitors," she said lightly.

"How about a movie Friday night? We'll run over to El Paso and eat supper before we go to the theater."

"Terrific," she agreed. He was loads of fun and she needed to get away.

"I won't get back until midnight, I guess," her father called out. "After we check that bull down at the Berry place, I want to look over Berry's books before the tax man gets them. Don't wait up."

"Okay. Have fun," she called back. It was a joke between them, because Jack Berry kept books that would have confounded a lawyer. It was almost estimated tax time, and Jack was the ranch's only bookkeeper. They should have hired somebody more qualified, but Jack was elderly and couldn't do outside work. Her father had a soft heart. Rather than see the old man on welfare,

Ben had hired him to keep the books. Which meant, unfortunately, that Ben had to do most of the figuring over again at tax time. His soft heart was one reason the ranch was in the hole. He didn't really have a business head like his own father had possessed. Without C.C.'s subtle guidance, the ranch would have gone on the auction block three years ago. It still might.

C.C. She frowned, turning toward the back door. She was worried about him. He hadn't seemed too drunk when she'd gone to check on him earlier, and that was unusual. His yearly binges were formidable. She'd better give him another look, before her father thought to check him out at midnight.

The bunkhouse was filling up. There were three men in it, now, the newest temporary hands. But C.C. wasn't there.

"He was pretty tight-lipped about where he was going, Miss Mathews," one of the men volunteered. "But I'd guess he was headed into Juárez from the direction he took."

"Oh, boy," she sighed. "Did he take the pickup or his own car?"

"His own car—that old Ford."

"Thanks."

It was a good thing she drove, she thought angrily. One of these days she'd be gone, and who'd take care of that wild-eyed cowboy then? The thought depressed her. He wouldn't have any trouble finding somebody to do that, not with his looks. And there was always Edie.

She turned off on the road that led to the border. The official at the border remembered the big white

Ford—there hadn't been a lot of traffic across, since it was a weekday night. She thanked him, went across and drove around until she found the white Ford parked with characteristic haphazardness in a parking space. She pulled in beside it and got out.

Fortunately she hadn't taken time to change. She was wearing jeans and a checked shirt with a pullover sweater and boots, just the outfit for walking around at night. She was a little nervous because she didn't like going places alone after dark. Especially the kind of place she was sure C.C. was going to be in. Too, she was worried in case her father came home and needed to ask her anything. Her closed bedroom door might fool him into thinking she was just asleep, but if he saw the pickup missing, he might get suspicious. She didn't want him to fire C.C. He liked the man, but if C.C. didn't tell him why he was drinking—and C.C. wouldn't—then her father was very likely to let him go anyway.

There was a bar not a block away from where she parked. She had a feeling that C.C. was in it, but when she looked inside, there were mostly Mexican men and only one or two young Americans. She walked the streets, peeking into bars, and almost got picked up once. Finally, miserable and worried, she turned and started back to the truck. On the way, she glanced into that first bar again—and there he was, leaning back in a chair at a corner table.

She walked in and went back to the corner table.

"Oh…" C.C. let out a word that he normally wouldn't have. He was cold and dangerous looking now, not the easily handled man of a few hours ago. She knew that her old tactics wouldn't work this time.

"Hi," she said gently.

"If you're here to drag me back, forget it," he drawled, glaring at her from bloodshot eyes. There was a half-empty tequila bottle on the table and an empty glass beside it. "I won't go."

"It's hot in here," she remarked, feeling her way. "Some air might help you."

He laughed drunkenly. "Think so? Suppose I pass out, tomboy. Will you throw me over your shoulder and carry me home?"

That hurt. He made her out to be some female Amazon. Perhaps that was how he thought of her—as just one of the boys. But she smiled. "I might try," she agreed.

He studied her with disinterested brevity. "Still in jeans. Always wearing something manly. Do you have legs, tomboy? Do you even have breasts—?"

"I'll bet you can't walk to the car by yourself," she cut him off, trying not to blush, because his voice carried and one or two of the patrons were openly staring their way.

He stopped what he was saying to scowl at her. "The hell I can't," he replied belligerently.

"Prove it," she challenged. "Let's see you get there without falling flat on your face."

He muttered something rough and got to his feet, swaying a little. He took out a twenty-dollar bill and tossed it onto the bar, his hat cocked arrogantly over one eye, his tall, lithe body slightly stooped. "Keep the change," he told the man.

Pepi congratulated herself silently on her strategy as he weaved out onto the street. He took off his hat and wiped his forehead hesitantly.

"Hot," he murmured. He shook his head, his breath coming hard and heavy. He turned to look at Pepi, frowning slightly. "I thought we were going for a walk."

"Sure," she said.

"Come here, then, sweet girl," he coaxed, holding out his arm. "I can't let you get lost, can I?"

It was the liquor talking, and she knew it. But it was so sweet to have his arm around her shoulder, his head bent to hers, his breath against her forehead. Even the scent of the tequila wasn't that unpleasant.

"So sweet," he said heavily, walking her away from the car, not toward it. "I don't want to go home. Let's just walk the night away."

"C.C., it's dangerous in this part of the city," she began softly.

"My name...is Connal," he said abruptly.

That was faintly shocking, to know that he had a real name. She smiled. "It's nice. I like it."

"Yours is Penelope Marie," he laughed roughly. "Penelope Marie Mathews."

"Yes." She hadn't known that he knew her full name. It was flattering.

"Suppose we change it to Tremayne?" he asked, hesitating. "Sure, why not? You're always looking after me, Penelope Marie Mathews, so why don't you marry me and do the thing right?" While she was absorbing the shock, he looked around weavingly. "Aha, sure, there's one of those all-night chapels. Come on."

"C.C., we can't…!"

He blinked at her horrified expression. "Sure we can. Come on, honey, we don't have to have any papers or anything. And it's all legal."

She bit her lower lip. She couldn't let him do this, she thought, panicking. When he sobered up and found out, he'd kill her. Not only that, she wasn't sure if a Mexican marriage was binding; she didn't know what the law was.

"Listen, now," she began.

"If you won't marry me," he threatened with drunken cunning, "I'll shoot up a bar and get us landed in jail. Right now, Pepi. This minute. I mean it."

Obviously he did. She gave in. Surely nobody in his right mind would marry them with him in that visibly drunken condition. So she went along with him, worried to death about how she was going to get him home. But she knew that he owned a Beretta and had a permit for it, and she couldn't be sure that he didn't have it on him. God forbid that he should shoot somebody!

He dragged her into the wedding chapel. Unfortunately the Mexican who married them spoke little English, and Pepi's halting Spanish was inadequate to explain what was going on. C.C., she recalled, spoke the language fluently. He broke in on her stumbling explanation and rattled off something that made the little man grin. The Mexican went away and came back with a Bible and two women. He launched into rapid-fire Spanish, cueing first Pepi and then C.C. to say *si* and then he said something else, grinned, and then a terrified Pepi was being hugged and kissed by the women.

C.C. scrawled his signature on a paper and rattled off some more Spanish while the little man wrote a few other things on the paper.

"That's all there is to it." C.C. grinned at Pepi. "Here. All nice and legal. Give me a kiss, wife."

He held out the paper, took a deep breath, and slid to the floor of the chapel.

The next few minutes were hectic. Pepi finally managed to convey to the Mexican family that she had to get him to the car. They brought in a couple of really mean-looking young men who lifted C.C. like a sack of feed and carried him out to the parking lot. Pepi had him put in the pickup truck. She handed the boys two dollar bills, which was all she had, and tried to thank them. They waved away the money, grinning, when they noticed the beat-up, dented condition of the old ranch pickup. Kindred spirits, she thought warmly. Poor people always helped each other. She thanked them again, stuck the paper in her pocket, and started the truck.

She made it to the ranch in good time. Her father's Jeep was still gone, thank God. She backed the pickup next to the bunkhouse, where it wasn't visible from the house, and knocked on the door.

Bud, the new hand she'd spoken to earlier, answered the knock. Apparently the men had been asleep.

"I need a favor," she whispered. "I've got C.C. in the truck. Will you toss him on his bunk for me, before my dad sees him?"

Bud's eyebrows rose. "You've got the boss in there? What's wrong with him?"

She swallowed. "Tequila."

"Whew," Bud whistled. "Never thought of him as a drinking man."

"He isn't, usually," she said, reluctant to go into anything more. "This was an unfortunate thing. Can you do it? He's heavy."

"Sure I can, Miss Mathews." He followed her out in his stocking feet, leaving the bunkhouse door open. "I'll try not to wake the other men. They're all dead tired, anyway. I doubt they'd hear it thunder."

"Heavens, I hope not," she said miserably. "If my dad sees him like this, his life's over."

"Your dad don't like alcohol, I guess," Bud remarked.

"You said it."

She opened the pickup door. C.C. was leaning against it, sound asleep and snoring. Bud caught him halfway to the ground and threw him over his shoulder in a fireman's lift. C.C. didn't even break stride; he kept right on snoring.

"Thanks a lot, Bud." Pepi grinned.

"My pleasure, miss. Good night."

She climbed into the pickup, parked it at the back of the house, and rushed upstairs to bed. Her father would be none the wiser, thank God.

She undressed to get into her gown, and a piece of paper fell to the floor. She unfolded it, and found her name and that of Connal Cade Tremayne on it along with some Spanish words and an official-looking signature. It didn't take much guesswork to realize that it was a marriage license. She sat down, gazing at it. Well, it wasn't worth the paper it was written on, thank

God. But she wasn't about to throw it away. In days to come, she could dream about what it could have meant if it had been the real thing. If C.C. had married her, wanted her, loved her. She sighed.

She put the license in her drawer and she lay down on the bed. Poor man, perhaps his ghosts would let him rest for a while now. She wondered how much of tonight he was going to remember, and hoped he wouldn't be too furious at her for going to get him or for leaving his dilapidated old Ford in Juárez. But with any luck, the old car would be fine, and he could get somebody to go with him to get it when he sobered up. Anyway, he ought to be grateful that she went after him, she assured herself. With winter coming on, it might be hard to get a new job. She didn't want to lose him. Even worshiping him from afar was better than never seeing him again. Or was it?

THE NEXT MORNING, she woke up with a start as a hard knock sounded on her door.

"What is it?" she asked on a yawn.

"You know damned good and well what it is!"

That was C.C. She sat up just as he threw open the door and walked in. Her gown was transparent and low-cut, and he got a quick but thorough look at her almost bare breasts before she could jerk the sheet up to her throat.

"C.C.!" she burst out. "What in heaven's name are you doing!"

"Where is it?" he demanded, his eyes coldly furious.

She blinked. "You'll have to excuse me, I don't read minds."

"Don't be cute," he returned. He was looking at her as if he hated her. "I remember everything. I'm not making that kind of mistake with you, Pepi Mathews. I may have to put up with being mothered by you, but I'll be damned if I'll stay married to you when I'm cold sober. The marriage license, where is it?"

It was a golden opportunity. To save his pride. To save her flimsy relationship with him. To spare herself the embarrassment of why she'd let him force her into the ceremony. Steady, girl, she told herself. The marriage wasn't legal in this country, she was reasonably sure of that, so there would be no harm done if she convinced him it had never happened.

"What marriage license?" she asked with a perfectly straight face and carefully surprised eyes.

Her response threw him. He hesitated, just for an instant. "I was in Mexico. In Juárez, in a bar. You came to get me... We got married."

Her eyes widened like saucers. "We did what?"

He was scowling by now. He fumbled a cigarette out of his pocket and lit it. "I was sure," he said slowly. "We went to this little chapel and the ceremony was all in Spanish... There was a paper of some kind."

"The only paper was the twenty-dollar bill you gave the bartender," she mused. "And if it hadn't been for Bud what's-his-name helping me get you to bed last night, you wouldn't still be working here. You know how Dad feels about booze. You were really tying one on."

He stared at the cigarette, then at her, intently. "I couldn't have imagined all that," he said finally.

"You imagined a lot of things last night," she laughed, making a joke out of it. "For one, that you were a Texas ranger on the trail of some desperado. Then you were a snake hunter, and you wanted to go out into the desert and hunt rattlers. Oh, I got you home in the nick of time," she added, lying through her teeth with a very convincing grin.

He relaxed a little. "I'm sorry," he said. "I must have been a handful."

"You were. But no harm done," she told him. "Yet," she added, indicating the sheet under her chin. "If my father finds you up here, things could get sticky pretty fast."

"Don't be absurd," he replied, frowning as if the insinuation disturbed him. "You're only a little tomboy, not a vamp."

Just what he'd said last night, in fact, along with a few other references that had set off her temper. But she couldn't let on.

"All the same, if you and Dad want breakfast, you'd better leave. And your car is still in Juárez, by the way."

"Amazing that it made it that far," he murmured dryly. "Okay. I'm sorry I gave you a hard time. Do I still get breakfast?"

She relaxed, too, grateful that she didn't have to lie anymore. "Yes."

He spared her one last scowling glance. "Pepi, you've got to stop mothering me."

"This was the last time," she promised, and meant it.

His broad shoulders rose and fell halfheartedly. "Sure." He paused at the open door with his back to her. "Thanks," he said gruffly.

"You'd have done it for me," she said simply.

He started to turn, thought better of it, and went out, closing the door behind him.

Pepi collapsed on the pillow with a heartfelt sigh. She'd gotten away with it! Now all she had to do was find out just how much trouble she was in legally with that sham marriage.

CHAPTER THREE

IT TOOK PEPI half the next day to work up enough nerve to actually phone an attorney and ask if she was really married to C.C. She had to be careful. It couldn't be a lawyer who knew her, so she called one in El Paso, giving the receptionist an assumed name. She was given an appointment for that afternoon, because the attorney had a cancellation in his busy schedule. She told the receptionist why she wanted to see the attorney, adding lightly that she'd gotten a Mexican marriage and thought it wasn't binding. The secretary laughed and said a lot of people thought that, only to find out to their astonishment that they were very binding in Texas. She reconfirmed the appointment, wished Pepi a nice day and hung up.

Pepi replaced the receiver with a dull thud and sat down heavily in the chair beside the telephone table in the hall. Her heart was beating madly. It would take having the lawyer look at the document to be sure, but it sounded as if his receptionist was right. Legally she was Mrs. C.C. Tremayne. She was Connal Tremayne's wife.

But he didn't know it.

The consequences of her deception could be far-reaching and tragic, especially if he decided to marry

Edie. He would be commiting bigamy, and he wouldn't even know it.

What should she do? If she told him now, after having denied it when he'd demanded the truth, he'd never believe anything she said again. He'd hate her, too, for trapping him into marriage. It didn't matter that he'd threatened to land them in jail if she didn't go along. He'd been intoxicated, not responsible for his actions. But she'd been sober. When he asked her why she'd gone through with it, how would she answer him? Would he guess that she was shamefully in love with him?

The questions tormented her. She burned lunch. Her father gave her a hard glare as he bit into a scraped grilled cheese sandwich.

"Tastes like carbon," he muttered.

"Sorry." She'd forgotten to buy cheese at the store on her latest shopping trip, so there had been only enough for three sandwiches. She'd managed to burn all three. All she could do was scrape them off and hope for the best.

"You've been preoccupied all morning," he remarked with intense scrutiny of the bright color in her cheeks. "Want to talk about it?"

She managed a wan smile and shook her head. "Thanks anyway."

He got down another bite of overdone grilled cheese sandwich. "Would it have anything to do with C.C.'s absence last night?"

She stared at him blankly. "What?"

"C.C.'s car was missing all night, and I understand that he had to have one of the hands drive him over to

Juárez to collect it this morning." He glared at the remainder of his sandwiches and pushed the plate away. "He was drinking, wasn't he, Pepi?"

She couldn't lie, but it wouldn't do to tell the truth, either. "One of the men said C.C. had a few in Juárez, but on his own time," she added quickly. "You can't really jump on him unless he does it on your time." She warmed to her subject. "Besides that, he only drinks once a year."

He frowned. "Once a year?"

"That's about the extent of it. And please don't ask me why, because I can't tell you." She laid a gentle hand on his forearm. "Dad, you know we owe the ranch to his business sense."

"I know," he muttered. "But damn it, Pepi, I can't have one set of rules for the men and another for him."

"He probably won't ever do it again," she said reassuringly. "Come on, you haven't actually caught him in the act, you know."

He grimaced. "I don't guess I have. But if I ever do...!" he added hotly.

"I know. You'll throw him off the roof." She grinned. "Drink your coffee. At least it isn't burned." She finished hers. "I, uh, have to go into El Paso this afternoon to pick up a package I ordered."

He scowled. "What package?"

"For your birthday," she improvised. That wasn't improbable; his birthday was only two weeks away.

"What is it?" he asked.

"I'll never tell."

He let the subject drop after that, and went back out

to work. Pepi washed up and then went to dress for her appointment. Jeans and a T-shirt weren't exactly the best outfit to wear to her own doom, she thought blackly.

She put on her full denim skirt with a blue print blouse and pinned her hair up on her head. She looked much more mature, she decided, although nothing could be done about the freckles on her nose. Not even makeup camouflaged them very well. She did the best she could, adding only a touch of makeup to her face and groaning over her voluptuous figure. If only she could lose enough weight to look like Edie...

With a moan, she slipped her hose-clad feet into taupe high heels, transferred the contents of her handbag into the pocketbook that matched the heels, and went downstairs.

As luck would have it, she ran right into C.C. on the front porch. He looked hungover and dusty. His batwing chaps were heavily stained, like the jeans under them and his chambray shirt. His hat had once been black, but now it was dusty gray. He glared down at her with black eyes.

"Brandon's out at the holding corral," he remarked in an oddly hostile tone. "I assume he's the reason for the fine feathers?"

"I'm going into El Paso to do some shopping," she replied. "How's your head?" Better to sound natural, she decided, and she even smiled.

"It was bad enough before I buried it in dust and bleating calves," he muttered. "Come in here a minute. I have to talk to you."

She knew her heart had stopped beating. With a

sense of awe, she felt the warmth of his lean, strong hand around her upper arm as he guided her back into the house and shut the door. He let go of her almost reluctantly.

"Look, Pepi, this has got to stop," he said.

"W-what has?" she faltered.

"You chasing me down on my yearly binges," he said irritably. He took off his hat and ran a grimy hand through his sweaty jet hair. "I've been thinking all day about what could have happened to you in Juárez last night. That part of town is a rough place in broad daylight, never mind at night. I told you before, I don't need a nursemaid. I don't want you ever pulling such a stupid stunt again."

"There's a simple solution. Stop drinking," she said.

He searched her uplifted face quietly, scowling. "Yes, I think I might have to. If my memory's as faulty as it was last night..."

She had to exert every ounce of will she had not to give anything away. "Your secrets are safe with me, C.C.," she said in a stage whisper, and grinned.

He relaxed a little. "Okay, squirt. Go do your shopping." His dark eyes slid over her body in a way they never had before, and she felt her knees going weak.

"Something wrong?" she asked huskily.

His eyes caught hers. "You kick around in jeans so much that I forget occasionally that you've even got legs." His gaze dropped to them and he smiled in a sensual kind of way. "Very nice legs, at that."

She flushed. "My legs are none of your business, C.C.," she informed him.

He didn't like that. His sharp glance told her so. "Why? Do they belong to the carrot-topped vet already? He acts more like a lover than a friend, despite your constant denials." His expression seemed to harden before her eyes. "You're twenty-two, as you keep telling me. And this is a permissive age, isn't it? No man can expect virginity in a wife anymore."

The mention of the word "wife" made her face pale. But she couldn't let him see how shaken she was. "That's right," she said. "It is a permissive age. I can sleep with a man if I like."

He looked briefly murderous. "Does your father know about that attitude?"

"What my father doesn't know won't bother him," she said uneasily. "I have to go, C.C."

His eyes mirrored his contempt. "My God, I thought you were old-fashioned, in that respect at least."

That hurt. She lowered her gaze to his shirt. "As you keep telling me, my private life is no concern of yours," she said in a tight voice. "You and Edie probably don't play bingo on your dates, either, and I don't make nasty remarks about your morals."

"I'm a man," he said shortly.

She lifted her eyes defiantly. "So what? Do you think being a man gives you some divine right to sleep with anybody you like? If men expect chaste women, then women have the right to expect chaste men!"

His thick eyebrows lifted toward the ceiling. "My God, where would you find one?"

"That's my point exactly. Sling mud and it sticks to your fingers. Now I'm going."

"If you aren't meeting the handsome vet, who are you meeting, dressed like that?" he asked curtly.

"It's just a skirt and blouse!"

"Not the way you fill them out, little one," he said quietly. His eyes made emphatic statements about that before he lifted them back up to capture hers.

"I'm overweight," she got out.

"Really?" He pulled out a cigarette and lit it, but his eyes had hers in a stranglehold and he wouldn't let her avert her gaze.

Her heart raged in her chest, beating painfully hard and fast. Her lips parted on a shaky breath and she realized that her hands were clutching her purse so hard that her nails were leaving marks in the soft leather.

He moved closer, just close enough to threaten her with the warm strength of his body. He was so much taller that she had to look up to see his eyes, but she couldn't manage to tear her gaze away.

The back of his forefinger touched her cheek in a slow, devastating caress. "I thought you were a total innocent, little Pepi," he said, his voice at least an octave deeper. "If that's not the case, you could find yourself in over your head very quickly."

Her lips parted. She was drowning in him, so intoxicated that she didn't even mind the smell of calf and burned hide that clung to him. Her eyes fell to his hard mouth, to its thin chiseled lines, and she wanted it with a primitive hunger. It occurred to her that she could entice him into her bed, that she could sleep with him. They were legally married, even if he didn't know it. She could seduce him. The delicious thought made her breath catch.

Then came the not-so-delicious thought of what would happen afterward. With the experience she was pretty sure he had, he might know that she was virginal, by her reactions if nothing else. Besides that, it might hurt, which would be a dead giveaway. And he didn't know they were married. All sorts of complications could arise. No, she thought miserably, she couldn't even have that consolation. Not even one night to hold in her memory. She had to keep him at arm's length until she could decide how to tell him the truth and what to do about it.

She backed away a little, forcing a smile. "I really have to go," she said huskily. "See you later."

He muttered something under his breath and opened the door for her, his dark eyes accusing as they watched her go. She was getting under his skin. It made him angry that her body enticed him, that he was hungry for her. It made him angrier that she was apparently experienced. He didn't want other hands touching her, especially the vet's. She'd been his caretaker for so long now that he'd come to look upon her with the same passion a winemaker felt for his best vintage. But he'd thought she was virginal, and she'd as good as told him she wasn't. That realization changed everything. He'd placed her carefully off limits for years, but if she wasn't innocent, then he didn't have to worry about his conscience. Odd, though, he thought as he watched her go, she could still blush prettily enough when he looked at her body. Maybe she wasn't very experienced, despite the redheaded veterinarian's attentions. C.C.'s black eyes narrowed. Brandon didn't have his experience, so that gave him an edge. Yes, it did. He lifted the cigarette to his mouth and smiled faintly as he watched Pepi climb into her father's old Lincoln and drive away.

Blissfully unaware of C.C.'s plotting, Pepi managed to get the car out of the driveway without hitting anything. Her hands on the steering wheel were still shaking from her unexpected confrontation. That was the first time that C.C. had ever made anything resembling a pass at her. Perhaps she should have been less emphatic about her experience—of which she didn't have any. But she'd felt threatened by the way C.C. had looked at her, and her mind had shut down. For one long second she agonized over the thought that he might take her off the endangered species list and start pursuing her himself. But, no, he had Edie to satisfy those needs. He wouldn't want an innocent like herself. And then she remembered that she'd told him she was no innocent. What would she do if he made a heavy pass at her? She loved him to distraction, but she didn't dare let things go that far. If the worst came to pass and they were really married, she could get an annulment without much difficulty. But if she admitted him to her bed, it would mean getting a divorce, and that would take much longer. She couldn't afford to give in to temptation, no matter how appealing it was....

THE ATTORNEY'S OFFICE was located adjacent to a new shopping center that had just opened on the outskirts of town. She pulled into a parking spot in front of the adobe facade of the office building and took a deep breath. This wasn't going to be very pleasant, she was afraid.

She went in and produced the document. The attorney took his time looking it over. He was bilingual, so the wording that had sent Pepi crazy trying to decipher with the help of a Spanish-English dictionary made perfect sense to him.

"It's legal, I assure you," he mused, handing it back. "Congratulations," he added with a smile.

"He doesn't know we're married." She groaned. She told him the particulars. "Doesn't that mean anything, that he was intoxicated?"

"If he was sober enough to agree to be married, to initiate the ceremony and to sign his name to a legal certificate of marriage," he said, "I'm afraid it is binding."

"Then I'll just have to get an annulment," she said heavily.

"No problem," he said, smiling again. "Just have him come in and sign—"

"He has to know about it!" she exclaimed, horrified.

"I'm afraid so," he said. "Even if he did apparently get married without realizing it, there's just no way the marriage can be dissolved without his consent."

Pepi buried her face in her hands. "I can't tell him. I just can't!"

"You really have to," he said. "There are all kinds of legal complications that this could create. If he's a reasonable man, surely he'll understand."

"Oh, no, he won't," she said on a miserable sigh. "But you're right. I do have to tell him. And I will," she added, rising to shake his hand. She didn't say when.

Pepi mentally flayed herself for not telling C.C. the truth when he'd demanded it. She'd only wanted to spare him embarrassment, and she hadn't thought any damage would be done. Besides that, the thought of being his wife, just for a little while, was so sweet a temptation that she hadn't been able to resist. Now she was stuck with the reality of her irresponsibility, and she didn't know what she was going to do.

For a start, she avoided C.C. With roundup in full swing, and the men working from dawn until long after dark, that wasn't too hard. She spent her own free time with Brandon, wishing secretly that she could feel for him what she felt for C.C. Brandon was so much fun, and they were compatible. It was just that there was no spark of awareness between them.

"I wish you wouldn't spend so much time with Hale," her father said at supper one night near the end of the massive roundup, during one of his rare evenings at home.

"There, there, you're just jealous because he's getting all your apple pies while you're out working," she teased.

He sighed. "No, it's not that at all. I want to see you in a happy marriage, girl. The kind your mother and I had. Hale's a fine young man, but he's too biddable. You'd be leading him around by the nose by the end of your first year together. You're feisty, like your mother. You need a man who can stand up to you, a man you can't dominate."

Only one man came immediately to mind and she

flushed, averting her eyes. "The one you're thinking of is already spoken for," she said tersely.

His eyes, so much like her own, searched her face. "Pepi, you're old enough now to understand why men see women like Edie. He's a man. He has...a man's needs."

She picked up her fork and looked at it, trying not to feel any more uncomfortable than she already did. "Edie is his business, as he once told me. We have no right to interfere in his private life."

"She's an odd choice for a ranch foreman, isn't she?" he mused, still watching her like a hawk. "A city sophisticate, a divorcée, a woman used to wealth and position. Don't you find it unexpected that she likes C.C.?"

"Not really. He's quite sophisticated himself," she reminded him. "He seems to fit in anywhere. Even at business conferences," she added, recalling a conference the three of them had attended two years ago. She and her father had both been surprised at the sight of C.C. in a dinner jacket talking stocks and bonds and investments with a rancher over cocktails. It had been an eye-opening experience for Pepi.

"Yes, I remember," her father agreed. "A mysterious man, C.C. He came out of nowhere, literally. I've never been able to find out anything about his background. But from time to time, things slip out. He's not a man unused to wealth and position, and at times he makes me feel like a rank beginner in business. He can manipulate stocks with the best of them. It was his expertise that helped me put the ranch into the black. Not to mention those new techniques in cattle management that he bulldozed me into trying. Embryo transplants, artificial insemination, hormone implants…although he and I mutually decided to stop the hormone implants. There's been a lot of negative talk about it among consumers."

"Negative talk never stopped C.C.," she said, chuckling.

"True enough, but he thinks like I do about it. If implants cut back beef consumption because people are afraid of the hormones, that cuts our profits."

"I give up," she said, holding up both hands. "Put away your shooting irons."

"Sorry," he murmured, and smiled back.

"Actually I agree with you," she confessed. "I just like to hear you hold forth. I'm going dancing with Brandon on Friday night. Okay?"

He looked reluctant, but he didn't argue. "Okay, as long as you remember that my birthday's Saturday night and you're going out with me."

"Yes, sir. As if I could forget. Thirty-nine, isn't it…?"

"Shut up and carve that apple pie," he said, gesturing toward it.

"Whatever you say."

She tried not to think about C.C. for the rest of the week, but it was impossible not to catch an occasional glimpse of him in the saddle, going from one corral to the next. He let the herd representatives ride in the Jeep—representatives from other ranches in the area checking brands to make sure that none of their cattle had crossed into Mathews territory. It was a common courtesy locally, because of the vast territory the ranches in south Texas covered. Her father ran over two thousand head of cattle, and when they threw calves, it took some effort to get them all branded, tattooed, ear-tagged and vaccinated each spring and fall. It was a dirty, hot, thankless chore that caused occasional would-be cowboys to quit and go back to working in textile plants and furniture shops. Cowboying, while romantic and glamorous to the unknowing, was low paying, backbreaking and prematurely aging as a profession. It meant living with the smell of cow chips, burning hide, leather and dirt—long hours in the saddle, long hours of fixing machinery and water pumps and vehicles and doctoring sick cattle. There was a television in the bunkhouse, but hardly ever any time to watch it except late on summer evenings. Ranch work was year-round with few lazy periods, because there was always something that needed doing.

The advantages of the job were freedom, freedom, and freedom. A man lived close to the earth. He had time to watch the skies and feel the urgent rhythm of life all around him. He lived as man perhaps was meant to live, without technology strangling his mind, without the smells and pressures of civilization to cripple his spirit. He was one with nature, with life itself. He didn't answer to an alarm clock or some corporation's image of what a businessman should be. He might not make a lot of money, he might risk life and limb daily, but he was as free as a modern man could get. If he did his job well and carefully, he had job security for all his life.

Pepi thought about that, and decided that it might not be such a bad thing after all, being a cowboy. But the title and job description, while it might fit C.C., sat oddly on his broad shoulders. He was much too sophisticated to look at home in dirty denims. It was easier now to picture him in a dinner jacket. All the same, he did look fantastic in the saddle, riding a horse as easily as if he'd been born on one. He was long and lean and graceful, even in a full gallop, and she'd seen him break a horse to saddle more than once. It was a treat to watch. He never hurt the horse's spirit in the process, but once he was on its back, there was never any doubt about who the master was. He stuck like glue, his hard face taut with strain, his eyes glittering, his thin lips smiling savagely with the effort as he rode the animal to submission.

The picture stuck in Pepi's mind, and brought with it disturbing sensations of another kind of conquest. She was no prude, and despite her innocence, she knew what men and woman did together in bed. But the sensation, the actual feelings they shared were alien to her. She wondered if C.C. would be like that in bed, if he'd have that same glittery look in his eyes, that same savage smile on his thin lips as he brought a woman to ecstasy under the driving force of his hard, sweat-glistened body...

She went scarlet. Fortunately there was nobody nearby to see her. She darted into the house and up the staircase to get dressed for her dinner date with Brandon.

They went to a restaurant in downtown El Paso, one famous in the area for the size of its steaks and for its view of the city at night from its fourteenth-floor location in a well-known hotel.

"I do love the view from up here," Pepi told Brandon, smiling at him as they were shown to a seat by the huge windows overlooking the Franklin Mountains. The Franklins, in fact, were responsible for the city's name, because the pass that separated the Franklins from the Juárez Mountains to the south was called *El Paso del Norte*—the path of the north. Part of the mountain chain was located in the city of El Paso itself. The only major desert city in Texas, El Paso shared much history with Mexico's Juárez, across the border. Pancho Villa lived in El Paso after his exile from his own country, and historically the Texas city, which sat on the Butterfield Overland stage route in the late nineteenth century, had been the site of Indian attacks and a replica of old Fort Bliss marked the former home of the cavalry that once fought the Apaches, including the famous Chief Victorio. Modern-day Fort Bliss was the home of the largest air defense center of the free world. Not far from the restaurant where Pepi and Brandon were eating was the Acme Saloon, where gunfighter John Wesley Hardin was shot in the back and killed.

On a less grim note, there was an aerial tramway up to Ranger Peak, giving tourists a view of seven thousand square miles of mountain and desert. There were one hundred parks in El Paso, not to mention museums, old missions, and plenty of attractions across the border in Mexico's largest border city, Juárez.

Pepi had lived near El Paso all her life, and she had the love of the desert that comes from living near it. Tourists might see an expanse of open land nestled between mountain ranges with no apparent life. Pepi saw flowering agave and prickly pear cactus, stately organ pipe cactus and creosote bushes, graceful mesquite trees and the wonder of the mountain ranges at sunset. She loved the desert surrounding the city. Of course, she loved her own home more. The land down near Fort Hancock where the ranch was located was just a bit more hospitable than this, and her roots were there.

"The view from up here is pretty great," Brandon agreed, drawing her out of her reveries. "But you suit me better than the desert and the mountains," he added, his gaze approving her simple mauve dress with its crystal pleats and cap sleeves. Her hair, in an elegant bun, drew attention to the exquisite lines of her face and the size of her pale brown eyes. She'd used more makeup than usual and she looked honestly pretty, freckles and all. But it was her figure that held Brandon's attention. When she dressed up, she was dynamite.

"What will you have to drink?" the waitress asked with a smile, diverting both of them.

"Just white wine for me," Pepi replied.

"I'll have the same," her escort added.

The waitress left and Brandon, resplendent in a dark suit, leaned his forearms on the spotless white tablecloth and stared at her warmly. "Why won't you marry me?" he asked. "Does it have something to do with the fact that I hang out with animals?"

She laughed. "I love animals. But I'm not quite ready for marriage yet." Then she remembered that she *was* married, and her heart dropped. She shifted back in her chair, feeling vaguely guilty at being out with Brandon when she was legally another man's wife. Of course, the man she was married to didn't know it. That made her feel a little better, at least.

"You're an old lady of twenty-two," he persisted. "You'll be over the hill before you know it."

"No, I won't. I haven't even decided what I want to do with my life yet." That was true. She'd never gone to college. Somehow, after she'd graduated from high school, there had been too much to demand her time at home. "I like figures," she murmured absently. "I thought I might take an accounting course or something."

"You could come and work for me. I need a bookkeeper," he said instantly.

"Sorry, but so does Dad. Jack Berry, our present bookkeeper, is hopeless. So is Dad. If I decide to take on bookkeeping, you'd better believe that Dad will scoop me up first. He hates having to redo Jack's figuring."

"I guess... Well, well, look at that dress!"

It was unusual for Brandon to be so wickedly interested in what any woman wore. Pepi turned her head slightly to follow his gaze and her heart froze in her chest.

Edie was just coming in the door, wearing a red dress that was cut to the waist in back and dipped in a faintly low V in front. Despite its length, it was an advertisement for her blonde beauty, and she drew eyes. Just behind her stood a bored-looking C.C. in a dark vested suit, his hard face showing lines of tiredness from the two weeks of work he'd just put in. Pepi could hardly bear to look at him.

He must have felt her stare because his head turned and even across the room she registered the impact of that level look. She averted her eyes and smiled at Brandon.

"You might as well keep your leering looks to your-self," she said more pleasantly than she wanted to. "C.C.'s pretty possessive of her."

"He's giving you a hard glare. Were you supposed to stay home tonight or something?"

"No. He's probably just tired," she emphasized, try-ing not to remember the last face-to-face confronta-tion she'd had with her father's foreman. It made her pulse leap and catch fire just to think about the way he'd talked to her, the things he'd said. She loved ev-erything about him, but if his attentiveness to Edie was anything to go by, the feeling was hardly mutual. She carefully avoided glancing at him again, oblivious to his angry scowl and preoccupied manner while he ate his own supper.

CHAPTER FOUR

IF PEPI HAD hoped that C.C. and his girlfriend would leave without saying anything, she was doomed to disappointment. After he and Edie had finished dessert, he went straight to Pepi's table, dragging the unwilling blonde along with him.

"Well, hello," Brandon said, smiling at them. "How does it feel to finally be through with roundup, C.C.? I'm royally sick of it myself, and I've still got two herds to examine tomorrow."

"It's nice to have a little free time," the older man said quietly. His black eyes were carving up Pepi's face. "I haven't laid eyes on you for two weeks," he told her curtly. "I wondered if you've been avoiding me."

Pepi was shocked by the sudden attack, as well as by the venom in his deep voice. She wasn't the only one. Brandon and Edie exchanged questioning glances, too.

"I haven't been avoiding you," Pepi said, but she couldn't quite meet those eyes with the memory of their last confrontation between them. "You've been out with the men all day and most of the night, just like Dad. I've had things of my own to do, keeping up with the cooking and helping Wiley organize supplies for the chuck wagon."

The Bar M was one of the few ranches that still operated a chuck wagon. The ranch was so big that it wasn't practical to have two dozen men trucking back and forth to the bunkhouse kitchen to be fed. Wiley, one of the older hands, cooked and Pepi helped him keep supplies in.

"You usually come out and watch us work," C.C. persisted, his eyes narrowing.

It was a question, and Pepi didn't want to answer it. She tangled her fingers in her napkin, vaguely aware of Edie's frown as she watched the byplay.

"I'm overweight," Pepi told him belligerently, glaring up at him. "All right? I find it hard to get in the saddle these days. Now are you satisfied!"

"You're not overweight," C.C. said shortly.

Edie took C.C.'s arm possessively. "We girls can be sensitive about our weight, aren't we, Penelope?" she said with a dry laugh. "Especially when it lands around our hips."

What hips? Pepi wanted to ask, because Edie looked more like a bean pole than a woman with her exaggerated thinness. The older woman's comments had hurt, and Pepi wished she knew why she'd ever brought the subject up in the first place. It had been clumsy and stupid; her usual condition when C.C. came close these days.

"I think Pepi's just right," Brandon murmured, smiling reassuringly at her. "She suits me."

"You angel," Pepi said, smiling at him.

"Why isn't your father with you?" C.C. asked suddenly, his face gone hard at the way Pepi was smiling at the redheaded vet.

Pepi started, her big eyes gaping up at him as if she feared for his sanity. "I don't usually take my father on dates, C.C.," she said.

"Tomorrow is his birthday," he reminded her with faint sarcasm, bristling with bad humor. He hated seeing her with Hale, hated having her avoid him. He felt that it was probably the things he'd said to her that had sent her running, but deeper still was resentment that she was more than likely sleeping with that clown next to her. The thought of Pepi in another man's bed drove him out of his mind. He'd been short-tempered and unapproachable almost the whole time he was working roundup because of the casual way she'd denied being innocent. God knew how many dreams he'd had about relieving her of that condition, and in the most tender way. Now his illusions were shattered, and he wanted to make her as miserable as she'd made him.

"I know tomorrow is his birthday." Pepi faltered. "Brandon and I are taking him to the *Diez Y Seis de Septiembre* parade in the morning. Aren't we, Brandon?" she added, almost frantic. They weren't taking her father anywhere, but she couldn't bear to tell C.C. that all she'd planned was a birthday cake and a nice supper. Not when he was looking at her as if she were public enemy number one and the most ungrateful daughter on earth.

"That's right," Brandon agreed immediately.

Hale, again, C.C. thought furiously. He lifted his chin and looked down his straight nose at her. He spared

Brandon a cold, barely civil glance. "I suppose he'll be grateful that you bothered about his birthday."

"What in the world's come over you?" Pepi asked defensively. Was he trying to start a fight, for heaven's sake? She stiffened in her chair, aware of Edie's surprised scrutiny of her escort.

"He's had a hard couple of weeks, that's what," Brandon said with a forced smile, trying to relieve the tension. "I ought to know. I've been out there most days."

"Roundup makes everybody bad-tempered," Pepi agreed. She looked up at Edie. "How are you? I love your dress."

"This old rag?" Edie chuckled. "Thanks. I thought it might cheer up my friend here, but it hasn't seemed to do much for him."

"Oh, hasn't it?" C.C. murmured, diverted at last. He glanced briefly at Pepi before he slid a possessive arm around Edie's shoulders and pulled her close, his eyes warm, his voice deep and sensuous. "Come along, and I'll see if I can't convince you that it has."

"Now there's an offer I won't refuse," Edie murmured huskily. "Good night, Penelope, Brandon."

They murmured their farewells and Pepi refused to watch them walk away. He was her husband. She wanted to stand up and shout it, to drag Edie away from him. They were going off somewhere to be alone, and she knew what would happen; she could see it in her mind. She ground her teeth together.

"Poor thing," Brandon said then, his blue eyes full of concern and sudden understanding. "So that's how it is."

"I've been looking out for him for a long time," Pepi

said defensively. "I'm overly protective. I have to stop it. He's not my chick, and I'm not his mother hen. Well, maybe once a year, but only then."

Brandon wasn't buying it. He covered her hand on the table with his own. "If you ever need a shoulder to cry on, you can use mine," he said gently. "And if you ever get over him…"

"Thanks," she said, forcing a smile.

"I guess you know that I can't take you and your father to the parade in the morning?" he added.

She nodded, smiling. "Sorry. I don't even know why I said it. He made me mad. I was going to bake my father a cake, that's all."

"I wouldn't mind helping him eat it, but I'm going to be out all day tomorrow with old man Reynolds's herd," he said ruefully. "I won't be home until after midnight, more than likely."

"I'll save you a piece of cake. Thanks for pulling my irons out of the fire."

"You're welcome." He frowned. "It's not like C.C. to start fights with you in public. Odd that he'd take you to task over your dad."

She couldn't tell him that C.C. had been spoiling for a fight ever since she'd gone overboard and lied about her maidenly condition. Anyway, it didn't matter. C.C.'s opinion didn't bother her. Not one bit!

"Maybe he's just frustrated because he's been away from Edie for two weeks," she said miserably and felt her heart breaking at the thought of how much lost time he could make up for tonight with his blonde attachment.…

She felt sick. "It's ever so complicated, Brandon," she sighed. "I've managed to get us into a terrible mess, and, no, I can't talk about it. Can we go, please? I've got a headache."

He took her home and she managed to get away without a good-night kiss. C.C.'s appearance had ruined the evening for her. She'd hoped to keep him out of her mind for a little while, but fate seemed to have other ideas.

She hardly slept. She got up with a dull headache and it got worse when C.C. came in smiling and looking like a hungry cat with canary feathers sticking out both sides of his mouth. She didn't need a scorecard to know why he was so smug and content. He'd probably had a hell of a sweet night with Edie, but while she'd always suspected what his relationship with the blonde actually was, her feelings overwhelmed her. She glared at C.C. with eyes that almost hated him, her freckles standing out in a pale, haunted face.

"What do you want?" she demanded testily.

His eyebrows arched. "Coffee, for now. And a word with your father before you and the happy vet take him off to town."

She'd told a bald-faced lie the night before, and now she was standing in the middle of it with nothing to say. Her face slowly flamed scarlet.

His black eyes narrowed. He pushed back the brim of his Stetson and leaned against the kitchen counter, his blue striped Western shirt complementing the darkness of his face and hair and eyes, his powerful leg muscles rippling under tight denims as he shifted his position.

"Are you taking him to the parade?" he asked, his tone less belligerent than it had been the night before.

She shook her head, wiping flour off her hands and dabbing at a streak of it on the denim skirt that she was wearing with a yellow tank top.

"Why did you say you were?" he added.

She glanced at him angrily. "Because you made me sound like a female Jack the Ripper last night, as if I didn't even care about my own father."

His eyes slid down her body and back up again, a visual touch that made her nerves sit up and scream. No man had ever looked at her like that, so sensually that she felt as if he'd stroked her bare breasts. She caught her breath.

He trapped her eyes with his, reading her response in them. So she wasn't immune to him. She might be experienced, but she was vulnerable just the same. A faint smile touched his hard mouth.

"I know you care about your father," he said. "I just don't like the amount of time you spend with Hale."

"Brandon is—"

"A clown," he finished for her, his smile fading. "Too irresponsible and flighty for a woman with your depth. He's probably never satisfied you once."

What he meant was evident in his tone, and she almost dropped the bag of flour in her haste to put it away. She kept her back to him while she made biscuits, hoping he'd go away.

"He makes me laugh," she said through her teeth.

He came up behind her, his body so close that she could feel the heat and strength of it at her back, smell the faint cologne he wore. She tensed all over, waiting for him to touch her, waiting for his lean hands to bite into her waist and jerk her back into his body, for those same hands to smooth up her rib cage to her full, throbbing breasts and cup them....

"What are you doing?" he asked.

Her eyes blinked. He wasn't touching her. She felt his breath on her nape, but he was just looking over her shoulder, that was all. But she was on fire to kiss his hard mouth, to touch him, to hold him against her. She had to clench her teeth to still the feverish excitement he created with his proximity. Perhaps he didn't realize how vulnerable she was, and she wanted to keep it that way.

"I'm making biscuits." Heavens, was that husky whisper really her voice?

"And ham? I like country ham."

"Yes, I know. I'm going to fry it while the biscuits cook. There's coffee on the stove if you want some."

"I noticed."

But he didn't move. She started pinching off biscuits and laying them neatly into the round baking pan in front of her, but her hands were trembling. He was tormenting her. She wanted to scream.

She turned her head helplessly and looked up into his eyes, and all at once she knew. That flicker of mocking amusement in his face was enough to convince her that he was all too aware of the effect he had on her.

"Do I bother you, Pepi?" he drawled, deliberately letting his gaze drop to her full, parted lips. "Surely I shouldn't if Hale is enough for you."

Her breath was ragged. She forced her head back

down so that she could concentrate on her biscuits. "Is Edie enough for you?" she countered outrageously.

"When I'm in the mood, anything with breasts is enough for me," he said curtly, angered by her refusal to admit her interest in him.

"C.C.!" she burst out, whirling.

His hands slid past her wide hips to rest on either side of her on the table, effectively trapping her. His gaze was relentlessly probing. "You don't want me to know that you're attracted to me. Why?"

"This isn't fair," she whispered. "I've looked out for you for years, I've done my best to make you comfortable, to help you when I could. Is this any way to pay me back for being your friend?"

He stared at her unblinkingly. "I told you, I don't need a nursemaid. But you've been avoiding me and I don't like it. I want to know why."

"And this is how you plan to find out?" she asked, her voice wobbling a little, because his nearness was devastating to her senses.

"It's the quickest way," he replied. "You've been backing away ever since that day in the hall." His eyes narrowed to glittering slits. "In fact, you've been backing away since that night in Juárez. What did I do to you, Pepi? Did I try to make love to you?"

"No!" she burst out.

"Then what happened?" he asked.

She couldn't tell him. She should, but she couldn't. She lowered her eyes to his broad chest. "You said I could probably throw you over my shoulder and carry you out of the bar," she said dully, repeating the blistering insult he'd thrown at her. "That I was nothing but a tomboy…"

He didn't remember. But he could see the hurt on her face, and that disturbed him. "I was drinking," he said gently. "You know I didn't mean anything I said."

She laughed painfully. "No? I thought people always told the truth when they drank, because they were uninhibited."

He drew in a slow, deep breath. "What else did I say?"

"That was more than enough. I closed my ears to the rest of it."

"And that's why you've been avoiding me?" he persisted, as if it mattered. In fact, it did. He'd been smarting ever since, hurt by her avoidance as he'd rarely been hurt by anything.

She hesitated. Then she nodded.

He bent his head and laid his cheek against hers, nuzzling it gently. The silence in the kitchen grew hot with restrained excitement. She could almost hear her own heartbeat…or was it his? She all but stopped breathing. He smelled of cologne and tobacco, and his cheek was rough and warm where it lay against hers. He didn't try to kiss her, or even pull her against him. But his face drew slowly against her own, and she felt his thick eyelashes against her cheek, her chin, her soft throat, felt the heat of his tobacco-scented breath on her breasts as his forehead rested on her collarbone and she felt the bridge of his nose on the bare swell of her breast where it slowly pushed the fabric out of the way.…

"Pepi, where the hell is the newspaper?"

C.C. lifted his head as her father's voice exploded

from the hall. He stared down at her shocked face with narrowed eyes in a face like honed steel. He edged away from the table, his lean hands at his sides, and his gaze dropped to the drooping neckline of the tank top, which her cold fingers fumbled to adjust.

She met C.C.'s gaze for one long, shattering instant and then she turned abruptly back to her biscuits with trembling hands and a heartbeat that shook her.

"There you are. Morning, C.C.," her father said with a chuckle. "I found the paper," he added, waving it as he went to the table and sat down. "Pepi had already brought it in."

"Happy Birthday," Pepi said with a forced smile. "I'm making breakfast."

"So I noticed. Do I get a cake?"

"Coconut, your favorite, and all your favorite foods for supper," she added.

"C.C., you can come over and help me eat it," he told the younger man.

"I'm afraid not," C.C. replied, glancing at Pepi's rigid spine. "I'm taking Edie to the parade, and then down to Juárez to spend the day shopping."

"Well, you'll enjoy that, I'm sure," Ben said slowly, aware of odd undercurrents in the kitchen.

"Come with us. You, too, Pepi," he added carelessly. "We'll celebrate your birthday in Mexico," he told Ben.

"Great idea! I haven't taken a day off since I don't know when. Pepi will enjoy it, too. We'll do it, then to-night you and Edie can come home with us and have supper, can't they, Pepi?"

She was going to die. She knew she was going to die.

Thank God nobody could see her face. "Of course they can," she said through her teeth. "We'll have a lovely time." What else could she say, she wondered. After all, it was Ben's birthday. He was entitled to spend it the way he pleased. But she was still going up in flames at the way C.C. had touched her, and the thought of watching him with Edie all day made her want to run screaming into the yard.

"Just the four of us," C.C. added as he sat down with a cup of coffee in his hand. "Not Hale."

She swallowed. "Brandon can't come anyway. He's going to be working all day and most of the night."

"I thought you liked Brandon," Ben Mathews remarked, eyeing C.C. curiously.

"I do. I just don't like him hanging around Pepi," C.C. replied honestly. He glanced at her rigid back and away. "She can do better."

Ben chuckled. Now the undercurrents began to make sense. He shot a curious look toward his daughter, not missing the flush on her cheeks and the way she fumbled biscuits into the oven. He wondered for a minute what he'd interrupted by bursting into the kitchen. Then C.C. asked him a question about the culled cattle he was selling off, and the moment was forgotten.

Almost all the biscuits went fast. Pepi had to grab to get one at all, and the ham and scrambled eggs went even faster.

"You're inhaling it!" she accused them.

"Can I help it if you're the best cook around?" C.C. asked innocently.

"A good cook beats a fashion plate any day," her father remarked bluntly. "Ought to marry this girl, C.C., before she takes her pots and pans elsewhere."

"Dad!" Pepi exclaimed, shattered. She went white with horror, remembering that marriage license in her bureau drawer.

C.C. frowned. That was an odd reaction for a woman who'd been as responsive as she had a few minutes ago. She was acting pretty oddly lately, and he didn't believe it was only because he'd hurt her feelings in Juárez. No, there had to be something more. Something had happened that night, he was sure of it. But what?

"I don't want to get married, to a good cook or a fashion plate," he murmured absently to Ben, scowling as he turned his attention back to the biscuit he was buttering. He missed the expression on Pepi's face.

"Don't you want kids?" Ben asked curiously.

Pepi could have cried when she saw the way that innocent question affected C.C. Her father didn't know what she did about their foreman's past.

"Have the last biscuit," she broke in, shoving the plate in her father's face with a scowl.

He was quick, was Ben. He realized instantly that he'd said something he shouldn't. "Well, where's the honey?" he demanded, camouflaging the brief silence. "You've eaten it all, haven't you? It was my honey!"

"It was your apple pie," she threw back. "You ate every bit of it and didn't even offer me any, so you can forget the honey, it's mine!" She clutched the jar to her breasts and glared at him across the table.

C.C. was touched by her attempt to protect him, even

now. He watched her quietly, thinking how attractive she was. She looked soft and rounded and sweet. He liked her freckles and the way her hair caught fire and burned like bronze and honey in the sun. He liked the way she talked, the way she smelled. He liked a lot of things about her. And if it hadn't been for the tormenting memories, for the wounds of the past, he might have considered marrying her. But no, marriage wasn't something he coveted. It was a part of life he'd already experienced. Despite his jealousy of Hale, the other man would probably be better for Pepi than he would.

He never should have touched her. Now he was going to have to undo the damage he'd just done by losing his head before Ben walked in. He'd have to play up to Edie to throw Pepi off the track, to make sure she didn't get any ideas about him. Friendship was all he had to offer, and the sooner he made that clear to her the better. But he was going to have to keep his emotions under control to accomplish that. She went to his head, more so every day. He'd said and done things that he'd never meant to; he'd deliberately made passes at her. He couldn't understand his loss of control, or his sudden fascination with Pepi. Perhaps the long hours and hard work of the past few weeks were telling on him. He frowned and studied his cooling coffee. Maybe what he needed was a vacation. God knew he hadn't taken one in three years. He might go back to Jacobsville, Texas, where he was born, and visit his three brothers who were running the family business in his absence. He might go and try to face the past, if he could.

"I said, when do you want to leave?" Ben asked him for the second time.

"About nine-thirty," he said, tossing down the rest of his coffee. "We don't want to get there too late for the parade."

"Are you sure you want both of us along?" Pepi asked hesitantly.

He got up and glared at her. "It's your father's birthday. Of course I'm sure. Edie and I will enjoy having company." His eyes narrowed. "After all, we're alone most of the time. As we will be tonight, when I take her home. I don't mind sharing her occasionally."

Ben chuckled, but Pepi felt as if she'd been slapped. Coming so close on the heels of C.C.'s ardor, it was painful to be reminded that he belonged to someone else. She got up and began to clear the table absently.

C.C. went out the door without looking back. He hated hurting her. He never should have touched her.

Pepi took her time dressing. She'd thought about wearing one of her colorful Mexican dresses for the parade, with their lavish embroidery so delicate against the bone-white cotton and lace. But if Edie was going along, she might as well not bother to look feminine. Beside the blonde, she felt like an oversized tank.

She put on gray slacks and a bulky khaki top, tying her hair back in a severe ponytail. She looked terrible, she thought as she saw her reflection, defiantly leaving off makeup as well. Good. That would show C.C. Tremayne what she thought of him!

It did. He scowled at the sight of her, no less than her father had when she'd come downstairs.

"What the hell happened to you?" C.C. demanded. He'd changed, too, into a very becoming yellow knit designer shirt and tan slacks, a creamy Stetson perched on his black hair.

"What do you mean? I look the way I always do," Pepi defended.

"You didn't look like that last night," he said accusingly.

"Last night, I dressed up for Brandon," she said, staring back at him. "You have Edie to dress up for you," she added meaningfully.

C.C. shifted his eyes uncomfortably. He'd deserved that. "Ready to go, Ben?" he asked the older man, who was dressed casually himself.

"Just let me get my hat." He glanced at his daughter and scowled. "You could have worn that Mexican dress, just for me. I thought it looked just right for a fiesta."

"It doesn't fit," she lied, averting her gaze from C.C. "Besides, I look like a hippo in it...."

"You don't look like a hippo," C.C. said angrily. "My God, will you stop harping on your weight? You're just right. At least you look like a woman. People don't have to stop and guess when you walk by!"

Pepi stared at him with raised eyebrows. He glared at her and turned away just as Ben joined them.

She wondered if she was ever going to understand him. He was acting so completely erratic these days, like a man in love. She sighed. Probably it was just a matter of time before he and Edie tied the knot, despite what he'd said at the breakfast table about not wanting to marry again. She turned, picking up her purse on the

way out the door. Anyway, why would he look twice
at her with someone as beautiful as Edie on his arm?

Edie was waiting in C.C.'s Ford, looking bored and
irritable.

"Finally!" she muttered. "It's hot out here!"

"Sorry. I had to find my hat," Ben mumbled as he
put Pepi into the backseat and climbed in beside her.

"I didn't mean to sound like that, Ben," Edie purred,
all smiles when C.C. climbed in under the wheel and
cranked the car. "You know we're delighted to have you,
and Pepi, with us today. Happy Birthday!"

"Thanks," Ben said. He glanced at his daughter's
quiet, sad face. She sat stiffly beside him, staring blankly
out the window. He was beginning to get the picture
about the way she felt. If she wasn't in love with C.C.,
she was giving a good imitation of a woman who was.

"Well, on to the parade," Edie mused, checking her
makeup in her compact mirror. "Want to borrow a lip-
stick, Pepi? I didn't realize I'd rushed C.C. that much."

"I'm not wearing any," Pepi replied, "but thank you."

Edie glanced at her and then shrugged.

The parade was colorful and there was a crowd. The
Diez Y Seis de Septiembre celebration was the annual
observance of Mexico's independence from Spain—
Mexico's Independence Day. Pepi always enjoyed the
music and the floats, and the carnival atmosphere, but
today she was preoccupied. She put on a happy face for
her father's benefit, hoping he wouldn't see through it.
But C.C.'s obvious interest in Edie was killing her. He
had a possessive arm around the blonde, and once he

bent and kissed her hungrily in full view of Pepi and the rest of El Paso.

Pepi turned away to buy a pinwheel from a passing vendor, glad for the diversion. She handed it to her father, deliberately keeping her eyes away from C.C.

"Happy Birthday, Dad," she said gently and smiled. "I've got your present at home. I thought you could have it with your cake after supper."

"That will be a nice touch." He patted her shoulder. "Sorry about this," he murmured, nodding toward an oblivious C.C. and Edie. "I should have refused."

"No, you shouldn't. It's your birthday." She smiled. "It's for the best, you know. I was wearing my heart out on him. It's just as well that I have to face how he really feels. Dreams are sweet, but you can't build a future on them."

"You've been different lately, Pepi," her father said surprisingly. "Is there anything you want to tell me?"

"A lot." She turned her eyes toward C.C. "But first I have to tell him something. I should have told him before, but it's not too late. The minute we get home I'll make it all right. Then," she said with a rueful smile, "I'm going to need a shoulder to cry on, I think."

"You aren't in trouble, or anything?" her father asked hesitantly.

She laughed. "Not the kind you're thinking, no." She sighed and watched the parade. "It will be all right," she said, trying to convince herself. "It's just a little thing. Just a minor inconvenience."

She hoped C.C. would see it like that. She had to tell him today, before she lost her nerve. He and Edie were getting involved, anybody could see that. She couldn't, in all good conscience, let him face a bigamy charge because of her own stubborn pride. Tonight, she'd tell him the truth, and hope for the best.

CHAPTER FIVE

THEY WENT PAST the border guards for the day trip into Mexico with no problem at all. The car was stopped, but Pepi knew why. The border guard, a rather squatty young man, had spotted Edie and asked her instead of C.C. what they were going to do in Juárez.

Edie ate up his attention, tossing her blond hair and laughing as she told him they were going shopping. He waved them through with flattering reluctance, still eyeing Edie, while C.C. chuckled softly under his breath. Edie did love to make a conquest. She seemed to enjoy letting C.C. know that she could attract other men quite easily.

Watching the woman, Pepi could have sworn that C.C. knew exactly what she was up to. He seemed so cynical about women, as if he knew them inside out and couldn't care less. She happened to glance at him then, and saw that bitter, half-mocking smile on his sensuous mouth. Before she could look away, he caught her eyes. It was like lightning striking. She had to drag her gaze away.

C.C. drove while Edie leaned over the backseat of his big Ford and talked animatedly to Ben. Pepi shook

her head. Even her father wasn't immune to Edie's flirt-
ing. He was grinning like a Cheshire cat.

It wasn't a long drive and minutes later, they were in
Juárez. And it was only thanks to C.C.'s experience that
they found their way around—Juárez was impossible
with a map, and worse without one.

The city was deliciously Mexican. They browsed
through the endless markets and Edie pleaded until C.C.
bought her a ridiculously expensive turquoise necklace. Pepi would have been easier to please. If C.C. had
handed her a pebble from the ground, she'd have slept
with it under her pillow for the rest of her life. But her
tastes were simpler than Edie's—she only wanted C.C.

Down the street was a magnificent cathedral, and
near that was a small boutique. Edie exclaimed at the
display in the window, and noticed that they honored
her charge card.

"I'll only be a few hours," she told C.C., tiptoeing to
kiss his lean cheek. "Penelope, want to come along?" she
called to Penelope, knowing full well that the younger
woman had little interest in fancy clothes and didn't
possess a charge card. She'd never gone further afield
than the small town she grew up in; Edie knew that, too.

"No, thanks," Pepi said amiably. "I'd rather sightsee."

"Good," her father said. "You can keep me company.
C.C. seems to be in another world."

He did, and when Pepi saw where his dark eyes were
riveted, she felt her stomach sink. He was mentally re-
tracing his steps the night he got drunk, she was sure
of it! His eyes went from the bar down the street to a

small chapel—the chapel where he'd drunkenly forced Pepi to stand in front of a priest.

"Well, well, a wedding chapel," Ben murmured. He glanced down at Pepi. "For a man who isn't interested in getting married, he does seem to find it fascinating, doesn't he?"

Pepi had a sick feeling when she saw C.C. jam his lean hands into his pockets and start toward the chapel. She moved forward instinctively to try to divert him. And just as she reached him, oblivious to her father's surprised expression, the two Mexicans who'd helped her bundle up C.C. and get him to the truck that night came sauntering out of the wedding chapel. Perhaps they were related to the priest…

Don't say anything, don't recognize him, please, she prayed, both her fingers crossed.

They did recognize him, though, and broke into wide grins. *"Felicitaciones,"* they laughed. *"¿Como quiere usted vida conjugal, eh? ¡Y alla esta su esposa! ¿Hóla, señora, coma 'sta?"*

"What?" Ben burst out, overhearing the conversation.

Pepi buried her face in her hands. "What did they say?" she asked through her fingers.

"They're congratulating him on being married!"

Ben didn't say another word. Rapid-fire Spanish exchanges led to an ominous silence, and seconds later, a furious C.C. was towering over her. He took her by both shoulders and shook her, hard, ignoring Ben's dazed presence.

"What the hell do they mean, congratulations on my marriage?" he demanded, his deep voice cutting and sharp. "You lied to me! We were married here that night, weren't we? Weren't we?"

"All right, yes," she whispered. "I didn't know it was legal," she tried to explain, her eyes big, tearful and anguished. "C.C., I didn't know it was legal!"

"You're married?" Ben burst out.

"Not for long," C.C. said, all but throwing Pepi away from him, as if the touch of her burned his hands. "My God, of all the low, contemptible, underhanded ways to get a husband! Get a man drunk and drag him in front of a minister, and then keep it a secret! You knew I'd never marry a plain little schemer like you if I was sober! You're nothing to look at, and you don't act or dress like a typical woman. It wouldn't surprise me if you told Hale every move to make when you get him in bed!"

"C.C., please," she pleaded, aware of the attention his loud, angry voice was attracting.

He seemed to realize that they were on display. "I'll get Edie. We're leaving, right now," he told Pepi. "The sooner this farce ends in an annulment, the better."

"You got him drunk and married him?" Ben asked, shaken by the revelation.

"He got drunk and threatened to land us in a Mexican jail if I didn't," she said heavily. "I didn't think it was binding anywhere except in Mexico or I'd never have gone through with it. You know what the criminal justice system is like down here, it's as slow as molasses. We could have spent weeks or months in jail before you could have managed to get us out...."

"I know that! What did he mean about you sleeping with Hale?" he demanded.

"I don't sleep with Brandon. I just let C.C. think it... Well, to throw up a smoke screen, I guess. Dad, it's such a mess! I had the best intentions...and on your birthday!" She burst into tears. "I should have said something, but I was scared. I thought I could get a quiet annulment, but the lawyer said he'd have to know...!"

Ben held her while she cried, awkwardly patting her back until a fire-eyed C.C. joined them with Edie in tow.

"What's the matter with Pepi?" Edie asked.

"Don't ask," Ben said heavily. "We have to go."

"Okay." She shrugged, eyeing the younger woman curiously. "Gosh, Pepi, are you sick?"

"If she is, she damn well deserves to be," C.C. said furiously. "Let's go."

Edie didn't dare question him. Pepi cried silently and Ben sat by helplessly while they got out of Juárez into El Paso and on the road to the ranch.

C.C. was out of sorts the whole way back home. He smoked in silence, letting Edie prattle on until she got disgusted with him and turned up the radio. Lost in thoughts of her own, Penelope just leaned back with her eyes closed, oblivious to the worried look on her father's face.

Instead of going to the ranch, C.C. stopped by Edie's apartment, escorted her to the door and left her there without a word. He didn't say another word all the way home. He didn't speed, or drive recklessly. Penelope wondered at his control. Even when he was furious, and she knew he was right now, he never lost that iron control. She wondered if he ever had.

Back at the ranch, C.C. headed for the stables the minute he parked the car, and Pepi felt sorry for any poor soul who was in there undefended. C.C. in a temper was a force to behold. Presumably he was going to work off some steam before he started on her again. She couldn't even blame him for being so angry. She should have told him in the very beginning. It was her own fault.

"Suppose you tell me the whole story?" her father asked while she made coffee in the kitchen.

She did, all about C.C.'s once-a-year bender and the reason for it, about the way she'd sobered him up— or thought she had—and the way she'd trailed him to Juárez and wound up married to him.

"The bottom line," she said, "is that I think he comes from money, despite the work he does here. He might think I deliberately maneuvered him into marriage for mercenary motives."

"C.C. knows you better than that," Ben scoffed.

"He knows the ranch hasn't been paying and that I don't have a job and my future looks pretty insecure," she said. "It isn't, but it looks that way. And I'm reasonably sure he knows that I'm attracted to him."

"Attracted, as in head over heels in love with?" her father mused.

She shook her head. "No, thank God, he doesn't know that." She jammed her hands into her slacks pockets with a heavy sigh. Her eyes were red-rimmed from crying. "It's not the end of the world. We can get an annulment pretty easily, and I'll even get a job and pay for it. Maybe someday he'll forgive me, but right now I guess he'd like to strangle me and I don't blame him. I just hope he doesn't tell Edie. I wouldn't like her to be hurt by it."

"What about you?" Ben asked angrily. "You're hurt by it, and it's his own damned fault. If he'd stayed sober…!"

"Dad, he loved his wife. I guess he's still grieving for her. Remember how you felt when Mom died?" she added.

He got a faraway look in his eyes. He sighed. "Yes, I can understand that. Your mama was my world. We were childhood sweethearts and we lived together for twenty-two years. I could never find anyone to measure up to her, so I never remarried. Maybe he feels like that."

"Maybe he does," she agreed.

He hugged her warmly and let her go. "Try not to brood. It will all pass over. C.C. will blow off steam and come to terms with it, and you'll get it worked out. I hope," he mused on a chuckle. "With times as hard as they are, I need to keep C.C.'s mind on business, with all due respect to you."

"Ever thought of selling shares in the property?" she asked seriously.

"Yes, I have. Or taking on a partner," he added. He glanced at her. "You wouldn't mind if I did that?"

"Of course not. I don't want to lose it, either," she added gently. "You do whatever you have to."

He sighed, looking around the rustic, spacious kitchen. "Then I think I'll do some discreet advertising. God knows, you can't go much longer without a new wardrobe," he added with a mischievous wink.

"Forget about my wardrobe," she returned. "I don't care what I wear. Not anymore," she added, turning back to see about the coffee.

"There's still Hale," he said, trying to comfort her as best he could. Her pain was tangible.

"Yes, there's still Brandon. He's taking me to a cattlemen's association dinner next Wednesday night," she said. "He's a nice man, don't you think?"

He studied her quietly. "Sure he is. But you don't love him. Don't settle for crumbs, honey. Go for the whole meal."

She laughed. "Old reprobate," she accused. "You do have a way with words."

"You have a way with food," he countered. "Will you hurry up and get some supper fixed? I'm starving!"

"Okay." She went back to her pots and pans. From the kitchen window, she could see the bunkhouse. C.C. came out suddenly, dressed in, of all things, a suit. He walked toward the house, big and lean and elegant, and she washed the same dish four times while she waited for the step at the kitchen door. C.C. never went to the front. He was too much like family. But right now he was her worst enemy. The suit bothered her. Was he quitting? She felt her heart stop beating momentarily while she brooded. Did he hate her that much…?

He came in without knocking, letting in a chilly burst of wind. Penelope shuddered.

"It's getting colder out there," Ben said to ease the sudden tension.

"Colder than you know," C.C. said. He had a smoking cigarette in his hand. He lifted it to his thin lips, glaring at Pepi. "I'll be away until early next week. I've got some personal business to see to. Including," he added icily, "getting an annulment underway. I want that marriage license, Penelope."

She wiped her hands on her apron, not looking at him. "I'll get it," she said in a subdued tone, and ran for the staircase.

Her hands trembled as she took the piece of paper out of her bureau drawer and looked at it. C.C. Tremayne. The name on the license said Connal Cade Tremayne. Connal. She'd never called him anything but C.C. Until that night in Juárez, she didn't know what the initials stood for. Now she said the name to herself and grieved for the dreams contained in that simple page of words. If only things had been different, and they'd married because he loved her.

She took one long, last look at the license and carried it back downstairs.

C.C. was waiting for her at the foot of the staircase, alone. His black eyes bit into her face, but she wouldn't meet them. She held out the paper in trembling, cold fingers until he took it and then she jerked her hand back before it touched his. She could imagine that he'd welcome her touch about as much as leprosy right now.

"I'm sorry," she said huskily, staring at her boot-clad feet. "It was just—"

"Just an outsize crush that got out of hand," he returned icily. "Well, it backfired, didn't it? You're underhanded and scheming and probably a gold digger to boot."

Hot tears stung her eyes. She didn't answer him. She edged past him and went into the kitchen, barely able to see the floor as she went back to the pots and pans on the stove.

He clenched the license in his lean hand, hating himself, hating her. He was taking the hide off her, and he knew he was being unreasonable, but she'd tricked him into marriage when he was too drunk to know what he was doing. He'd thought better of her. She had no right to land him in this predicament. He'd taken Edie out, he'd… And he was married! What if he'd decided to take Edie to a minister? He'd have been committing unwitting adultery and bigamy all at once!

"She's paying for it," Ben said quietly, joining the younger man in the hall. "Don't make it any worse on her. She didn't do it deliberately, regardless of what you think."

"She should have told me," he returned curtly.

"Yes," Ben agreed. "She should have. But she didn't know how. She didn't think it was legal. And to give her credit, she did call an attorney about a quick, quiet annulment. But she found out she'd need your signature for that."

"Did you know?" C.C. demanded.

Ben shook his head. "Not until today. I thought she was in some kind of trouble, but I had no idea what it was."

C.C. stared at the paper in his hand with angry, troubled eyes. Marriage. A wife. He couldn't forget Marsha, he couldn't forget her determination to go down that river with him. She'd always been headstrong, hell-bent in her own way. He should have insisted, especially since she was sick so often and dizzy. He hadn't known she was pregnant. It had been horrible enough to have to identify her body, but to know that she'd been carrying their first child…

He groaned aloud. He'd all but killed her. His wealth had been tied to hers, a joint venture that had paid off in the embryo transplant science. He'd been too sickened by the accident to take up the reins again, leaving his oldest brothers in charge and the younger one to help while he went in search of peace of mind. He'd found it here. He'd enjoyed helping Ben build up a ranch that had been headed for receivership. He'd enjoyed Pepi's bright, undemanding company. And now she'd stabbed him in the back. He had to get away, from her and the memories she'd brought on him again.

"Where are you going?" Ben asked. "Or is that a question I shouldn't ask?"

"What do you mean?"

Ben shrugged. "Pepi said she thought you probably came from money. You blurted a lot out to her that time you were delirious and she nursed you. She thought maybe you'd been punishing yourself for your wife's death and that's why you stayed here." C.C. didn't answer. Ben lifted an eyebrow. "Whatever the reason, you're welcome here if you want to come back. I'm grateful for all you've done for me."

C.C. felt doors closing. Ben was talking as if he wasn't coming back. He glanced toward the kitchen, but Pepi was not visible there. He felt a sudden shock of panic at the thought of not seeing her again. God, what was wrong with him?

He folded the marriage license. "I don't know what I'm going to do. I might go home and see my people. I need to make an appointment with a lawyer about this," he added, fingering the paper. Odd how it seemed more like a treasure than an unwanted legal tie.

"Well, if you decide not to come back, I won't blame you," Ben said wearily. "Not much hope for this place, and we both know it. You've got us in the black, but cattle prices are down and I had to go in the hole for more equipment. I'm getting too old to manage, anyway."

That didn't sound like Ben. C.C. scowled. "My God, you're barely fifty-five!"

"Wait until *you're* fifty-five and say that," Ben chuckled. He held out a hand and C.C. shook it. "Thanks for giving me a shot at keeping the place. But you've got your own life to live." His eyes narrowed. "Maybe it's time you faced your ghosts, son. I had to do that, when I finally came to grips with my drinking problem and the fact that it cost me Pepi's mother. I survived. So will you."

"Marsha was pregnant," C.C. said curtly.

Ben nodded. "That's the worst of it for you, I imagine. You're a young man, C.C. Comparatively young, anyway. You can have other children."

"I don't want children. I don't want a wife," he said angrily, shaking the marriage license. "Least of all one I didn't choose!"

In the kitchen, Pepi heard his words, and tears rolled silently down her cheeks. She remembered what he'd said to her in Juárez. It certainly wiped out all the former compliments he'd given her, about being womanly looking. She wished she could crawl in a hole and die.

Out in the hall, Ben could imagine Pepi's pain. He herded C.C. toward the front door instead of the back one, to spare Pepi any more anguish.

"Take a few days," Ben suggested. "You've had two hard weeks of roundup and you haven't had a real vacation in over three years. Some time off is just the thing."

C.C. relaxed a little. "I guess I do need it." He stared at the folded license and, involuntarily, his eyes went back down the hall. He'd been harder on Pepi than he probably should have been. He frowned, remembering what he'd said to her. She was little more than a child in some ways. He was beginning to wonder if her so-called experience wasn't just a figment of her imagination. The way she'd reacted to him in the kitchen that morning hadn't been indicative of sophistication. Could she have lied about that, too?

His jaw clenched. He'd never be able to trust her again. If she'd lie to him once, she'd do it twice. God, why had she done this to him?

"Go on," Ben said gently, wary of new explosions. "I can handle things until you get back. Or until I have to look for a new foreman. I won't pressure you."

He frowned, thinking about something Ben had said. "You said she knew I had money."

Ben grimaced. "Yes, I did. And she was sure you'd think the marriage was because of it." He shook his head. "You're doing your damnedest to paint her evil through and through, aren't you, son?"

C.C. blinked. Was he? He moved restlessly. "I'll be in touch. Sorry to leave you in the lurch like this. God knows, it's not your fault."

"It's not Pepi's, either," Ben said enigmatically. "When you want to know the whole story, you might ask her side of it. But cool down first. And have a safe trip."

C.C. started to say something, but he closed his mouth. "Take care of yourself. Happy Birthday," he added, withdrawing a small package from his breast pocket. "I wish it could have been a happier one."

"I'm getting a whole coconut cake," Ben reminded him. He grinned. "Nothing makes me happier than not having to share it."

C.C. chuckled softly. "Okay. See you."

"Yes. I hope so," Ben added under his breath when the younger man had gone. He opened the package. It was a tie tack with a gold maverick head. He grinned. Leave it to C.C. to pick something he really liked.

He went back into the kitchen, hesitant about approaching Pepi. But she was calm enough, dishing up supper.

"Ready to eat?" she asked pleasantly. Only the faint redness of her eyes attested to her earlier misery.

"Sure. You all right?" Ben asked.

She nodded. "Right as rain. There's just one thing. I don't want to talk about it. Ever. Okay?"

He agreed. And she was her old self, on the surface at least. What Ben couldn't see was the agony under her calm expression, the pain in her heart. She was sure she didn't love C.C. now. A man who could be that cruel didn't deserve to be loved, and it was his fault anyway.

He was the one who'd forced her to get married. But he made it sound like she'd trapped him! Well, they'd see about that when he came back again. He'd never have to worry about having her heart at his feet ever again!

She served her father his favorite foods for supper and gave him his present—a new pipe and a special lighter for it—with a huge slice of coconut cake. She pretended to be happy, and hoped he wouldn't see the truth. She didn't want to spoil the rest of his birthday.

"There's just one thing you might think about," he said before she went up to bed later. "A man who's caught against his will isn't going to give in without a fight."

"I didn't catch—!" she fumed.

"You aren't listening. I mean a man who's fighting his own feelings, Pepi. I think he's got a case on you, and he doesn't want to face it. He won't take it lying down. He'll give you hell until he accepts it."

She knew better than to let herself dream again. She couldn't take another disappointment in love. "I don't want him anymore," she said bluntly. "I should have married Brandon in the first place. At least he doesn't yell at me and accuse me of things I didn't do. He's fun to be with and even if I don't love him, I like him. I sure as hell don't like C.C. Tremayne!"

"Don't marry one man trying to forget another one," Ben cautioned. "It'll only hurt Brandon and yourself."

She sighed. "I guess so. But I might learn to love him. I'm going to do my best to love him. I hope C.C. Tremayne never comes back!"

"God forbid. If that happens, the ranch will go under," Ben chuckled.

She threw up her hands and climbed the staircase.

But she didn't sleep. She wondered if she ever would again. She felt sick all over, hearing C.C.'s angry words every time she closed her eyes. Eventually she gave up even trying to go to sleep. She got up and cleaned the kitchen until dawn, an exercise that proved adequate to take her mind off C.C.—for two-minute stretches, at least.

By the time Ben had finished his breakfast, she was dressed for church. He didn't say a word. He went and put on his suit and they drove to the little Methodist church five miles down the road.

When they got home, with Pepi still brooding and withdrawn, Brandon Hale's car was parked at the front steps. She got out of her father's car and ran to Brandon as fast as her legs would carry her.

Ben, watching, frowned. Trouble was sitting on the horizon, and he wondered where this new complication was going to land them all.

CHAPTER SIX

BRANDON GAPED AT Pepi when she told him what was going on. They'd just finished a sparse lunch and her father was bringing the coffee tray into the living room where they were sitting.

"You're married?" Brandon groaned.

"Not really," she said quickly. She fingered her skirt while she gave him the details. "So, you see, it's just legal on paper, and only until I can get it annulled."

"C.C. knows, I guess?" Brandon persisted.

"Boy, does he know!" Ben Mathews muttered. He brought in a tray with three cups of black coffee on it. "If any of you want cream, you can go get it," he added as he put it down on the coffee table in the early American decor of the living room.

"Well, what did he say?" the younger man asked.

"You couldn't repeat it in mixed company." Ben sighed.

"He was furious," Pepi volunteered. She stared at her skirt. "I guess I can't blame him. He doesn't know the whole story, and I was too upset to try to make him listen. It doesn't matter anyway," she said miserably. "He said he sure didn't want to be married to somebody like me."

"He was in shock," Ben said stubbornly, staring at

her averted face. "A man has to have time to adjust to news like that."

"How long will an annulment take?" Brandon asked.

"I'll find out in the morning. I'm going to see our attorney," Pepi told him. "Maybe it won't take long. Heaven knows, C.C. will do his best to rush it through. I hope I don't have to have the marriage license," she added, frowning. "C.C. took it with him."

"Where'd he go?" Brandon asked.

"¿Quien sabe?" Ben shrugged.

"At least it's not a real marriage," Brandon said gently, patting Pepi's soft hand in her lap. "You scared the life out of me."

"Well, it's definitely not real, so you can relax," Pepi said. "Drink your coffee, Brandon. Then we can go riding. I need to get out of the house."

"Good idea," Ben seconded. "And I can start on the books."

"It's Sunday!" she protested.

"I know that. I'll eat my cake while I work on them. That will make it all right. Besides," he chuckled wickedly, "we went to church first."

She threw up her hands and went to change into jeans and a T-shirt.

Brandon stayed until late, and Pepi was glad of his company. She hardly slept that night, and early the next morning she went to see the family attorney.

Mr. Hardy was sixty and very abrupt, but under his bespectacled, dignified manner, he was the best friend that the Mathews family had ever had.

"Don't have the license, hmm?" he murmured when

Pepi had told him the whole story. "No matter. I'll go ahead and draw up the papers for the annulment. Have C.C. come in and sign them Friday. Meanwhile, don't worry about it. Just one of those things. But if I were him, I'd keep away from liquor from now on," he added dryly.

She smiled. "I'll try to make sure he does that," she replied gently.

There, she told herself later, it was done. The wheels were in motion. In no time, she'd be plain old Penelope Mathews again, not Penelope Tremayne. The thought depressed her. She'd wanted so badly to keep the name, to have the marriage real and wanted. But C.C. had made no secret of his feelings on the matter, or of his patent disgust with the idea of Pepi as a wife. She wondered if she was ever going to be able to forget the wounding things he'd said to her.

On an impulse, she stopped by the local department of labor office to see what kinds of jobs were going for women with minimal typing skills. Fate was kind. There was a receptionist's job open with a local insurance agency. She went over to inquire about it, and was hired. She was to start on the following Monday, a week away—on the condition that their valued receptionist, who'd just had a baby, stuck to her decision not to return. They couldn't refuse her if she wanted her job back, and they promised to call Pepi if she wasn't needed.

Well, if that didn't work out, she'd find something else, she promised herself. There was just no way she could stay on the ranch now that this fiasco had occurred. Every time she saw C.C., it would rip her heart open. And if he made fun of her, or taunted her about the almost-marriage, it would be unbearable. Probably he still hated her. That might make it easier. Ben needed him, so she couldn't demand that he be fired. She'd just have to find a graceful way out of the dilemma for all of them. Despite the hurt, she loved C.C. more than her own life. She could leave the ranch and find a room in El Paso, and a job. That way her father could have his very necessary foreman and she could have peace of mind. Besides, Brandon lived in El Paso. He'd look out for her. She might even marry him. He was kind and he cared about her. Surely that was better than living alone.

By Wednesday afternoon, C.C. still hadn't come back. Wednesday night, Brandon took Pepi to a cattlemen's association meeting with him. It was a dinner meeting, and Pepi enjoyed not only the meal but the discussion about range improvement methods that followed it.

She'd worn a new mustard-colored rayon skirt with her knee-high lace-up Apache moccasins and a Western-cut patterned blouse. Her reddish-brown hair was around her shoulders for a change, and she'd put on enough makeup to embellish her face. She looked pretty, and Brandon's interest was echoed by several single men present.

Her drooping spirits got quite a lift. She smiled and talked and laughed, and by the time they left the meeting, she was relaxed and happy.

That mood lasted until they got to the front porch and Brandon bent to kiss her good-night. Before he reached her lips, a coldly unapproachable C.C. sauntered into the light from the darkened corner where he'd been sitting.

"Oh, hello, C.C.," Brandon said hesitantly. He raked a hand through his red hair, glancing worriedly at Pepi's suddenly white face. "I'll call you in the morning, Pepi. Good night!"

He darted off the porch. Pepi watched him go so that she wouldn't have to look at C.C. One glimpse told her that he was wearing a charcoal-gray suit with a pearly Stetson, and that he looked dangerous. Smoke from the cigarette in his lean fingers drifted past her nose as Brandon waved and drove out of the yard.

"Where have you been?" he asked, his deep voice accusing.

"I've been to a cattlemen's association meeting, C.C.," she replied, moving unobtrusively away from the threat of his powerful body. She turned and went into the house, leaving C.C. to close the door behind them.

"No word of welcome?" he asked sarcastically.

She didn't look at him. She couldn't bear to see the expression in his eyes. She started toward the staircase, but he reached out to catch her arm.

Her reaction caught him off guard. She jerked her arm away from his lean hand and backed against the staircase, her wide, dark eyes accusing and frightened.

His thin lips parted on a sharp breath. "My God, you're not afraid of me?" he asked, scowling.

"I'm tired," she said, averting her face. "I just want to go to bed. Mr. Hardy says you can come in and sign the annulment papers Friday," she added. "I started proceedings and I'll pay for them. You won't have to be out a penny. Is Dad in his study?"

He frowned as he lifted the cigarette to his lips. "He's

over at the bunkhouse, talking to Jed. I don't want you seeing Hale while you're legally married to me."

She hesitated, but it wasn't really much to ask. And she was too tired to argue with him. "All right, C.C.," she replied dully. "Maybe the annulment won't take too long."

His eyes narrowed to angry slits. "In a hurry to put Hale's ring on your finger?" he asked.

"I don't want to fight with you," she said quietly, meeting his gaze with an effort. It disturbed her, the way he was looking at her. It made her heart race, her knees tremble under her. "I've got a job," she told him. "I start Monday. Then I'll look for a room or something in El Paso. You won't… You won't have to worry about running into me all the time around here."

"Pepi!" he said huskily.

She whirled. "Good night, C.C.!"

She ran all the way upstairs and into her room, closing the door with hands that trembled, with tears running down her pale cheeks. So he was back. Back, and spoiling for trouble. That didn't bode well for the future.

She got into her gown, washed her face, and climbed into bed with a long sigh. She was reaching for the bedside light when her door suddenly opened and C.C. came in, closing it behind him.

Pepi froze with her hand out, all too aware of the way the almost transparent green gown she was wearing outlined her body, left the upper curve of her breasts bare. With her hair around her pale shoulders, she looked very soft and feminine, and C.C. was getting an eyeful.

"What do you want?" she asked uneasily.

"To talk," he replied. He pulled up a chair beside the bed and dropped into it. There were new lines in his face, and he looked as tired as she felt. He'd discarded his suit coat and tie and rolled up the sleeves of his exquisite cotton shirt, its neck unbuttoned to his collarbone. Dark curly hair peeked out between the loose buttons and Pepi had to force her eyes back up to his face. She didn't like being reminded of his vibrant masculinity. She wasn't his type, and he didn't want her. She had to remember that.

"About the annulment?" she asked hesitantly. She sat up against her pillow, demurely pulling the sheet over her breasts, an action that C.C.'s faintly amused eyes didn't miss.

He watched her hungrily. The days he'd been away, a lot of things had been settled in his mind. He'd brooded about his own situation until he'd given some thought to Pepi's. That was when he'd realized how much he owed her. She'd been the best friend he had, ever since he'd come to the ranch. But he'd repaid her loyalty by hurting her, making her feel unwanted. Now he had to put things right, if he could. Perhaps telling her the truth about his past might be a good first step. If she understood him, she might be able to forgive the things he'd said to her before he left.

"No," he said after a minute. "I don't want to talk about the annulment right now. I want to tell you about me." He leaned back in the chair and crossed one long leg over the other. "I was born in Jacobsville, down near Victoria," he began, watching her while he lit a cigarette and fished for an ashtray on the dresser. He grimaced as he emptied jewelry out of it and put it in his lap. "I have three brothers, two older, one younger than I am. We're in the cattle business, too, except that we deal in purebred cattle—Santa Gertrudis. Our land came from one of the early Spanish land grants, and we've always had money."

She watched him, astonished at the revelation.

"I got married years ago. I was getting older, I was lonely." He shrugged. "I wanted her. She was my age, and a wild woman from the word go. We both liked dangerous sports, like shooting the white water." His fingers clenched on the cigarette, and there was suddenly a faraway, tormented look in his dark eyes. "She went everywhere with me. But that weekend, I wanted to get away. She had this tendency to smother me; had to be with me every minute, night and day. After the first few weeks we were married, it got so I couldn't stand and talk to one of my brothers without having her in my pocket. She was insanely jealous, but I hadn't realized that until it was too late. Well, I signed up for a rafting trip down the Colorado and went without her. But when I got to the river with the rest of the group, she was there waiting. We argued. It didn't do any good. She was hell-bent on going." He took a draw from the cigarette. "The raft capsized on a bad stretch and she went under. We searched for the better part of an hour, but by the time we found her, it was too late." He looked straight at Pepi, his eyes cold. "She was three months pregnant."

"I'm sorry," she said quietly. "That must have been the worst of it, for you."

He was surprised at her perceptiveness, although God knew why he should have been. Pepi always managed to see things that other people missed. "Yes, that was the worst of it," he confessed. "I was never able to find out if she knew about her condition, or if she didn't care. She was a free spirit. She wasn't really suited to marriage. If she'd stayed single, she'd probably still be alive."

"I'm a fatalist," Pepi said, her voice gentle. "I think God chooses when we die, and the circumstances."

"Perhaps you're right. But it's taken me three years to come to grips with it. I inherited her estate, and she was as wealthy as I was. That was one reason I came here, started over again from scratch with your father. I wanted to get away from money and see what I could do by the sweat of my own brow. I inherited most of what I had. It's been fun, making my own way."

"It's been a lifesaving experience for us," Pepi said. "We owe you a lot. And you were a mystery to us, but you always seemed to fit in very well."

"Except for one day a year," he mused sadly. "Every year on the day it happened, I go a little crazy. I didn't know how much I wanted a child until it was too late."

She searched for the right words to comfort him. "C.C., you're still young enough to marry again and have children," she said hesitantly.

His eyes narrowed. "But I am married, Pepi. To you."

She felt her cheeks stinging with heat. She averted her wounded eyes to the coverlet. "Not for long. Mr. Hardy said an annulment would be no problem at all."

"I'd like to know what happened that night," he said after a minute.

"Not a lot. You were stinking drunk in a bar in Juárez. I went in to get you out, you made a lot of insulting remarks, and then you said since I seemed to be forever nursemaiding you, I might as well marry you. In fact, you threatened to land us in jail if I didn't."

His eyebrows arched. "I did?"

"You did," she muttered. "I wasn't sure what to think. You were pretty loud and you sounded serious to me. Mexican jails are easy to get into and hard to get out of. I had visions of us languishing down there for months while Dad went nuts trying to get us out."

"My God! Why didn't you tell me that?"

"You didn't want to listen," she replied doggedly. "You were too busy telling me what an underhanded little gold digger I was!"

He sighed angrily. "I know plenty about gold diggers," he said defensively. "Until I married, I fielded them like baseballs."

"You never had to field me!" Pepi returned. She glared at him from the depths of her feather pillow. "I looked after you when you needed it and I liked to think we were friends, but that's all it was," she lied, salvaging what she could of her pride. "I never wanted to marry you!"

His dark eyes narrowed as he turned that statement over in his mind and examined it. He didn't believe her. She'd been vulnerable to him before he'd hurt her pride so badly. If any feeling was still there, he might be able to reach it if he was careful, and slow.

"I remember telling you once that I had nothing left of love in me," he said. "It felt like that, for a long time.

I got numb, I think, because of the guilt. I wouldn't let myself feel."

She lowered her eyes to his chest. "Yes, I can understand that," she said gently. "But I was never any threat to you, C.C."

"Weren't you?" he mused, smiling faintly. "You were the most caring little thing I'd ever met. You mothered me. Funny, how much I enjoyed that after a while. Apple pie when I was broody, hot stew when I was cold, unexpected things like puff pastries in my saddlebags when I went out to roundup. Oh, you got under my skin, Pepi, right from the beginning. The miracle is that I didn't realize how far."

"You don't have to baby me," she muttered, glaring at him. "What you said when you found out we were married was the truth. It was honest. I always knew you wouldn't want a fat frump like me...."

"Pepi!"

"Well, I am one," she said doggedly, her fingers clenching in the cover. "Ugly and overweight and country to the bone. Dad used to say that you were sophisticated enough for a debutante, and he was right. Edie's just your style."

He leaned back in his chair. "Edie doesn't want a house in the country and two or three kids," he said quietly.

So that was it. He couldn't have Edie, so he might be willing to settle for second-best—for Pepi. She lowered her eyes. She'd wanted him for so long that she was almost ready to take him on any terms, even on the rebound. But she couldn't forget the things he'd said about her, and to her.

"You might be able to change her mind," she said.

He scowled, watching her. "I don't want to change it," he said surprisingly. "Pepi, we're married."

She colored. "That isn't a hurdle. I told you, I've already seen Mr. Hardy. All you have to do is sign the papers on Friday and he'll get the annulment underway."

He felt that statement to his bones. He shifted in the chair, his gaze on her flushed face. "You haven't considered the options. Your father is still just barely operating in the black. I could put the ranch back on its feet for good. You might find a few things that you wanted, too. After all, I'm rich."

"I don't care about your money," she returned, her pale brown eyes accusing. "I like having food in the house and a roof over my head, but I couldn't care less about how much money I've got, and you know it!"

His breath sighed out roughly. "Is it Hale?" he demanded. "Is he why you're in such a rush to get an annulment?"

Her eyes dilated. "*You're* the one who was demanding a speedy end to the marriage!"

"Yes, well, I've had second thoughts." He uncrossed his legs and sprawled, one hand loosely grasping the almost-finished cigarette as he stared at her. "If I'm already married, I won't have to fend off potential brides, will I?" he added.

She sat up straight in bed. "Now, you listen here, C.C., I'm not going to become a human sacrifice to save you from the altar! Marrying you sure wasn't my idea!"

"You could have called my bluff," he reminded her, his dark eyes faintly twinkling. "Why didn't you?"

"I told you! Because I didn't want to spend the rest of my life in a Mexican jail!"

"If I was drunk enough to pass out, I was too drunk to cause much trouble," he continued. "Besides, I didn't have a gun."

She drew up her knees angrily and clasped her arms around them. "You've got all the answers, haven't you?"

"Not quite all," he said. "But I'm getting there." He took his time, stabbing out his cigarette in the ashtray. "You said once that you and Hale were lovers. Are you?" he asked, lifting his eyes back to hers.

She gave him a wary look, hoping he hadn't seen through the lie. If he thought she and Brandon were close, it might keep him at bay until she could decide how to cope with this newest complication. "That's none of your business."

"The hell it's not. You're mine."

Electricity danced through her veins, but she didn't let him see the reaction in her eyes. "No, I am not. You're only married to me because of an accident. That means Brandon is none of your concern."

He got up with deceptive laziness and put the ashtray back on the side table. "I'm making him my business." He paused at her bedside, narrow eyes assessing, threatening. "You aren't sleeping with him again," he said shortly. "And no more dates, either. From now on, you'll stay at home where you belong."

Her eyes opened wide. "Who do you think you are?" she demanded.

"Your husband," he said, "*Mrs*. Tremayne."

"Don't call me that," she grumbled. "It's not my name."

"Oh, yes, it is. And you can forget that annulment. I won't sign the papers."

"But you have to!" she said helplessly.

"Really? Why?" he asked, and looked interested.

"Because it's the only way to get rid of me!"

He pursed his lips and let his eyes slide over her. "Do I want to do that? After all, you've been looking out for me for the past three years, through thick and thin. You're a treasure, Pepi. I don't intend giving you up to the redheaded vet. You can tell him I said so."

"I don't want to be married to you," she yelled.

He lifted his eyebrows. "How do you know that? I haven't made love to you yet."

She went scarlet. Her fingers grasped the covers in a death grip and she stiffened when he took a step closer to the bed, her eyes as wide as saucers in her flushed face.

He shook his head and made a clicking sound with his tongue. "My God, if you keep up this attitude, it's going to be damned hard for us to have children together."

"I won't have children!" she whispered.

"Well, not like that," he murmured, grinning. "You *do* know how women get them?"

"Sure," she said hesitantly. "From the hospital."

"That comes later," he reminded her. He smiled. "Afterward."

That slow, meaningful smile made her nervous. "I don't want to sleep with you," she told him.

"We won't sleep," he promised.

"Will you get out of here!"

Before he could reply, the bedroom door opened suddenly and her father glanced from one of them to the other, scowling. "For God's sake, what's all the yelling about?"

"I've been explaining the facts of life to Pepi." C.C. shrugged. "She thinks babies came from the hospital. Did you tell her that?"

Ben looked flustered. "Well, not exactly... Look here, what are you doing in her bedroom?"

"We're married," C.C. reminded him. He produced an envelope. "The marriage license is in here."

"But you don't want to be married to her," Ben returned. "You said so. You went off to get an annulment."

"I changed my mind. She's a good cook, she's nice looking, and she doesn't have any bad habits. I could do worse."

"I could do better!" Pepi shouted, red-faced. "You get out of here, Connal Tremayne! I'm getting that annulment, and you can go to hell!"

C.C. exchanged an amused glance with Ben. "I suppose you taught her to swear, too?" he asked the older man. "For shame!"

"She taught me," Ben said defensively. "And I don't think she wants to stay married to you, C.C."

"Sure she does!" he replied. "It's just going to take a little time to convince her of it. Meanwhile—" he threw an arm across the older man's shoulder "—I want to talk to you about some improvements I have in mind for the house and the ranch."

"Don't you listen!" Pepi raged. "He's trying to buy us!"

"I am not!" C.C. said indignantly. "I'm trying to overcome your objections. Your father wouldn't mind a partner, I'll bet. Especially when it's his own brand-new son-in-law. Right, Dad?" he added, smiling with crocodile intensity at the older man.

"Right, son!" Ben agreed, grinning back. "I hadn't thought about that," he mused to himself. "I'll finally have a son of my own!"

"Are you both forgetting something?" Pepi asked haughtily.

"I don't think so," C.C. replied.

"I'm not staying married to you!" she told him. "I'm getting an annulment."

"Don't worry, Dad," C.C. told Ben encouragingly. "She has to have my cooperation for that, and I'll never agree. Imagine a woman hard-hearted enough to try to get rid of a man even before the honeymoon!"

"Say, that's right, you haven't had a honeymoon," Ben agreed.

"C.C. can go on the honeymoon by himself," Pepi said. "I hear it's nice in Canada this time of year. Don't they have grizzly bears up there...?"

"We don't have time for a honeymoon just now," C.C. replied easily. "We've got too much work to do fixing up the ranch. First, I thought we'd get a contractor over here and let him look at the house. I'm inviting my brothers up from Jacobsville to talk to us about getting one or two Santa Gertrudis seed bulls..."

"Stop!" Pepi held up her hand. "I won't agree to this!"

"What do you have to do with it?" C.C. asked innocently. "Your father and I are going to be partners."

"Dad, you can't let him do this," she pleaded with her parent.

Ben lifted his eyebrows. "Why not?" he asked.

"She's only frustrated," C.C. said, leading the older man out the door. "A little loving will put her on the right track in no time."

"You try it and I'll crack your head with a tire iron!" she raged.

C.C. grinned at her from the doorway. "I do like a woman with spirit," he murmured.

"Will you please leave?" she said, admitting defeat. "I want to go to sleep."

"You might as well. Maybe it will improve your mood," he said as he closed the door.

"Improve my mood," she muttered, glaring at the closed door. "First he insults me, then he storms off in a snit demanding an annulment and now he wants to go partners with Dad. I will never understand men as long as I live!"

She put her head under the pillow. But despite her best attempts, it was early morning before she finally got to sleep.

CHAPTER SEVEN

IT WASN'T AT all unusual for C.C. to have breakfast with
Pepi and her father, but in recent months he'd kept very
much to himself. Even so, Pepi wasn't surprised to find
him sitting in the dining room with her father when she
came down to breakfast. She was surprised to find food
on the table, waiting for her, right down to a fresh pot of
coffee.

"Shocked, are we?" C.C. murmured dryly, his dark
eyes sliding possessively down her body, clad in jeans
and boots and a white blouse with a yellow knit pullover
sweater. "Think men are helpless, do we?"

She glanced around, looking to see how many people
he was talking to.

"Cute," he chuckled. "Sit down and eat, before it gets
cold."

She took the chair across from him, next to her father.
Her gaze went restlessly from C.C. in working clothes—
denim and chambray—to her father in a suit.

"Are you planning to be buried before the end of
the day, or are you going somewhere?" she asked Ben.

"I'm going to the bank to pay off the note on the
place," he said hesitantly.

"With what?" she cried.

"We can talk about it later," C.C. interrupted. "Eat your eggs."

"With what?" she persisted, glaring at her father. He looked guilty. Her eyes went to a smug C.C., leaning back like a conqueror with his shirt straining over a muscular chest and broad shoulders while he watched her. "You did it. You gave him the money to pay off the note, didn't you?" she demanded.

"He's my father-in-law," C.C. said easily. "Not to mention my partner. We're having the papers drawn up today. Your father is seeing about it while he's in town."

"You aren't going with him?" she asked warily.

He shrugged. "We've got a new shipment of cattle coming in. Somebody has to be here to sign for them and oversee the unloading."

"New cattle?" She knew her eyes were bulging. "What new cattle?"

"Some heifers to add to our replacement heifers, that's all," C.C. assured her. He grinned. "But we're going to have two purebred Santa Gertrudis bulls. My brothers are coming up tomorrow."

"There are more like you?" she wondered aloud, recalling his vague reference to them the night before.

"Three," he reminded her.

"God help us all. Are they married?"

His dark eyes narrowed. "One of them is. The youngest. The older two are still single, and don't get any ideas. You've already got a husband."

"Only until I can get your signature on a document," she replied sweetly.

"And hell will freeze over, first," he returned.

"Can't we save the arguing for later?" Ben moaned. "I want to enjoy my breakfast."

"He's got a point. Have some salsa."

She gave up. She spooned the brilliant red salsa over her eggs and savored the spicy flavor they gave the perfectly cooked scrambled eggs. The bacon was neatly done, too, and the biscuits were even better than her own.

She frowned at C.C. She knew that he, like most of the men, could whip up a meal when he had to. But this was beyond the scope of most men who weren't professional chefs. "You cooked all this?"

"Did I say that?" C.C. asked innocently.

"Well, no…"

"Consuelo did it," Ben told her. "We thought you might like a late morning, what with all the excitement last night."

"Excitement," she muttered. "First he wants an annulment and now he doesn't want one."

"Let's just say that I came to my senses in time," C.C. said lazily, smiling at her over a forkful of eggs. His gaze went to her full lips and lingered there, before it slid back up to catch and hold hers. "I know a good thing when I see it."

Her heart went crazy. It wasn't fair, to do this to her. "Why do you need me to ward off prospective brides?" she managed in a husky tone.

"Because I'm going to start a small branch of the family business over here," he replied. "Most people in southeastern Texas know the Tremayne properties. Pretty soon they'll know them in El Paso, and I'll be on the endangered species list. That's where you come in. If I have too many money-hungry women after me, all I have to do is produce my sweet little wife to ward them off."

"I'm not sweet and I'm not little." She put down her fork. "I'm plain and fat, you said so."

His jaw clenched. "I said a lot of things I regret," he replied. "I hope you're not going to spend the next twenty years throwing them in my face every time you get hot under the collar."

She stared at him until she had to drop her eyes to her plate in self-defense. That level, unblinking stare of his had backed down grown men in a temper. She shifted under it. "You said you didn't want to get married."

"I didn't. But it's something of a *fait accompli*, now, isn't it?"

"A what?" She frowned.

He lifted an eyebrow. "It's French. It means an accomplished fact. You don't speak French, I gather. I do. I'll teach you. It's a sexy language. So is Spanish."

She cleared her throat and sipped coffee. "I don't have a facility for languages."

"A few words won't hurt you. Especially," he added softly, "the right kind of words."

She knew what he was insinuating. Her gaze went helplessly to his face and slid to his thin, firm mouth. She'd always wondered how it would feel on hers, but in three years he'd never really kissed her, unless she counted a peck on the lips under the mistletoe that time, and that was as impersonal as a smile. She'd dreamed and dreamed about his arms around her, the pleasure of having him kiss her in a fever of passion. Of course, she wasn't the kind of woman who inspired passion in men. Edie was.

Edie. She thought about the other woman and felt uneasy all over again. She had a pretty good idea what C.C. had seen in Edie and she wondered if he planned to continue that relationship. The marriage was by no means a real one. He could claim that Pepi had no right to tell him what he could and couldn't do, and he'd be right. They were only married in name.

She put down her fork, her appetite gone. If only he loved her. If only he'd married her voluntarily, and not because of a drunken rampage.

"What's the matter now?" her father muttered, watching her expression change. "You look like the end of the world."

"I couldn't sleep," she said defensively.

"Dreaming about me." C.C. grinned.

She glared at him. "I was not!"

"That's right, Pepi, fight it. But I'll win," he added quietly, getting to his feet to stare down at her. "And you know it."

She didn't understand his new attitude, or that look in his dark eyes, either. She looked up at him helplessly.

"All at sea, aren't you, little one?" he murmured. "Well, it's going to take some time, but you'll get the idea eventually. See you later, Ben." He tossed down the rest of his coffee, retrieved his Stetson from the counter and slanted it across his eyes. "Why don't you come down to the loading dock and watch us move the cattle in?" he asked Pepi.

It was the first such invitation he'd ever extended to

her, almost as if he'd welcome her company. She didn't know how to respond to it, so she hesitated.

"Suit yourself," he said on a heavy sigh. "If you change your mind, you know where I'll be."

He went out the door and Pepi exchanged a puzzled glance with her father.

"What's going on?" she asked him.

"Damned if I know, except that he's sure done a hard about-face," Ben replied. "I can't say I'm sorry, in one respect. This land has been in our family since just after the Civil War. I'd hate like hell to lose it, because of my own financial incompetence."

Pepi knew how much the ranch meant to her father, and she felt a twinge of guilt for putting up a fight when C.C. was the answer to all his problems. But he was the root of all hers.

"How do you really feel about this?" Ben asked quietly.

She fingered her coffee cup. "I think he's just making the most of a bad situation," she said. "Or maybe he feels that getting an annulment would be a reflection on his masculinity." She shrugged. "Maybe it's even what he said, to keep prospective brides off his back when his monied background gets around. But how I feel about it is uneasy. He's too smooth about it for a man who was ranting and raving like a madman when he found out what happened in Juárez."

"He was away for several days," Ben said thoughtfully. "Maybe he came to grips with it then."

She remembered what C.C. had told her about his wife, and she wasn't sure about that. He'd mentioned wanting a family, that Edie didn't. He could just be thinking about how easily Pepi could be cast in the mold he wanted—housewife and mother and cook, somebody in the background of his life, somebody he could walk away from without his emotions being involved if the marriage dissolved for any reason. She knew he didn't love her. He'd made that all too obvious already. He might want her. She wasn't even sure about that, because he only let things show on his face that he wanted people to see. He might be playing a game. He might be getting even.

"You're doing it again," Ben observed. "Brooding," he added when she frowned with curiosity. "Stop brooding. Live one day at a time and see what happens."

She wanted to argue, but there was really no reason to. "Okay," she said easily. "I've got a job," she said.

"A what?"

"A job. Well, I've almost got a job," she amended. "There's one going in El Paso, if the receptionist who just had a baby doesn't come back." She told him about it, puzzled by his worried look. "What's wrong with my having a job?" she demanded.

"You've got enough to do around here," he muttered. "I'll have to give up my apple pies and cakes if you go to work. Who'll take care of me?"

Her eyebrows arched. "But, Dad, I can't stay at home forever!"

"Could if you stayed married to my new son-in-law," he said curtly. "No reason why you shouldn't. He's a great catch. Rich, good-looking, smart…"

"…hardheaded, autocratic, unreasonable…" she amended.

"...and best of all, he likes kids," he concluded firmly. "I like kids. Would have had more than just you if we could have, you know. Nothing in the world I'd enjoy more than a houseful of grandkids."

"Great. When I get free from C.C. and marry Brandon, we'll make sure you have lots. All redheaded," she said with a smug grin.

"I don't want his grandkids!" he raged.

"Too bad," she sighed, finishing her breakfast. "Because I'm not going to spend the rest of *my* life helping C.C. ward off women."

"Hasn't it occurred to you that he might have other reasons for wanting you to stay with him?" her father asked after a minute. "More personal reasons than he's given?"

She searched his face. "You mean because of his wife, and the baby?" she asked.

He nodded. "Hard for him, losing her like that, and her pregnant at the time. I can see why he's haunted. I know all about guilt, sweetheart, I felt it for years because I was drinking the night of the wreck that killed your mother. I learned finally that you can't live in the past. You have to shoulder your mistakes and regrets and go on. He's learning that. Maybe he's ready to start over, too."

"Maybe he is, but it's not enough, Dad," she said wearily. "I can't be just a healing balm in his life, you know? I have to be loved, wanted, needed."

"He needs you, all right, we've all seen that over the years," Ben reminded her.

"Sure. Good old Pepi, keeping him out of trouble,

making sure he wears his raincoat, watching over his meals…but that isn't what he needs, Dad. He needs a woman he can love. Edie would be a better choice than I am, at least they've got a relationship of sorts. C.C. and I—well, he's never even kissed me," she muttered with a faint flush.

"You might ask him to, then," Ben said with a twinkle in his eyes. "Just to sample the goods, so to speak."

She went redder and lowered her brown eyes to her plate. "I don't want to kiss him, I don't know where he's been."

"You won't know what you're missing until you try," he said. "After all, you've lived like a saint for the past few years, despite the best efforts of the redheaded vet."

"You didn't tell C.C. that!" she exclaimed.

"He figured it for himself," he said easily. "C.C.'s been around. Even a blind man could tell that you haven't. You blush too much."

"I'll dot my face with rice powder and wear a mask over my eyes from now on, that's for sure!" she grumbled. "Men!"

"Now, now. We only want what's best for you."

"And the fact that he can get the ranch out of debt is like icing on the cake, huh?"

He smiled placatingly. "I won't say no. This land is a legacy. We'll hand it down for years to come now, and the history that goes with it. John Wesley Hardin slept in this very house. A Comanche war party raided the ranch and killed one of the cowboys. The cavalry used to bivouac on the bottoms on its way to various cam-

DIANA PALMER 115

paigns toward the Pasa del Norte and back. Yes, girl, this land is full of history. I'd like your kids to inherit it."

She reached out and lightly touched his wrinkled hand. "I understand that. But marriage seems to be hard enough when you love someone. When you don't..."

"But you do," Ben replied knowingly. "I've seen the way you watch him, the way you light up when he comes into a room. He doesn't see it because he's not looking. But the fact that he doesn't want an annulment gives you hope, doesn't it?"

"He doesn't want it for the right reasons," she moaned. "Any woman would suit him, don't you see?"

"No, I don't." He tugged his pocket watch out by its gold chain and looked at it. "And I don't have time to make you see it right now, I'm late. Won't be in for lunch, so don't worry about me. C.C. mentioned he might be in for it, though."

"I'll be sure I leave him something on the table," she muttered.

"Now, now. Is that any way to treat the man who's getting your worried old father out of debt?"

She grimaced. "I guess not. All right, I'll try to look suitably grateful. Now if you'll excuse me," she added, getting up to stack the dishes, "I've got some chores to do. And I'm not giving up that job, either," she tossed over her shoulder. "If they hire me, I'm going!"

Ben threw up his hands and went toward the door.

Pepi did the dishes and cleaned the house. All the while she was thinking about C.C.'s impromptu invitation to come out to the loading docks and watch them process the new heifers. He'd probably be through long before lunch, and he hadn't pressed his invitation. But she went, anyway, riding lazily down the unpaved ranch road toward the loading docks; the wooden chutes down which arriving cattle were driven into the ranch's only fenced pasture.

As she rode, her mind was comparing this valley land with the mostly desert country farther to the northwest, toward El Paso. The desert country around El Paso was deceptive. Beautiful, in its stark way, and its barren appearance only disguised a multitude of life, animal and plant. The prickly pear cactus could inflict enough hairy thorns to keep a man busy with tweezers and a flashlight for the better part of an hour, but it put forth some of the most elegant blossoms of any desert plant. The rain kindled more blossoms, so that the desert came alive with them. Even the tough mesquite tree put out its own heavenly bloom. Animal life abounded, and not just rattlesnakes and lizards. There were other stretches where only the creosote bushes grew, spreading like miniature orchards, with no vegetation nearby because of their toxic root secretions, which killed any vegetation that tried to grow up around them. After a rain, their pungent, spicy smell was a treat to the senses. Old pioneers made medicines and glue out of them.

But where the Mathews ranch sat, near the site of old Fort Hancock, southeast of El Paso in Hudspeth County, the Rio Grande was close enough to make the area fertile and there was plenty of grazing land for the cattle. The U.S. Army had situated a number of forts along the Rio Grande in the mid and late 1800s in accordance with the settlement of the southern boundary of Texas against the Mexican border. The United States accepted responsibility for stopping Indian attacks across the border, so a number of forts were located along the river. One of those was Fort Hancock, named for General Winfield Scott Hancock. Pepi had played on the site of it on trips with her parents, the eternal history buffs. They'd known every point of historical interest in the area, which was why she knew about the Salt War, provoked by the salt deposit at the base of Guadalupe Peak, which resulted in some fierce gun battles between people who thought the salt should be free and others who argued the advantages of private mineral rights. She knew about the Indian hot springs on the Sierra Blanca road, and nearby Fort Quitman, another of the early forts—although no real ruins were left of it, only an adobe scale model on private land.

As a girl, she used to wander around those historic spots imagining war parties of elegant Comanche warriors on horseback—the best light cavalry in the world, they'd been called. She could imagine men on long cattle drives, and Mexican bandits like Pancho Villa, and Apache and Yaqui raiders. Her imagination had kept her from brooding about being an only child.

Pepi wondered if C.C. liked history. She'd never asked him. She frowned as the mare picked up her pace as they approached the bottoms near what they privately called Mathews Creek, a tributary of the Rio Grande. This area was known to flood when the spring rains came, otherwise it was the haunt of such creatures as pronghorn antelope and white-tailed deer. Her father occasionally allowed hunting on his land, but only if he knew the people involved. Since man had killed off most of the predators that once kept the browsing animals in check, man now had to arrange a less natural way of reducing the number of antelope and deer. Otherwise they overgrazed the land and threatened the survival of the cattle and even themselves.

She felt her heart climb into her throat when she saw the big trucks still unloading new stock, because C.C. was straddling the fence supervising the operation. He must have sensed her approach, because he looked straight at her. Even at the distance, she could see the smile.

He jumped down from the fence and moved toward her, lean and rangy and dangerous. She wondered if there had ever been a man like him. He was certainly the stuff her dreams were made of.

"So you decided to join us," he mused. "Well, come on down."

She swung out of the saddle and fell into step beside him, the reins loosely in her hand. The mare followed noisily behind them.

"That's a lot of cattle," she mentioned when they'd tied the mare to the fence a little farther along.

He glanced down at her. "It takes a lot of cattle to make a living these days," he reminded her. "Especially for ranchers like your father and me, who aren't taking shortcuts."

She frowned. "Shortcuts?"

"Hormone implants, super vitamins, that kind of thing."

"Didn't I read in Dad's market bulletin that some

foreign countries were refusing to import cattle with hormone implants that make them grow faster and bigger?" she asked.

He grinned. "Did your homework, I see," he mused. He lit a cigarette and pushed back the brim of his battered tan Stetson. "That's right. People are becoming more health conscious. We have to raise leaner beef in more natural ways to fit the market. Even the pesticides we use on our grain is under fire."

"Not to mention branding," she murmured, darting a glance upward.

"Don't get me started," he began gently. "It isn't cruel, but it is necessary. A freeze-dried brand won't last or be visible after a year or so. Even a burnt brand fades after the cattle shed their coats a few times. Ear tags can be removed. Hot branding is the only way a rancher can protect his investment and mark his cattle. Anything less is an open invitation to rustlers to come and wipe us out."

"I can hear the giggles now. Rustlers, in the space age."

"You know as well as I do that rustling is big business, even if they do it with trucks instead of box canyons," he muttered. "Damn it, we're under the gun from every side these days. People may have to choose between meat and tubes of food paste one day, but until they're willing to pass up a juicy steak, some concessions are going to have to be made."

"I still don't think they ought to torture animals unnecessarily," she said doggedly. "Not just out of curiosity, or to make cosmetics safer for women."

He chuckled. "You and your soft heart. You'd make pets of all my steers and name the chickens, wouldn't you? A hundred years ago you'd have starved to death. And I'll remind you of a time when children died by the thousands or were crippled by endless diseases. How do you think the researchers found cures for those diseases?"

"By using animals for their experiments, I guess," she said uneasily.

"Damned straight. And a hundred years ago, if you couldn't kill an animal, you starved." He stared out over the range. "Cruelty is a part of life. Like it or not, you and I are predators, animals. Man is just a savage with the edges smoothed over. Put him in a primitive environment with an empty belly, and he'll kill every time."

"Can we talk about something less violent?" she asked. "Are your brothers like you?"

He turned, staring down at her appreciatively, from her loosened reddish hair to her rounded figure in jeans. "Evan is," he said finally. "He's the eldest. We look alike, although he's more reserved than I am. Harden is closest to my age, but he's blue-eyed. My youngest brother is Donald—he got married just before I left to come here. Nice girl. Her name is Jo Ann."

"Are your parents still alive?" she asked.

"Our father died when we were just boys. Mother's still around, though." He hooked his thumbs in his wide leather belt and looked down at Pepi. "Her name is Theodora," he said, his gaze falling to Pepi's mouth. "If we have a daughter, I'd like to name her after my mother. She's a special woman. Gritty and capable and loving. She'd like you, Penelope Mathews Tremayne."

She felt her face going hot. He was much too close, and the threat of that lean, fit body made her nervous. She shifted away a little, but he moved with her, his smile telling her that he knew very well how he affected her.

"I'm not a Tremayne for long," she said defensively.

"For as long as I say so, you are," he murmured. "Marriage isn't something to be taken lightly. If you didn't want to marry me, you should never have let me convince you to go into that Mexican wedding chapel."

He had a point there, but she couldn't admit it. She stuck her hands into her pockets to keep them still. She couldn't get her eyes up past his shirt. It was blue-checked, Western cut, and drawn taut across that broad expanse of chest. She could see the shadow of hair under it. She'd seen him without his shirt once or twice, but only from a distance. She couldn't help wonder what he looked like up close, and when she realized what she was thinking, her face flamed.

He lifted an eyebrow. "My, my, aren't we unsettled?" he mused with a slow smile. "Want me to take it off, Pepi?" he drawled softly.

Her eyes shot up to his, glanced off them and darted away to the cattle. Her heart almost shook her with its beat and her mouth went bone-dry as she searched for poise. "I was…admiring the color," she stammered.

"You were undressing me, you mean," he said casually, lifting the cigarette to his mouth. "Why don't you?" he murmured. "We're married. I don't mind if you touch me."

She actually gasped and started to move away, but

he caught a long strand of her hair between his hard fingers and stayed the movement effectively.

"Don't run from me," he said, his voice deep and slow, carrying even over the bawling of the cattle and the shouts of the nearby cowboys who were unloading them. A big cattle trailer had been backed in, shielding them from the men with its bulk. "It's time you faced up to the reality of our situation."

"Our situation would resolve itself if you'd agree to an annulment." She choked out the words.

His hand moved, tangling in her hair. He turned her, lifted her face to his with the pressure of it, and his dark eyes had an odd, new glint in their narrowed depths. "Annulments are for people who can't work out their problems. You and I are going to give this marriage a chance, starting now, here."

"We're what... C.C.!"

His mouth covered her startled cry. When she returned the kiss, he threw the cigarette in the dirt and his free arm gathered her up against the length of his hard-muscled, fit body. The warm strength of it weakened her will. Slowly she became aware of her hands gripping his muscular arms frantically, her breathing almost stifled. Then she began to feel the slow warmth of his mouth against her own, the sensual movements growing gentler and more insistent by the second.

Brandon had kissed her. So had other boys. But it had been nothing like this. She barely felt the hot sun on her head or heard the noise around them or smelled the dust. She hesitated in her struggles for an instant and gave in to the steely arm around her back. He moved

her closer, and she shivered a little with the newness
of letting a man hold her like this, in an embrace that
was nothing short of intimate.

His mouth lifted, brushed, touched the corners of
hers as he felt her resistance slackening. She melted into
him unexpectedly and his cheek drew slowly against
hers, lifting fractionally so that he could see her eyes.
The dazed pleasure in them made him hungry. Soft,
pale darkness under those long, thick lashes, pierced
with curiosity and need.

"The...men," she managed halfheartedly.

He turned her just fractionally, so that she could see
that they were shielded from view by the cattle trailer.
"What men, little one?" he whispered. His mouth settled on hers like the brush of a butterfly's wing. Lifted.
Teased. "Slide your arms under mine," he murmured
as he nibbled her lower lip. "Come close."

She obeyed him helplessly, sinking into a sweet
oblivion that throbbed with new sensations. Her hands
flattened against his shoulder blades. Odd, she thought
dazedly, how well they fit together, despite his superior height.

"Kiss me, Mrs. Tremayne," he whispered, coaxing
her lips apart.

She went under. His mouth was gentle, and then not
gentle. She moaned as the pressure and insistence grew
to shocking hunger, and she felt her legs begin to tremble against the hard pressure of his.

He let her go unexpectedly and drew back, his jaw
clenched, his eyes strange and glittery. "Wrong time,
wrong place," he said huskily. He took a slow breath and

surveyed his handiwork, nodded as he saw the unmistakable signs of arousal. "Yes, you want me," he said under his breath. "That's a start, at least."

She swallowed. Her lips felt bruised and when she closed them, she tasted him. She wanted to ask him why, but he took her hand and tugged, pulling her along with him.

"These are Herefords," he said as if nothing at all had happened. "You know that we cross Brahman cattle with shorthorns to produce Santa Gertrudis. Well, this is another kind of cross," he said, and proceeded to give her a refresher course in cattle breeding.

She listened, but her eyes were all over his face, and her body was burning.

He lit a cigarette while he talked, and once he smiled down at her in a way that made her heart beat heavily. They seemed to have crossed some new bridge, quite unexpectedly, and she felt a sense of excitement that she'd never anticipated. Even when he had to leave her to go back to work, and she was riding home again on the mare, the excitement lingered. She only wished she knew where they were headed together.

As she gazed at him, drinking in his sharp features, his dark complexion and lithe, muscular build, she wondered what a child of theirs would look like.

The thought embarrassed her and she dragged her eyes away. There would be plenty of time for that kind of curiosity later, if and when things worked out between them.

CHAPTER EIGHT

LIFE GOT MORE complicated very quickly. Brandon came by to see Pepi the next morning, a little hesitant because she was still technically married to C.C. Brandon didn't quite understand what was going on. Pepi had told him that the marriage was a mistake, but C.C. was glaring daggers at him from across the living-room coffee table, and he felt like a buck under the sights of a marksman.

"I, uh, thought we might take in a movie tomorrow night, that is, if C.C. doesn't mind," Brandon added quickly.

Pepi hadn't seen C.C. until Brandon showed up, but here he sat, self-appointed chaperone, and the way he was watching Brandon made her nervous.

C.C. leaned back in his chair and smoked his cigarette with arrogant self-confidence. "Pepi is my wife," he told the younger man. "I don't think married ladies should date other men. Just a little quirk of mine," he added with faintly dangerous eyes.

Brandon's eyes widened. "I thought... Pepi said," he faltered, glancing at her and finding no help, "that it was all a mistake."

"It might have started that way," C.C. replied. "But

Pepi and I are determined to make the most of our unfortunate situation. Aren't we, Penelope?"

She looked at him uncertainly. She hadn't felt like herself since the day before, when C.C. had kissed her with such passion. He was backing her into a corner, and she couldn't see the way out.

"Now, look here, C.C.," she began.

He smiled at her lazily. "Connal, sweetheart, remember? Her memory comes and goes, poor little squirt," he told Brandon.

"It does not!" she raged at him. "I never forget anything!"

"Just a few minutes ago, you forgot you were married." He shrugged. "Can't blame a man for worrying when his own wife forgets her own wedding."

Pepi fumed while Brandon shifted uncomfortably in the chair. He looked as if his world was coming down around his ears. "I wanted to have another look at those two heifers with the parasites," he told C.C., changing the subject. "How are those calves that we're treating for scours?"

"They're better," the older man replied. "But I'd feel easier if we had more time to watch them. We've had a lot of sick cattle. I don't like it."

"Might not hurt to check the graze," Brandon suggested. "They may be getting into something toxic."

"I had the same idea." C.C. nodded. "I'm going to have those tanks checked today, too. There may be something leaching into the water supply."

"Just thank your lucky stars we aren't up near the

Guadalupe Mountains, where the salt flats are," Brandon murmured dryly.

"I do, every day." C.C. got to his feet. "I'll walk you out. We've got company coming today, so I don't have a lot of time to spare. I'll let Darby go with you to see about the calves."

Pepi didn't like the expression on his face. She jumped up. "I'll go, too."

C.C. lifted an eyebrow, but he didn't say anything. Pepi went out behind Brandon, who was looking more than a little flustered.

They walked toward the barn, where Darby, the wizened little wrangler, was working. C.C. left Brandon with him and came back to where Pepi was waiting and watching. He took her arm and led her around the corner of the house, where his Ford sat by the deserted bunkhouse a few hundred yards from the back barn.

"Where are we going?" she asked.

"To the airport to meet my brothers, have you forgotten?" he asked conversationally.

"Yes, I guess I had," she said. "But I didn't know I was going with you to get them," she added meaningfully. "I'm not properly dressed...."

"You look fine to me," he murmured, his eyes approving the long denim skirt she was wearing with her high-topped moccasins and a pullover knit blouse. "I like your hair down like that."

"Does it really matter how I wear it?" she asked coolly.

His breath stilled. He caught her hand and turned her toward him, his black eyes quiet and steady on her face.

"I regret saying that most of all," he told her, "because you please me exactly the way you are. I wanted to hurt you." He looked down at her small hand in his. "God help me, I said things I never meant to. It was a shock, and not a very pleasant one at the time. I didn't know the circumstances, if that's any excuse. I don't expect you to get over it very soon. But maybe the wounds will heal in time. I have to hope so, Pepi."

Her pale brown eyes fell to his thin, sensuous mouth and lifted again to meet his eyes. "We were friends," she began. "I wish we could be again."

"Do you?" He moved a little closer, his expression as much a threat as his taut, fit body. "After yesterday, I doubt either of us is going to be able to settle for just friendship." His eyes fell to her soft mouth. "I want you."

She moved back a step, her face mirroring her indecision. "You want Edie, too."

He frowned. "In the same way you wanted Hale?" he probed suspiciously. "Some suitor, rushing out the door without you. I'd have laid my head open with a stick and taken you off to safety if I'd been him."

"I'd like to see you lay your own head open with a stick," she muttered.

He chuckled. "That wasn't what I meant." He lifted his chin and, with one eye narrowed, he looked down his nose at her. "Did you want him, little one?" he asked very softly. He let go of her hand and lifted his, knuckles down, to her collarbone. He trailed it slowly over the fabric, the sound of it loud in the stillness of early morning, his eyes assessing her sudden color, the rustle of her breath.

"C.C...." she whispered uncertainly, but she didn't try to move away.

"It's all right," he said quietly. "I'm your husband."

She couldn't think, which was just as well. The back of his hand moved down ever further, over the knit blouse to the swell of her breast—back and forth with delicate tenderness, until she felt as if her whole body was on fire. Her breath caught in her throat; she was burning with need.

As if he sensed her hunger, his forefinger bent and he brushed it down to her nipple, making it go suddenly hard and exquisitely sensitive. She gasped audibly.

He saw the heat in her cheeks and felt her faint shudder with a sense of shocking satisfaction.

"It was a lie," he said curtly. "You haven't had Hale. You haven't had a man at all."

She couldn't deny it. But she couldn't move, either. He was casting a spell over her. She loved the pleasure his touch was giving. She was getting drunk on it, in fact.

He glanced around them, frustrated and hungry to teach her more than this cursory lesson, but there were damned cowboys everywhere, coming out of the woodwork, and any minute they were going to be heading for that back barn. His brothers were due in thirty minutes. He wanted to throw something.

He looked back down at Pepi, his hard face showing new lines. "This will have to do, for now," he said huskily. He slid his free hand under the thick fall of her hair and lifted her mouth. "God, it hurts...!" he groaned.

She didn't understand. His mouth settled on hers

in soft, teasing movements and his hand went slowly under her breast to lift its soft weight while his thumb slid roughly over the taut nipple.

"Oh!" she groaned against his mouth, but it wasn't pain that dragged the sound out of her, and he knew it.

"Open your mouth," he ground out at her lips.

She fit her lips to his and lifted her arms around him, shivering, trying to get closer to that expert hand on her breast. But all at once, he moved both hands to her hips and jerked.

Her shocked exclamation went into his mouth. He moved her thighs in a quick rotation against his aroused body and then put her away from him.

"No," he said shortly when she tried, dazed, to move back into his arms. "Come on," he said, catching her arm to pull her along with him toward the car.

His hand was rough on her soft flesh, but she hardly felt it. She was shaking all over. So that was what it felt like to make love. She was sure there was a lot more to it, like having their clothes out of the way. Her skin went hot and she sighed huskily at the thought of C.C.'s lean, hard hands on her naked body.

"Miss Experience," he bit off, glaring down at her. "My God, why did you lie to me?"

"I thought it would make me less vulnerable," she said without thinking.

His eyes darted from her swollen, parted lips back up to her shocked face. "You look less vulnerable, all right," he said mockingly.

"You needn't make fun of me, C.C.," she whispered. "I can't help the way you make me feel."

He opened the passenger door of the Ford and stood aside to let her get in. "I'm not making fun of you," he replied. "If you want the truth, it arouses me like hell to have you cave in when I touch you."

She looked up at him, her pale brown eyes curious and a little afraid. He seemed very adult and worlds ahead of her in experience. "What you...did to me," she asked hesitantly, trying not to stammer. "Does it feel like that, in bed?"

His heart stopped beating. Then it went wild, and his body strung him out. He searched her soft eyes in a silence that throbbed with promise.

"Why don't you come to me tonight, and I'll show you?" he asked quietly.

Her eyes widened until the pupils seemed to blot out their color. "You mean...sleep with you?" she whispered.

He nodded. "The bunkhouse is empty, now that we're through roundup. You're my wife," he added, feeling the words all the way to his toes. "There's no shame in it, Pepi," he added when he saw her hesitation. "It would only be the consummation of our wedding vows." He lifted her hand and drew its palm hungrily to his lips. "Until you sleep with me," he added huskily, "we're not legally married. Did you know that?"

"No. I mean, no, I didn't," she faltered. The look in his eyes was melting her ankles. She could hardly stand up. It was hard to remember that he didn't love her. She had to try to keep that in mind, but it was difficult to keep anything in mind with his eyes piercing hers like that.

"Afraid of it?" he asked quietly.

"Yes, a little," she whispered.

"I'll be careful with you." He drew her hand to his chest and pressed it there, palm down, so that she could feel the powerful beating of his heart under his shirt.

"It will hurt," she blurted out.

"Maybe," he agreed. "But you won't care."

She searched his eyes curiously.

"You may find bruises on your hips tomorrow because I was rough with you on the way here," he replied, his voice deep and slow. "I didn't intend to be that rough, but you were fighting to get back into my arms afterward, not to get out of them."

Her lips parted. She'd forgotten the steely bite of his fingers into her soft flesh. "So it's like that," she whispered.

"Yes. It's like that. A fever that burns so wild and so high, you can't even feel pain through it." His face hardened. "I'll make you so damned hungry for me that you won't care what I do to you."

"But what about Edie...." she whispered painfully.

He framed her face in his hands and bent to kiss her forehead with breathless tenderness. "Edie was a pleasant, and a very innocent, diversion," he whispered, sliding his cheek against hers so that his breath was warm at her ear. "I haven't slept with her."

"But...you must have wanted to," she began again.

He lifted his head, and his dark eyes searched hers slowly. "Pepi, I don't really understand why, but maybe the guilt made it difficult for me to deal with relationships. I...haven't wanted sex since Marsha died. At least, not until yesterday."

"You wanted me," she whispered with growing wonder.

"Oh, yes, I did," he said with undisguised hunger. "I still do, more every day." His eyes slid down her body and he drew her against him, his lean hands on her shoulders. "Do you want to give me a baby?" he asked.

It was the first time anyone had asked her that. She felt her body burning with heat, and she knew her freckles were standing out like crazy in her face. "Now?" she asked uncertainly.

"If you don't want to get pregnant, I'll have to do something to prevent it," he explained gently.

"Oh." She averted her eyes. "Well, I... I don't know." Things were moving fast. Almost too fast. She felt hunted.

"Don't look like that," he said, his voice almost tender as he tipped her face up to his eyes. "You don't have to, if you don't want to. I'm in no hurry. We've got the rest of our lives. If you want to spend some time getting used to me first, that's all right. I'll never rush you."

"C.C.," she said softly, and she smiled at him. "You're a nice man."

"That's what I've been trying to tell you. It's just that I haven't quite tried to prove it, yet," he added with a smile full of self-mockery. "And my name is Connal."

"Yes. Connal." She reached up hesitantly and paused, but he caught her fingers and drew them to his face, letting her trace his dark eyebrows, his straight nose, the hard curve of his thin mouth.

"We'll take one day at a time," he assured her solemnly. "No pressure."

"Thank you."

He smiled and put her in the car, sliding in beside her with apparent good humor to start the engine.

She fastened her seat belt and studied his profile hungrily. "Connal?" she asked.

He glanced at her and lifted an eyebrow.

"Do you… I mean, is a child important to you?" she asked quietly.

He frowned. She made it seem as if he wanted her because she could bear him one. He wasn't certain what to say to reassure her. She'd said that she wasn't in love with him, although she was certainly attracted to him. God knew, he didn't want to frighten her off.

"Eventually, yes," he compromised. "Don't you want children?"

"Yes, I do," she said huskily, meeting his eyes. "I want them very much."

His chest began to swell. He hoped against hope that someday she'd want them because she loved him. But it would take time, he reminded himself. He mustn't be impatient.

He didn't say anything else. He nodded and turned his attention back to the road.

The airport was crowded, and Pepi clung to C.C.'s lean hand on the way through the crush of people.

"Everybody decided to come on the same day," he mused, moving aside with her to let the embarking passengers get by. For a brief moment, they were alone in the corridor. He chuckled and drew her along with him, his spurs "making music" as the cowboys like to call it.

"I'd forgotten what spurs sounded like," she murmured.

"I forgot to take them off this morning," he recalled. "Back in the old days, the Mexican spurs were so big that vaqueros had to take them off just to walk," he replied. "God knows how their mounts survived."

"You use spurs when you help break horses," she reminded him.

He smiled down at her. "Sure I do. But you know we use special spurs that don't break the skin or injure the horse's hide. To a horse, it's like being tickled. That's why he jumps and sunfishes."

Her hand felt very small and helpless in his. It wasn't a feeling she'd have liked with another man, but with C.C. it seemed very natural.

She looked down, marking the size of her foot and his. He had big feet, too, but they suited him because he was so tall.

"I don't have big feet," he remarked, accurately reading her mind.

"Did I say anything?" she protested.

He chuckled. "You didn't have to. There they are!" he said suddenly, looking over the crowd in front of them. "Evan! Harden!"

Two men who looked very much like C.C. moved toward them. They weren't wearing working clothes, though. They were in suits. The taller man had on a pearl-gray vested suit with a matching Stetson. He was huskily built. He looked like a wrestler, with dark eyes and dark hair and a complexion that was even darker than C.C.'s. The other man was only fractionally shorter, dressed in dark slacks with a white open-necked shirt with a sports jacket. He wore a black Stetson at a cocky angle over his equally black hair, and when he came closer, Pepi noticed that his eyes were a pale, glittery blue under thick black lashes. He had a leaner look than Evan, and a wiry frame that was probably deceptive, because he looked as fit as C.C.

C.C. greeted his brothers and then drew them to where Pepi stood waiting awkwardly, her uncertainty evident in her nervous face.

"Evan, Harden, this is my wife, Penelope," C.C. introduced her, sliding a casual but possessive arm around her shoulders.

"She looks just the way you described her," Harden murmured dryly, extending a lean hand. His pale blue eyes assessed her and gave nothing away. "You're a rancher's daughter, I gathered."

Penelope nodded. "I grew up around horses and cattle," she said quietly, and smiled nervously. "Hereford cattle, of course," she added. "I guess our stock will look pretty mangy to you by comparison with your purebred Santa Gerts."

"Oh, we're not snobs," Harden murmured. He stuck his hands deep in his pockets and glanced at C.C. "Except when it comes to Old Man Red."

"The foundation sire of our herd," Evan added. He extended a hand the size of a plate and shook Pepi's with firm gentleness. His dark eyes narrowed. "You look threatened. No need. We're domesticated, and we've had our shots."

Pepi's rigid stance relaxed and she laughed, her whole face lighting up. Evan didn't smile, but his dark eyes did, and she felt at home for the first time.

"Speak for yourself," Harden drawled, and his blue eyes were briefly cold. "The day I get domesticated you can bury me."

"Harden is a card-carrying bachelor," Evan mused.

"Look who's talking," Harden replied.

"Not my fault that women can't appreciate my superior good looks and charm." The eldest Tremayne shrugged. "They trample me trying to get to you."

Pepi laughed with pure delight. They were nothing like she'd imagined.

"Come on. You can fight out at the ranch," C.C. said. He took Pepi's arm.

"Pity you had to walk off with Penelope before she got a look at us," Evan said, shaking his head. "I'm a much better proposition, Pepi. I still have all my own teeth."

"That's true," Harden agreed. "But only because you knocked out two of Connal's."

"Fair trade," Connal returned. "I got three of his."

"It was a long time ago," Evan said. "We've all calmed down a lot since then."

"C.C. hasn't been very calm lately," Pepi murmured. "He was so mad when he found out we were married."

"Served him right for getting drunk," Evan said curtly. "Mother would lay a tire tool across his head for that."

"Oh, Pepi threatened to," C.C. chuckled. "Still a tee-totaler, I see, Evan?"

"He carries it to sickening extremes," Harden murmured. "Justin and Shelby Ballenger will never invite him to another dinner party. He actually got up from the table and carried the glass of wine the waiter accidentally poured back to the kitchen."

C.C. burst out laughing. "Well, Justin never was much of a drinker himself, as I recall. Not in Calhoun's league, anyway."

"Calhoun's gotten as bad as Evan," Harden told him. "He doesn't want to set a poor example for the kids, or so he says."

"Alcohol is a curse," Evan said as they reached the car.

"My father will love you," Pepi said, grinning up at him.

When they got to the ranch, Ben seemed to take to Evan even before he knew about the eldest brother's temperance stance. But he was less relaxed with Harden. In fact, so was Pepi. The blue-eyed brother moved lazily and talked lazily, but Pepi sensed deep, dark currents in him.

The men talked business while Pepi whipped up a quick lunch, but the brothers only stayed for two hours and had to catch a plane right back to Jacobsville. Pepi didn't ride with C.C. to take them to the airport, though. She had a call from her prospective employer just as they were going out the door, and she waved them on to take it.

The insurance company's receptionist had decided

that she did want her old job back. They were very apologetic, and promised to let Pepi know the minute they had another opening. She was disheartened, but it was probably just as well.

"We're going to get a bull." Ben Mathews was all but dancing as he told her. "One of the new crop of young bulls out of Checker. Remember reading about him in the trade paper? He's one of the finest herd sires in years!"

"And his progeny cost plenty, I don't doubt," Pepi said. "C.C.'s going to fund the addition, I gather."

"He's a full partner," Ben reminded her. "And we're all in this to make the ranch pay, aren't we?"

"Yes, I guess we are. How do you like his brothers?"

"Oh, Evan's a card. He's very obviously the financial brains of the outfit. Knows his figures."

"And Harden?" she added.

He sat down in his chair and crossed his legs. "Harden is a driven man. I don't know why, but he strikes me as a bad man to have for an enemy. He's charming, but underneath it, there's a darkness of spirit."

"A deep kind of pain—" Pepi nodded "—and a terrible anger."

"Exactly. I hope we'll be doing most of our business with Evan. He's more like C.C."

"He's more like two of C.C.," Pepi laughed. "I wonder what the other brother looks like, the one who's married?"

"Just like C.C. and Evan, from what I gather. Harden's the odd one, with those blue eyes. He doesn't really favor the others very much."

"Probably a throwback to another generation, like Aunt Mattie who had dark-haired parents and was a blonde."

"No doubt."

"My job didn't come through," she said after a minute. "They don't need me."

"Then why don't you do some bookkeeping and typing for the ranch?" Ben asked. "Connal said we're going to have to keep proper books now, and there'll be a lot of correspondence. He was going to hire somebody, but you're a good typist and you aren't bad with figures. We can keep it in the family."

"I guess I could," she said. "I like typing."

"You can talk to Connal when he gets back."

She cleaned up the kitchen and made an apple pie. By the time she took it out of the oven, Connal had returned.

"Did they get off all right?" she asked him.

"Like clockwork." He paused by the counter where she was placing a cloth over the pie. "For supper?" he asked hopefully.

She smiled at him shyly. "Yes. I like your brothers," she said.

"They liked you, too. Evan was particularly impressed."

"Evan is easier to get along with. Harden..." She hesitated. "He's...different."

"More different than you know," he said quietly. He moved closer, taking a strand of her hair in his fingers and twirling it around one. "How about supper and a movie tonight?"

"I have to get supper for Dad," she said, hesitating.

"We'll take him with us," he chuckled.

"On a date?" She lifted her eyebrows. "He'd love that. Besides, this is his checkers night with old man Dill down the road. No, I'll fix something for him before we go. He won't mind."

"If you're sure." He sighed heavily, watching her. "Pepi, how would you feel about moving into a house with me?" he added, frowning.

"But...but what about Dad?" she asked.

"Consuelo can cook and clean for him. She could go on salary. And there's a house, the Dobbs house. They moved back East last month," he reminded her. "Your father was renting them the house. It's small, but it would be just right for the two of us."

She couldn't cope with so much at once. Things were happening with lightning speed, and her mind was whirling.

"You mean, live with you all the time," she faltered. "Even at night?"

"That's the general idea," he replied. "A wife's place is with her husband."

"You didn't want a wife. You said so..."

"...with alarming repetition, yes, I know," he finished for her. "Will you try to understand that I've changed my mind? That marriage is no longer the terror it was for me?"

"Well, yes, I'll try. But you didn't have much choice about ours, did you?"

He let go of her hair. "Not much," he agreed. "But

looking back, I wouldn't have wanted to marry anyone. Surely you realized that?"

"You were pretty adamant about it." She nodded. "I just wish we'd gone about things in the normal way. I'll always feel that you were trapped into a relationship you really didn't want."

"So were you," he replied. "But the thing we have to do now is make the most of it. An annulment would disgrace us both, Pepi, especially your father. Now that he and I are in partnership, the best way to cement it is to make the marriage a real one."

"Is it what you really want, Connal?" she asked worriedly.

"Of course it is," he said.

She couldn't help feeling that he was only saying that to put her at ease. It would hurt his pride to get an annulment. People might think he wasn't enough of a man to fulfill his wedding vows. Too, he might still have in mind using her to ward off other contenders for his hand in marriage.

"Could I have a little more time?" she asked hesitantly.

He stared down at her. After the afternoon, he'd thought she'd be immediately receptive to his advances, but perhaps she'd had too much time to think and she'd gotten cold feet. The last thing he could afford to do was to rush her.

"Okay," he said after a minute. "You can have a little more time. But you and I are going to start doing things together, Pepi. If we don't live together, we're at least going to start acting like married people in public."

"That's all right with me," she said. But afterward, she worried about Edie. Had Connal told her about his marriage? And was his relationship with Edie really as innocent as he'd said it was?

CHAPTER NINE

CONNAL TOOK HER to the same exclusive restaurant in El Paso where she'd gone with Brandon the night before her father's birthday. She was wearing a plain gray jersey dress with a pretty scarf, her hair down around her shoulders, and Connal had told her that she looked delightfully pretty. Even if he was lying, it was exciting to go on a real date with him, to have his dark eyes possessive on her face as they walked to their table.

He looked elegant in a dinner jacket and dark slacks, his white silk shirt a perfect foil for his dark complexion and darker eyes and hair. Pepi loved to look at him. She thought that in all the world, there couldn't be a more handsome man.

He seated her and then himself, and she smiled at him until a movement caught her eye and she saw Edie sitting at a nearby table all alone, staring pointedly at Connal.

"I'd better have a word with her," he told Pepi, his eyes narrowing. "I won't be a minute."

He got up and went to the other table, smiling at an Edie who became suddenly radiant. The blonde was wearing a simple black sheath dress cut almost to the navel in front, and Pepi despaired of the way she probably compared to the sophisticated older woman.

She couldn't tear her eyes away from them. They did look so right together, and despite C.C.'s determination to make the most of a bad situation—their marriage—she felt guilty and ashamed that he'd had to be trapped into marrying her when he'd have been so much better off with Edie. Pepi was just a country girl. She had no sophistication. She didn't even know how to choose the kind of clothes that were proper for a place like this. Inevitably she was going to be a dismal disappointment for a man like Connal, who was born to wealth and high society.

Edie's face suddenly went rigid. She stared at Pepi blankly for an instant, and then with quickly concealed rage. Her attention went back to C.C. and she seemed to come apart emotionally. She started crying.

C.C. got her up out of her chair and put a comforting arm around her as he led her gently out of the restaurant.

Obviously he'd told her about the marriage. Did he tell her, Pepi wondered, that it had been a forced one, and not of his choosing? Was he going to take her home now or get her a cab?

Ten minutes passed and Pepi grew more upset as she realized he'd more than likely driven Edie home. He'd comfort her, surely. Maybe more than that. He and Edie were close, even if they weren't lovers. Or had he stretched the truth about that, too?

The waiter hovered and Pepi went ahead and ordered soup du jour and a chef's salad. It was all she had any appetite for.

She'd just finished when C.C. came back, his expression telling her nothing as he sat down across from her.

"Is she all right?" Pepi asked quietly.

"Not really, but she'll do. I should have picked a better place to tell her," he said shortly. "God, I never expected that kind of reaction."

"She's been your only steady date for a long time," Pepi said with downcast eyes. "It's understandable that she had hopes of her own."

C.C. hated scenes. It brought back unpleasant memories of times when Marsha had put away too many cocktails and did her best to embarrass him. She'd never succeeded. Neither had Edie, but it touched off his temper.

"Women always have hopes," he said with cold bitterness. "Of course, not all of them are fortunate enough to catch a man drunk and drag him into a Mexican wedding chapel."

Pepi closed her eyes. She shouldn't let him get to her like this. Despite his ardor, his desire for her, underneath there was always going to be resentment that he'd been less than sober when he signed the marriage license. He was never going to let Pepi forget, either, and what kind of life was that going to be for either of them?

"I wouldn't exactly call it fortunate," Pepi replied without looking at him.

"Thank you," he replied acidly. "I can return the compliment."

The waiter came and C.C. ordered a steak and salad. He sipped the coffee he'd ordered and glared at Pepi. It wasn't her fault, he knew, but he was furious at Edie's theatrics and Pepi's meek acceptance of his bad humor. He wanted a fight, and he couldn't seem to start one. If Pepi continued to knuckle under like this, marriage was going to be impossible for her.

"Nothing to say?" he prodded.

She tightened her fingers around the water glass. "What would you like to hear?" She lifted the glass, her pale brown eyes glittering with dislike. "Or would you prefer something nonverbal but just as enlightening?"

His eyes began to twinkle. "Go ahead. Throw it."

She glanced around at the elegant diners surrounding them and thought better of it. There were some priceless antiques decorating the place. With her luck she'd hit something irreplaceable and land them in debt for years. She put the water glass down.

"It's not my fault," she said coldly. "You're the one who threatened to shoot up Juárez."

"And you knew I didn't have a gun," he countered.

"No, I didn't," she returned. "Dad told me once that you have a Beretta and a license to carry it. I had no way of knowing there wasn't one in your pocket, and I wasn't about to frisk you."

"God forbid," he said with mock horror. "Imagine having to touch a live man like *that*!"

"Cut it out," she muttered, reddening.

"You are a greenhorn and a half, aren't you?" he mused. "Don't know how to kiss, don't know how to make love, wouldn't dream of touching a man below the belt…"

"Stop!" She glanced around quickly to make sure

nobody had heard him, her face beet-red. "Somebody might hear you!"

"So what? We're married." His eyes narrowed. "Till death do us part," he added mockingly.

Her own eyes narrowed and she smiled sweetly. "In that case, do check your bed at night, dear man. I'll see if I can find a couple of rattly bedmates for you."

"One of your ranch hands did that, the first night I was here," he recalled, grinning at her shock. "Didn't they ever tell you?"

"Somebody put a live rattlesnake in your bed?" she gasped.

"Indeed they did," he replied. "Fortunately they'd de-fanged him first, but it was an interesting experience."

"What did you do?"

"You didn't hear the gunshot, either, I gather?" he mused.

"You shot it?"

"Uh-huh," he agreed. "Right through the head, the mattress, and the bunkhouse floor."

"Poor old snake," she said.

He gave her a hard glare. "Aren't you the one who leaped up onto the hood of a truck from a standing start when one came slithering past your foot this summer?"

"I didn't say I liked them," she emphasized. "But I think it's horrible to kill things without reason. What could the poor thing have done to you—gummed you to death?"

"You're forgetting I didn't know he'd had his fangs pulled."

"Oh. I guess not."

The waiter brought his meal and he ate it in silence, noticing that Pepi's eyes wandered back to the window and the sharp, dark outline of the mountains in the distance. She was brooding, and he felt bad that he'd attacked her without reason.

"I suppose Edie was angry?" she said, fishing.

He finished the last bit of his steak and washed it down with steaming black coffee. "That's an understatement. She had a lot to say when I told her how our marriage had come about."

"Including advising you on the quickest way to have it annulled, I imagine?" she asked miserably.

"I told her we couldn't get an annulment," he murmured dryly.

"But of course we can," she said without thinking. "We haven't—" She broke off, gasping.

He watched her eyes widen when she realized what he was saying.

"You didn't tell Edie that?" she burst out.

"Why not?" His black eyes probed hers. "Regardless of how they got said, I consider marriage vows binding. That means I don't have women on the side. As for what we haven't done yet, you'll sleep with me, eventually. You're as hungry for it as I am. Maybe even hungrier. I remember how I ached before my first time. And I wanted Marsha so much that I couldn't sleep at night."

Neither could she, but she wasn't about to admit that to him. She lowered her eyes to the table. "I suppose your first wife loved you?" she asked idly.

"She loved the idea of my money, just like the ones who came after her, up to and including Edie," he replied with a cynicism that shocked Pepi. He looked at that moment like a man who'd known every conceivable kind of woman and trusted none of them.

"Did Edie know who you were?" Pepi asked.

He nodded. "Through a mutual friend. So you see, it wasn't love eternal on her part. She enjoyed a good time and eating in the best places. But she'll find someone else. There are plenty of well-heeled bachelors around."

"Are you as cynical as you sound?" she asked.

"Every bit," he replied narrowly. "Even Marsha married me as much for what I have as what I was. She told me she couldn't endure being married to a man who worked for wages. She was pretty and I wanted her. But long before the accident, I regretted marrying her."

Would it be that way with her, too, she wondered. Would he be that resentful of her? He already disliked the way they'd been married.

"You must have missed her, though," she said gently.

"I missed her," he agreed. "I missed the child more. God, it was hard living with that! If I'd had any idea, any idea at all that she was pregnant, I'd never have let her in the raft. But she was too possessive to let me go alone. There were two other women in the rafting party, and she'd convinced herself that I wanted both of them."

She studied his hard face. "Didn't she know that you aren't the kind of man who'd forsake any vow he made?" she said after a minute.

His head came up and his dark eyes glittered into hers. "If you believe that, why did you look so accusing when I came back from taking Edie home? Were you picturing me in bed with her?"

She blushed. "There's a big difference between taking a vow voluntarily and taking one when you're out of your mind on tequila," she said with wan pride. "You didn't get married out of choice, this time." She picked up her napkin and stroked the embossed design. "It's not going to work, C.C.," she added wearily.

"Oh, hell, yes, it is," he said tersely. He finished his coffee. "I'm still in the adjustment stage, that's all. Until recently I thought of you as Ben's tomboy teenage daughter."

So that was it. Probably she still acted like one, too. But it was beyond her abilities to pretend a sophistication she didn't have.

"Or your nursemaid," she mused, smiling a little. "That's what you said in Juárez, that since I was always playing nursemaid, we might as well get married so I'd have an excuse."

"You've always looked out for me," he said quietly. "I never thought of you in a physical way, Pepi. It was as much a shock for me as it was for you that morning in the kitchen when your father interrupted us," he added, his eyes glittery under his thick lashes.

She averted her gaze. She remembered, too. It had been the sexiest kind of lovemaking, but he hadn't even kissed her.

"If things had happened naturally," he continued, his voice deepening, "it wouldn't have affected me the way it did."

"They wouldn't have happened naturally, and you know it, C.C.," she told him, her eyes a little sad as they met his. "You'd never in a million years have wanted somebody like me. I guess if this hadn't come up, you'd have married Edie eventually."

"Didn't you hear a word I just said, about why Edie kept going out with me?" he asked irritably.

"Edie loves you," she muttered. "I'm not blind, even if you're trying to be. She genuinely cared about you. No woman is completely mercenary, and there's a lot more to you than just the size of your wallet."

He lifted an eyebrow. "Really? Name something."

"You're kind," she said, taking the sarcasm at face value. "You don't go out of your way to start fights, but you'll stand your ground when it's necessary. You're fair and open-minded when it counts, and you have a lot of heart."

He stared at her. "I thought you didn't care enough about me to want to stay married to me?" he murmured, touched by her opinion of him.

"And I'll remind you again that you're the one who wanted the annulment and went storming off in a snit to get it," she shot back. "I still don't understand what changed your mind while you were away."

"Evan did," he said after a minute. "He accused me of running from commitment." He paused to light a cigarette, staring absently at his lighter before he re-pocketed it. "I guess in a way he was right. I couldn't bear the thought of another Marsha, another possessive woman smothering me. I couldn't bear the thought, either, that tragedy could repeat itself, because I was still working out the guilt I felt over Marsha's death. Evan said that I should keep you, if you were brave enough to take me on," he added, staring at her quietly. "He thought you sounded like exactly the kind of woman I needed. And maybe he was right, Pepi. The last thing you are is possessive."

She could have laughed out loud at that! Of course she was possessive; she loved him. But he obviously didn't want a woman who cared deeply about him. He wanted a shallow relationship that would allow him to remain heart-free and independent, and she couldn't settle for that.

"All the same, I'm not sure I can handle this," Pepi confessed. "You'll never get over the fact that it was an accidental marriage. Even a few minutes ago, when you were upset about Edie, you threw it up to me."

"Haven't you been doing the same thing, about what I said to you before I left to visit my brothers in Jacobsville?" he countered.

She shrugged. "I guess I have. But we're two pretty different people, C.C., and I won't ever get used to a rich lifestyle or high society," she said honestly. "I'm not a social animal."

His face went hard. "You don't think you can live with me as I am?"

"I could have lived very well with my father's foreman, who was just an ordinary working man," she replied. "I'm made for cooking and cleaning, for taking care of a house and raising a family. I'm just not cut out for society bashes, and no matter how hard you try to change me, you'll never get the country out of me."

He lifted his chin, his eyes narrowing on her face. "Do I strike you as the kind of man who lives from party to party?" he asked.

"You've been hiding out for three years," Pepi reminded him, "living a lifestyle that probably wasn't a patch on the one you left behind. I don't know anything about that side of your life at all."

"Would you like to?" he asked. "We could go to Jacobsville and visit my family for a few days."

She hesitated. Harden intimidated her, but she liked Evan well enough. "What's your mother like?" she asked.

He smiled. "She's like Evan," he replied. "She's dry and capable and easy to like. She'll like you, too."

"Harden doesn't like me," she said.

"Harden doesn't like women, sweetheart," he said gently. "Despite the fact that he's got a face like a dark angel and the charm to match, he's the original woman-hater."

"Then it wasn't just me," she said, a little relieved.

"It wasn't. He hates our mother most of all," he added quietly. "That's why he doesn't live at home. Evan does, because it's too much of a burden for Mother, but Harden has an apartment in Houston, where our offices are located."

She wanted to follow up on that, but it probably wasn't the best time to start probing into family secrets.

"I guess we'd have to stay in the same room?" she asked worriedly.

His dark eyes searched hers in a warm silence. "Yes."

"Twin beds?" she asked hopefully.

He shook his head.

"Oh." She toyed with her fork, going warm all over at the thought of sleeping with him.

"Want to back out?" he challenged softly.

She lifted her eyes to his and hesitated. Then she gave in, all at once. She loved him. If he wanted to try to make their marriage work, this was the first step. He seemed adamant about not getting an annulment, and she didn't really want one, either.

"No," she said. "I don't want to back out."

His face tautened and he seemed to have a hard time breathing. "Brave words," he said huskily. "Suppose I have more in mind than sharing a pillow with you?"

She gnawed on her lower lip. "That's inevitable, isn't it?" she asked hesitantly. "If we stay married, I mean."

He nodded. "I won't settle for a platonic marriage. I want a child, Pepi," he added, his voice deeper, slower as he stared into her eyes.

She stared at her hands, neatly folded in front of her on the table. "I'd like that. I'm just a little nervous about it, that's all. Most women these days are experienced."

"You can't imagine what a rare and exquisite thing a virgin bride is to me," he said quietly. "Your innocence excites me, Pepi. Just thinking about our first time makes my knees go weak."

It made hers go weak, too, but she didn't think she should admit it. Her eyes glanced off his and away again. "When did you plan for us to visit your family?" she asked instead, changing the subject.

"Tomorrow. My mother wants to meet you. It wouldn't hurt to let her see that I haven't let history repeat itself."

"As if you had much choice." She sighed. "Oh, C.C., I'm so sorry I got us into this mess," she groaned, meeting his dark gaze levelly. "I didn't know what to do.

Edie or somebody like her could have coped with it better."

"Edie or somebody like her would have been laughing like hell at my predicament and adding up the settlement all at the same time," he replied. "They wouldn't have flayed themselves with attacks of conscience."

"Wouldn't you like to get an annulment, anyway?" she asked him. "Then you'd have the right to choose…"

"Is it the damned redheaded vet after all?" he shot back, suddenly dark-faced with rage. "Well, is it?"

"What do you mean?" she faltered, staggered by the venom in the attack.

He leaned forward, his eyes like black fires burning in his lean face. "You know what I mean. He's in love with you. Was it mutual? Is he why you're so single-minded about that annulment, so you can dump me and marry him?"

"Brandon did ask me to marry him, but…" she began.

"But you did your Florence Nightingale act and followed me to Juárez," he said angrily. "Well, don't hold your breath until I let you go. We're married, and we're staying married. And I'd better not catch Hale hanging around you, either!"

She gaped at him. "That's not fair!" she tossed right back. "Even if it wasn't a conventional marriage, I take my vows seriously, too!"

"Do you? Prove it," he said tersely.

"Prove it?" she echoed blankly.

"You know where the bunkhouse is," he said with a mocking smile.

She averted her angry face. He'd told her that before

and she'd refused, asked for time. Now here he was rushing her again, and it felt almost as if he were requesting something horribly immoral. She couldn't help her reticence. She still didn't feel married to him.

"So you still have cold feet?" he taunted. "All right, then. Save your pride. But you'll sleep with me when I take you to visit my family. You gave your word."

"Yes, I know," she said huskily. She folded her napkin neatly and laid it beside her plate. "Could we go now?"

"Of course." He got up and pulled out her chair, pausing to look down at her with troubled dark eyes. "You're going to fight me every step of the way, aren't you?" he asked deeply. "You'll never forget the things I said when I found out about the marriage license."

"It wasn't any surprise, C.C.," she replied, looking up at him with quiet pride. "I always knew I wasn't your type of woman. You even warned me once, that morning I came to make black coffee for you when you were hungover. You said you didn't have anything to give and told me not to break my heart over you. There was no need to worry. My heart isn't breaking." That was true. It had already been broken by his cold indifference.

He let out a rough sigh. He'd closed all his doors and now he didn't know how to open them again. All he knew was that if he lost Pepi, there wouldn't be much left of his life.

He paid the bill and led her out to the car. He didn't say anything, driving quickly and efficiently down the long road paralleling the Rio Grande until they were on the turnoff to the ranch. It was wide-open country here, and deserted most all the time.

Pepi sat beside him in a rigid silence, toying with her purse. There was a tension between them that disturbed her. Despite his apparent unconcern as he drove, smoking his cigarette without talking, she sensed that he was boiling underneath. Maybe Edie had upset him and he couldn't get over having lost her. She didn't take his remarks about Brandon seriously, because he had to know she wasn't crazy about their vet. Besides, if he'd been jealous, that would mean he cared. And he'd already said he didn't.

She leaned her head back with a faint sigh, anxious to be home, to get this turbulent evening into the past where it belonged.

But C.C. suddenly pulled off into a small grove of trees, their outline dark against the night sky, and cut off the engine.

She opened her eyes and looked at him. In the pale light from the half moon, his eyes looked glittery and dangerous.

"Afraid?" he asked softly.

"N-no," she faltered.

He put out his cigarette and unfastened first his seat belt, then hers. He took the purse out of her hands and laid it on the dash. With deft sureness, he lifted her body across his legs and eased her head back onto the hard muscle of his upper arm.

"Liar," he said quietly, searching her oval face. "You're scared to death. Physical love isn't something to be afraid of, Pepi. It's an exquisite sharing of all that two people are, an intimate expression of mutual respect and need."

He sounded more gentle than he ever had, and some of her apprehension drained away. She rested her cool hand on his dinner jacket as she searched the hard face above hers. Once she'd dreamed of lying in his arms like this, being totally alone with him and wanted by him. But so much had happened in the meantime that it seemed somehow unreal.

"Do you really want me, that way?" she asked, her voice sounding strained and high-pitched.

"You greenhorn," he murmured. He shifted her so that her belly lay against his, and he rotated her hips sharply, letting her feel what happened to him almost instantly. He heard her gasp and felt her stiffen against him. "Does this answer your question?" he asked outrageously, and his steely hand refused to let her draw away from the stark intimacy. "Would you like to know how many years it's been since a woman could turn me on this fast?"

Her fingers clenched on his dinner jacket, but she stopped trying to pull away. The feel of him was drugging her. Her own body began to betray her, reacting unexpectedly to the evidence of his need and lifting closer to it.

He caught his breath. "Pepi!" he ground out.

She felt him tremble with a sense of wonder. She watched his face and repeated the tiny movement of her hips. Yes, he liked it. She could tell by the way his jaw tautened, by the sudden catch of his breath, the stiffening shudder of his body against her.

"Do you...like that?" she whispered shyly.

"Yes, I like it!" he groaned. He bent, his free hand tangling in her thick, soft hair, the other going to the base of her spine to hold her even closer. "Do it again, baby," he whispered against her lips. "Do it again, hard...!"

His mouth invaded hers. She felt the sudden sharp thrust of his tongue and her body arched as his hand went under the skirt of her dress and up against her stocking-clad leg. He touched her inner thighs, his mouth teasing now, nibbling at her lips while his hand slowly discovered the most intimate things about her trembling body. She couldn't even protest. She loved what he was doing to her.

His hand withdrew and went up her back to the zipper of the dress, to loosen it before he did the same thing with the catch of her lacy bra.

"Don't be afraid," he said softly when she tried feebly to stay the downward movement of his hands. "I want to look at your breasts, Pepi. I want to touch them."

She trembled all over with the words, her eyes lost in his. She gave way, and the dress fell to her waist along with the thin wisp of lace that had hidden her from his rapt stare.

He held her a little away from him, and his dark eyes feasted on her nudity in the dim light. She could feel the tension in him. He didn't move or speak for the longest time, and as she watched, her nipples began to harden under that piercing stare. She didn't understand the contraction, or the way her body arched up faintly, as if enticing him to do more than look.

"It isn't enough, is it, little one?" he asked tenderly.

His hands slid under her bare back and he bent his dark head to her body. "You smell of gardenias, Pepi," he whispered. His lips touched the silken swell of her breast, lightly brushing it, and she shivered. He liked that reaction, so he did it again, and again, working his way around, but not touching the hard nipple. Pepi's hands clenched against his chest and she felt her body beginning to throb in a new and scary way.

"C.C.," she moaned. "Please…it aches so! Make it… stop!"

One lean hand slid up her rib cage to tease at the outside edge of her breast. His lips teased some more, until she actually shuddered with the need and began to beg him.

"Sweet," he breathed roughly. And his mouth suddenly opened, taking the hard nipple inside, closing on it with a warm, slow suction that made her cry out. It was like a tiny climax. Her hands tangled convulsively in his hair and she wept, gasping as the pleasure went on and on and on.

"Oh, God…!" he ground out, shocked at her capacity for lovemaking. If she could be this aroused when he'd barely touched her, he could hardly imagine how it would be in bed, with her naked body under his, her long, elegant legs enclosing him, holding him, welcoming him as a lover.

"Connal," she whispered shakily. Her lips touched his forehead, his closed eyes, trembling. "Connal, please. Please."

"I can't," he bit off, lifting his head. He could barely speak, his lean hand unsteady on her breast where it rested like a brand of fire while he looked down at his handiwork. "Not here."

"No one would see us," she moaned.

"I can't take the risk," he said heavily. He pulled her to him, wrapping up her bare breasts against the silky fabric of his dinner jacket, rocking her. "Anyone could drive up here, including the county police," he murmured at her ear. His lips brushed her earlobe. "I don't want anyone to see you without your clothes except me. And when we go all the way, I want it to be in a bed, not the front seat of a car."

She shivered, nestling closer. "Does it feel like this, when you go all the way?" she asked huskily.

"Yes," he breathed at her ear. "But it's much more intense." He bit her earlobe and his hands smoothed over her bare back with slow sensuality. "Has Hale seen you like this?" he whispered.

"No," she whispered back. "Nobody has, except you."

He lifted his head and looked down at her, making a meal of her bareness. He touched her nipple, very gently, and watched it harden, felt her shiver. His eyes caught hers. "Much more of this," he said roughly, "and I'll take you sitting up, right here. We'd better go home."

Her body exploded with heat as he lifted her back into her own seat. "Could we do it, like that?" she asked hoarsely.

His face tautened and for one insane instant, he was tempted. "Yes, we could." He banked down the fires. "But we're not going to. We're married. We don't have to make out in cars. Here, sweetheart, let me help you."

He forced himself to control the singeing need in

his body as he put her bra and dress back in place, delighted with her headlong response and the certainty that their marriage had a chance after all.

"I don't want to stop," she whispered.

"Neither do I. But we'll wait a while, all the same," he said curtly. He searched her face. "Before we both get blinded and sidetracked by intimacy, I want a little time for us to get to know each other. We'll go see my family and we'll do some things together. Then we'll sleep together."

She was stunned. That had to mean he cared a little, it had to! "I'd like that, Connal," she said.

He smiled at her. "Yes. So would I." He started the car and waited until she fastened her seat belt to drive off. But he held her hand the rest of the way home.

CHAPTER TEN

PEPI AND C.C. left the next morning for Jacobsville. Ben waved them off, muttering something about not knowing how he was going to keep from bursting with all that freedom and being alone with the apple pie Pepi had baked him that morning.

She hadn't been sure what to pack, so she put in her finest clothes and hoped for the best. None of her things were very expensive. She had a feeling that where she was going, they'd look like rags. But she didn't say that to C.C. He was suddenly very distant as he drove.

"You're not having second thoughts, are you?" she asked hesitantly. "About taking me to meet your mother, I mean?"

He glanced at her, astonished. "Why should I?"

She shifted and glanced out at the flat horizon. "Well, C.C., I don't know a lot about fancy place settings and etiquette, and I stayed up half the night worrying about what would happen if I got flustered and spilled coffee on her carpet or something."

He reached over and found her hand, entwining her cold, nervous fingers with his strong, warm ones.

"Now, listen. My mother is a ranch wife. She's as down-to-earth as your father, and she doesn't have one

of those houses that get featured in the designer maga-
zines. If you spilled coffee she'd just point you toward
the kitchen and tell you where she keeps the spot re-
mover. Fancy place settings aren't necessary, because
Jeanie May cooks such great meals that nobody cares
about formal etiquette once they get to the table. The
only real hazard is going to be my brother Harden,
who'll go off into a black study at the thought of having to help entertain you."

"Who hurt him like that, made him so bitter?" she
asked.

He glanced at her. "Well, you'll hear it sooner or
later. Better you hear it from me. About a year after
Evan was born, my mother and father got a separation.
During that time, she met and fell in love with another
man. There was a brief affair. Her lover was killed in
Vietnam and she came back to my father finally because he kept pleading with her. She was pregnant with
Harden, so Dad adopted him. But Jacobsville is a small
town, and inevitably, Harden found out the hard way
that he wasn't Dad's son."

"And he blames your mother."

"That's right, he does. Despite the fact that she's a
pillar of the community now, Harden can't forget that
she took a lover while she was still legally married. He
can't forgive her for making him conspicuous, an out-
cast as he calls it."

"But your father adopted him, doesn't that count for
anything?" she asked.

He shook his head. "Harden has the most rigid views
of any of us. He's an old-line conservative with Nean-

derthal principles." He glanced toward her with a rueful smile. "I'd bet you that he's still a virgin. I don't think he's even had a woman."

Her eyes widened. She remembered Harden's astonishing good looks, his physique, his rugged personality. Harden a virgin? She burst out laughing. "Not nice," she accused. "Teasing me like that."

"I'm not teasing, as it happens, I'm serious," he replied. "Harden is a deacon in the church and he sings in the choir. In fact, there was a time when he seriously considered being a minister."

"How old is he?"

"Thirty-one."

"A year older than you?" she asked.

He nodded. "Mother and Dad had a rather physical reunion when she came home. They were happy together, but I don't think she ever really got over the other man. And despite the fact that Harden hates her, he's her favorite even now."

"Forgiveness is a virtue," she said. "I guess not everybody is capable of it, but I'm sorry for your mother."

"You won't be, when you meet her. She's spunky. Like you."

She leaned her head back and smiled at him, her eyes faintly possessive. Memories of the night before streamed back to fire her blood and lingered in her pale brown eyes.

He stopped at an intersection and looked back at her, his own eyes kindling with what he read in that level stare.

"Remembering?" he asked huskily.

"Yes," she whispered.

His breath came more quickly, his brown sports shirt rising and falling roughly over his broad chest. His gaze went down to her breasts under the pale green shirtwaist dress she was wearing and lingered there. "You were like warm silk under my mouth," he bit off.

She gasped.

His eyes lifted back to hers and time stopped. "This isn't the place," he said tightly.

"No."

He glanced around and behind them. Not a single car in sight. "On the other hand, what the hell," he murmured and threw the car out of gear. "Come here."

He snapped open her seat belt and pulled her to him, his hard mouth crushing down over hers in a fever of ardent need. She circled his head with her arms and held on for dear life, giving him back the kiss hungrily. Her body throbbed with need of him, her mouth shaking as his tongue penetrated it insistently.

He dragged his head up at the distant sound of a big truck coming closer and spotted it in the rearview mirror. "Obviously he's not a married man," he muttered, putting a radiant, breathless Pepi back in her seat and buckling her in. "Damn it." He put the car in gear again, his hands slightly unsteady on the wheel, looked both ways and pulled out onto the highway.

He glanced at her hungrily. "Tonight, I'm going to have you. One way or the other, the waiting's over."

Her lips parted on a rough breath. "Are the walls very thin?" she asked hesitantly.

"We'll be in a room away from the others," he said

curtly. "You can scream if you want to, nobody will hear you."

"I... I can't seem to be quiet when you start touching me," she said gently. "I lose control."

"So do I," he replied tersely.

She flushed. He made it sound very intimate and she wanted him. Her body blazed with the need, even now.

He glanced at her. "Baby, if you don't stop looking at me like that, I'll park the damned car and make love to you on the roadside," he threatened huskily.

"Anywhere," she said shakily. "Oh, Connal, I want you so much, it's like a fever."

His jaw tautened. He actually shivered. His eyes went to a small crossroads where a motel was situated. Without thinking, he pulled off and cut the engine. "Do you want me enough?" he asked, staring at her.

The fever was so high that even her shyness didn't faze it. "Yes," she whispered huskily, flushing.

He got out, went inside the office and came out with a key. He didn't say another word until they were in the room, with the door locked.

"Do you want me to use anything?" he asked before he touched her.

She knew what he was asking. She loved him. If a child came of this, it would be all right. He wanted one desperately, she knew.

"No," she said, going close to him. "Don't use anything."

He drew her slowly to him, already so aroused that his tall, fit body was shaking. "I don't know how long I can hold out," he breathed at her lips. "But I'll try to arouse you enough to make it bearable. And later, afterward, I'll make it up to you if I lose control."

She didn't understand what he was saying. His hands were on the buttons of her dress and she stood very still, letting him peel the clothing from her body until she was totally nude.

Her skin felt blazing hot. She was shy, and the way he was looking at her burned her, but it made her proud, too, because his pleasure in her body was evident in the glitter of his black eyes and the tenderness of his smile.

He jerked back the covers on the big double bed and picked her up, putting her down gently against the pillows. Then he set about removing his own clothing.

Pepi had seen pictures of naked men, but nothing had prepared her for the sight of Connal without clothing. He was magnificent, all lean hard muscle and black, curling hair. Aroused, his body was faintly intimidating and she held her breath when he came toward her.

"Don't panic," he said gently as he slid onto the bed beside her. "By the time we start, you'll be ready for me. Your body is like a pink rosebud, all silky and tightly furled. I'm going to open the petals, one by one, and make you bloom for me." He bent his mouth and took hers, very softly. One lean hand slid down her rib cage to her hips and over her thighs and back up to tease around her breast.

The embarrassment and shyness faded as he began to touch her, his fingers delicate and deft and sure on her untaught body. He lifted his head and looked at her, watched her reactions as he feathered caresses over her taut breasts, down her flat belly, to that place where she was most a woman. He touched her there and she shivered and tried to get away.

"No," he whispered tenderly, kissing her eyes closed. "This is part of it. You have to give yourself completely, or I could hurt you even without meaning to. I want to show you how it's going to feel. Relax, little one. Give me your body."

His lips coaxed lazily, and she gave in to the slow, tender probing of his fingers, shivering as she permitted the extraordinary intimacy. Her body reacted to him with headlong delight, arching and throbbing as he made it feel incredible sensations with his deft touch.

"It won't even be difficult for you," he whispered, smiling against her mouth. "Now it begins, little one. Now..."

The kiss grew deeper, invasive. His hand tormented and then began to move with a slow, torturously sweet rhythm that made her lift and tremble with each touch. She gasped and then little cries began to purr out of her. She reached for him, her nails digging into his upper arms as the pleasure built beyond anything she'd ever dreamed.

He smiled through his own fierce pleasure at the look on her face. His head bent to her breasts and he took one into his mouth with the same rhythmic movement his fingers were teaching her. All at once, she began to convulse.

And at that moment, he lifted his body completely over hers, nudging her long, shivering legs aside, and thrust down with one fierce, smooth movement.

She cried out, her eyes meeting his at the instant he

took possession of her. But she didn't draw back, even at the faintly piercing pain that quickly diminished in the face of a slow, anguished pleasure that fed on itself and grew and grew with each sharp, downward movement of his body.

Somewhere along the way, his taut face became a blur, and she shuddered into oblivion just as she heard his hoarse cry and felt the deep, dragging convulsions of his body.

She opened her eyes at last, feeling new, reborn. Her skin was damp and cool. So was his. He was lying over her, dead weight now that the passion had drained out of him, and her arms enfolded him tenderly, holding him to her. She moved and felt him move with her, awed by the fusion of her female body with his male one, with the devastating intimacy of lovemaking.

"Did it hurt very much?" he asked at her ear, his voice drowsy with pleasure.

"No." Her arms contracted. "Do it again."

He chuckled. "I need a few minutes," he whispered. "Men aren't blessed with the capacity of women."

"Really?" She looked into his eyes as he lifted his dark, sweaty head. "You cried out."

"So did you," he said lazily. "Or don't you remember?"

"It all sort of blurred at the last," she replied. Her eyes mirrored her awe. "I hope I get a baby," she whispered. "It was so beautiful."

His face tautened and to his astonishment he felt his body react to the words with sudden, sharp capability.

She gasped. "Connal! You said—"

"Never mind what I said," he bit off against her mouth. His arms caught his weight and he began to move hungrily. "Help me this time," he whispered, and taught her how. "Yes, like that, like…that," he gasped, shivering as the wave began to catch him all over again. Impossible, he thought while he could. His teeth clenched. He could feel her eyes on him. She was… watching him…and he was so caught up in the fevered need that he didn't even mind. Her body, soft like down, silky, hot, absorbed him into it, holding him…

He arched, hoping against hope that she was still with him as he felt the sensation blind him with pleasure.

"Are you all right?"

He heard her voice and managed to open his eyes. She was above him, now, her face concerned, her pale brown eyes curious and gentle.

His heart was still slamming wildly against his chest. He could barely breathe. He pushed back his damp hair and drew her mouth down to his, kissing her tenderly.

"Yes, I'm all right," he whispered.

"You looked scary," she managed. "Like you were being killed. And you cried out…"

He laughed wearily. "My God, honey, why do you think the French call it the little death?" he asked. He drew her hand to his mouth. "You look the same way," he added, smiling. "I watched you, the first time."

"Oh." She colored a little. "I watched you, the second."

"Yes, I know." His dark eyes held hers. "It's all right," he said when she looked faintly guilty. "Total intimacy is a gift, something that two people share. Don't be embarrassed by anything you say or do when you're with me like this. I'll never ridicule you with it. I want you to feel completely uninhibited when we make love, as free to take me as I am to take you."

Her eyes widened. "Could I?"

"Well, not right now," he murmured ruefully.

"I didn't mean right now. You'd let me?"

He frowned slightly. "Of course I'd let you. You're my wife."

"And you...won't mind if I get pregnant right away?" she persisted.

"I told you I wanted a child," he said simply. His dark eyes narrowed. "They say a woman can tell at the instant of conception," he murmured.

She smiled down at him gently. "I don't think I can," she said. The smile faded and she traced his thin lips with a trembling forefinger. "Connal, what if I can't give you a child?" she asked worriedly. "Will you want a divorce...?"

"No!" He dragged her down to him and kissed her roughly. His eyes blazed at her. "It isn't a conditional marriage," he said firmly. "If you can't, it won't matter, so stop thinking up things to worry about."

"All right." She relaxed against him, sighing with pleasure as she felt the crisp hair on his broad chest tickling her breasts. She laughed softly and moved deliberately from side to side. "That feels good," she whispered.

"Yes, indeed, it does," he murmured, indulging her. "But you've had enough for one day. You're much too new to the art for long sessions in bed."

She opened her eyes and stared across his hair-covered chest to the window beyond. "Connal, it's addictive, isn't it?" she asked lazily. "Once you know what it's like, you want it more every time."

"Yes." His arms contracted. "No regrets?"

"Not even one," she whispered. She closed her eyes and nestled closer, smoothing one of her long legs against his powerful, hair-roughened one. "I ache."

"So do I," he confessed. "But we have to stop."

She sat up, her eyes slow and possessive on his body, openly curious. He watched her with evident amusement as she learned him by sight.

"I've never seen a man without his clothes before," she said.

"I'm glad. You won't be able to compare me unfavorably with anyone else," he mused.

She laughed. "As if anybody could compare with you," she murmured. "You're beautiful, Connal. You're just beautiful."

He sat up and kissed her warmly. "Men aren't beautiful," he said firmly, and got up to dress.

"Handsome, then. Physically devastating." She stretched hugely, enjoying the way his eyes slid over her appreciatively. "I used to think about being with you, like this, but it was always night and the lights were out."

"What a shock you were in for," he said dryly.

She stood up, smiling at him. "It was a very nice shock, actually," she said.

He pulled her gently into his arms and kissed her. "I hope I gave you half as much pleasure as you gave me," he whispered. "The fact that you came to me a virgin is something I'll treasure all my life."

She hugged him fiercely. "You make me glad that I waited," she murmured. "None of my friends did. They used to make fun of me."

"I never will," he said, tapping her gently on the nose. His eyes were brilliant with some inner feeling. "Get your clothes on."

"Fancy telling a woman that," she sighed. "And after she's given you everything she has."

"Oh, I'd keep you like that forever," he murmured, tracing her soft lines with his eyes. "But people are bound to stare if you go out like that."

"I get your point." She put her clothes on again and brushed her hair. Connal was waiting when she came out of the bathroom.

"Is this dress all right?" she asked worriedly. "I won't look too out of place, will I?"

He tilted her face up and kissed her. "You look just right, Mrs. Tremayne."

"I like the way that sounds," she whispered, thinking that it would be even more special if he loved her as much as she loved him. But he'd been gentle, and he must care for her a little to have been so tender.

"Legally mine," he murmured. His eyes darkened. "So don't give Evan any ideas."

Her face mirrored her shock. "I've only seen him once," she began.

"He thinks you're the berries," he replied. "And he's a lonely man. Don't encourage him."

"I noticed you didn't mention Harden. Don't you want to protect him, too?"

He ignored the sarcasm, shocked by his own possessiveness, his sudden sharp jealousy. "Harden's immune. Evan isn't."

"Listen here, C.C. Tremayne, just because I liked sleeping with you is no reason to accuse me of being a loose woman…!"

"Point one," he said, covering her lips with a firm forefinger, "I am not accusing you of anything. And point two, what we just did together had nothing, not a damned thing, to do with sleeping."

"Ticky, ticky," she returned.

He searched her eyes slowly. "I've never had it like that," he said curtly. "Not with anyone. Not so bad that I cried out and damned near fainted from the force of the pleasure when you satisfied me. I don't know that I like losing control that savagely."

She felt a fierce pride that she'd done that to him, and her eyes told him so. "Suppose I make you like it?" she whispered huskily.

His heart began to thunder against his ribs all over again at her sultry tone. "Think you could?" he challenged.

She moved closer, her finger toying with one of the pearly buttons at his throat. "Wait and see," she said softly. She reached up and teased his lips with hers, a fleeting touch that aroused without satisfying.

He watched her go to the door with a feeling of having given up a part of himself that he was going to miss like hell one day. She knew how he reacted to her, and that gave her a weapon. She enjoyed lovemaking, that was obvious, but she'd said she didn't love him. If she ever realized how hopelessly in love with her he was, she'd have him on the end of a hook that he'd never get free from. He almost shivered with apprehension. Accidental marriage or not, he wanted this woman with blind obsession. Whatever happened now, he wasn't going to give her up.

They drove the rest of the way to Jacobsville in a tense silence. C.C. smoked cigarettes until Pepi had to let down a window in self-defense. He seemed nervous, and she wondered if it was coming home that had him in such a state, or bringing her here. Despite his denials, she wondered how she was going to be received by his family. He was used to wealth and society people, and she wasn't. Would they even accept her?

He drove past a huge feedlot, through the country and down a long winding paved road until he reached an arch that boasted a sign that read Tremayne.

"Home," he murmured, smiling at her. He sped down the driveway in the Ford, while Pepi clenched her hands in her lap and hoped that she could cope. There were white fences on either side of the driveway, and far in the distance sat a white Victorian house with a long porch and beautiful gingerbread latticework. There were flower beds everywhere, and right now assorted chrysanthemums were blooming in them.

"It's beautiful," she said, her eyes lingering on the tall trees around the house.

"I've always thought so. There's Mother."

Theodora Tremayne was small and thin and dark,

with silver hair that gleamed in the sun. She was wearing jeans and a sweatshirt with an apron. She rushed out to meet them.

"Thank God you're home," she said, hugging Connal. "You must be Pepi, I'm so glad to meet you." She hugged Pepi, too, before she turned back to her tall son. "The sink in the kitchen is stopped up and I can't find Evan anywhere! Can you fix it?"

"Don't you have a plumber's helper?" Connal asked with a wry smile.

"Of course. What do you want with it?" she asked blankly.

"She had a flat tire on the wheelbarrow," he told Pepi.

"Go ahead, blurt out all the shameful family secrets at once!" Theodora raged at him. "Why don't you tell her about the mouse under the sink that I can't catch, and the snake who insists on living in my root cellar?"

Pepi burst out laughing. She couldn't help it. She'd been so afraid of some rich society matron who'd make fun of her, and here instead was Theodora Tremayne, who was nothing short of a leprechaun.

"I'm glad to see you have a sense of humor, Pepi," Theodora said approvingly. "You'll need it if you have to live with my son. He has no sense of humor. None of my sons do. They all walk around like thunderheads, glowering at everybody."

"Nobody glowers except Harden," C.C. said defensively.

"He's enough," Theodora said miserably. "He gets worse all the time. Well, come in and fix the sink, son. Pepi, do you like ham sandwiches? I'm afraid that's all

I could get together in a hurry. I've been out helping
Evan and the boys brand new calves and things are in
a bit of a mess."

She went on mumbling ahead of them. Connal caught
Pepi's hand.

"No more worried thoughts?" he asked with an
amused smile.

"None at all. She's a treasure!" she said.

He slid his arm around her and hugged her close.
"She isn't the only treasure around here," he whispered,
and bent to kiss her.

Pepi went inside with him, her feet barely touching
the floor. She wondered if she wouldn't float right up
to the ceiling, she was so happy. He had to care a little.
He just had to!

CHAPTER ELEVEN

But Connal's earlier warmth seemed to disintegrate as the day wore on. He fixed his mother's sink, leaving Pepi to help a flustered Theodora set the dining-room table.

"I'm so glad he's coming out of the past," Theodora told the younger woman with sincere gratitude. "You don't know how it's been for us, watching him beat himself to death over something he couldn't have helped. He came to see us, occasionally, and there were phone calls and letters. But it's not the same thing as regular contact."

"We never knew anything about his past; Dad and I, that is," Pepi said. "But C.C. always had class. You couldn't miss it. I used to wonder why he buried himself on a run-down place like ours."

"He speaks highly of your father," Theodora said. "And he, uh, had a lot to say about you, too, the last time he was here."

Pepi blushed, lowering her eyes to the plate she was putting on the table. Thank God she knew where the knife, fork and spoon went, and it wasn't one of those elaborate settings that she couldn't figure out. "I guess he did," she answered Theodora. "He was furious when he left the ranch. I didn't blame him, you know," she said, lifting quiet brown eyes to the other woman's face.

"He had every right to hate me for not telling him the truth."

Theodora searched those soft eyes. "He's hurt you badly, hasn't he?" she asked unexpectedly. "Does he know how you feel?"

The blush got worse. Pepi's hand shook as she laid the silverware. "No," she said in a whisper. "If he even considers it, he probably thinks I'm in the throes of physical attraction. And for right now, it's safer that way. I'm not convinced that I can ever be the kind of wife he needs. You see," she added worriedly, "I'm not sophisticated."

Theodora impulsively went around the table and hugged her, warmly. "If he lets you get away from him, I'll beat him with a big stick," she said forcefully. "I'll go and bring in the sandwiches and call the boys in. Don't look so worried, Penelope, they won't take any bites out of you!" she said with a grin.

Pepi sat down where Theodora had indicated, and a minute or so later, the older woman came back with a huge platter of sandwiches, closely followed by her three towering sons.

"Hello, again," Evan said warmly, seating himself beside Pepi. "What a treat, having something pretty to look at while I eat," he added, with a meaningful glance toward his brother Harden.

Harden lifted a dark eyebrow, glancing with cold indifference at Pepi. "I've told you before, if you don't like looking at me while you eat, wear a blindfold."

"God forbid, he'd probably eat the tablecloth!" Theodora chuckled. "Sit down, Connal, don't dither."

"Yes, ma'am," he murmured, but his smile wasn't re-

flected in his eyes as he glanced with open disapproval
at Evan sitting beside Pepi.

"Say Grace, Harden," Theodora said.

He did, and everyone became occupied with sandwiches and coffee preparation. Evan told Pepi about
the ranch and its history while Harden ate in silence
and Theodora quizzed Connal about his future plans.

Pepi couldn't hear what Connal was saying, but she
did feel the angry lash of his eyes. She wondered what
she'd done to make him so cold toward her. Could he be
regretting that impulsive stop at the motel? She flushed
a little, embarrassed at the memories that flooded her
mind. She still ached pleasantly from the experience.
But perhaps it was different for a man, if he didn't love
a woman he slept with. Connal had wanted her with a
raging passion, she couldn't have mistaken that. But
afterward he might have regretted his loss of control,
the lapse that had turned an accidental marriage into
a real one. He might be having second thoughts about
Edie even now. He looked odd, too. Very taciturn and
quiet. Pepi knew that mood very well. It was the one that
caused the men to keep well away from him, because
when he got broody, he got quick-tempered, too. Pepi
hoped he wasn't spoiling for a fight with her.

"I always wanted a sister," Evan murmured dryly.
"What I got was Connal and Donald and...him," he
shuddered as he glanced at Harden.

Harden kept eating, totally impervious to the insult.

"You won't get through his hide with insults," Theodora told her son. "I tend to think he thrives on them."

"You should know," Harden told her, his blue eyes as cold as the smile he bent on her.

"Not now," she told him firmly. "We have guests."

"Family," Evan corrected.

"Yours, not mine," Harden said with a pointed glare at his mother. "No offense," he added to Connal.

"You plan to carry the vendetta to your grave, I gather," Theodora muttered.

"I've got to get back to work," Harden said, rising. "I'll see you tonight, Connal."

He walked out, lean and lithe and arrow-straight, without a backward glance.

"Now that the company has improved, what do you think of our quaint little place?" Evan asked Pepi.

She replied automatically, her mind on the awkward conversation that had gone before. If this was any indication of how things were going to go for the duration of her visit, she wasn't at all sure she wanted to stay.

But it got better, without Harden's difficult presence. Evan took her in hand before Connal could protest and drove off with her in the ranch Jeep.

"What about Connal...?" she asked uneasily, glancing back to where he stood with Theodora glaring after them.

"Now, now, all I have in mind is a little brotherly chat," Evan replied, and the teasing was abruptly gone. As he glanced at her without smiling, she saw in Evan the same steely character that had intimidated her first in C.C. and then in Harden.

He pulled the Jeep off on the side of the ranch road when they were out of sight of the house, and cut the engine. "Edie called here this morning, looking for Connal," he said without preamble.

"Oh. I see." She studied the broad, leonine features quietly. He and Connal looked alike. Although Evan's hair was more brown than black, he had the same piercing, unsmiling sternness as his brother.

"I don't think you do," Evan replied. "Edie isn't the kind of woman to take a rebuff lying down. She didn't believe him when he told her he was married. She thought he was being tricked by a fake license, and she told me so."

She sighed heavily. "Well, it's easy enough to check, you know," she said.

"Undoubtedly. I did, when Connal showed us the license." He smiled ruefully at her glare. "No offense, child, but he stands to inherit a hell of a fortune when Mother passes on. He's not exactly a poverty case now, and I didn't know you from a peanut when he came storming in here waving that damned license and cursing at the top of his lungs."

"But Connal said it was you who changed his mind about staying married to me," she faltered.

He leaned back against the Jeep door, big and elegant-looking for a cattleman, his Stetson pushed back over his broad forehead. "Sure I did," he mused. "One of these days I'll let you read what my private detective said about you. You're the kind of woman mothers dream about finding for their sons. A walking, talking little elf with domestic skills and a gentle heart. In this oversexed, undercompassionate generation, you're a miracle. I told Connal so. Eventually he began to realize that he could do a lot worse."

"I wonder." She sighed.

"Edie doesn't seem to agree, so watch out," he cautioned sternly. "Don't let her spring any surprises on you. Forewarned is forearmed, right?"

"Right. Thanks, Evan."

"Connal deserves a little happiness," he said tersely. "He never had much with Marsha, and she couldn't bear to have him out of her sight five seconds. It's time he stopped beating himself to death."

"I think so, too," she said gently. "I'll take good care of him, Evan." *If I get to,* she added silently.

He smiled almost tenderly. "I gather that you've been doing that very well for the past three years," he said, his deep voice warm with affection. "We'd better get back. I thought you ought to know what the competition was up to so there wouldn't be any unexpected surprises."

"I'll watch my back," she promised.

Evan drove her around the ranch and pointed out herd sires along the way. He seemed to have a phenomenal memory for their names, because he never seemed to draw a blank. He was in a jovial mood for the rest of the way home.

But Connal was in a furious one when they got there. He gave his brother a glare that would have fried a defenseless egg, and the one he bent on Pepi made her feel like backing away.

Theodora pretended not to notice the tension. She herded them into her four-by-four and they drove into Jacobsville to get some more supplies for roundup.

She seemed to know everyone. Pepi lost her nervousness as she was introduced to several people at the hardware store, including a harassed young woman herding three small children through the aisles, followed by a tall blond man.

"The Ballengers," Theodora told Pepi, "Abby and Calhoun. That's Matt…no, it's Terry…and that's Edd," she said, trying to identify each child.

"You've got it just backward, Theodora," Calhoun drawled. "Terry, Edd and Matt."

"Between your kids and your brother Justin's children, I can't keep the names straight!"

"And Justin and Shelby have another one on the way," Calhoun chuckled. "Shelby's sure this one is going to be a girl."

"After two boys I can understand her determination," Theodora replied.

"We gave up," Abby sighed. "I like boys and I'm tired of the maternity ward, not to mention never being able to get one word in edgewise. They'd trample my dead body to get to their daddy."

"They sure would, but I still love you," Calhoun murmured and kissed her forehead warmly.

She melted against him, almost visibly a part of him. Pepi felt a twinge of sadness that she might never know that kind of devotion. Apparently desire was all she aroused in C.C., and the way he was acting, he might not even feel that anymore. His lean face was as hard as if it had been carved out of granite, and he didn't move a step closer to Pepi when she was introduced as his wife.

It was hard to pretend that everything was fine, that she was divinely happy, when her heart was breaking.

Later, Theodora took her on a tour of Jacobsville, named after Shelby Ballenger's family, and pointed out the huge Ballenger feedlot and the old Jacobs's home, now owned by a new resident. Back at the ranch, Theodora produced photo albums, while the men went out to check on the progress of the branding.

There was little conversation over the supper table. The pert, gangly cook made some acid comments about the enormous male appetites and grinned on her way back to the kitchen.

"She's been here for so long that she owns the kitchen," Theodora explained merrily. "She loves clean platters after a meal."

"She's a wonderful cook," Pepi mused.

"I hear you make wonderful apple pies," Evan commented dryly.

"I don't know about that," Pepi said shyly. "My dad seems to think they're pretty good, because he sure hates sharing them."

"I don't blame him." Evan glared at Harden and his mother. "I hardly ever get my fair share of any dessert around here."

Theodora's eyebrows arched. "Penelope, his idea of a fair share is two-thirds of the pie."

"I'm going seedy, anybody can see that," Evan protested. "Wasting away from starvation…"

Pepi laughed delightedly, her eyes twinkling at Evan, who was sitting beside her.

Across the table, Connal wasn't laughing. He was

tormenting himself with that smile and reading all sorts of ridiculous ideas into it. She'd been attracted to Evan since the first time she'd seen him, and today she'd gone off with him all too willingly. Now she was hanging on his every word. He was losing Pepi. If all she'd felt for him was a sensual curiosity, now that he'd satisfied that, she might have no interest left in him. God, what if she fell in love with Evan? His face contorted and he averted it quickly, before anyone saw his anguish.

After supper, Theodora produced a new video as a special treat, a first-run comedy that Pepi had been dying to see. But her enthusiasm quickly waned when C.C. left in the middle stating that he needed to make a few business calls.

Pepi excused herself shortly thereafter and went toward the study, hoping to have it out with C.C. But he wasn't there. With a leaden sigh, she went out the front door, pulling her sweater closer around her, and sat alone on the steps to look out over the dark horizon.

The door opened and closed. Expecting, hoping, that it was C.C., she got to her feet. But it was Harden.

Of all the men she'd ever met, he made her the most nervous.

"Am I intruding?" he asked quietly.

"No. I...just wanted a little air," she stammered. "I'd better go back in now."

He caught her arm, very gently, and held her in place. "There's no need to be afraid of me," he said softly. "None of my vendettas, as Theodora calls them, involve you."

She relaxed a little when he let her go and lit a cigarette.

"Connal's been watching you all night," he said after a minute. "Brooding. Did you argue before you came here?"

"No," she said, glad of the dark because she blushed remembering what they'd done before they came here. "We were getting along better than we had in some time, in fact. Then when we got here, he closed up."

"About the time you went off with Evan," he suggested.

"Well…yes."

"I thought so."

"But that was so Evan could tell me about the phone call," she said, puzzled.

He moved into the light from the windows, frowning. "What phone call?"

"There's this lady C.C. used to go around with," she said wearily. "Edie. Evan says she called here looking for C.C. because she thinks I faked the marriage license."

"Sour grapes, I expect," he mused. "Did you tell Connal why you went off with Evan?"

"I haven't had a chance. He seems to be avoiding me. I guessed maybe he was having second thoughts, again. He was sure mad when he found out the marriage was valid," she said, grimacing. "I thought he'd never speak to me again as long as he lived. Then when I agreed to an annulment and started the wheels turning, he showed up again and said he didn't want one." She threw up her hands. "I don't know what he wants anymore. Maybe he's missing Edie and angry because he's stuck with me."

"Maybe he's jealous," he murmured dryly. "I see that

thought hadn't occurred to you," he added when she gaped at him.

"C.C.'s never been jealous of me," she faltered. "My gosh, he never wanted me. Well, not for a wife, I mean…" She averted her red face when she remembered who she was talking to.

Harden actually laughed, the sound deep and pleasant in the night air. "He's a man. And it does rather go with marriage."

"I suppose so," she murmured. "But he doesn't have any reason to be jealous of Evan. I always wanted a big brother, you see."

"And Evan is a teddy bear, right?"

"Well, yes…"

"That particular teddy bear has some nasty fangs and a temper you're better off not knowing about," he advised. "He likes you, but Marsha wouldn't come near the place because of him. He hated her from head to heels and made no secret of it."

"But he's so nice," she said.

"You're not doing business with him," he chuckled. "Evan's deep. Just don't put too much stock in that boyish charm. I'd hate to have you totally disillusioned when he throws somebody over a fence."

"Evan?" she gasped.

"One of the new men took a short quirt to a filly and drew blood. Evan heaved him over the fence and jumped it himself. The last we saw of the man, he was tearing through the blackberry thicket like a scalded dog trying to outrun Evan."

She was beginning to get a good idea of what the

Tremayne men were really like. She whistled silently. "My, my, and here I thought you were the terror of the outfit." She grinned.

"Oh, I'm right down the line behind your husband and Evan."

"And Donald, is that his name, the youngest?"

"Donald puts Tabasco sauce on his biscuits," he replied. "And I have personally seen him skin men at five feet when he's angry."

"I don't know that I want to be related to you savages," she said, tongue in cheek.

"Sure you do," he replied. "Once you get to know us, you'll feel right at home. Any woman who'll take on Connal has to be a hell-raiser in her own right. God knows Jo Ann is, or she'd never have lasted three years with Donald."

She laughed. "I can't wait to meet them."

"They're away for two weeks on business, I'm sorry to say. Another time."

"Yes." She glanced toward the front door. "I suppose I'd better go and try to find my husband."

"That's a step in the right direction. Good night, Penelope."

"Good night, Harden," she replied, smiling as he went down the steps and out to his car. He was nice. Like the rest of C.C.'s family.

She said good night to the others and went upstairs, wondering if she could work up enough nerve to seduce her own husband.

CHAPTER TWELVE

IT WAS BARELY ten o'clock, but when Penelope got to the room where Connal had taken their suitcases, it was to find him already in bed and apparently asleep.

She hesitated. The lamp by the king-size bed was on, but the bare chest half-covered by the plaid sheet was rising and falling regularly.

"Connal?" she asked softly, but he didn't answer.

With a long sigh, she got out her gown and took it into the bathroom to put it on. This was not the night she'd envisioned, and her courage failed her when she walked back into the bedroom minutes later wearing the long green nylon gown.

She climbed slowly into bed beside him, gave his dark head and his hair-covered muscular chest a long look, and resignedly turned out the light.

But she couldn't sleep. She tossed and turned, remembering so vividly the ardor she'd shared with C.C. only hours before. Her body had never ached so when she'd been unawakened. Now she knew what desire was, and she felt it so acutely that it was almost pain.

"Can't you sleep?" he asked, his voice deep and clear, not muffled with drowsiness.

"Not very well," she said. She lay on her side, looking toward the dark shape that was his head. Dim light from the safety lights by the barn shone in through the curtains. "I guess it's because I'm not used to sleeping with anyone," she added.

"Neither am I, just lately." He reached out and drew her slowly against him. Her hand came in contact with his bare hip and she realized belatedly that he wasn't wearing pajamas.

He felt her stiffen unexpectedly and chuckled under his breath. "You saw me nude just this morning," he reminded her. "And I saw you. Is it still such a shock? Or is it just that I'm the wrong man?" he added sarcastically.

"The wrong man?" she echoed.

"You've been hanging on Evan all day," he said. His hands smoothed up her body, his thumbs edging out to rub against her sensitive nipples. "Are your marriage vows uncomfortable all of a sudden?"

"C.C., that's not true," she said quietly. "I like Evan very much, but I haven't been hanging on him."

His fingers bit into her sides. "I wouldn't really expect you to admit it. Maybe I can't even blame you. One way or another, I got us into this mess."

A mess. He was admitting that it was that, in his eyes. Her heart plummeted. "I thought you were making a phone call. I went looking for you," she said, making a clean breast of it.

"I made it up here," he said. "I had to call Edie."

Her heart stopped beating. She wanted to hit him. So Evan's warning had been right on the money, had it? That woman wasn't going to give up, and if C.C.

had no qualms about calling her from his family home, then he must have misgivings about breaking off with her in the first place.

Connal felt her go rigid and his heart jumped. That was the first hopeful sign he'd ever had that she might care a little for him. God, if only it were true!

"Nothing to say?" he chided.

She ground her teeth together. "I think I can sleep now," she said through them.

"Can you?" He moved the covers away and while she was dealing with that unexpected action, his lips came down squarely over her breast, taking the nipple and the fabric that covered it into the hot darkness of his open mouth.

The cry that tore out of her throat was music to his ears. He shifted and while his mouth made intimate love to hers, he stripped the gown down her trembling body and his hands relearned its soft, sweet contours with a lazy thoroughness that had her moaning in his arms.

"Can I have you without hurting you?" he whispered at her ear, his breath as hot as the body threatening hers.

"Yes," she whimpered. Her nails bit into his shoulders, tugging at them, her legs already parting to admit him, her body lifting to meet the fierce, heated descent of his. "Connal…!"

"Take me," he ground out against her mouth as his hips thrust down in one long, invasive movement.

She whimpered under the sharp pleasure, clinging to him as his body enforced its possession with increasing urgency. "Don't stop, Connal, don't…stop…!"

His mouth bit at hers. "You're noisy," he breathed

huskily. "I like it. I like the way you feel, the way you taste. Tell me you want me."

"I…want…you!" She could barely get the words out. He was killing her. The pleasure was too sweet to bear and she was going to die of it.

She said so, her voice breaking as he fulfilled her with savage urgency, finding his own shuddering release seconds later.

She couldn't stop trembling. She clung to his damp body, frightened by the force of the satisfaction he'd given her.

He felt tears against his cheek and lifted his head. His heartbeat was still shaking him, his arms trembling as they supported him above her. He couldn't see her face, but he could feel the convulsive shudders of her body, feel how disturbed she was from the grip of her hands.

"Don't be afraid," he whispered. "We went very high this time. Give yourself time to come down again. It's all right." His fingers smoothed back her damp hair and he kissed her eyes closed, kissed her cheeks, her trembling mouth in a warm, soft silence that gradually took the fear away.

"You said… I was noisy," she whispered.

"Didn't I say that I liked it?" he murmured. He bit her lower lip gently. "Touch me."

He guided her hand to him, and smiled when she hesitated shyly.

"We're married," he said. He opened her fingers and spread them, pressing them slowly against him. "You won't hurt me, if that's why you're so tense," he whispered. He kissed her gently and in between kisses, he

guided and coaxed and in soft whispers, explained to
her everything she needed to know about a man's body.

The lesson was sweet and lazy and slow, and as her
eyelids began to fall drowsily, he joined her body tenderly, intimately, to his and pulled her over him to cra-
dle her softness on his strength. Incredibly, she slept.

THEY WENT HOME the next day. Connal was less rigid,
and seemed perfectly happy all the way back to the
ranch. But he was preoccupied again by the end of the
day, and he didn't mention sharing her bed that night.

It became a routine for several days. He was friendly
enough, even affectionate, but he didn't touch her or
kiss her. He did watch her, with brooding, narrow eyes
as if he couldn't decide what to do.

She was still worried about the phone call he said
he'd made to Edie, and if his desire for her had waned
because of the other woman.

"What's going on between you and my new son-in-
law?" Ben Mathews finally demanded one morning in
the kitchen after breakfast.

"What do you mean?" she hedged. She had her hair
in a ponytail and she was wearing a sweater and jeans
and scuffs, less than elegant attire. C.C. hadn't even
come in for breakfast for the second time in as many
days.

"I mean, you and Connal are married, but you don't
act like it," he said bluntly. "And ever since you came
home from his family's ranch, you've both gone broody.
Why?"

"He called Edie," she said quietly. "I don't know if

he's looking for a way out or trying to make me get a divorce. He hasn't said. But he's not happy, I know that." She glanced at him, hoping to forestall any more personal questions. "Don't you have to be in El Paso at eleven for a meeting?" she asked.

"Yes, I do, and I'm going any minute. Why not an annulment?"

She blushed and put her hands back in the warm, soapy dishwater. "For the obvious reason," she said demurely.

"Then if that's the case, why aren't you living together? There's a furnished house going spare, if that's the problem."

She felt tears stinging her eyes. "It's more than that."

"What?"

She dropped a pan and in the ensuing noise, nobody heard C.C. come in the front door and down the hall. He was standing right outside the door, about to make his presence known, when he heard Pepi's choked voice.

"I'll tell you what," she wept. "He doesn't love me. He never did, and I didn't expect it, you know. But I had hoped…"

Ben pulled her gently into his arms and held her while she cried. "You poor kid," he sighed, patting her back comfortingly. "I don't guess you ever told him you were dying for love of him?"

Connal felt his body go rigid with the shock. He couldn't have moved if his life had depended on it.

"No, I never told him," Pepi sobbed. "Three years. Three long, awful years. And we got married by accident, and I knew he wouldn't want somebody plain and tomboyish like me, but oh, God, Papa, I love him so much! What am I going to do?"

Connal moved into the room, white-faced, his dark eyes blazing. "You might try telling him," he said harshly.

Ben let her go and moved away, a smug grin on his face that he quickly hid from them. "I'm late. Better be off. See you kids after lunch."

They didn't even hear him leave. Connal was still staring at her with an expression she could barely see through her tears.

"Oh, mother!" she wailed. "Why did you have to stand out there and listen!"

"Why not?" He moved closer, catching her arms and jerking her close, his bat-wing chaps hard and cold even through her jeans, like the tan checked Western shirt her hands rested against. "Say it to my face. Tell me you love me," he dared, his taut expression a challenge in itself, giving nothing away of his own feelings.

"All right. I love you!" she burst out. "There, are you satisfied?" she raged, red-faced.

"Not yet," he murmured in a low, sexy tone. "But I think I can take care of that little problem right here..."

His mouth settled on hers in slow, arousing movements. It had been so long. Days of polite conversation, tormented lonely nights aching for what had been. She went wild in his arms, pressing close against him, welcoming the intimate touch of his hands on her breasts, their pressure at her thighs as he moved her urgently against his hips.

"Just a minute," he whispered gruffly, as he locked the door.

His hand then went to the chaps. He stripped them off and threw them on the floor, his hands going to her blouse and then her jeans. Somehow he managed to get them off along with the scuffs she'd been wearing instead of boots. He sat down in the chair at the kitchen table and pulled her over him.

There was a metallic sound as his belt hit the floor and the rasp of a zipper. He pulled her down on him, watching her eyes as she absorbed him easily, quickly.

"Forgive me," he whispered jerkily. "I can't wait."

"Neither can I," she whispered back, meeting his lips halfway. "I love you, Connal," she whimpered as he moved under her.

"I love you," he said huskily. "Oh, God, I love you more than my own life…!" He heard her shocked gasp and said it again and again, his hands insistent, demanding as he rocked her, lifted and pushed her in a rhythm that eventually shook the floor and the heavens.

She trembled uncontrollably. So did he. The explosion they'd kindled had all but landed them on the floor. He laughed huskily, lifting his head to meet her wickedly amused eyes.

"So much for new techniques borne of desperation," he murmured. "Now let's go upstairs and do it properly."

Hours later she nestled her cheek against his damp chest and opened her eyes. "We really ought to get dressed. Dad will be home eventually."

He kissed her forehead lazily. "I locked the door, remember?"

"So you did." She sighed, loving the new closeness

they were sharing. "Harden said you were jealous of Evan."

"I was. Blind jealous, of him, of Hale, of any man who came near you. All these years together, and I didn't know that I loved you. Evan knew it instantly. And when I realized it, it was almost too late to stop you from getting an annulment." He shook her gently. "God, you've led me a merry chase! Even our first time, I was convinced that you were just curious about sex. I didn't think you gave a damn about me except physically."

"I've loved you since the first time I saw you," she whispered. "You became my world."

His arm tightened around her. "You were mine, too. It just took a while for me to realize it. Until that happened, I said some pretty harsh things to you. I hope in time you'll be able to forget them. I was running as fast as I could. It's taken me a long time to get over Marsha, but I think I have. I had to be whole again before I had anything to offer you. I had to stop being afraid of commitment, and it wasn't easy."

"Dad said that. I wasn't so optimistic. I thought you hated me."

"Wanted you, not hated you. And resented it like hell. Eventually you stayed on my mind so much that I burned from morning till night wanting you. It's becoming an obsession."

"Wanting isn't loving."

He chuckled. "I know that, too, but you have to admit, it's a big part of it." He kissed her closed eyelids. "I'd die for you, Penelope," he whispered huskily. "Will that do?"

"Oh, yes." She nuzzled her head against his chin. "Why did you call Edie?"

"I thought we'd come to that," he said, and grinned. "Evan told me what she was up to, so I phoned and told her that my marriage was perfectly legitimate and furthermore, I was desperately in love with my wife. I don't think we'll hear any more from her."

She lifted up, searching his face while he made a meal of her breasts with his eyes. "That's why Evan took me riding, to warn me that she'd called, looking for you!"

"Well, I'll be!" he burst out, diverted. "And he never said a word."

"Harden said you were jealous," she murmured dryly. "That gave me the first hope I'd had."

"How do you think I felt that night we spent together when you grumbled about Edie?" he laughed softly. "God, I'll never forget the way we made love then!" he whispered at her temple.

"Neither will I." She looked down into his eyes, her own fever kindling as she stared at him, her body tautening visibly. "Connal…" she whispered, her voice shaking.

His jaw tautened. He caught her waist and lifted her over him, pulling her down on his hips. "Yes," he whispered. "I need you, too. Again, little one."

"I don't think I can, this way…" She hesitated.

"Yes, you can," he said huskily. "I'll teach you. Like this, Pepi…"

She was shocked to discover that she could, indeed, and it was a long time before she was able to get up and dress afterward.

"Shy little country girl, hmmm?" he mused as they sat in the dining room sipping coffee and eating apple pie. "What an about-face!"

"It's the company I'm keeping," she murmured. "And we have a problem."

"You're pregnant?" he asked hopefully.

"That isn't a problem, and I may be but I don't know yet," she said. "I mean, we're married, but I don't have a wedding ring."

He grinned and pulled a box out of his jeans pocket. "Don't you?"

He held it out and she opened it, producing a beautiful set of rings—one with a big diamond, the other a gold band with inlaid diamonds that matched it.

"It's lovely," she said huskily. "But where's yours?" She glared at him. "You're wearing a ring, Connal Cade Tremayne. I won't have every lonely spinster in south Texas trying to trespass on my preserves!"

"Well, well," he murmured dryly. "Okay. We'll go into town and buy me one."

The front door slammed and her father came walking into the dining room, stopping suddenly. "My God!" he wailed.

"You noticed my rings, did you?" Pepi grinned.

"Tell him that we're moving into the vacant house this afternoon, that'll unfreeze him," Connal dared.

"We are," she told her father. She frowned. "What's the matter with you? Aren't you happy that our marriage is going to work out and Connal and I are going to live together and you're going to have grandchildren at last? Aren't you happy about all that?"

"Of course I am, Pepi," he groaned. "It's just…"

"Just?" Connal prompted.

"Just?" Pepi seconded.

"Damn it," he raged, slamming his hat down. "You've eaten my apple pie!"

SEVERAL WEEKS LATER, Pepi made him a present of three freshly baked pies and the news that he was going to become a grandfather. She told Connal afterward that she wasn't sure which of her presents made him smile the widest.

* * * * *

HARDEN

CHAPTER ONE

THE BAR WASN'T CROWDED. Harden wished it had been, so that he could have blended in better. He was the only customer in boots and a Stetson, even if he was wearing an expensive gray suit with them. But the thing was, he stood out, and he didn't want to.

A beef producers' conference was being held at this uptown hotel in Chicago, where he'd booked a luxury suite for the duration. He was giving a workshop on an improved method of crossbreeding. Not that he'd wanted to; his brother Evan had volunteered him, and it had been too late to back out by the time Harden found out. Of his three brothers, Evan was the one he was closest to. Under the other man's good-natured kidding was a temper even hotter than Harden's and a ferocity of spirit that made him a keen ally.

Harden sipped his drink, feeling his aloneness keenly. He didn't fit in well with most people. Even his in-laws found him particularly disturbing as a dinner companion, and he knew it. Sometimes it was difficult just to get through the day. He felt incomplete; as if something crucial was missing in his life. He'd come down here to the lounge to get his mind off the emptiness. But he felt even more alone as he looked around him at the laughing, happy couples who filled the room.

His flinty pale blue eyes glittered at an older woman nearby making a play for a man. Same old story. Bored housewife, handsome stranger, a one-night fling. His own mother could have written a book on that subject. He was the result of her amorous fling, the only outsider in a family of four boys.

Everybody knew Harden was illegitimate. It didn't bother him so much anymore, but his hatred of the female sex, like his contempt for his mother, had never dwindled. And there was another reason, an even more painful one, why he could never forgive his mother. It was much more damning than the fact of his illegitimacy, and he pushed the thought of it to the back of his mind. Years had passed, but the memory still cut like a sharp knife. It was why he hadn't married. It was why he probably never would.

Two of his brothers were married. Donald, the youngest Tremayne, had succumbed four years ago. Connal had given in last year. Evan was still single. He and Harden were the only bachelors left. Theodora, their mother, did her best to throw eligible women at them. Evan enjoyed them. Harden did not. He had no use for women these days. At one time, he'd even considered becoming a minister. That had gone the way of most boyish dreams. He was a man now, and had his share of responsibility for the Tremayne ranch. Besides, he'd never really felt the calling for the cloth. Or for anything else.

A silvery laugh caught his attention and he glanced

at the doorway. Despite his hostility toward anything in skirts, he couldn't tear his eyes away. She was beautiful. The most beautiful creature he'd ever seen in his life. She had long, wavy black hair halfway down her back. Her figure was exquisite, perfectly formed from the small thrust of her high breasts to the nipped-in waist of her silver cocktail dress. Her legs were encased in hose, and they were as perfect as the rest of her. He let his gaze slide back up to her creamy complexion with just the right touch of makeup, and he allowed himself to wonder what color her eyes were.

As if sensing his scrutiny, her head abruptly turned from the man with her, and he saw that her eyes matched her dress. They were the purest silver, and despite the smile and the happy expression, they were the saddest eyes he'd ever seen.

She seemed to find him as fascinating as he found her. She stared at him openly, her eyes lingering on his long, lean face with its pale blue eyes and jet-black hair and eyebrows. After a minute, she realized that she was staring and she averted her face.

They sat down at a table near him. The woman had obviously been drinking already, because she was loud.

"Isn't this fun?" she was saying. "Goodness, Sam, I never realized that alcohol tasted so nice! Tim never drank."

"You have to stop thinking about him," the other man said firmly. "Have some peanuts."

"I'm not an elephant," she said vehemently.

"Will you stop? Mindy, you might at least pretend that you're improving."

"I do. I pretend from morning until night, haven't you noticed?"

"Listen, I've got to—" There was a sudden beeping sound. The man muttered something and shut it off. "Damn the luck! I'll have to find a phone. I'll be right back, Mindy."

Mindy. The name suited her somehow. Harden twisted his shot glass in his hand as he studied her back and wondered what the nickname was short for.

She turned slightly, watching her companion dial a number at a pay phone. The happy expression went into eclipse and she looked almost desperate, her face drawn and somber.

Her companion, meanwhile, had finished his phone call and was checking his watch even as he rejoined her.

"Damn," he cursed again, "I've got a call. I'll have to go to the hospital right away. I'll drop you off on the way."

"No need, Sam," she replied. "I'll phone Joan and have her take me home. You go ahead."

"Are you sure you want to go back to the apartment? You know you're welcome to stay with me."

"I know. You've been very kind, but it's time I went back."

"You don't mind calling Joan?" he added reluctantly. "Your apartment is ten minutes out of my way, and every second counts in an emergency."

"Go!" she said. "Honest, I'm okay."

He grimaced. "All right. I'll phone you later."

He bent, but Harden noticed that he kissed her on the cheek, not the lips.

She watched him go with something bordering on relief. Odd reaction, Harden thought, for a woman who was obviously dating a man.

She turned abruptly and saw Harden watching her. With a sultry laugh she picked up the piña colada she'd ordered and got to her feet. She moved fluidly to Harden's table and without waiting for an invitation, she sat down, sprawling languidly in the chair across from him. Her gaze was as direct as his, curious and cautious.

"You've been staring at me," she said.

"You're beautiful," he returned without inflection. "A walking work of art. I expect everyone stares."

She lifted both elegant eyebrows, clearly surprised. "You're very forthright."

"Blunt," he corrected, lifting his glass in a cynical salute before he drained it. "I don't beat around the bush."

"Neither do I. Do you want me?"

He cocked his head, not surprised, even if he was oddly disappointed. "Excuse me?"

She swallowed. "Do you want to go to bed with me?" she asked.

His broad shoulders rose and fell. "Not particularly," he said simply. "But thanks for the offer."

"I wasn't offering," she replied. "I was going to tell you that I'm not that kind of woman. See?"

She proffered her left hand, displaying a wedding band and an engagement ring.

Harden felt a hot stirring inside him. She was married. Well, what had he expected? A beauty like that would be married, of course. And she was out with a man who wasn't her husband. Contempt kindled in his eyes.

"I see," he replied belatedly.

Mindy saw the contempt and it hurt. "Are you…married?" she persisted.

"Nobody brave enough for that job," he returned. His eyes narrowed and he smiled coldly. "I'm hell on the nerves, or so they tell me."

"A womanizer, you mean?"

He leaned forward, his pale blue eyes as cold as the ice they resembled. "A woman hater."

The way he said it made her skin chill. She rubbed warm hands over her upper arms. "Oh."

"Doesn't your husband mind you going out with other men?" he asked mockingly.

"My husband…died," she bit off the word. She took a sudden deep sip of her drink and then another, her brows drawn together. "Three weeks ago." Her face contorted suddenly. "I can't bear it!"

She got up and rushed out of the bar, her purse forgotten in her desperate haste.

Harden knew the look he'd just seen in her eyes. He knew the sound, as well. It brought him to his feet in an instant. He crammed her tiny purse into his pocket, paid for his drink, and went right out behind her.

It didn't take him long to find her. There was a bridge nearby, over the Chicago River. She was leaning over it, her posture stiff and suggestive as she held the rails.

Harden moved toward her with quick, hard strides, noticing her sudden shocked glance in his direction.

"Oh, hell, no, you don't," he said roughly and abruptly dragged her away from the rails. He shook her once, hard. "Pull yourself together, for God's sake! This is stupid!"

She seemed to realize then where she was. She looked at the water below and shivered. "I...wouldn't really have done it. I don't think I would," she stammered. "It's just that it's so hard, to go on. I can't eat, I can't sleep...!"

"Committing suicide isn't the answer," he said stubbornly.

Her eyes glittered like moonlit water in her tragic face as she looked up at him. "What is?"

"Life isn't perfect," he said. "Tonight, this minute, is all we really have. No yesterdays. No tomorrows. There's only the present. Everything else is a memory or a daydream."

She wiped her eyes with a beautifully manicured hand, her nails palest pink against her faintly tanned skin. "Today is pretty horrible."

"Put one foot forward at a time. Live from one minute to the next. You'll get through."

"Losing Tim was terrible enough, you see," she said, trying to explain. "But I was pregnant. I lost the baby in the accident, too. I was... I was driving." She looked up, her face terrible. "The road was slick and I lost control of the car. I killed him! I killed my baby and I killed Tim...!"

He took her by the shoulders, fascinated by the feel of her soft skin even as he registered the thinness of them. "God decided that it was his time to die," Harden corrected.

"There isn't a God!" she whispered, her face white with pain and remembered anguish.

"Yes, there is," he said softly. His broad chest rose and fell. "Come on."

"Where are you taking me?"

"Home."

"No!"

She was pulling against his hand. "I won't go back there tonight, I can't! He haunts me...."

He stopped. His eyes searched her face quietly. "I don't want you physically. But you can stay with me tonight, if you like. There's a spare bed and you'll be safe."

He couldn't believe he was making the offer. He, who hated women. But there was something so terribly fragile about her. She wasn't sober, and he didn't want her trying something stupid. It would lie heavily on his conscience; at least, that was what he told himself to justify his interest.

She stared at him quietly. "I'm a stranger."

"So am I."

She hesitated. "My name is Miranda Warren," she said finally.

"Harden Tremayne. You're not a stranger anymore. Come on."

She let him guide her back to the hotel, her steps not quite steady. She looked up at him curiously. He was wearing an expensive hat and suit. Even his boots looked expensive. Her mind was still whirling, but she had enough sense left to realize that he might think she was targeting him because he had money.

"I should go to my own apartment," she said hesitantly.

"Why?"

He was blunt. So was she. "Because you look very well-to-do. I'm a secretary. Tim was a reporter. I'm not at all wealthy, and I don't want you to get the wrong idea about me."

"I told you, I don't want a woman tonight," he said irritably.

"It isn't just that." She shifted restlessly. "You might think I deliberately staged all this to rob you."

His eyebrows rose. "What an intriguing thought," he murmured dryly.

"Yes, isn't it?" she said wryly. "But if I were planning any such thing, I'd pick someone who looked less dangerous."

He smiled faintly. "Afraid of me?" he asked deeply.

She searched his hard face. "I have a feeling I should be. But, no, I'm not. You've been very kind. I just had a moment's panic. I wouldn't really have thrown myself off the bridge, you know. I hate getting wet." She shifted. "I really should go home."

"You really should come with me," he replied. "I won't rest, wondering if you've got another bridge picked out. Come on. I don't think you're a would-be thief, and I'm tired."

"Are you sure?" she asked.

He nodded. "I'm sure."

She let him lead her into the hotel and around to the elevator. It was one of the best hotels in the city, and he went straight up to the luxury suites. He unlocked the door and let her in. There was a huge sitting room that led off in either direction to two separate bedrooms. Evan had planned to come up with Harden from Texas.

At the last minute, though, there'd been an emergency and Evan had stayed behind to handle it.

Miranda began to feel nervous. She really knew nothing about this man, and she knew she was out of control. But there was something in his eyes that reassured her. He was a strong man. He positively radiated strength, and she needed that tonight. Needed someone to lean on, someone to take care of her, just this once. Tim had been more child than husband, always expecting her to handle things. Bills, telephone calls about broken appliances, the checkbook, groceries, dry cleaning, housekeeping—all that had been Miranda's job. Tim worked and came home and watched television, and then expected sex on demand. Miranda hadn't liked sex. It was an unpleasant duty that she tried to perform with the same resignation that she applied to all her other chores. Tim knew, of course he did. She'd gotten pregnant, and Tim hadn't liked it. He found her repulsive pregnant. That had been an unexpected benefit. But now there was no pregnancy. Her hand went to her stomach and her face contorted. She'd lost her baby....

"Stop that," Harden said unexpectedly, his pale blue eyes flashing at her when he saw the expression on her face. "Agonizing over it isn't going to change one damned thing." He tossed his hotel key on the coffee table and motioned her into a chair. "I keep a pot of coffee on. Would you like a cup?"

"Yes, please," she said with resignation. She slumped down into the chair, feeling as if all the life had drained out of her. "I can get it," she added quickly, starting to rise.

He frowned. "I'm perfectly capable of pouring coffee," he said shortly.

"Sorry," she said with a shy smile. "I'm used to waiting on Tim."

He searched her eyes. "Had you trained, did he?" he asked.

She gasped.

He turned. "Black, or do you like something in it?"

"I... I like it black," she stammered.

"Good. There's no cream."

She'd never been in a hotel penthouse before. It was beautiful. It overlooked the lake and the beachfront, and she didn't like thinking about what it must have cost. She got to her feet and walked a little unsteadily to the patio door that overlooked Chicago at night. She wanted to go outside and get a breath of air, but she couldn't get the sliding door to work.

"Oh, for God's sake, not again!" came a curt, angry deep voice from behind her. Lean, strong hands caught her waist from behind, lifting and turning her effortlessly before he frog-marched her back to her chair and sat her down in it. "Now stay put," he said shortly. "I am not having any more leaping episodes tonight, do you understand me?"

She swallowed. He was very tall, and extremely intimidating. She'd always managed to manipulate Tim when he had bad moods, but this man didn't look as if he was controllable any way at all. "Yes," she said through tight lips. "But I wasn't going to jump. I just wanted to see the view—"

He cut her off. "Here. Drink this. It won't sober you up, but it might lighten your mood a bit."

He pushed a cup and saucer toward her. The smell of strong coffee drifted up into her nostrils as she lifted the cup.

"Careful," he said. "Don't spill it on that pretty dress."

"It's old," she replied with a sad smile. "My clothes have to last years. Tim was furious that I wasted money on this one, but I wanted just one nice dress."

He sat down across from her and leaned back, crossing his long legs before he lit a cigarette and dragged an ashtray closer. "If you don't like the smoke, I'll turn the air-conditioning up," he offered.

"I don't mind it," she replied. "I used to smoke, but Tim made me quit. He didn't like it."

Harden was getting a picture of the late Tim that *he* didn't like. He blew out a cloud of smoke, his eyes raking her face, absorbing the fragility in it. "What kind of secretary are you?"

"Legal," she said. "I work for a firm of attorneys. It's a good job. I'm a paralegal now. I took night courses to learn it. I do a lot of legwork and researching along with typing up briefs and such. It gives me some freedom, because I'm not chained to a desk all day."

"The man you were with tonight…"

"Sam?" She laughed. "It isn't like that. Sam is my brother."

His eyebrows arched. "Your brother takes you on drinking sprees?"

"Sam is a doctor, and he hardly drinks at all. He and Joan—my sister-in-law—have been letting me stay with them since…since the accident. But tonight I was going home. I'd just come from an office party. I certainly didn't feel like a party, but I got dragged in because everyone thought a few drinks might make me feel better. They did. But one of my coworkers thought I was feeling too much better so she called Sam to come and get me. Then I wanted to come here and try a piña colada and Sam humored me because I threatened to make a scene." She smiled. "Sam is very straitlaced. He's a surgeon."

"You don't favor each other."

She laughed, and it was like silvery bells all over again. "He looks like our father. I look like our mother's mother. There are just the two of us. Our parents were middle-aged when they married and had us. They died within six months of each other when Sam was still in medical school. He's ten years older than I am, you see. He practically raised me."

"His wife didn't mind?"

"Oh, no," she said, remembering Joan's kindness and maternal instincts. "They can't have children of their own. Joan always said I was more like her daughter than her sister-in-law. She's been very good to me."

He couldn't imagine anybody not being good to her. She wasn't like the women he'd known in the past. This one seemed to have a heart. And despite her widowed status, there was something very innocent about her, almost naive.

"You said your husband was a reporter," he said when he'd finished his coffee.

She nodded. "He did sports. Football, mostly." She smiled apologetically. "I hate football."

He chuckled faintly and took another draw from his cigarette. "So do I."

Her eyes widened. "Really? I thought all men loved it."

He shook his head. "I like baseball."

"I don't mind that," she agreed. "At least I understand the rules." She sipped her coffee and studied him over the rim of the cup. "What do you do, Mr. Tremayne?"

"Harden," he corrected. "I buy and sell cattle. My brothers and I own a ranch down in Jacobsville, Texas."

"How many brothers do you have?"

"Three." The question made him uncomfortable. They weren't really his brothers, they were his half brothers, but he didn't want to get into specifics like that. Not now. He turned his wrist and glanced at his thin gold watch. "It's midnight. We'd better call it a day. There's a spare bedroom through there," he indicated with a careless hand. "And a lock on the door, if it makes you feel more secure."

She shook her head, her gentle eyes searching his hard face. "I'm not afraid of you," she said quietly. "You've been very kind. I hope that someday, someone is kind to you when you need help."

His pale eyes narrowed, glittered. "I'm not likely to need it, and I don't want thanks. Go to bed, Cinderella."

She stood up, feeling lost. "Good night, then."

He only nodded, busy crushing out his cigarette. "Oh. By the way, you left this behind." He pulled her tiny purse from his jacket pocket and tossed it to her.

Her purse! In her desperate flight, she'd forgotten all about it. "Thank you," she said.

"No problem. Good night." He added that last bit very firmly and she didn't stop to argue.

She went quickly into the bedroom—it was almost as large as the whole of the little house she lived in—and she quietly closed the door. She didn't have anything to sleep in except her slip, but that wouldn't matter. She was tired to death.

It wasn't until she was almost asleep that she remembered nobody would know where she was. She hadn't called Joan to come and get her, as she'd promised Sam she would, and she hadn't phoned her brother to leave any message. Well, nobody would miss her for a few hours, she was sure. She closed her eyes and let herself drift off to sleep. For the first time since the accident, she slept soundly, and without nightmares.

CHAPTER TWO

MIRANDA AWOKE SLOWLY, the sunlight pouring in through the wispy curtains and drifting across her sleepy face. She stretched lazily and her eyes opened. She frowned. She was in a strange room. She sat up in her nylon slip and stared around her, vaguely aware of a nagging ache in her head. She put a hand to it, pushing back her disheveled dark hair as her memory began to filter through her confused thoughts.

She got up quickly and pulled her dress over her head, zipping it even as she stepped into her shoes and looked around for her purse. The clock on the bedside table said eight o'clock and she was due at work in thirty minutes. She groaned. She'd never make it. She had to get a cab and get back to her apartment, change and fix her makeup—she was going to be late!

She opened the door and exploded into the sitting room to find Harden in jeans and a yellow designer T-shirt, just lifting the lid off what smelled like bacon and eggs.

"Just in time," he mused, glancing at her. "Sit down and have something to eat."

"Oh, I can't," she wailed. "I have to be at work at

eight-thirty, and I still have to get to my apartment and change, and look at me! People will stare…!"

He calmly lifted the telephone receiver and handed it to her. "Call your office and tell them you've got a headache and you won't be in until noon."

"They'll fire me!" she wailed.

"They won't. Dial!"

She did, automatically. He had that kind of abrasive masculinity that seemed to dominate without conscious effort, and she responded to it as she imagined most other people did. She got Dee at the office and explained the headache. Dee laughed, murmuring something about there being a lot of tardiness that morning because of the office party the night before. They'd expect her at noon, she added and hung up.

"Nobody was surprised," she said, staring blankly at the phone.

"Office parties wreak havoc," he agreed. "Call your brother so he won't worry about you."

She hesitated.

"Something wrong?" he asked.

"What do I tell him?" she asked worriedly, nibbling her lower lip. "'Hi, Sam, I've just spent the night with a total stranger'?"

He chuckled softly. "That wasn't what I had in mind."

She shook her head. "I'll think of something as I go." She dialed Sam's home number and got him instead of Joan. "Sam?"

"Where the devil are you?" her brother raged.

"I'm at the Carlton Arms," she said. "Look, I'm late

for work and it's a long story. I'll tell you everything later,
I promise…"

"You'll damned well tell me everything now!"

Harden held out his hand and she put the phone into
it, aware of the mocking, amused look on his hard face.

She moved toward the breakfast trolley, absently
aware of the abrupt, quiet explanation he was giving
her brother. She wondered if he was always so cool
and in control, and reasoned that he probably was. She
lifted the lid off one of the dishes and sniffed the delicious bacon. He'd ordered breakfast for two, and she
was aware of a needling hunger.

"He wants to talk to you," Harden said, holding out
the phone.

She took it. "Sam?" she began hesitantly.

"It's all right," he replied, pacified. "You're apparently in good hands. Just pure luck, of course," he added
angrily. "You can't pull a stunt like that again. I'll have
a heart attack."

"I won't. I promise," she said. "No more office parties. I'm off them for life."

"Good. Call me tonight."

"I will. Bye."

She hung up and smiled at Harden. "Thanks."

He shrugged. "Sit down and eat. I've got a workshop
at eleven for the cattlemen's conference. I'll drop you
off at your place first."

She vaguely remembered the sign she'd seen on the
way into the hotel about a beef producers seminar. "Isn't
the conference here?" she stammered.

"Sure. But I'll drop you off anyway."

"I don't know quite how to thank you," she began, her silver eyes soft and shy.

He searched her face for a long, long moment before he was able to drag his eyes back to his plate. "I don't care much for women, Miranda," he said tersely. "So call this a momentary aberration. But next time, don't put yourself in that kind of vulnerable situation. I didn't take advantage. Most other men would have."

She knew that already. She poured herself a cup of coffee from the carafe, darting curious glances at him. "Why don't you like women?"

His dark eyebrows clashed and he stared at her with hard eyes.

"It won't do any good to glower at me," she said gently. "I'm not intimidated. Won't you tell me?"

He laughed without humor. "Brave this morning, aren't we?"

"I'm sober," she replied. "And you shouldn't carry people home with you if you don't want them to ask questions."

"I'll remember that next time," he assured her as he lifted his fork.

"Why?" she persisted.

"I'm illegitimate."

She didn't flinch or look shocked. She sipped her coffee. "Your mother wasn't married to your father." She nodded.

He scowled. "My mother had a flaming affair and I was the result. Her husband took her back. I have three brothers who are her husband's children. I'm not."

"Was your stepfather cruel to you?" she asked gently.

He shifted restlessly. "No," he said reluctantly.

"Were you treated differently from the other boys?"

"No. Look," he said irritably, "why don't you eat your breakfast?"

"Doesn't your mother love you?"

"Yes, my mother loves me!"

"No need to shout, Mr. Tremayne." She grimaced, holding one ear. "I have perfect hearing."

"What business of yours is my life?" he demanded.

"You saved mine," she reminded him. "Now you're responsible for me for the rest of yours."

"I am not," he said icily.

She wondered at her own courage, because he looked much more intimidating in the light than he had the night before. He made her feel alive and safe and cosseted. Ordinarily she was a spirited, independent woman, but the trauma of the accident and the loss of the baby had wrung the spirit out of her. Now it was beginning to come back. All because of this tall, angry stranger who'd jerked her from what he'd thought were the waiting jaws of death. Actually jumping had been the very last thing in her mind on that bridge last night. It had been nausea that had her hanging over it, but it had passed by the time he reached her.

"Are you always so hard to get along with?" she asked pleasantly.

His pale blue eyes narrowed. Of course he was, but he didn't like hearing it from her. She confused him. He turned back to his food. "You'd better eat."

"The sooner I finish, the sooner I'm out of your hair?" she mused.

"Right."

She shrugged and finished her breakfast, washing it down with the last of her coffee. She didn't want to go. Odd, when he was so obviously impatient to be rid of her. He was like a security blanket that she'd just found, and already she was losing it. He gave her peace, made her feel whole again. The thought of being without him made her panicky.

Harden was feeling something similar. He, who'd sworn that never again would he give his heart, was experiencing a protective instinct he hadn't been aware he had. He didn't understand what was happening to him. He didn't like it, either.

"If you're finished, we'll go," he said tersely, rising to dig into his pocket for his car keys.

She left the last sip of coffee in the immaculate china cup and got to her feet, retrieving her small purse from the couch. She probably looked like a shipwreck survivor, she thought as she followed him to the door, and God knew what people would think when they saw her come downstairs in the clothes she'd worn the night before. How ridiculous, she chided herself. They'd think the obvious thing, of course. That she'd slept with him. She flushed as they went down in the elevator, hoping that he wouldn't see the expression on her face.

He didn't. He was much too busy cursing himself for being in that bar the night before. The elevator stopped and he stood aside to let her out.

It was unfortunate that his brother Evan had decided to fly up early for the workshop Harden was conducting on new beef production methods. It was even more unfortunate that Evan should be standing in front of the elevator when Harden and Miranda got off it.

"Oh, God," Harden ground out.

Evan's brown eyebrows went straight up and his dark eyes threatened to pop. "Harden?" he asked, leaning forward as if he wasn't really sure that this was his half brother.

Harden's blue eyes narrowed threateningly, and a dark flush spread over his cheekbones. Instinctively he took Miranda's arm.

"Excuse me. We're late," he told Evan, his eyes threatening all kinds of retribution.

Evan grinned, white teeth in a swarthy face flashing mischievously. "You aren't going to introduce me?" he asked.

"I'm Miranda Warren," Miranda said gently, smiling at him over Harden's arm.

"I'm Evan Tremayne," he replied. "Nice to meet you."

"Go home," Harden told Evan curtly.

"I will not," Evan said indignantly, towering over both of them. "I came to hear you tell people how to make more money raising beef."

"You heard me at the supper table last month—just before you volunteered me for this damned workshop!" he reminded the other man. "Why did you have to come to Chicago to hear it again?"

"I like Chicago." He pursed his lips, smiling appreciatively at Miranda. "Lots of pretty girls up here."

"This one is off-limits, so go away," Harden told him.

"He hates women," Evan told Miranda. "He doesn't even go on dates back home. What did you do, if you don't mind saying? I mean, you didn't drug him or hit him with some zombie spell...?"

Miranda shifted closer to Harden involuntarily and slid a shy hand into his. Evan's knowing look made her feel self-conscious and embarrassed. "Actually—" she began reluctantly.

Harden cut her off. "She had a small problem last night, and I rescued her. Now I'm taking her home," he said, daring his brother to ask another question. "I'll see you at the workshop."

"You're all right?" Evan asked Miranda, with sincere concern.

"Yes." She forced a smile. "I've been a lot of trouble to Mr. Tremayne. I...really do have to go."

Harden locked his fingers closer into hers and walked past Evan without another word.

"Your brother is very big, isn't he?" Miranda asked, tingling all over at the delicious contact with Harden's strong fingers. She wondered if he was even aware of holding her hand so tightly.

"Evan's a giant," he agreed. "The biggest of us all. Short on tact, sometimes."

"Look who's talking," she couldn't resist replying.

He glared down at her and tightened his fingers. "Watch it."

She smiled, sighing as they reached his car in the garage. "I don't guess I'll see you again?" she asked.

"Not much reason to, if you don't try jumping off bridges anymore," he replied, putting up a cool front. Actually he didn't like the thought of not seeing her again. But she was mourning a husband and baby and he didn't want involvement. It would be for the best if he didn't start anything. He was still wearing the scars from the one time he'd become totally involved.

"I had too much to drink," she said after he'd put her in the luxury car he'd rented at the airport the day before and climbed in beside her to start the engine. "I don't drink as a rule. That last piña colada was fatal."

"Almost literally," he agreed, glancing at her irritably. "Find something to occupy your mind. It will help get you through the rough times."

"I know." She looked down at her lap. "I guess your brother thinks I slept with you."

"Does it matter what people think?"

She looked over at him. "Not to you, I expect. But I'm disgustingly conventional. I don't even jaywalk."

"I'll square it with Evan."

"Thank you." She twisted her purse and stared out the window, her sad eyes shadowed.

"How long has it been?"

She sighed softly. "Almost a month. I should be used to it by now, shouldn't I?"

"It takes a year, they say, to completely get over a loss. We all mourned my stepfather for at least that long."

"Your name is Tremayne, like your brother's."

"And you wonder why? My stepfather legally adopted me. Only a very few people know about my background. It isn't obvious until you see me next to my half brothers. They're all dark-eyed."

"My mother was a redhead with green eyes and my father was blond and blue-eyed," she remarked. "I'm dark-haired and gray-eyed, and everybody thought I was adopted."

"You aren't?"

She smiled. "I'm the image of my mother's mother. She was pretty, of course…"

"What do you think you are, the Witch of Endor?" he asked on a hard laugh. He glanced at her while they stopped for a traffic light. "My God, you're devastating. Didn't anyone ever tell you?"

"Well, no," she stammered.

"Not even your husband?"

"He liked fair women with voluptuous figures," she blurted out.

"Then he should have married one," he said shortly. "There's nothing wrong with you."

"I'm flat-chested," she said without thinking.

Which was a mistake, because he immediately glanced down at her bodice with a raised eyebrow that spoke volumes. "Somebody ought to tell you that men have varied tastes in women. There are a few who prefer women without massive…bosoms," he murmured when he saw her expression. "And you aren't flat-chested."

She swallowed. He made her feel naked. She folded her arms over her chest and stared out the window again.

"How long were you married?" he asked.

"Well…four months," she confessed.

"Happily?"

"I don't know. He seemed so different before we married. And then I got pregnant and he was furious. But I wanted a baby so badly." She had to take a breath before she could go on. "I'm twenty-five. He was the first man who ever proposed to me."

"I can't believe that."

"Well, I didn't always look like this," she said. "I'm nearsighted. I wear contact lenses now. I took a modeling course and learned how to make the most of what I had. I guess it worked, because I met Tim at the courthouse while I was researching and he asked me out that same night. We only went together two weeks before we got married. I didn't know him, I guess."

"Was he your first man?"

She gasped. "You're very blunt!"

"You know that already." He lit a cigarette while he drove. "Answer me."

"Yes," she muttered, glaring at him. "But it's none of your business."

"Any particular reason why you waited until marriage?"

The glare got worse. "I'm old-fashioned and I go to church!"

He smiled. It was a genuine smile, for once, too. "So do I."

"You?"

"Never judge a book by its cover," he murmured. His pale eyes glanced sideways and he laughed.

She shook her head. "Miracles happen every day, they say."

"Thanks a lot." He stopped at another red light. "Which way from here?"

She gave him directions and minutes later, he pulled up in front of the small apartment house where she lived. It was in a fairly old neighborhood, but not a bad one. The house wasn't fancy, but it was clean and the small yard had flowers.

"There are just three apartments," she said. "One upstairs and two downstairs. I planted the flowers. This is where I lived before I married Tim. When he…died, Sam and Joan insisted that I stay with them. It's still hard to go in there. I did a stupid thing and bought baby furniture—" She stopped, swallowing hard.

He cut off the engine and got out, opening the door. "Come on. I'll go in with you."

He took her arm and guided her to the door, waiting impatiently while she unlocked it. "Do you have a landlady or landlord?"

"Absentee," she told him. "And I don't have a morals clause," she added, indicating her evening gown. "Good thing, I guess."

"You aren't a fallen woman," he reminded her.

"I know." She unlocked the door and let him in. The apartment was just as she'd left it, neat and clean. But there was a bassinet in one corner of the bedroom and a playpen in its box still sitting against the dividing counter between the kitchen and the dining room. She fought down a sob.

"Come here, little one," he said gently, and pulled her into his arms.

She was rigid at first, until her body adjusted to being held, to the strength and scent of him. He was very strong. She could feel the hard press of muscle against her breasts and her long legs. He probably did a lot of physical work around his ranch, because he was certainly fit. But his strength wasn't affecting her nearly as much as the feel of his big, lean hands against her back, and the warmth of his arms around her. He smelled of delicious masculine cologne and tobacco, and her lower body felt like molten liquid all of a sudden.

His fingers moved into the hair at her nape and their tips gently massaged her scalp. She felt his warm breath at her temple while he held her.

Tears rolled down her cheeks. She hadn't really cried since the accident. She made up for it now, pressing close to him innocently for comfort.

But the movement had an unexpected consequence, and she felt it against her belly. She stiffened and moved her hips demurely back from his with what she hoped was subtlety. All the same, her face flamed with embarrassment. Four brief months of marriage hadn't loosened many of her inhibitions.

Harden felt equally uncomfortable. His blood had cooled somewhat with age, and he didn't have much to do with women. His reaction to Miranda shocked and embarrassed him. Her reaction only made it worse, because when he lifted his head, he could see the scarlet blush on her face.

"Thanks again for looking after me last night," she said to ease the painful silence. Her hands slid around to his broad chest and rested there while she looked up into pale, quiet eyes in a face like stone. "I won't see you again?" she asked.

He shook his head. "It wouldn't be wise."

"I suppose not." She reached up hesitantly and touched his beautiful mouth, her fingertips lingering on the full, wide lower lip. "Thank you for my life," she said softly. "I'll take better care of it from now on."

"See that you do." He caught her fingers. "Don't do that," he said irritably, letting her hand fall to her side. He moved back, away from her. "I have to go."

"Yes, well, I won't keep you," she managed, embarrassed all over again. She hadn't meant to be so forward, but she'd never felt as secure with anyone before. It amazed her that such a sweeping emotion wouldn't be mutual. But he didn't look as if he even liked her, much less was affected by her. Except for that one telltale sign...

She went with him to the door and stood framed in the opening when he went out onto the porch.

He turned, his eyes narrow and angry as he gazed down at her. She looked vulnerable and sad and so alone. He let out a harsh breath.

"I'll be all right, you know," she said with false pride.

"Will you?" He moved closer, his stance arrogant, his eyes hot with feeling. His body throbbed as he looked at her. His gaze slid to her mouth and he couldn't help himself. He wanted it until it was an obsession. Reluctantly he caught the back of her neck in his lean hand and tilted her face as he bent toward her.

Her heart ran wild. She'd wanted his kiss so much, and it was happening. "Harden," she whispered helplessly.

"This is stupid," he breathed, but his mouth was already on hers even as he said it, the words going past her parted lips along with his smoky breath.

She didn't even hesitate. She slid her arms up around

his neck and locked her hands behind his head, lifting herself closer to his hard, rough mouth. She moaned faintly, because the passion he kindled in her was something she'd never felt. Her legs trembled against his and she felt the shudder that buffeted him as his body reacted helplessly to her response.

He felt it and moved back. He dragged his mouth away from hers, breathing roughly as he looked down into her dazed eyes. "For God's sake!" he groaned.

He pushed her back into the apartment and followed her, elbowing the door shut before he reached for her again.

He wasn't even lucid. He knew he wasn't. But her mouth was the sweetest honey he'd ever tasted, and he didn't seem capable of giving it up.

She seemed equally helpless. Her body clung to his, her mouth protesting when he started to lift his. He sighed softly, giving in to her hunger, his mouth gentling as the kiss grew longer, more insistent. He toyed with her lips, teasing them into parting for him before his tongue eased gently past her teeth.

He felt her gasp even as he heard it. His hand smoothed her cheek, his thumb tenderly touching the corner of her mouth while his lips brushed it, calming her. She trembled. He persisted until she finally gave in, all at once, her soft body almost collapsing against him. His tongue pushed completely into her mouth and she shivered with passion.

The slow, rhythmic thrust of his tongue was so suggestive, so blatantly sexual, that it completely disarmed her. She hadn't expected this from a man she'd only met the day before. She hadn't expected her headlong reaction to him, either. She couldn't seem to let go, to draw back, to protest this fierce intimacy.

She moaned. The sound penetrated his mind, aroused him even more. He felt her legs trembling against his blatant arousal, and he forced his mouth to lift, his hands to clasp her waist and hold her roughly away from him while he fought for control of his senses.

Her face was flushed, her eyes half closed, drowsy with pleasure. Her soft mouth was swollen, still lifted, willing, waiting.

He shook her gently. "Stop it," he said huskily. "Or I'll have you right here, standing up."

She stared up at him only half comprehending, her breath jerking out of her tight throat, her heart slamming at her ribs. "What…happened?" she whispered.

He let go of her and stepped back, his face rigid with unsatisfied desire. His chest heaved with the force of his breathing. "God knows," he said tersely.

"I've… I've *never*…" she began, flustered with embarrassment.

"Oh, hell, I've 'never,' either," he said irritably. "Not like that." He had to fight for breath. He stared at her, fascinated. "That can't happen again. Ever."

She swallowed. She'd known that, too, but there had been a tiny hope that this was the beginning of something. Impossible, of course. She was a widow of barely one month, with emotional scars from the loss of her husband and child, and he was a man who obviously didn't want to get involved. Wrong time, wrong place, she thought sadly, and wondered how she was going to cope with this new hurt. "Yes. I know," she said finally.

"Goodbye, Miranda."

Her eyes locked with his. "Goodbye, Harden."

He turned with cold reluctance and opened the door again. He could still taste her on his mouth, and his body was taut with arousal. He paused with the door-knob in his hand. He couldn't make himself turn it. His spine straightened.

"It's too soon for you."

"I…suppose so."

There had been a definite hesitation there. He turned and looked at her, his eyes intent, searching.

"You're a city girl."

That wasn't quite true, but he obviously wanted to believe it. "Yes," she said.

He took a slow, steadying breath, letting his eyes run down her body before he dragged them back up to her face.

"Wrong time, wrong place," he said huskily.

She nodded. "Yes. I was thinking that, too."

So she was already reading his mind. This was one dangerous woman. It was a good thing that the timing was wrong. She could have tied him up like a trussed turkey.

His gaze fell to her flat belly and it took all his will-power not to think what sprang to his mind. He'd never wanted a child. Before.

"I'll be late for the workshop. And you'll be late for work. Take care of yourself," he said.

She smiled gently. "You, too. Thank you, Harden."

His broad shoulders rose and fell. "I'd have done the same for anyone," he said, almost defensively.

"I know that, too. So long."

He opened the door this time and went through it, without haste but without lingering. When he was back in the car, he forced himself to ignore the way it wounded him to leave her there alone with her painful memories.

CHAPTER THREE

EVAN WAS WAITING for Harden the minute he walked into the hotel. Harden glowered at him, but it didn't slow the other man down.

"It's not my fault," Evan said as they walked toward the conference rooms where the workshop was to be held. "A venomous woman hater who comes downstairs with a woman in an evening gown at eight-thirty in the morning is bound to attract unwanted attention."

"No doubt." Harden kept walking.

Evan sighed heavily. "You never date anybody. You're forever on the job. My God, just seeing you with a woman is extraordinary. Tell me how you met her."

"She was leaning off a bridge. I stopped her."

"And...?"

Harden shrugged. "I let her use the spare room until she sobered up. This morning I took her home. End of story."

Evan threw up his hands. "Will you talk to me? Why was a gorgeous girl like that jumping off a bridge?"

"She lost her husband and a baby in a car accident," he replied.

Evan stopped, his eyes quiet and somber. "I'm sorry. She's still healing, is that it?"

"In a nutshell."

"So it was just compassion, then." Evan shook his head and stuck his big hands into his pockets. "I might have known." He glanced at his half brother narrowly. "If you'd get married, I might have a chance of getting my own girl. They all walk over me trying to get to you. And you can't stand women." He brightened. "Maybe that's the secret. Maybe if I pretend to hate them, they'll climb all over me!"

"Why don't you try that?" Harden agreed.

"I have. It scared the last one off. No great loss. She had two cats and a hamster. I'm allergic to fur."

Harden laughed shortly. "So we've all noticed."

"I had a call from Mother earlier."

Harden's face froze. "Did you?"

"I wish you wouldn't do that," his brother said. "She's paid enough for what she did, Harden. You just don't understand how it is to be obsessively in love. Maybe that's why you've never forgiven her."

Evan had been away at college during the worst months of Harden's life. Neither Harden nor Theodora had ever told him much about the tragedy that had turned Harden cold. "Love is for idiots," Harden said, refusing to let himself remember. He paused to light a cigarette, his fingers steady and sure. "I want no part of it."

"Too bad," Evan replied. "It might limber you up a bit."

"Not much hope of that, at my age." He blew out a cloud of smoke, part of his mind still on Miranda and the way it had felt to kiss her. He turned toward the con-

ference room. "I still don't understand why you came
up here."

"To get away from Connal," he said shortly. "My
God, he's driving me crazy."

Harden lifted an amused eyebrow. "Baby fever. Once
Pepi gives birth, he'll be back to normal."

"He paces, he smokes, he worries about something
going wrong. What if they don't recognize labor in time,
what if the car won't start when it's time to go to the
hospital!" He threw up his hands. "It's enough to put a
man off fatherhood."

Fatherhood. Harden remembered looking hungrily at
Miranda's waist and wondering how it would feel to father a child. Incredible thought, and he'd never had it before in his life, not even with the one woman he'd loved
beyond bearing…or thought he'd loved. He scowled.

He had a lot of new thoughts and feelings with Miranda. This wouldn't do. They were strangers. He lived
in Texas, she lived in Illinois. There was no future in
it, even if she wasn't still in mourning. He had to bite
back a groan.

"Something's eating you up," Evan said perceptively,
narrowing one dark eye. "You never talk about things
that bother you."

"What's the use? They won't go away."

"No, but bringing them out in the light helps to get
them into perspective." He pursed his lips. "It's that
woman, isn't it? You saved her, now you feel responsible for her."

Harden whirled, his pale blue eyes glaring furiously
at the other man.

Evan held up both hands, grinning. "Okay, I get the message. She was a dish, though. You might try your luck. Donald and Connal and I can talk you through a date...and the other things you don't know about."

Harden sighed. "Will you stop?"

"It's no crime to be innocent, even if you are a man," Evan continued. "We all know you thought about becoming a minister."

Harden just shook his head and kept walking. Surely to God, Evan was a case. That assumption irritated him, but he wouldn't lower himself enough to deny it.

"No comment?" Evan asked.

"No comment," Harden said pleasantly. "Let's go. The crowd's already gathering."

Despite Harden's preoccupation with Miranda, the workshop went well. He had a dry wit, which he used to his advantage to keep the audience's attention while he lectured on the combinations of maternal and carcass breeds that had been so successful back home. Profit was the bottom line in any cattle operation, and the strains he was using in a limited crossbreeding had proven themselves financially.

But his position on hormone implants wasn't popular, and had resulted in some hot exchanges with other cattlemen. Cattle at the Tremayne ranch weren't implanted, and Harden was fervently against the artificial means of beef growth.

"Damn it, it's like using steroids on a human," he argued with the older cattleman. "And we still don't know the long-range effects of consumption of implanted cattle on human beings!"

"You're talking a hell of a financial loss, all the same!" the other argued hotly. "Damn it, man, I'm operating in the red already! Those implants you're against are the only thing keeping me in business. More weight means more money. That's how it is!"

"And what about the countries that won't import American beef because of the implants?" Harden shot back. "What about moral responsibility for what may prove to be a dangerous and unwarranted risk to public health?"

"We're already getting heat for the pesticides we use leaching into the water table," a deep, familiar voice interrupted. "And I won't go into environmentalists claiming grazing is responsible for global warming or the animal rights people who think branding our cattle is cruel, or the government bailing out the dairy industry by dumping their tough, used-up cows on the market with our prime beef!"

That did it. Before Harden could open his mouth, his workshop was shot to hell. He gave up trying to call for order and sat down to drink his coffee.

Evan sat back down beside him, grinning. "Saved your beans, didn't I, pard?" he asked.

Harden gestured toward the crowd. "What about theirs?" he asked, indicating two cattlemen who were shoving each other and red in the face.

"Their problem, not mine. I just didn't want to have to save you from a lynch mob. Couldn't you be a little less opinionated?"

Harden shrugged. "Not my way."

"So I noticed." Evan stood up. "Well, we might as

well go and eat lunch. When we come back we can worry about how to dispose of the carnage." He grimaced as a blow was struck nearby.

Harden pursed his lips, his blue eyes narrowing amusedly. "And leave just when things are getting interesting?"

"No." Evan stood in front of him. "Now, look here…"

It didn't work. Harden walked around him and right into a furious big fist. He returned the punch with a hard laugh and waded right into the melee. Evan sighed. He took off his Stetson and his jacket, rolled up the sleeves of his white cotton shirt and loosened his tie. There was such a thing as family unity.

Later, after the police came and spoiled all the fun, Harden and Evan had a quiet lunch in their suite while they patched up the cuts.

"We could have been arrested," Evan muttered between bites of his sandwiches.

"No kidding." Harden swallowed down the last of his coffee and poured another cup from the carafe. He had a bruise on one cheek and another, with a cut, lower on his jaw. Evan had fared almost as badly. Of course, the competition downstairs looked much worse.

"You had a change of clothes," Evan muttered, brushing at blood spots on his white shirt. "I have to fly home like this."

"The stewardesses will be fascinated by you. You'll probably have to turn down dates all the way home."

Evan brightened. "Think so?"

"You look wounded and macho," Harden agreed. "Aren't women supposed to love that?"

"I'm not sure. I lost my perspective when they started carrying guns and bodybuilding. I think the ideal these days is a man who can cook and do housework and likes baby-sitting." He shuddered. "Kids scare me to death!"

"They wouldn't if they were your own."

Evan sighed, and his dark eyes had a faraway look. "I'm too old to start a family."

"My God, you're barely thirty-four!"

"Anyway, I'd have to get married first. Nobody wants me."

"You scare women," Harden replied. "You're the original clown. All smiles and wit. Then something upsets you and you lose your temper and throw somebody over a fence."

Evan's dark eyes narrowed, the real man showing through the facade as he remembered what had prompted that incident. "That yellow-bellied so-and-so put a quirt to my new filly and beat her bloody. He's damned lucky I didn't catch him until he got off the property in his truck."

"Any of us would have felt that way," Harden agreed. "But you're not exactly what you seem to be. I may scare people, but I'm always the same. You're not."

Evan dropped his gaze to his coffee, the smile gone. "I got used to fighting when I was a kid. I had to take care of the rest of you, always picking on guys twice your size."

"I know." Harden smiled involuntarily at the memories. "Don't think we didn't appreciate it, either."

Evan looked up. "But once I put a man in the hospital, remember? Never realized I'd hit him that hard. I haven't liked to fight since."

"That was an accident," Harden reminded him. "He fell the wrong way and hit his head. It could have happened to anyone."

"I guess. But my size encourages people to try me. Funny thing, it seems to intimidate women." He shrugged. "I guess I'll be a bachelor for life."

Harden opened his mouth to correct that impression, but the phone rang and claimed his attention. He picked it up and answered, listening with an amused face.

"Sure. I'll be down in ten minutes."

He hung up. "Imagine that. They want me to do another hour. My audience has been bragging that this was the best workshop they'd ever attended. Not boring, you see."

Evan burst out laughing. "Well, you owe that to me."

Harden glared at him. "You can only come back if you promise to keep your mouth shut."

"Bull. You enjoyed it." He stretched hugely. "Anyway, it got your mind off the woman, didn't it?"

Harden was actually lost for words. He just stared at the bigger man.

"It's the timing, isn't it?" Evan asked seriously. "She's newly widowed and you think she's too susceptible. But if she was in that kind of condition, she sure as hell needs someone."

"It's still the wrong time," he replied quietly.

Evan shrugged. "No harm in keeping the door open until it is the right time, is there?" he asked with a grin.

Harden thought about what Evan had said for the rest

of the afternoon, even after the other man had caught his
flight back to Jacobsville. No, there wouldn't really be
any harm in keeping his door open. But was it what he
wanted? A woman like Miranda wasn't fit for ranch life,
even if he went crazy and got serious about her. She was
a city girl from Chicago with a terrible tragedy to put
behind her. He was a loner who hated city life and was
carrying around his own scars. It would never work.

But his noble thoughts didn't spare his body the anguish of remembering how it had been with Miranda
that morning, how fiercely his ardor had affected both
of them. All that silky softness against him, her warm,
sweet mouth begging for his, her arms holding fast. He
groaned aloud as he pictured that slender body naked
on white sheets. As explosive as the passion between
them was, a night with her would surpass his wildest
dreams of ecstasy, he knew it would.

It was the thought of afterward that disturbed him.
He might not be able to let her go. That was what
stopped him when he placed his hand hesitantly over
the telephone and thought about finding her number
in the directory and calling her. Once he'd known her
intimately, would he be capable of walking away? He
stared at the telephone for a long time before he turned
away from it and went to bed. No, he told himself. He'd
been right in the first place. The timing was all wrong,
not only for Miranda, but for himself. He wasn't ready
for any kind of commitment.

Miranda was thinking the same thing, back at her
own apartment house. But she had the number of the
Carlton Arms under her nervous fingers. She stared

at it while she sat on her sofa in the lonely apartment, and she wanted so badly to phone, to ask for Harden Tremayne, to…

To what? she asked herself. She knew she'd already been enough trouble to him. But she'd just finished giving her baby furniture to a charity group, and she was sick and depressed. Even though she wasn't in love with Tim anymore, she grieved for the child she was carrying. It would have been so wonderful to have a baby of her own to love and care for.

None of which was Harden's problem. He'd been reluctantly kind, as he would have been to anybody in trouble. He'd said as much. But she was remembering the way they'd kissed each other, and the heat of passion that she'd never felt with anyone else. It made her so hungry. She'd expected love and forever from marriage. She'd had neither. Even sex, so mysterious and complicated, hadn't been the wonderful experience she'd expected. It had been painful at first, and then just unpleasant. Bells didn't ring and the earth didn't move. In fact, she was only just able to admit to herself that she'd never felt any kind of physical attraction to Tim. She'd briefly imagined herself in love with him, but he'd been a stranger when they married. As she lived with him, she began to see the real man under the brash outgoing reporter, and it was a person she didn't like very much. He was selfish and demanding and totally insensitive.

Harden didn't seem to be that kind of man at all. He was caring, even if he was scary and cold on the surface. Underneath, he was a smoldering volcano of emotion and she wanted to dig deeper, to see how consuming a fire they could create together. With him, intimacy would be a wondrous thing. She knew it. Probably he did, too, but he was keeping his distance tonight. Either he wasn't interested or he thought it was too soon after her loss.

He was right. It was too soon. She crumpled the piece of paper where she'd written the number of the hotel. She was still grieving and much too vulnerable for a quick love affair, which was probably all he'd be able to offer her. He'd said he was a loner and he didn't seem in any hurry to marry. He'd been all too eager to get away from her, in fact. She put the paper in the trash can. It was just as well. She'd managed to get through work today without breaking down, and she'd manage the rest of her life the same way. It wasn't really fair to involve another person in the mess her mind was in.

She put on her nightgown and climbed under the covers. Finally she slept.

CHAPTER FOUR

HARDEN SLEPT BADLY. When he woke, he only retained images of the torrid dreams that had made him so restless. But a vivid picture of Miranda danced in front of his eyes.

He was due to go home today. The thought, so pleasantly entertained two days before, was unpalatable today. Texas was a long way from Illinois. He probably wouldn't see Miranda again.

He dragged himself out of bed, hitching up the navy-blue pajama trousers that hung low on his narrow hips. He rubbed a careless hand over his broad, hair-matted chest and stared out the window, scowling. Ridiculous, what he was thinking. There were responsibilities at home, and he'd already told himself how impossible it was to entertain ideas about her.

Impossible. He repeated the word even as he turned and picked up the telephone directory. He didn't know Miranda's maiden name, which made phoning her brother to ask where she worked out of the question. His only chance was to call her apartment and catch her before she left.

He found Tim Warren's name in the new directory and dialed the number before he could change his mind.

It rang once. Twice. Three times. He glanced at his
watch on the bedside table. Eight o'clock. Perhaps she'd
left for work. It rang four times. Then five. With a long
sigh, he started to hang it up. Maybe it was fate, he
thought with disappointment.

Then, just as the receiver started down, her soft voice
said, "Hello?"

His hand reversed in midair. "Miranda?" he asked
softly.

Her breath caught audibly. "Harden!" she cried as if
she couldn't believe her ears.

His chest expanded with involuntary pleasure, because she'd recognized his voice instantly. "Yes," he replied. "How are you?"

She sat down, overcome with excited pleasure. "I'm
better. Much better, thank you. How are you?"

"Bruised," he murmured dryly. "My brother helped
me into a free-for-all at the workshop yesterday."

"Somebody insulted Texas," she guessed.

"Not at all," he replied. "We were discussing hormone
implants and the ecology at the time."

"Really?"

He laughed in spite of himself. "I'll tell you all about
it over lunch."

She caught her breath. It was more than she'd dared
hope for. "You want to take me to lunch?" she asked
breathlessly.

"Yes."

"Oh, I'd like that," she said softly.

He didn't want to have to admit how much he'd like

it himself. He put on his watch. "When should I pick you up? And where?"

"At eleven-thirty," she said. "I go early so that we won't be all out of the office at the same time. It's in the Brant building. Three blocks north of your hotel." She gave him directions and the office number. "Can you find it?"

"I'll find it."

He hung up before she had time to reply. This was stupid, he told himself. But all the same, he had a delicious feeling of anticipation. He phoned the ranch to tell them he wouldn't be home for another day or two.

His mother, Theodora, answered the phone. "Harden?" she asked. "The car won't start."

"Did you put it in Park before you tried to start it?" he asked irritably.

There was a long pause. "Just because I did that once...!" she began defensively.

"Six times."

"Whatever. Well, no, actually, I guess it's in Drive."

"Put it in Park and it will start. Is Donald back?"

"No, he won't be home until next week."

"Then tell Evan he'll have to manage. I'm going to be delayed for a few days."

There was another pause. "Evan's got a split lip."

"I've got a black eye. So what? You have to expect a little spirit when you get a roomful of cattlemen."

"I do wish you wouldn't encourage him to get into fights."

"For God's sake, Theodora, he started it!" he raged.

"Can't you ever call me Mother?" she asked in an unconsciously wistful tone.

"Will you give the message to Evan?" he replied stiffly.

She sighed. "Yes, I'll tell him. You wouldn't like to explain what's going on up there, I suppose?"

"There's nothing to tell."

"I see. I don't know why I keep hoping for the impossible from you, Harden," she said dully. "When I know full well that you'll never forgive me."

Her voice was sad. He felt guilty when he heard that note in her voice. Theodora was flighty, but she had a big heart and a sensitive spirit. Probably he hurt her every time he talked to her.

"Evan can reach me here at the hotel if he needs me," he said, refusing to give in to the impulse to talk—to really talk—to her.

"All right. Goodbye, Son."

She hung up and he stared at the receiver, the dial tone loud in his ears. He'd never asked her about his father, or why she hadn't thought of an abortion when she knew she was carrying him. Certainly it would have made her life easier. He wondered why that thought occurred to him now. He put down the receiver and got dressed.

At eleven-thirty sharp, he walked into the law office where Miranda worked. He was wearing a tan suit, a subdued striped tie, a pearly Stetson and hand-tooled leather boots. He immediately drew the eyes of every woman in the office, and Miranda got up from her desk self-consciously. She couldn't tear her eyes away from him, either.

In her neat red-patterned rayon skirt and white blouse with a trendy scarf draped over one shoulder she looked pretty, too. Harden glared at her because she pleased his senses. This whole thing was against his will. He should be on his way home, not hanging around here with a recently widowed woman.

Miranda felt threatened by the dark scowl on his face. He looked as if he'd rather be anywhere but here, and she felt a little self-conscious herself at what amounted to a date only weeks after she was widowed. But it was only lunch, after all.

"I'll just get my purse," she murmured nervously.

"I could go with you and carry it," Janet, her coworker, volunteered in a stage whisper. She grinned at Harden, but he had eyes for no one except Miranda. He gave the other employee a look that could have frozen fire.

"Thanks, anyway," Miranda murmured when Janet began to appear threatened. She grabbed her purse, smiled halfheartedly at the other woman, and rushed out the door.

"Does your friend always come on to men like that?" he asked as he closed the door behind her.

"Only when they look like you do," she said shyly.

He cocked an eyebrow and pulled his hat lower over his eyes. "I don't take one woman out and flirt with another one."

"I'm absolutely sure that Janet won't forget that," she assured him.

He took her arm as they got into the elevator. "What do you feel like? Hamburgers, fish, barbecue, or Chinese?"

"I like Chinese," she said at once.

"So do I." He pushed the Down button and stared

at her from his lounging posture against the wall as it
began to move. Her hair was done in some complicated
plait down her back, but it suited her. So did the dan-
gly silver earrings she was wearing. His eyes slid down
to the dainty strappy high heels on her pretty feet and
back up again.

"Will I do?" she asked uncertainly.

"Oh, you'll do," he agreed quietly. His eyes narrowed
with faint anger while he searched hers. "I'm supposed
to be on a one o'clock flight home."

She swallowed. "Are you?" she asked, and her face
fell.

He noticed her disappointment. It had to mean that
she was as fascinated by him as he was by her, but it
didn't do much for his conscience. This was all wrong.

"Do you have time to take me to lunch?" she asked
worriedly.

"I canceled the flight," he said then. He didn't add
that he hadn't yet decided when he was going home. He
didn't want to admit how drawn he was to her.

Her silver eyes went molten as they met his and she
couldn't hide her pleasure.

That made it worse, somehow. "It's insane!" he said
roughly. "Wrong time, wrong place."

"Then why aren't you leaving town?" she asked.

"Why didn't you say no when I asked you out to
lunch?" he shot right back.

She felt, and looked, uncertain. "I couldn't," she replied hesitantly. "I...wanted to be with you."

He nodded. "That's why I'm here," he said.

The elevator stopped while they were staring at each

other. His pale blue eyes glittered, but he didn't make a move toward her, even though it was killing him to keep the distance between them.

The doors opened and he escorted her out the front door, his fingers hard on her upper arm, feeling the thinness through the blouse.

"You've lost weight, haven't you?" he asked as they walked down the crowded street toward the Chinese restaurant he'd seen on the way to her building.

"A little. I've always been thin."

A small group of people came rushing past them and knocked against Miranda. Even as she lost her footing, Harden's arm was around her, pressing her against him.

"Okay?" he asked softly, his eyes watchful, concerned.

She couldn't look away from him. He hypnotized her. "Yes. I'm fine, thanks."

His fingers contracted on her waist. She was wrapping silken bonds around him. He didn't know if he liked it, but he couldn't quite resist her.

Her heart hammered crazily. He looked odd; totally out of humor, but fascinated at the same time.

In fact, he was. His own helplessness irritated him.

Neither of them moved, and he almost groaned out loud as he forced himself to turn and walk on down the street.

Miranda felt the strength in his powerful body and felt guilty for noticing it, for reacting to it. She walked beside him quietly, her thoughts tormenting her.

The restaurant wasn't crowded. Miranda settled on the day's special, while Harden indulged his passion for sweet-and-sour pork. When he reached for the hot mustard sauce for his egg roll, she shuddered.

"You aren't really going to do that, are you?" she asked. "You might vanish in a puff of smoke. Haven't you ever heard of spontaneous combustion?"

"I like Tabasco sauce on my chili," he informed her, heaping the sauce on the egg roll. "I haven't had taste buds since 1975."

"I still can't watch."

He smiled. "Suit yourself."

He ate the egg roll with evident enjoyment while she sipped more hot tea. When he finished she stared at him openly.

"I'm waiting for you to explode," she explained when his eyebrows lifted in a question. "I think that stuff is really rocket fuel."

He chuckled. It had been a long time since he'd felt like laughing. It surprised him that Miranda was the catalyst, with all the grief she'd suffered so recently. He searched her eyes curiously as a new thought occurred to him.

"You forget when you're with me, don't you?" he asked. "That's why you came back to the hotel night before last instead of insisting that I take you home."

She stared at him. Finally she nodded. "I stop brooding when I'm around you. I don't understand why, really," she added with a quiet sigh. "But you make it all go away."

He didn't reply. He stared down at his cup with eyes that hardly saw it. She attracted him. He'd thought it was mutual. But apparently he was only a balm for her grief, and that disturbed him. He should have followed his instincts and gone home this morning.

"Did I even say thank you?" she asked.

"You said it." He finished his tea and studied her over the rim of the small cup. "When do you have to be back?"

She glanced at the big face of his watch. "At one-thirty." She hesitated. "I guess you think I'm only using you, to put what happened out of my mind," she said suddenly. "But I'm not. I enjoy being with you. I don't feel so alone anymore."

She might have read his mind. The tension in him relaxed a little. He finished his tea. "In that case, we'll go to the park and feed the pigeons."

Her face lit up. That would mean a few more precious minutes in his company. It also meant that he wasn't angry with her.

"No need to ask if you'd like to," he murmured dryly. "Finish your tea, little one."

She drained the cup obediently and got up, waiting for him to join her.

They strolled through the park overlooking the lake. The wind was blowing, as it always did, and she enjoyed the feel of it in her hair. He bought popcorn from a vendor and they sat on a bench facing the water, tossing the treat to the fat pigeons.

"We're probably giving them high-blood pressure, high cholesterol, and heart trouble," she observed as the birds waddled from one piece of popcorn to the next.

He leaned back on the bench, one arm over the back,

and looked down at her indulgently. "Popcorn is healthier than bread. But you could ask them to stop eating it."

She laughed. "I'd be committed."

"Oh, I'd save you." He tossed another kernel to the pigeons and stared out at the lake, where sailboats were visible in the distance. "Jacobsville doesn't have a lake this size," he murmured. "We have a small one on the ranch, but we're pretty landlocked back home."

"I've gotten used to seeing the sailboats and motorboats here," she sighed, following his gaze. "I can see them out the office window on a clear day." She tucked loose strands of hair back behind her ear. "The wind never stops. I suppose the lake adds to it."

"More than likely," he replied. "I used to spend a good bit of time down in the Caribbean. It blows nonstop on the beach, as well."

"And out on the plains," she murmured, smiling as she remembered her childhood on a ranch in South Dakota. Something she hadn't told him about.

"Pretty country," he said. "We had an interest in a ranch up in Montana, a few years back. It folded. Bad water. Salt leaching killed the land."

"What kind of cattle do you raise?" she asked.

"Purebred Santa Gertrudis mostly. But we run a cow-calf operation alongside it. That means we produce beef cattle," he explained.

She knew that instantly, and more. She'd grown up in ranching country and knew quite a bit about how beef was produced, but she didn't say so. It was nicer to let him explain how it worked, to sit and listen to his deep, quiet voice.

Her lunch hour was up before she realized it. She got to her feet with real reluctance. "I have to go," she said miserably.

He stood up beside her, his pale blue eyes on her downbent head. He rammed his hands into his pockets and glowered at the dejected picture she made. He knew what he had to do, though.

"I'm going home, Miranda," he said shortly.

She wasn't surprised. He'd acted as if he was here against his better judgment, and she couldn't blame him. Her conscience was beating her over the head, because it didn't feel right to be going on a date when her husband was only dead a month.

She looked up. His expression gave nothing away, but something was flickering in his eyes. "I don't know what would have happened to me if it hadn't been for you," she said. "I won't forget you."

His jaw went taut. He wouldn't forget her, either, but he couldn't put it into words.

He turned, beginning the long walk back to her office. It shouldn't have felt so painful. In recent years, there hadn't been a woman he couldn't take in his stride and walk away from. But Miranda looked lost and vulnerable.

"I'm a loner," he said irritably. "I like it that way. I don't need anyone."

"I suppose I'm not very good at being alone," she replied. "But I'll learn. I'll have to."

"You were alone before you married, weren't you?" he asked.

"Not really. I lived with Sam and Joan. Then I de-

cided that enough was enough, so I improved myself
and found Tim." She sighed wearily. "But I guess I was
alone, if you stop and think about it. Even after Tim and
I got married, he always had someplace to go without
me. Then I got pregnant, but that wasn't meant to be."
She felt her body tauten. It was still hard to think about
the child she'd lost; about her part in its loss. She felt a
minute's panic at losing Harden, now that she'd begun
to depend on him. She glanced at him. "I married too
quickly and I learned a hard lesson: there are worse
things than your own company."

"Yes." He let his pale eyes slide down to meet hers.
"You've given me a new perspective on women. I suppose there are some decent ones in the world."

She smiled sadly. "High praise, coming from you."

"Higher than you realize. I meant it. I hate women,"
he said curtly.

That was sad. She knew it was probably because of
his mother, and she wondered if he'd ever tried to understand how his mother had felt. If he'd never loved,
how could he?

"You've been very kind to me."

"I'm not a kind man, as a rule. You bring out a side
of me I haven't seen before."

She smiled. "I'm glad."

"I'm not sure I am," he said. "Will you be all right?"

"Yes. I've got Sam and Joan, you know. And the
worst of it is over now. I'll grieve longer for the baby
than I will for Tim, I'm afraid."

"You're young. There can be other babies."

Her eyes turned wistful. "Can there? I'm not so sure."

"You'll marry again. Don't give up on life because you had some hard knocks. We all have them. But we survive."

"I never found out what yours were," she reminded him.

He shrugged. "It does no good to talk about them." He stopped in front of her office building. "Take care of yourself, Miranda."

She looked up at him with quiet regret. He was a very special man, and she was a better person for having known him at all. She wondered how different her life would have been if she'd met him before Tim. He was everything Tim hadn't been. He was the kind of man a woman would do anything for. But he was out of her reach already. It made her sad.

"I will. You, too." She sighed. "Goodbye, Harden."

He searched her eyes for a long minute, until her body began to throb. "Goodbye."

He turned and walked away. She watched him helplessly, feeling more lost and alone than ever before.

Harden was feeling something similar. It should have been easy to end something that had never really begun, but it wasn't. She'd looked so vulnerable when he'd left her. Her face haunted him already, and he was only a few yards away.

If only his mind would stop remembering the softness of Miranda's silver eyes, looking up at him so trustingly. He'd never had a woman lean on him before. He was surprised to find that he liked it. He felt himself hesitating.

His steps slowed. He muttered a harsh curse as he

turned. Sure enough, Miranda was still standing there, looking lost. He felt himself walking back to her without understanding how it happened. A minute later, he was towering over her, seeing his own helpless relief mirrored in her soft gray eyes.

Her eyes searched his in the silence that followed.

"What time do you get off—five?" he asked tersely.

She could hardly get the word out. "Yes."

He nodded. "I'll pick you up."

"The traffic is terrible..."

He glared at her. "So what?"

She reached out and touched his arm. "You came back."

"Don't think I wanted to," he told her flatly. "But I can't seem to help myself. Go to work. We'll find some exotic place for supper."

"I can cook," she volunteered. "You could come to my apartment."

"And let you spend half the night in the kitchen after you've worked all day?" he asked. He shook his head. "No way."

"Are you sure?"

He smiled faintly. "No. But we'll manage. I'll be out front when you get off. Are you usually on time?"

"Always," she said. "The boss is a stickler for promptness, even when it comes to getting off from work." She stared up at him for a long moment, ignoring passersby, her heart singing. "Oh, I'm glad you stayed!" she said softly.

"Even if it was against my better instincts?"

"Will it help if I tell you that you might have saved my sanity, if not my life?" she replied.

He studied her for a long moment. "It will help. I'll see you later."

He watched her go inside the building, his face still taut with reluctant need. It surprised him that he could feel at all, when his emotions had lived in limbo for so long.

After he left her, he spent the rest of the day getting acquainted with the city. It was big and busy and much like any other city, but he enjoyed the huge modern sculptures and the ethnic restaurants and the museums. He felt like any tourist by the time he'd showered and changed and gone back to pick up Miranda.

She was breathless when she got to him in the lobby.

"I ran all the way," she panted, holding on to the sleeves of his gray suit coat as she fought for breath. "We were late today, of all days!"

He smiled faintly. "I would have waited."

"I guess I knew that, but I hurried, all the same."

He escorted her to the car and put her inside. "I found a Polynesian place. Ever had poi?"

"Not yet. That sounds adventurous. But I really would like to change first…"

"No problem." He remembered without being told where her apartment was. He drove her there, finding a parking spot near the house—a miracle in itself, she told him brightly.

He waited in the living room while she changed. His curiosity got the best of him and he browsed through her bookshelf and stared around, learning about her. She liked biographies, especially those that dealt with the late nineteenth century out West. She had craft books and plenty of specific works on various Plains Indian tribes. There were music books, too, and he looked around instinctively for an instrument, but he didn't find one.

She came out, still hurriedly fastening a pearl necklace over the simple black sheath dress she was wearing with strappy high heels. Her hair was loose, but neatly brushed, hanging over her shoulders like black silk.

"Is this all right?" she asked. "I haven't been out much. Tim liked casual places. If I'm overdressed, I can change, but you're wearing a suit and I thought—!"

He moved close to her during the rush of words and quietly laid his thumb square over her pretty lips, halting them.

"You look fine," he said. "There's no reason to be nervous."

"Isn't there?" she asked, forcing a smile. "I'm all thumbs. I feel as if I'm eighteen again." The smile faded. "I shouldn't be doing this. My husband has only been dead a few weeks, and I lost my baby. I shouldn't go out, I should still be in mourning," she stammered, trying to make sense of what was happening to her.

"We both know that," he agreed. "It doesn't help very much."

"No," she replied with a sad smile.

He sighed heavily. "I can go back to my hotel and pack," he said, "or we can go out to dinner, which is the best solution. If it helps, think of us as two lonely people helping each other through a bad time."

"Are you lonely, Harden?" she asked.

He drew in a slow breath and his hand touched her hair very lightly. "Yes, I'm lonely," he said harshly. "I've never been any other way."

"Always on the outside looking in," she murmured, watching his face tauten. "Yes, I know how it feels, because in spite of Sam and Joan, that's how it was with me. I thought Tim would make it all come right, but he only made things worse. He wanted what I couldn't give him."

"This?" he asked, and slowly traced around the firm, full curve of her mouth, watching her lips part and follow his finger helplessly. She reacted to him instantly. It made his head spin with delicious sensations.

She caught his wrist, staying his hand. "Please," she whispered, swallowing hard. "Don't."

"Does it make you feel guilty to let me pleasure you?" he asked quietly. "It isn't something I offer very often. I meant what I said, I detest women, as a rule."

"I guess I do feel guilty," she admitted. "I was driving and two lives were lost." Her voice broke. "It was *my* fault…!"

He drew her to him and enveloped her in his hard arms, holding her while the tears fell. "Give yourself time. Desperation won't solve the problem or stop the pain. You have to be kind to yourself."

"I hate myself!"

His lips brushed her temple. "Miranda, everyone has a secret shame, a searing guilt. It's part of being human. Believe me, you can get through the pain if you just think past it. Think ahead. Find something to look forward to, even if it's just a movie or eating at a special restaurant or a holiday. You can survive anything if you have something to look forward to."

"Does it work?"

"It got me through my own rough time," he replied.

She drew back, brushing at her tear-streaked cheeks. "Want to tell me what it was?" she asked with a watery smile.

He smiled back, gently. "No."

She sighed. "You're a very private person, aren't you?"

"I think that's a trait we share." He drew back, pulling her upright with him. The neckline of her dress was high and very demure and he lifted an eyebrow at it.

"I dress like a middle-aged woman, isn't that what you're thinking?" she muttered.

He laughed out loud. "I'm afraid so. Don't you have something a little more modern in your closet?"

She shifted her shoulders. "Yes. But I can't wear low necklines because…"

He tilted her chin up. "Because…?"

She flushed a little and dropped her eyes. "I'm not exactly overendowed. I, well, I cheat a little and if I wear something low cut, you can tell."

He pursed his lips and dropped his eyes to her bodice. "Now you've intrigued me."

She moved a little away from him, feeling shy and naive. "Hadn't we better go?"

He smiled. "Nervous of me, Miranda?"

"I imagine most women are," she said seriously, searching his hard face. "You're intimidating."

"I'll try not to intimidate you too much," he promised, and held the door open for her. As she passed him on the way out, he wondered how long he could contain his desire for her without doing something irrevocable.

CHAPTER FIVE

FOR THE NEXT few days, Harden tried not to think about the reasons he shouldn't be with Miranda. She was in his blood, a sweet fever that he couldn't cure. The more he tried to resist her, the more his mind tormented him. Eventually, he gave in to it, because there was nothing else he could do.

Work was piling up back at home because he wasn't there to help Evan. His mind was anywhere except on the job these days. More and more, his waking and sleeping hours were filled with the sight of Miranda's lovely face.

He hated his obsession with her. He was a confirmed bachelor, well able to resist a pretty face. Why couldn't he escape this one? Her figure was really nothing spectacular. She was pretty, but so were plenty of other women. No, it was her nature that drew him; her sweet, gentle nature that gave more than it asked. She enveloped him like a soft web, and fighting it only entangled him deeper.

During the past few days, they'd been inseparable. They went out to dinner almost every night. He took her dancing, and last night they'd gone bowling. He hadn't done that in years. It felt unfamiliar to be throwing balls down alleys, and when he scored, Miranda was as enthusiastic as if she'd done it herself.

She laughed. She played. He was fascinated by the way she came out of her shell when she was with him, even if he did get frequent and disturbing glimpses of the anguish in her silver eyes.

He didn't touch her. That was one luxury he wouldn't allow himself. They were too explosive physically, as he'd found out the morning he'd taken her home from the hotel. Instead, they talked. He learned more about her, and told her more about himself than he'd shared with anyone else. It was a time of discovery, of exploration. It was a time between worlds, and it had to end soon.

"You're brooding again," she remarked as he walked her to her door. They'd been out to eat, again, and he'd been preoccupied all night.

"I've got to go back," he said reluctantly. He looked down at her with a dark frown. "I can't stay any longer."

She turned and unlocked her door slowly, without glancing his way. She'd expected it. It shouldn't have surprised her.

"I'm a working man, damn it," he said shortly. "I can't spend my life wandering around Chicago while you're in your office!"

She did look at him then, with soft, sad eyes. "I know, Harden," she said softly.

He shoved his hands into his pockets. "Can you write a letter?"

She hesitated. "A letter? Well, yes… I've never had anybody to write to, of course," she added.

"You can write to me," he said, his voice terse with impatience and irritation. "It isn't the same as having time to spend together, but it's better than phone calls.

I can't talk on the phone. I can never think of anything to say."

"Me, too," she said, smiling up at him. Her heart raced. He had to be interested if he was willing to keep in touch. It lifted her spirits.

"Don't expect a letter a day," he cautioned her. "I'm not that good at it."

"I don't have your mailing address," she said.

"Get me a piece of paper. I'll write it down for you."

He followed her into the apartment and waited while she produced a pad and pen. He scribbled the ranch's box number and zip code in a bold, black scrawl and gave it to her.

"This is mine," she said, taking the pad and writing down her own address. She put the pad aside and looked up at him. "You've made life bearable for me. I wish I could do something that nice for you."

His teeth clenched. He let his eyes run down the length of the black strappy dress she was wearing to long legs encased in nylon and sling-back pumps with rhinestone buckles. His gaze came back up to her loosened dark hair and her soft oval face and her trusting silver eyes.

"You could, if you wanted to," he said huskily.

She swallowed. Here it was. She hadn't mistaken his desire for her, and now he was going to ask something that she didn't know if she could give.

"Harden… I… I don't like intimacy," she said nervously.

His eyebrows arched. He hadn't expected her to be so blunt. "I wasn't going to ask you to come to bed with me," he murmured dryly. "Even I have more finesse than that."

She took a steadying breath. "Oh."

"But while we're on the subject," he said, pushing the door shut behind him, "why don't you like intimacy?"

"It's unpleasant," she said flatly.

"Painful?" he probed.

She put her purse on a table and traced patterns on it, without looking at him. Harsh memories flooded into her mind. "Only once," she said hesitantly. "I mean unsatisfying, I guess. Embarrassing and unsatisfying. I never liked it."

He paused behind her, his lean hands catching her waist and turning her, so that she faced him.

"Did he arouse you properly before he took you?" he asked matter-of-factly.

She gasped. Her wide eyes met his as if she couldn't believe what he'd said.

He shrugged. "I don't find it uncomfortable to talk about. Neither should you, at your age."

"I haven't ever talked about it, though," she stammered.

"Your brother is a doctor," he pointed out.

"But, my goodness, Sam is worse than I am," she exclaimed. "He can't even say the word sex in front of people. He's a very repressed man. Straitlaced, isn't that the word? And Joan is a dear, but you can't talk to her about…intimacy."

"Then talk to me about it," he replied. "That first morning, when I kissed you, you weren't afraid of being intimate with me, were you?"

She nibbled her lower lip. "No," she said, her face flaming.

"Was it like that with your husband?"

She hesitated. Then she shook her head.

"There's a chemistry between people sometimes," he said, watching her face. "An explosive need that pulls them together. I haven't felt it often, and never quite like this. I gather that you've never felt it at all before."

"That's...fairly accurate."

He tucked his hand under her chin and lifted her shy eyes to his. "Sex, in order to be good, has to have that explosive quality. That, and a few other ingredients— like respect, trust, and emotional involvement. It's an elusive combination that most people never find. They settle for what they can get."

"Like I did, you mean," she said.

He nodded. "Like you did." He lifted one lean hand to her face and very lightly traced her mouth, watching it part, watching her breathing change suddenly. "Feel it?" he asked softly. "That tightening in your body when I touch your mouth, the way your breath catches and your pulse races?"

"Yes." She swallowed. "Harden, do you feel it?"

"To the soles of my feet," he replied. He bent and lifted her, very gently, in his arms, his eyes on her face. "Let me make love to you. Set any limits you like."

The temptation made her heart race. She dropped her eyes to his thin mouth and wanted it beyond bearing. "Don't...don't make me pregnant," she whispered. "I don't have anything to use."

His body shuddered. It humbled him that she'd let him

go that far. "I don't have anything to use, either, so we can't go all the way together," he said unsteadily. "Does that reassure you?"

"Yes."

He moved toward the bedroom, and stopped when he noticed her eyes darting nervously to the bed.

"He made love to you there," he said suddenly, his eyes blazing as he guessed the reason for her hesitation. He looked down into her face. "Was it always there?"

"Yes," she whispered.

"How about on the sofa?"

Her body tensed with anticipated pleasure. "No."

He whirled on his heel and carried her to the long, cushy sofa. He put her down on it and stood looking at the length of her with eyes that made her body move restlessly.

She felt uneasy. He was probably used to women who were voluptuous and perfectly figured, and she had plenty of inhibitions about her body that Tim had given her. The padded bra had been his idea, because he never thought she was adequate.

Harden saw the hesitation in Miranda's big eyes and wondered at it. He unfastened his tie and tossed it into the chair beside the sofa. His jacket followed. He held her eyes while his hand slowly unbuttoned the white shirt under it, revealing the breadth and strength of his hair-matted chest. He liked the way Miranda's eyes lingered on his torso, the helpless delight in them.

"Do you like what you see?" he asked arrogantly.

"Can't you tell?" she whispered.

He sat down beside her, his hand sliding under her

back to find the zipper of her dress. "We'll compare notes."

But her hands caught his arms as she realized what he was going to do. All her insecurities flamed on her face.

He frowned. And then he remembered. His thin mouth pulled into a soft, secretive smile. "Ah, I see. The padded bra," he whispered.

She blushed scarlet, but he only laughed. It wasn't a cruel laugh, either. It was as if he was going to share some delicious secret with her, and wanted her to enjoy it, too.

His hand slowly pulled the zipper down. He ignored the nervous hands trying to stop him. "Will it help if I tell you that size only matters to adolescent boys who never grow up?" he asked softly.

"Tim said…"

"I'm not Tim," he whispered as his mouth gently covered hers.

She felt the very texture of his lips as he brushed them lightly over and around hers. He caught her top lip between his teeth and touched it with his tongue, as if he were savoring the taste of the delicate inner flesh. Her breath stopped in her throat because it was very arousing.

And meanwhile, he was sliding the dress off her shoulders, along with her bra straps.

"You…mustn't," she protested just once.

He hesitated as the dress slid to the upper curves of her firm breasts. "Why?" he asked softly, his lips touching her mouth as he spoke.

"It's…it's too soon," she said, her voice sounding panicky.

"No, that's not the reason," he murmured. He lifted his head and searched her silver eyes. "You think I'll be disappointed when I look at you." He smiled. "You're beautiful, Miranda, and you have a heart as big as all outdoors. The size of your breasts isn't going to matter to me."

The color came into her cheeks again. Even Tim had never said anything so intimate to her.

"So innocent," he said solemnly, all the humor gone. "He didn't leave fingerprints, did he? But I promise you, I will." His hands moved, drawing the fabric away from her firm, high breasts, and he looked down at them with masculine appreciation.

She didn't even breathe. Her heart was racing madly, and she felt her nipples become hard under that silent, intent scrutiny. She might be small, but he wasn't looking at her as if he minded. His eyes were finding every difference in color, in texture, sketching her with the absorption of an artist.

"Sometimes I think God must be an artist," he said, echoing her silent thoughts. "The way He creates perfection with just the right form and mix of colors, the beauty of His compositions. I get breathless looking at a sunset. But I get more breathless looking at you." His eyes finally lifted to hers. "Why are you self-conscious about your size?"

"I…" She cleared her throat. Incredible, to be lying here naked from the waist up and listening to a man talk about her breasts! "Well, Tim said I was too little."

He smiled gently. "Did he?"

He seemed to find that amusing. His hands moved again, and this time she did protest, but he bent and gently brushed her eyelids shut with his mouth as he eased the rest of the fabric down her body. In seconds, he had her totally undressed.

He lifted his head then and looked at her, his eyes soft and quiet as she lay trembling, helpless.

"I won't even touch you," he whispered. "Don't be embarrassed."

"But... I've *never*—!" she stammered.

"Not even in front of your husband?" he asked.

"He didn't like looking at me," she managed unsteadily.

He sighed softly, his eyes on her breasts, the curve of her waist, her flat belly and the shadow of her womanhood that led to long, elegant legs. "Miranda, I fear for the sanity of any man who wouldn't like looking at you," he said finally. "I swear to God, you knock the breath right out of me!"

Her eyes fell in shocked delight, and landed on a point south of his belt that spoke volumes. She gasped audibly and averted her gaze to his chest.

"I've always tried to hide that reaction with other women," he said frankly. "But I don't mind very much if you see it. I want you very badly. I'm not ashamed of it, even if it is the wrong time. Look at me, Miranda. I don't think you've ever really looked at a man in this condition."

His tone coaxed her eyes back to his body, but she lifted her gaze a little too quickly and he smiled.

"Doesn't it make you uncomfortable?" she blurted out.

"What? Letting you look, or being this way?"

"Both."

He touched her mouth with a lean forefinger. "I'm enjoying every second of it."

"So am I," she whispered as if it were a guilty secret.

"Will you let me touch you?" he asked softly, searching her eyes. "It has to be because you want it. In this, I won't do anything that even hints of force or coercion."

Her head was whirling. She looked at him and fires kindled in her body. She wanted to know what it felt like to have his hands on her, to feel pleasure.

"Will I like it?" she whispered.

He smiled gently. "Oh, I think so," he murmured.

He bent, and very lightly brushed his lips over one firm breast, his teeth grazing the nipple.

She gasped and shivered. "You...didn't tell me you were going to do that!" she exclaimed, her silver eyes like saucers.

He lifted his head and searched them. "Didn't I?" He smiled again. "Is it all right?"

Having him ask her that made her go boneless. Tim had always taken, demanded, hurt her. The funny thing was that she'd thought it would be like pleading if a man asked first, but Harden looked impossibly arrogant and it didn't sound anything like pleading. Her whole body trembled with shocked pleasure.

"Yes," she whispered. "It's all right."

"In that case..."

His lean hands lifted her body in an arch so that his lips could settle and feed on her soft breasts. She couldn't believe what was happening to her. She'd never felt pleasure before. What she'd thought was desire had been nothing more than infatuation, and this was the stark reality. It was hot and sharp-edged and totally overwhelming. She was helpless as she'd never been, living only through the hard mouth that was teaching her body its most sensitive areas, through the hands that were so gently controlling her.

Her hands were in his thick, dark hair and his mouth was suddenly on hers, forcing her lips apart with a tender ferocity that made her totally his.

"Don't panic," he whispered.

She didn't understand until she felt him touch her in a way that even Tim never had. She cried out and arched, her body going rigid.

Harden looked down at her, but he didn't stop, even when he felt her hands fighting him. "Just this, sweetheart," he whispered, watching her eyes. "Just this. Let it happen. It won't hurt."

She couldn't stop. It was like going over a cliff. She responded because it was impossible not to, her face taut with panic, her eyes wild with it. She was enjoying it, and she couldn't even pretend not to. He watched her face, smiling when she began to whimper, feeling her responses, feeling her pleasure. When it spiraled up suddenly and arched her silky body, when she wept and twisted and then cried out, convulsing, he felt as if he'd experienced everything life had to offer.

He cradled her in his arms while she cried, his lips gentle on her closed eyes, sipping away the tears.

"Amazing, what a man can do when he sets his mind

to it," he whispered against her mouth. "I'm glad to see that my instincts haven't worn out. Although I've read about that, I've never done it before."

Her eyes flew open. She was still trembling, but through the afterglow of satisfaction, she could see the muted pleasure in his eyes.

"Never?" she exclaimed.

"Why are you shocked?" he asked. "I'm no playboy. Women are still pretty much a mystery to me. Less so now," he added with a wicked gleam in his eyes.

She blushed and hid her face in his throat. His hair-roughened chest brushed her breasts and she stiffened at the pleasurable sensations that kindled in her. Involuntarily she pressed closer, pushing her hard nipples into the thick hair so that they brushed his skin.

He went taut against her. "No," he whispered.

He sounded threatened, and she liked his sudden vulnerability. He'd seen her helpless. She wanted to see him the same way. She brushed against him, drawing her breasts sensually across his broad chest until she felt him shudder. His big hands caught her arms and tightened, but he didn't try to make her move away.

"Here." He lifted her, so that she sat over his taut body, facing him, and then his hands bruised her hips and pulled her closer, so that the force of his arousal was blatant against her soft belly. He wrapped her up, crushing her breasts into his chest, and sat rocking her hungrily.

"Harden," she whispered.

His jaw clenched. He was losing it. "Touch me, sweetheart."

Her hands smoothed over his chest.

"No," he ground out. "Touch me where I'm a man."

She hesitated. His mouth whispered over her closed eyes. He caught one of her hands and slowly smoothed it down over his flat stomach, his breath catching when he pressed it gently to him.

Her heart ran away with her. She'd never touched Tim like that. The intimate feel of Harden's body made her throb all over. She liked touching him. But when he began to slide the zipper down, she jerked her fingers away and buried her hot face in his throat.

"You're right," he said roughly, fastening it back. "I'm letting it go too far. Much too far."

He eased her away and got up, his tall body shivering a little with residual desire as he fumbled a cigarette out of his pocket and lit it. "Put your things back on, little one," he said huskily.

She stared at him with her black dress in her hands. "You don't want me to," she whispered.

His eyes closed. "My God, no, I don't want you to," he ground out. He turned, his face rigid with unsated passion, his body blatant with it. "I want to bury myself inside you!"

She trembled at the stark need. Her lips parted helplessly. "I… I'd let you," she said fervently.

His gaze dropped to her breasts and beyond it, to her flat belly. She'd had a baby there. She'd lost the baby and her husband, and he shouldn't be doing this to her. He shouldn't be taking advantage of her vulnerability.

He closed his eyes again and turned away. "Miranda,

you aren't capable of making that kind of decision right now. It's too soon."

Too soon. Too soon. She came back to herself all at once. This was the apartment she'd shared with Tim. She'd been pregnant. She'd lost control of the car and killed her husband and her unborn child. And only minutes before, she'd been begging another man to make love to her.

She dragged the black dress over her head and fumbled the zipper up, her face white with reaction. She bundled up the rest of her things and pushed them down beside the sofa cushion, because she was shaking too hard to put them on. What had she done!

Harden had fastened his shirt and put his tie and jacket in place by the time she dressed.

He looked down at her with quiet, somber eyes in a face as hard as stone. "I won't apologize. It was too sweet for words. But it's too soon for lovemaking."

She couldn't meet his eyes. "But, we did…"

"I pleasured you," he replied quietly. "By lovemaking, I mean sex. If I stay around here much longer, you'll give yourself to me."

"You make me sound like a terrible weakling." She laughed mirthlessly.

He knelt just in front of her, his hands beside her hips on the sofa. "Miranda, it isn't a weakness or a sin to want someone. But you've got a tragedy to work through. By staying here, I'm only postponing your need to put it behind you, not to mention clouding your grief with desire. I want you, baby," he said huskily, his eyes fierce as they met hers. "I want you just as desperately as you want me, but you've got to be sure it's not just misplaced grief or a crutch. Sex is serious business to me. I don't sleep around, ever."

She wanted to ask him if he ever had. He seemed very experienced, but he didn't sound as if sex was a minor amusement to him. He might be even more innocent than she was, and that made her feel less embarrassed about what she'd let him do.

She searched his face. "Harden, I might not have acted like it, but it's serious business to me, too. Tim was the only man I ever slept with."

"I know." He caught her hand and held the soft palm to his mouth hungrily. "But he never satisfied you, did he?"

She swallowed. Finally she gave in to that blatant stare. "Not like you did, no." She hesitated.

"You want to ask me something," he guessed from that odd look. "Go ahead. What is it?"

"Would it feel like that if I gave myself to you? If we went all the way?" she asked slowly.

His fingers clenched on hers. "I think it might be even more intense," he said gruffly. "Watching you almost sent me over the edge myself."

She reached out and touched his face, adoring the strength of it under her cool fingers. "You…had nothing," she exclaimed belatedly.

He only smiled. "Don't you believe it," he said with a deep, somber look in his pale blue eyes. "And now, I've got to go. I've put it off as long as I can."

He got to his feet. Miranda let him pull her up and her heart was in her eyes as she gazed up at him.

"I'll miss you more than ever, now," she confessed.

He sighed. "I'll miss you, too, little one," he said curtly. "Write to me. I'm as close as the telephone, if you just want to talk. You'll get through this, Miranda. All you need is a little time."

"I know. You made it so much easier, though."

He brushed his fingers through her unruly hair and tilted her face up to his hungry eyes. "It isn't goodbye. Just so long, for a while."

She nodded. "Okay. So long, then."

He bent and kissed her, so tenderly that she almost cried. "Be good."

"I can't be anything else. You won't be here. Harden," she said as he opened the door.

He looked back, his eyebrow arching in a question.

"Just remember," she said with forced humor. "You saved my life. Now you're responsible for it."

He smiled gently. "I won't forget."

He didn't say goodbye. He gave her one long, last look and went out the door, closing it gently behind him. He hadn't really saved her life, she knew, because she hadn't meant to jump off the bridge. But it made her feel good to think that she owed it to him, that he cared enough to worry about her.

She had his address, and she'd write. Maybe when she was through the natural grieving process, he'd come back, and she'd have a second chance at happiness. She closed her eyes, savoring the intimacy she'd shared with him. She wondered how she was going to live until she saw him again.

CHAPTER SIX

HARDEN WAS GRUMPY when he got home. Not that anybody noticed, because he was *always* grumpy. His irritation didn't improve, either, when his brother Connal showed up.

"Oh, God, no, here he comes again!" Evan groaned when the car pulled up just as he and Harden were coming down the steps.

"That's no way to talk about your brother," Harden chided.

"Just wait," the bigger man said curtly.

"I can't stand it!" Connal greeted them, throwing up his hands. "We get all the way to the hospital, I make all the necessary phone calls, and they say it's false labor! Her water hasn't even broken!"

Evan and Harden exchanged glances.

"He needs help," Evan said. "Broken water?"

"You wouldn't understand," Connal said heavily, his lean, dark face worn and haggard. "I've just left her sleeping long enough to ask Mother to come back with me. Pepi needs a woman around right now."

"We'll starve," Evan said miserably.

"No, you won't," Harden muttered. "We have a cook, remember."

"Mother tells Jeanie May what to cook. You'd better worry, too," Evan said shortly. "Even if you don't live here, you're always around when the food goes on the table."

"Don't you two start, I've got enough problems," Connal muttered darkly.

Evan's eyebrows arched. "Don't look at me. You're the one who made Pepi pregnant."

"I wanted children. So did she."

"Then stop muttering and go home."

Connal glared at the bigger man. "Your day will come," he assured Evan. "You'll be walking the streets dreading your own Waterloo in the delivery room, wait and see!"

Evan's face clouded. His usual carefree expression went into eclipse. "Will I?" he asked on a hard laugh. "Don't bet on it."

Connal started to question that look, but Harden stepped in.

"Theodora's in the study looking up something about how to repair bathrooms," he said.

"The plumber will love that," Connal said knowingly. "Don't worry, I'll have her out of here before she bursts another pipe."

"Last one flooded the back hall," Evan recalled. "I opened the door and almost got swept down to the south forty."

"She's got no business trying to fix things. My God, she had a flat tire on the wheelbarrow!" Harden exclaimed.

"Takes talent," Evan agreed. "But don't keep her too long, will you? She takes my side against him," he jerked a thumb at Harden.

"That's nothing new," Harden said, lighting a cigarette. "She knows how I feel about her."

"One day you'll regret that," Connal said. It wasn't something he usually mentioned, but Harden's attitude was getting to him. Part of the reason he'd come for Theodora was that he'd noticed her increasing depression since Harden had come home from his unexplained stay in Chicago.

"Tell Pepi we asked about her," Harden said easily, refusing to rise to the bait.

"I'll do that."

Connal asked about Donald, who was away again with his wife, and after a minute he said goodbye and went into the house, leaving Harden and Evan to go about their business.

Harden climbed behind the wheel before his brother could protest.

"I'm not riding with you," he told Evan flatly. "Your foot's too heavy."

"I like speed," Evan said bluntly.

"Lately, you like it too much." Harden glanced at him and away. "You haven't been yourself since that girl you were dating broke up with you."

Evan's face set and he glanced out the window without speaking.

"I'm sorry," he told Evan. "I'm sorry as hell. But there has to be a woman for you somewhere."

"I'm thirty-four," Evan said quietly. "It's too late. You used to talk about being a minister. Maybe I should consider it myself."

"A minister isn't necessarily celibate," his brother replied. "You're thinking of a priest. You aren't Catholic," he added.

"No, I'm not. I'm the giant in Jack and the Beanstalk," he said wearily. He put his hat back on. "I'm sorry I don't smoke," he murmured, eyeing Harden's smoke. "It might keep me as cool as it seems to keep you."

"I'm not cool." Harden stared out the windshield. "I've got problems of my own."

"Miranda?" Evan asked slowly.

Harden stiffened. His dreams haunted him with the images of Miranda as she'd let him see her that last night at her apartment. The taste of her mouth, the exquisite softness of her body made him shiver with pleasure even in memory. He missed her like hell, but he had to be patient.

He glanced at Evan. He sighed, then, letting it all out. Evan was the only human being alive he could talk to. "Yes."

"You came home."

"I had to. She's so damned vulnerable. I could never be sure it was me she wanted and not a way to avoid coping with the grief."

"Do you want her?"

Harden took a draw from the cigarette and turned his head. His eyes were blazing as the memories washed over him. "Like I want to breathe," he said.

"What are you going to do?"

The broad shoulders lifted and fell. "I don't know. I'll write to her, I guess. Maybe I'll fly to Chicago now and again. Until she's completely over her grief, I don't dare push too hard. I don't want half a woman."

"Strange," Evan said quietly, "thinking about you with a woman."

"It happens to us all sooner or later, didn't Connal say?"

Evan smiled. "Well, Miranda's a dish. When you finally decide to get involved, you sure pick a winner."

"It's more than the way she looks," came the reply. "She's...different."

"*The* woman usually is," Evan said, his dark eyes sad in his broad face. "Or so they say."

"You'll find out yourself one day, old son."

"Think so? I can hope, I suppose."

"What we both need is a diversion."

Evan brightened. "Great. Let's go to town and wreck a bar."

"Just because you hate alcohol is no reason to do a Carrie Nation on some defenseless bar," his brother told him firmly.

Evan shrugged. "Okay, I'm easy. Let's go to town and wreck a coffee shop."

Harden chuckled softly. "Not until my eye heals completely," he said, touching the yellowish bruise over his cheekbone.

"Spoilsport. Well, I guess we can go to the hardware store and order that butane we need to heat the branding irons."

"That's better."

HARDEN GOT HIS first letter from Miranda the very next day. It didn't smell of perfume, and it was in a perfectly respectable white envelope instead of a colorful one, but it was newsy and warm.

She mentioned that she'd had dinner with her brother and sister-in-law twice, and that she'd started going to their church—a Baptist church—with them on Sunday. He smiled, wondering if he'd influenced her. She wasn't a Baptist, but he was; a deacon in his local church, where he also sang in the choir. She missed seeing him, her letter concluded, and she hoped that he could make time to write her once in a while.

She was going to be shocked, he decided as he pulled up the chair to his desk and started the word processing program on his computer. He wrote several pages, about the new bulls they'd bought and the hopes he had for the crossbreeding program he'd spoken about at the conference in Chicago. When he finished, he chuckled at his own unfamiliar verbosity. Of course, reading over what he'd written, he discovered that it was a totally impersonal letter. There was nothing warm about it.

He frowned, fingering the paper after he'd printed it out. Well, he couldn't very well say that he missed her like hell and wished he was still in Chicago. That would be overdoing it. With a shrug, he signed the letter with a flourish and sealed it before he could change his mind. Personal touches weren't his style. She'd just have to get used to that.

MIRANDA WAS SO thrilled when she opened the letter two days later that she didn't at first notice the impersonal style of it. It was only after the excitement subsided that she realized he might have been writing it to a stranger.

Consequently she began to wonder if he was really interested in her, or if he was trying to find a way of letting her down, now that they were so far apart. She remembered how sweet it had been in his arms, but that had only been desire on his part. She knew men could fool themselves into thinking they cared about a woman when it was only their glands getting involved. She'd given Harden plenty of license with her body, and it still made her uneasy that she'd been that intimate with him so soon after Tim and the baby. Her own glands were giving her fits, because she couldn't stop remembering how much pleasure Harden had given her. She missed him until it was like being cut in half. But this letter he'd written to her didn't sound like he was missing her. Not at all.

She sat down that night as she watched television and tried to write the same sort of note back. If he wanted to play it cool, she'd do her best to follow his lead. She couldn't let him know how badly she wanted to be with him, or make him feel guilty for the physical closeness they'd shared. She had to keep things light, or she might inadvertently chase him away. She couldn't bear that. If he wanted impersonal letters, then that's what he'd get. She pushed her sadness to the back of her mind and began to write.

From there, it all began to go downhill. Harden frowned over her reply and his own was terse and brief. Maybe she was regretting their time together. Maybe grief had fed her guilt and she wanted him to end it. Maybe what they'd done together was wearing on her conscience and she only wanted to forget. He'd known he was rushing her. Why hadn't he taken more time?

Once he was back at his apartment in Houston, he

was putting things into perspective. There was no future with someone like Miranda, after all. She was a city girl. She'd never fit into ranching. He had his eye on a small ranch near Jacobsville and he'd already put a deposit on it. The house wasn't much. He was having it renovated, but even then it wouldn't be a showplace. It was a working ranch, and it would look like one. Miranda would probably hate the hardship of living on the land, even if he did make good money at it.

He stared out his window at the city lights. The office building where the family's corporate offices were located was visible in the distance among the glittering lights of downtown Houston. He sighed wearily, smoking a cigarette. It had been better when he'd kept to himself and brooded over Theodora's indiscretion.

For the first time, he allowed himself to wonder if his mother had felt for his father the way he felt with Miranda. If her heart had fallen victim to a passion it couldn't resist. If she'd loved his father so much that she couldn't refuse him anything, especially a child.

He thought about the child Miranda had lost, and wondered how it would be to give her another, to watch her grow big with it. He remembered her soft cries of pleasure, the look of utter completion on her face. His teeth ground together.

He turned away from the window angrily. Miranda wrote him the kind of letter his brothers might, so how could he imagine she cared? She was closing doors between them. She didn't want him. If she did, why hadn't her later letter been as sweet and warm as that first one?

The more he thought about that, the angrier he got.

Days turned to weeks, and before he realized it, three months had passed. He was still writing to Miranda, against his better judgment, but their letters were impersonal and brief. He'd all but stopped writing in the past two weeks. Then a client in Chicago asked Evan to fly up and talk to him.

Evan found an excuse not to go. Connal, a brand-new father with a baby boy to play with, was back on the ranch he and Pepi's father owned in West Texas. Donald and Jo Ann were just back from overseas, and Harden's youngest brother said flatly that he wasn't going anywhere for months—he and Jo Ann had had their fill of traveling.

"Looks like you're elected," Evan told Harden with a grin. "Call it fate."

Harden looked hunted. He paced the office. "I need to stay here."

"You need to go," Evan said quietly. "It hasn't gotten better, you know. You look terrible. You've lost weight, and you're working yourself to death. She's had time to get herself back together. Go and see if the magic's still there."

"She writes me business letters. She's probably dating somebody else by now."

"Go find out."

Harden moved irritably. The temptation was irresistible. The thought of seeing Miranda again made him feel warm. He studied the older man. "I guess I might as well."

"I'll handle things here. Have a good trip."

Harden heard those words over and over. He deliberately put off calling Miranda. He met the client, settled his business, and had lunch. He went to a movie. Then, at five, he happened to walk past her office building just about time for her to come out.

He stood by a traffic sign, Western looking in a pale gray suit with black boots and Stetson, a cigarette in his hand. He got curious, interested looks from several attractive women, but he ignored them. He only had eyes for one woman these days, even if he wasn't sure exactly how he felt about her.

A siren distracted him and when he glanced back, Miranda was coming out of the entrance, her dark hair around her shoulders, wearing a pale green striped dress that made his temperature soar. Her long legs were encased in hose, her pretty feet in strappy high heels. She looked young and pretty, even if she was just as thin as she'd been when he left her.

She was fumbling in her purse for something, so she didn't look up until he was standing directly in her path.

Her expression told him everything he wanted to know. It went from shock to disbelief to utter delight in seconds, her huge silvery eyes like saucers as they met his.

"Harden!" she whispered joyously.

"No need to ask if you're glad to see me," he murmured dryly. "Hello, Miranda."

"When did you get here? How long can you stay? Do you have time to get a cup of coffee with me…!"

He touched his forefinger to her soft mouth with a smile, oblivious to onlookers and pedestrians and motorists that sped past them. "I'll answer all those questions later. I'm parked over here. Let's go."

"I was fumbling for change for the bus," she stammered, red-faced and shaken by his unexpected appearance. Her eyes adored him. "I didn't have it. Have you been here long?"

"A few minutes. I got in this morning." He looked down at her. "You're still thin, but you have a bit more color than you did. Is it getting easier?"

"Yes," she said, nodding. "It's amazing what time can accomplish. I think I have things in perspective now. I'm still sad about the baby, but I'm getting over it."

He paused at his rented Lincoln and opened the passenger door for her. "I'm glad."

She waited until he got in beside her and started the car before she spoke. "I didn't know if I'd see you again," she confessed. "Your letters got shorter and shorter."

"So did yours," he said, and his deep voice sounded vaguely accusing.

"I thought maybe my first one made you uncomfortable," she confessed with a smile. "I sort of used yours as a pattern."

He smiled, too, because that explained everything. Now he understood what she'd done, and why.

"I don't know how to write a letter to a woman," he said after a minute, when he'd pulled into traffic and was negotiating lanes. "That was the first time I ever had."

Her face brightened. "I didn't know."

He shrugged. "No reason you should."

"How long can you stay?"

"I had to see a client," he replied. "I did that this morning."

"Then, you're on your way home. I see," she said

quietly. She twisted her purse on her lap and stared out at traffic. Disappointment lined her face, but she didn't let him see. "Well, I'm glad you stopped by, anyway. It was a nice surprise."

He cocked an eyebrow. Either she was transparent, or he was learning to read her very well. "Can't wait to get rid of me, can you?" he mused. "I had thought about staying until tomorrow, at least."

Her face turned toward his, and her eyes brightened. "Were you? I could cook supper."

"I might let you, this time," he said. "I don't want to waste the whole evening in a restaurant."

"Do you need to go back to your hotel first?" she asked.

"What for? I'm wearing the only suit I brought with me, and I've got my wallet in my pocket."

She laughed. "Then we can just go straight home."

He remembered where her apartment house was without any difficulty. He parked the car as close to it as he could get, locked it, and escorted her inside.

While she was changing into jeans and a pink knit top, he wandered around her living room. Nothing had changed, except that there were more books. He picked up one of the paperbacks on the table beside the couch and smiled at her taste. Detective stories and romance novels.

"I like Erle Stanley Gardner," he remarked when she was busy in the kitchen.

"So do I," she told him, smiling over her shoulder as she put coffee on to perk. "And I'm crazy about Sherlock Holmes—on the educational channel, you know."

"I watch that myself."

He perched himself on a stool in front of her break-fast bar and folded his arms on it to study her trim figure as she worked. She produced an ashtray for him, but as she put it down, he caught her waist and pulled her between his legs.

"Kiss me," he said quietly, holding her gaze. "It's been a long, dry spell."

"You haven't been kissed in three months?" she stammered, a little nervous of the proximity.

He smiled. "I hate women, remember? Kiss me, before you start on the steak."

She smiled jerkily. "All right." She leaned forward, closed her eyes, and brushed her mouth softly against his.

His lean hand tangled in her long hair and held her there, taking over, parting her lips, deepening the kiss. His breath caught at the intensity of it, like a lightning bolt in the silence of the kitchen.

"It isn't enough," he said tersely, drawing back just long enough to crush out his cigarette. Both arms slid around her and brought her intimately close, so that her belly was against his, her face on an unnerving level with his glittery blue eyes. "I've missed you, woman," he whispered roughly.

His mouth met hers with enough force to push her head back against his hand. He was rough because he was starved for her, and it was a mutual thing. She hesitated only for a second before her arms went around his neck and she pressed close with a soft moan, loving the warm strength of his body as she was enveloped against it. She could hear his breath sighing out as his mouth grew harder on hers, bruising her lips, pushing them apart to give him total access to their moist inner softness.

All at once, his tongue pushed past her lips and into her mouth, and a sensation like liquid fire burst in her stomach. It was as intimate as lovemaking. She felt her whole body begin to throb as he tasted her in a quick, hard rhythm. She made a sound she'd never heard from her throat in her life and shuddered as she moved closer to him, her legs trembling against his.

"Yes," he breathed unsteadily into her mouth. "Yes, sweetheart, like…that…!"

He stood up, taking her with him, one lean hand dropping to her hips to grind them into his own. She stiffened at his fierce arousal, but he ignored her instinctive withdrawal.

"It's all right," he whispered. "Relax. Just relax. I won't hurt you."

His voice had the oddest effect on her. The struggle went out of her all at once, and she gave in to him with an unsteady sigh. Her hands pressed gently into his shirt front and lingered there while the kiss went on and on and she felt a slight tremor in his own powerful legs.

He lifted his head finally and looked down at her, breathing unsteadily, fighting to control what he felt for her.

His hands at her waist tightened and the helpless, submissive look on her soft face pushed him over the edge. "Is there anything cooking that won't keep for a few minutes, Miranda?" he asked quietly.

She swallowed. "No. But..."

He bent and lifted her gently into his arms and carried her out of the kitchen. "Don't be afraid, little one," he said quietly.

"Harden, I don't... I'm still not using anything," she stammered.

He didn't look at her as he walked into her bedroom. "We won't make love."

Her lips parted. They felt sore and they tasted of him when she touched them with her tongue. He laid her down on the bed and stood looking at her for a long moment before he sat down beside her and bent to take her mouth softly under his once again.

The look in his eyes fascinated her. It was desire mingled with irritation and something darker, something far less identifiable. His gaze fell to the unsteady rise and fall of the knit top she was wearing and his hand moved to smooth down her shoulder to her collarbone.

"No bra tonight?" he asked bluntly, meeting her eyes.

She flushed. "I..."

He put a long forefinger on her lips. "What we do together is between you and me," he said solemnly. "Not even my own brothers know anything about my personal life. I want very badly to touch you again, Miranda. I think you want it just as much. If you do, there isn't really any reason we can't indulge each other."

She searched his eyes quietly. "I couldn't sleep, for dreaming about how it was between us, last time," she whispered.

"Neither could I," he replied. His hands moved to her

waist and brought her into a sitting position. Gently he removed the pink knit top and put it aside, letting his eyes adore her pink and mauve nudity. He smiled when her nipples went hard under the scrutiny.

Her hands touched his lean cheeks hesitantly and she shivered as she drew his face toward her, arching her back to show him what she wanted most.

"Here?" he whispered, obliging her.

She drew in her breath as his mouth opened over her breast, taking almost all of one inside. The faint suction made her tremble, made her nails bite into the shoulders of his suit jacket.

"Too…many clothes, Harden," she whispered.

He lifted his head and pressed a soft kiss on her mouth before he stood up. "Yes. Far too many."

He watched her while he removed everything above his belt, enjoying the way her eyes sketched over him.

"Harden," she began shyly, her eyes falling to the wide silver belt.

"No," he said, reading the question in her eyes. He sat down beside her and drew her gently across his lap, moving her breasts into the thick mat of hair over his chest. "If I take anything else off, we'll be lovers."

"Don't you want to?" she asked breathlessly.

"Yes," he said simply. "But it's still too soon for that." He looked down where her pale body was pressed to his darkly tanned one. "I want you to come home with me, Miranda."

CHAPTER SEVEN

MIRANDA DIDN'T BELIEVE at first that she'd heard him. She stared at him blankly. "What?"

He met her eyes. "I want you to come home with me," he said, shocking himself as much as he was obviously shocking her. "I want more than this," he added, dragging her breasts sensually against his bare chest. "As sweet as it is, I want to get to know all of you, not just your body."

"But...my job," she began.

"I have in mind asking you to marry me, once we've gotten used to each other a little more," he said then, driving the point home. "And don't look so shocked. You know as well as I do that we're going to wind up in bed together. It's inevitable. I'm no more liberated than you are, so we have to do something. Either we get married, or we stop seeing each other altogether. That being the case, you have to come home with me."

"And stay...with you?" she echoed.

"With Theodora. My mother," he clarified it. "I'm buying a place in Jacobsville, but it isn't ready to move into. Even if it was," he added with a rueful smile, "things aren't done that way in Jacobsville. You'd stay with Theodora anyway, to keep everything aboveboard.

Or didn't I mention that I was a deacon in our Baptist church?"

"No," she stammered. "You didn't."

"I thought about being a minister once," he murmured, searching her rapt eyes. "But I didn't feel called to it, and that makes the difference. I still feel uncomfortable with so-called modern attitudes. Holding you like this is one thing. Sleeping with you—my conscience isn't going to allow that."

"I was married," she began.

"Yes. But not to me." He smiled gently, looking down to the blatant thrust of her soft breasts with their hard tips brushing against his chest. "And it didn't feel like this, did it?"

"No," she admitted, going breathless when he brushed her body lazily against his. "Oh, no, it didn't feel anything like this!" She pressed even closer, gripping his shoulders tightly. "But you say you hate women. How are you going to manage to marry me?"

"I didn't say I hated you," he replied. His hands tangled in her hair and raised her face to his quiet eyes. "I've never wanted anyone like this," he said simply. "All I've done since I left Chicago is brood over you. I haven't looked at another woman in all that time."

She drew back a little, tingling with pleasure when the action drew his eyes immediately to her breasts. She didn't try to hide them this time.

After a minute, he lifted his eyes to hers and searched them, reading with pinpoint accuracy the pride and pleasure there. "You like it, don't you?" he asked quietly. "You like my eyes on you."

"Yes," she said hesitantly.

"Shame isn't something you should feel with me," he told her. "Not ever. I know too much about you to think you're easy."

She smiled then. "Thank you."

His lean hands smoothed down to her waist, and he shook his head. "I can't imagine being able to do this anytime I please, do you know that?" he said unexpectedly. "I've never had…anyone of my own before." It surprised him to realize that it was true. He'd thought he had, once, but it had been more illusion than reality and he was only discovering it.

"Actually, neither have I," she said. Her eyes ran over his hair-roughened chest down to the ripple of his stomach muscles above his belt and back to the width of his shoulders and his upper arms. "I love to look at you," she said huskily.

"It's mutual." His fingers brushed over the taut curve of one breast, tracing it lovingly. "Don't you *ever* put on a padded bra again," he said shortly, meeting her eyes. "Do you hear me, Miranda?"

She laughed breathlessly. "Yes."

He laughed, too, at his own vehemence. "Too small. My God. Maybe he was shortsighted." He stood up, drawing her with him, his eyes eloquent on her body. "I don't suppose you'd like to cook supper like that…" He sighed heavily.

"Harden!"

"Well, I like looking at you," he said irritably. "Touching you." His fingers brushed over her breasts lovingly, so that she gasped. "Kissing you…"

He bent, caressing her with his mouth until she began to burn. Somehow, they were back on the bed again, and his mouth was on her breasts, his hands adoring her while he brushed her silky skin with his lips.

"It won't...be enough," she moaned.

"My God, I know that," he said unsteadily.

He moved, easing his body over hers so that she could feel his arousal, his eyes holding hers as he caught his weight on his forearms and pressed his hips into hers.

"You'd let me, right now, wouldn't you?" he asked roughly.

"Yes." She let her hands learn the rigid muscles of his back, delighting in the slight roughness of his skin.

His mouth bent to hers and nibbled at her lower lip. "This is really stupid."

"I don't care. I belong to you."

He shuddered. The words went through him with incredible impact. He actually gasped.

"Well, I do," she whispered defensively. Her mouth opened under his. "Lift up, Harden."

He obeyed the soft whisper, feeling her hands suddenly between them. His shocked eyes met hers while she worked at the fastening of his belt. "My God, no!" he burst out. He caught her hand and rolled onto his back, shivering.

She sat up, her eyes curious. "No?"

"You don't understand," he ground out.

Her soft eyes searched his face, seeing the restraint that was almost gone. "Oh. You mean that if I touch you that way, the same thing will happen to you that happened to me when...when you did it?"

"Yes." His cheeks went ruddy. He stared at her with desire and irritation and pain mingling. "I can't let you do that."

"Why?" she asked quietly.

"Call it an overdose of male pride," he muttered, and threw his long legs off the side of the bed. "Or a vicious hang-up. Call it whatever the hell you like, but I can't let you."

She watched him get to his feet and come around the bed, his eyes slow and quiet on her bare breasts as she sat watching him. "I let you," she pointed out.

"You're a woman." He drew in a jerky breath. "My God, you're all woman," he said huskily. "We'll set the bed on fire our first time."

She flushed. "You're avoiding the issue."

"Sure I am." He pulled her up, grabbed her knit top, and abruptly helped her back into it. "I'm an old-fashioned man with dozens of hang-ups—like being nude in front of a woman, like allowing myself to be satisfied with a woman seeing me helpless, like... Well, you get the idea, don't you?" he asked curtly. He shouldered into his shirt and caught her hand, tugging her along with him. "Feed me. I'm starving."

Her head whirled with the things she was learning about him as he led her into the kitchen. He was the most fascinating man she'd ever known. But she was beginning to wonder just how experienced he was. He didn't act like a ladies' man, even if he kissed like one.

The memory of the baby still nagged at the back of her mind. She was sorry about Tim, too, but as she went over and over the night of the wreck, she began to realize that no one could have done more than she had. She was an experienced driver, and a careful one. And Tim had been drinking. She couldn't have allowed him behind the wheel. The roads were slick, another car pulled out in front of her without warning, and she reacted instinctively, but a fraction of a second too late. It was fate. It had to be.

He watched her toy with her salad. "Brooding?" he asked gently.

She lifted her gray eyes to his and pushed back a long strand of disheveled dark hair. "Not really. I was thinking about the accident. I've been punishing myself for months, but the police said it was unavoidable, that there was nothing I could have done. They'd know, wouldn't they?"

"Yes," he told her gently. "They'd know."

"Tim wasn't good to me. All the same, I hate it that he died in such a way," she said sadly. "I regret losing my baby."

"I'll give you a baby," he said huskily, his pale eyes glittering with possession.

She looked up, surprised, straight into his face, and saw something that she didn't begin to understand. "You want children?" she asked softly.

His eyes fell to her breasts and back up to her mouth. "We're both dark haired. Your eyes are gray and mine are blue, and I'm darker skinned than you are. They'll probably favor both of us."

Her face brightened. "You...want a child with me?" she whispered.

He wondered about that wide-eyed delight. He knew

she was still grieving for her child. If he could give her another one, it might help her to get over it. Even if she didn't love him, she might find some affection for him after the baby came. If he could get her pregnant. He knew that some men were sterile, and he'd never been tested. He didn't want to think about that possibility. He had to assume he could give her a child, for his own peace of mind. She was so terribly vulnerable. He found himself driven to protect her, to give her anything she needed to keep going.

"Yes," he said solemnly. "I want a child with you."

She beamed. Her eyes softened to the palest silver as they searched his hard face.

"But not right away," he said firmly. "First, you and I are going to do some serious socializing, get to know each other. There are a lot of hurdles we have to jump before we find a minister."

Meaning her marriage and her loss, she assumed. She managed a smile. "All right. Whatever you say, Harden."

He smiled back. Things were going better than he'd ever expected.

MIRANDA WAS NERVOUS when he drove from the airport back to the Tremayne ranch. She barely heard what he said about the town and the landmarks they passed. His mother was an unknown quantity and she was half afraid of the first meeting. She'd seen Evan, his eldest brother, at the hotel, so he wouldn't be a stranger. But there were two other brothers, and both of them were married. She was all but holding her breath as Harden pulled the car onto the ranch road and eventually stopped in front of a white, two-story clapboard house.

"Don't fidget," Harden scolded gently, approving her white sundress with its colorful belt and her sexy high-heel sandals. "You look pretty and nobody here is going to savage you. All right?"

"All right," she said, but her eyes were troubled when he helped her out of the car.

Theodora Tremayne was hiding in the living room, peeking out of the curtains with Evan.

"He's brought a woman with him!" she burst out. "He's tormented me for years for what happened, first about his real father and then about that…that girl he loved." She closed her eyes. "He threatened once to bring me a prostitute, to get even, and that's what he's doing right now, isn't he, Evan? He's going to get even with me by bringing a woman of the streets into my home!"

Evan was too shocked to speak. By the time he finally realized that his mother knew nothing about Miranda, it was too late. He could even understand why she'd made such an assumption, because he'd heard Harden make the threat. Miranda was a city girl, and she dressed like one, with sophistication and style. Theodora, with her country background, could easily mistake a woman she didn't know for something she wasn't.

The front door opened and Miranda was marched into the living room by Harden.

"Miranda, this is my mother, Theodora," he said arrogantly, and without a word of greeting, which only cemented Theodora's horrified assumption.

Miranda stared at the small, dark woman who stood with clenched hands at her waist.

"It's...very nice to meet you," Miranda said, her voice shaking a little, because the older woman hadn't said a word or cracked a smile yet. She looked intimidating and furiously angry. Miranda's face flushed as she recognized the blatant hostility without understanding what had triggered it. "Harden's been kind to me..."

"I'll bet he has," Theodora said with uncharacteristic venom in her voice.

Miranda wasn't used to cruelty. She didn't quite know how to handle it. She swallowed down tears. "I... I guess I really should go, Harden," she blurted out, flushing violently as she met Harden's furious eyes. "I..."

"What kind of welcome is this?" he asked his mother.

"What kind did you expect?" Theodora countered, her eyes flashing. "This is a low-down thing to do to me, Harden."

"To you?" he growled. "How do you think Miranda feels?"

"I don't remember extending any invitations," Theodora replied stiffly.

Miranda was ready to get under the carpet. "Please, let's go," she appealed to Harden, almost frantic to leave.

"You just got here," Evan said shortly. "Come in and sit down, for God's sake."

But Miranda wouldn't budge. Her eyes pleaded with Harden.

He understood without a word being spoken. "All right, little one," he said gently. His hand slid down to take hers in a gesture of quiet comfort. "I'm sorry about this. We'll go."

"Nice to…to have met you," Miranda stammered, ready to run for it.

Harden was furious, and looked it. "Her husband was killed in a car wreck a few months back," he told his mother, watching her face stiffen with surprise. "She lost the baby she was carrying at the same time. I've been seeing her in Chicago, and I wanted her to visit Jacobsville. But considering the reception she just got, I don't imagine she'll miss the introductions."

He turned, his fingers caressing Miranda's, while Evan fumed and Theodora fought tears.

"Oh, no! No, please…!" Theodora spoke in a rush, embarrassed at her unkindness. The younger woman looked as if she'd been whipped, and despite Harden's lack of courtesy in telling her about this visit, she couldn't take it out on an innocent person. It was her own fault that she'd leaped to conclusions.

"I really have to go home," Miranda replied, her red face saying far more than the words. "My job…!"

Harden cursed under his breath. He brought her roughly to his side and held her there, his eyes protective as they went from her bowed head to his mother's tormented face.

"I asked Miranda down here to let her get to know my family and see if she likes it around here," he said with a cold smile. "Because if she does, I'm going to marry her. We can accomplish that without imposing on your hospitality," he told Theodora. "I'm sure the local motel has two rooms to spare."

Miranda looked up into Harden's face. "Don't," she said softly. "Please, don't. I shouldn't have come. Take me to the airport, please. I was wrong to come."

"No, you weren't," Evan said curtly. He glared at Theodora and then at Harden. "Look at her, damn it! Look what you're doing to her!"

Two pairs of eyes saw Miranda's white face, her huge, tragic eyes with their unnatural brightness.

"Evan's right," Theodora said with as much dignity as she could gather. "I'm sorry, Miranda. This isn't your fight."

"Which is why she's leaving," Harden added. He drew Miranda against him and turned her, gently maneuvering her out the door and back to the car.

"Where are you going?" Theodora asked miserably.

"Chicago," Harden said without breaking stride.

"She hasn't met Donald and Jo Ann, or Connal and Pepi," Evan remarked from the porch. He stuck his big hands into his pockets. "Not to mention that she hasn't had time to say hello to the bulls in the barn or learn to ride a horse, or especially, to get to know me. God knows, I'm the flower of the family."

Harden raised his eyebrows. "You?"

Evan glowered at him. "Me. I'm the eldest. After I was born, the rest of you were just an afterthought. You can't improve on perfection."

Miranda managed a smile at the banter. Evan was kind.

Theodora came down the steps and paused in front of her son and the other woman. "I've done this badly, and I'm sorry. You're very welcome in my home, Miranda. I'd like you to stay."

Miranda hesitated, looking up at Harden uncertainly.

"You'll never get to see all my sterling qualities if you leave now," Evan said.

She smiled involuntarily.

"And I just baked a chocolate cake," Theodora added with an unsteady smile. "And made a pot of coffee. You probably didn't have much to eat on the plane."

"We didn't," Miranda confessed. "I was too nervous to eat."

"Not without cause, either, it seems," Harden said with a glare at his mother.

"Cut it out, or we'll go for a walk behind the barn," Evan said with a smile that didn't touch his dark eyes. "Remember the last one?"

"You lost a tooth," Harden said.

"I was thinking about your broken nose," came the easy reply.

"You can't fight," Theodora told them. "Miranda probably already thinks she's been landed in a brawl. We should be able to be civil to each other if we try."

"For a few days, anyway," Evan agreed. "Don't worry, honey, I'll protect you from them," he said in a stage whisper.

She did laugh, then, at the wicked smile on his broad face. She clung to Harden's hand and went back into the house.

Theodora was less brittle after they'd had coffee, but it wasn't until Evan took Harden off to see some new cattle that she really warmed up.

"I'm sorry about all this," she told Miranda earnestly. "Harden…likes to make things difficult for me, you see. I didn't know you were coming with him."

Miranda paled. "He didn't tell you?!"

Theodora grimaced. "Oh, dear. You didn't know, did you? I feel even worse now." She didn't, couldn't add, that she'd thought Miranda was a woman of the streets. That tragic young face was wounded enough without adding insult to injury.

"I'm so sorry… I can get a room in the motel," she began almost frantically.

Theodora laid a gentle hand on her arm. "Don't. Now that Donald and Jo Ann have their own home, like Connal and Pepi, I never have much female company. I'll enjoy having someone to talk to." She studied Miranda's wan face. "Harden's never brought a woman home."

"He feels sorry for me," Miranda said bluntly. "And he wants me." Her thin shoulders rose and fell. "I don't know why he wants to marry me, really, but he's relentless, isn't he? I was on the plane before I knew it."

Theodora smiled. "Yes, he's relentless. And he can be cruel." She drew in a steadying breath. "I can't pretend that he doesn't have a reason for that. I…had an affair. Harden was the result."

"Yes, I know," she replied, her voice gentle. "He told me."

Theodora's eyes widened. "That's a first! I don't think he's ever told anyone else."

"I suppose he isn't on his guard so much with me," Miranda said. "You see, I haven't had much spirit since the accident."

"It must have been terrible for you. You loved your husband?" she asked.

"I was fond of him," Miranda corrected. "And sorry that he had to die the way he did. It's my baby that I miss the most. I wanted him so much!"

"I lost two," Theodora said quietly. "I understand. Time will help."

Miranda's eyes narrowed as she looked at the older woman. "Forgive me, but it's more than just the circumstances of Harden's birth between the two of you, isn't it?" she asked very gently. "There's something more…"

Theodora caught her breath. "You're very perceptive, my dear. Yes, there is something more."

"I don't mean to pry," Miranda said when Theodora hesitated.

"No. It's your right to know. I'm not sure that Harden would ever talk about it." She leaned forward. "There was a girl. They were very much in love, but her parents disapproved. They had planned to elope and get married." Theodora's eyes went dull and sad with the memory. "She called here one night, frantic, begging to speak to Harden." She grimaced. "He'd gone to bed, and I thought they'd had a quarrel or something and it could wait until morning. Harden and I have never been really close, so I knew nothing of their plans to elope, or even that he was honestly in love with her. She seemed to be forever calling at bad times. I was trying to finish up in the kitchen because it was late, and I was tired. I lied. I told her that he didn't want to talk to her at the moment, and I hung up."

Miranda frowned slightly, not understanding.

Theodora looked up. "Her parents had found out about the elopement and were making arrangements to send her to a school in Switzerland to get her away from Harden. I can only guess that having Harden refuse to speak to her, as I made it sound, was the last straw. She walked out onto the second-story balcony of her house and jumped off, to the stone patio below. She died instantly."

Miranda's eyes closed as she pictured how it would have been for Harden after that. He was sensitive, and deep, and to lose someone he'd loved that much because of a thoughtless phone call must have taken all the color out of his world.

"Yes, you understand, don't you?" Theodora asked quietly. "He stayed drunk for weeks afterward." She dabbed at tears. "I've never forgiven myself, either. It was twelve years ago, but it might as well have been yesterday as far as Harden is concerned. That, added to the circumstances of his birth, has made me his worst enemy and turned him against women with a vengeance."

"I'm sorry, for both of you," Miranda said. "It can't have been an easy thing to get over."

Theodora sipped coffee before she spoke. "As you see, Miranda, we all have our crosses," she mused.

"Yes." She picked up her own coffee cup. "Thank you for telling me."

Theodora's eyes narrowed. "Do you love him?"

The younger woman's face flushed, but she didn't look away. "With all my heart," she said. It was the first time she'd admitted it, even to herself.

"Harden is very protective of you," Theodora observed. "And he seems to be serious."

"He wants me very badly," Miranda said. "But whether or not he feels anything else, only he knows. Desire isn't enough, really."

"Love can grow out of it, though. Harden knows how to love. He's just forgotten." Theodora smiled. "Perhaps you can reeducate him."

Miranda smiled back. "Perhaps. You're sure you don't mind if I stay with you? I was serious about the motel."

"I'm very sure, Miranda." Theodora watched the young face relax, and she was glad she hadn't made the situation worse than it was.

Evan and Harden were on their way back to the house before Evan said anything about Miranda's arrival.

"I can't believe you brought her home," he murmured, grinning at his younger brother. "People will faint all over Jacobsville if you get married."

Harden shrugged. "She's young and pretty, and we get along. It's time I married someone." His eyes ran slowly around the property. "Even if there are four of us, we'll need sons to help us keep the place. I'd hate to see it cut up into subdivisions one day."

"So would I." Evan shoved his big hands into his pockets. "Mother thought you were bringing that streetwalker you threatened her with once. Not that I expect you'd know a streetwalker if you saw one," he murmured dryly, "considering your years of celibacy."

Harden let the insinuation go, as he always did, but he frowned. "You didn't tell Theodora who Miranda was?"

"I started to, but there wasn't time." His expression

sobered. "You should have called first. No matter what
vendettas you're conducting against Mother, you owe
her a little common courtesy. Presenting her with a
houseguest and no advance notice is unforgivable."

Harden, surprisingly, agreed. "Yes, I know." He
broke off a twig from the low-hanging limb of one of
the pecan trees as they passed through the small orchard
and toyed with it. "Has Theodora ever talked about my
real father?" he asked suddenly.

CHAPTER EIGHT

EVAN'S EYEBROWS SHOT up and he stopped walking. Harden had never once asked anything about his real father. He hadn't even wanted to know the man's name.

"What brought on that question?" he asked.

Harden frowned. "I don't know. I'm just curious. I'd like to know something about him, that's all."

"You'll have to ask Mother, then," Evan told him. "Because she's the only one who can tell you what you want to know."

He grimaced. "Wouldn't she love that?" he asked darkly.

Evan turned. "She'll die one day," he said shortly. "You're going to have to live with the way you treat her."

Harden looked dangerous for a minute, but his eyes calmed. He stared out over the land. "Yes, I know," he confessed. "But she's got some things to deal with herself."

"I have a simpler philosophy than you," Evan said quietly. "I believe that the day we die is preordained. That being the case, I can accept tragedy a little better than you can. If you think Theodora played God that night, think again. You of all people should know that nobody can interfere if God wants someone to live."

Harden's heart jumped. He scowled, but he didn't speak.

"Hadn't considered that, had you?" Evan asked. "You've been so eaten up with hatred and vengeance that you haven't even thought about God's hand in life. You're the churchgoer, not me. Why don't you try living what you preach? Let's see a little forgiveness, or isn't that what your religion is supposed to be all about?"

He walked ahead of Harden to the house, leaving the other man quiet and thoughtful.

SUPPER THAT EVENING was boisterous. Donald and Jo Ann were live wires, vying with Evan for wisecracks, and they made up for Harden's brooding and Theodora's discomfort.

Donald was shorter and more wiry than his brothers, although he had dark hair and eyes like Evan. Jo Ann was redheaded and blue-eyed, a little doll with a ready smile and a big heart. They took to Miranda at once, and she began to feel more at home by the minute, despite Harden's lack of enthusiasm for the gathering.

After the meal, Harden excused himself and went outside. He didn't ask Miranda to join him, but she did.

He glanced back at her, startled. "I thought you were having the time of your life with the family."

She smiled at his belligerence. It was uncanny, how well she understood him. He was the outsider; he didn't fit in. He was on his guard and frankly jealous of the attention she was getting from the family he pretended he wasn't a part of. She couldn't let on that she knew that, of course.

She moved to join him on the porch swing, where he was lazily smoking a cigarette.

"I like your family very much," she agreed. "But I came here because of you."

He was touched. He hadn't been wrong about her after all. She seemed to know things about him, emotionally, that he couldn't manage to share with her in words.

Hesitantly he slid his free arm around her and drew her close, loving the way she clung, her hand resting warmly over his chest while the swing creaked rhythmically on its chains.

"It's so peaceful here," she said with a sigh.

"Too peaceful for you, city girl?" he teased gently.

She started to tell him about her background, but she decided to keep her secret for a little longer. He had to want her for herself, not just because she could fit in on a ranch. She didn't want to prejudice his decision about marrying her until she was sure of his feelings.

"I travel a good deal. And I'll keep the apartment in Houston. You won't get too bored," he promised her. He stared at her dark head with new possession. "Lift your face, Miranda," he said, his voice soft and deep in the quiet. "I'm going to kiss you."

She obeyed him without conscious thought, waiting for his mouth. It was smoky from the cigarette, and still warm from the coffee he'd had with supper. But most of all, it was slow, and a little rough, and very thorough.

A soft moan broke the silence. She lifted her arms, startled by the onrush of passion that made her desperate for more of him than this.

If she felt it, so did he. The cigarette went over the banister as he lifted her across him, and the kiss went from a slow exploration to a statement of intent in seconds.

She heard him curse under his breath as he fought the buttons of her shirtwaist dress, and then his hand was on her, possessive in its caressing warmth.

"Miranda," he whispered into her mouth. His hand was faintly tremulous where it traced the swollen contours of her breast.

He lifted his head and drew the dress away from her body, but the porch was too dark to suit him. He stood up with Miranda in his arms and moved toward the settee against the wall, where the light from the living room filtered through the curtains onto the porch.

"Where are we going?" Miranda asked, dazed by the force of her own desire.

"Into the light," he said huskily, "I have to see you." He sat down with Miranda in his arms, turning her so that he could see her breasts. "I have to look at you… Yes!"

"Harden?" She barely recognized her own high-pitched voice, so shaken was she by the look on his face.

"You're beautiful, little one," he whispered, meeting her eyes. His hand moved and she shivered. His head bent to her mouth, brushing it tenderly. "Do you have any idea what you do to me?"

"The same thing you do to me, I hope," she whispered. Her body arched helplessly. "Harden," she moaned. "Someone could come out here. Oh, can't we go somewhere…?"

He caught his breath and looked around almost desperately. "Yes." He got up and buttoned her deftly back into her dress, only to catch her hand and lead her along with him. His mind was barely working at all. Nowhere in the house was safe, with that crowd. Neither was the barn, because two calving heifers were in there, being closely watched as they prepared to drop pure-bred calves.

His eyes found his car, and he sighed with resignation as he drew Miranda toward it. He put her inside and climbed in with her, turning her into his arms the instant the door was closed.

"Now," he breathed against her waiting mouth.

He unbuttoned the dress again and found her with his hands, and then with his mouth. Her arms clung to him, loving the newness of being with him like this, of enjoying physical intimacy. She slid her hands inside his shirt and found the hard, hair-roughened warmth of his chest, liking the way he responded to her searching touch.

"Here," he said curtly, unfastening the shirt all the way down. He gathered her to him inside it, pressing her soft breasts into the hard muscles of his chest. He lifted his head and looked down at where they touched, at the contrasts, in the light that glared out of the barn window.

He moved her away just a little, so that he could see the hard tips of her breasts barely touching him, their deep mauve dusky against his tanned skin. His forefinger touched her there, and his blue eyes lifted to her silvery ones when she gasped.

"Why do you...watch me like that?" she whispered.

"I enjoy the way you look when I touch you," he said

softly. "Your eyes glow, like silver in sunlight." His gaze went to her swollen mouth, down her creamy throat to her breasts. "Your body…colors, like your cheeks, when I touch you intimately. Each time is like the first time you've known a man's lovemaking. That's why."

"It's the first time I ever felt like this," she replied. "It always embarrassed me with Tim. I felt…inadequate." She searched his narrow eyes. He looked very sensuous with his shirt unbuttoned and his hair disheveled by her hands. "I've never been embarrassed with you."

"It's natural, isn't it?" he asked quietly. "Like breathing." His forefinger began to trace the hard nipple and she clutched his shirt and shuddered. "Addictive and dangerous," he whispered as his mouth hovered over hers and his touch grew more sensual, more arousing. "Like…loving…"

His mouth covered hers before she could be certain that she'd heard the word at all, and then it was too late to think. She gave him her mouth, all of her body that he wanted, abandoned and passionately in love, totally without shame.

"No, don't!" she wept frantically when he pulled back.

He stilled her hands and drew her close, rocking her against him. He was shivering, too, and his voice was strained. "I hurt, little one," he whispered. "Be still. Let me calm down."

She bit her lower lip until she almost drew blood, trembling in his arms. He whispered to her, soothed her with his voice and his hands until she calmed and lay still against him, trying to breathe.

He let out a long breath. "My God, it's been a long time since I've been that excited by a woman. A few more seconds and I couldn't have pulled back at all."

She nuzzled her face into his hot throat. "Would it be the end of the world if we went all the way?" she whispered boldly.

"No. Probably not. But as my brother Evan reminded me about something else tonight, it's time I started practicing what I preach. I want a ring on your finger before I make love to you completely."

"You're a hopeless Puritan," she murmured dryly.

"Yes, I am," he agreed. He raised his cheek from her dark hair. "And a pretty desperate one. Name a date."

She stared at him worriedly. She was sure. But it was his body that wanted her most, not his heart. "Harden, you have to be sure."

"I'm sure."

"I know how badly you want me," she began, frowning uncertainly. "But there has to be more than just that."

He didn't listen. He was looking down his nose at her with glittery blue eyes. "You can have two weeks to make up your mind."

"And, after that?" she asked slowly.

"After that, I'll pick you up, fly you down to Mexico, and you'll be married before you have time to argue about it."

"That's not fair!" she exclaimed.

"I don't feel fair," he shot back. "My God, I'm alive, really alive, for the first time in my life, and so are you. I'm not going to let you throw this away."

"But what if it's all just physical?" she groaned.

"Then it's still more than four out of five couples have. You'll get used to me. I won't pretend that it's going to be easy, but you will. I'll never lift a hand to you, or do anything to shame you. I won't stifle you as a person. All I'll expect from you is fidelity. And later, perhaps, a child."

"I'd like to have a family," she said quietly. She lowered her eyes. "I suppose sometimes we do get second chances, don't we?"

He'd been thinking the same thing. His fingers touched her cheek, smoothing down to her mouth. "Yes. Sometimes we do, Miranda." He brushed her lips gently with his before he rearranged their disheveled clothing and led her back to the house.

MIRANDA FELT LIKE an actress playing a part for the next few days. Determined to find out if Harden could accept her as he thought she was, she played the city ingenue to the hilt. Leaving the jeans and cotton shirts she'd packed still in their cases, she chose her best dress slacks—white ones, of course—and silk blouses to wear around the ranch. She did her makeup as carefully as if she were going to work. She acted as if she found the cattle smelly and frightening.

"They won't hurt you," Harden said, and it was taking a real effort not to react badly to this side of her. He didn't know what he'd expected, but it wasn't to find her afraid of cattle. That was a bad omen. Worse, she balked when he offered to take her riding.

"I don't like horses," she lied. "I've only been on them once or twice, and it's uncomfortable and scary. Can't we go in the truck?"

Harden had to bite his tongue. "Of course, we can," he said with gentlemanly courtesy. "It doesn't matter."

It did, though, she could tell. She clung to his arm as they walked back from the barn, because she was wearing high heels.

"Honey, don't you have some less dressy slacks and some flat shoes?" he asked after a minute, frowning down at her. "That's really not the rig to wear around here. You'll ruin your pretty things."

She smiled at the consideration and pressed closer. "I don't care. I love being with you."

His arm slid around her, and all his worries about her ability to fit in disappeared like fog in sunlight. "I like being with you, too," he said quietly. He held her against his side, aware of mingled feelings of peace and riotous desire and pleasure as he felt her softness melt into his strength so trustingly.

"It bothers you, doesn't it, that I'm not a country girl?" she asked when they reached the truck.

He frowned. His pale blue eyes searched her gray ones. "It isn't that important," he said stubbornly. "After all, you won't be expected to help me herd cattle or pull calves. We have other common interests."

"Yes. Like walks in the park and science fiction movies and quiet nights at home watching television," she said, grinning up at him.

The frown didn't fade. He couldn't put it into words, but it was a little surprising that a woman who liked the park and loathed parties wouldn't be right at home on a ranch.

He shrugged it off and put her into the cab of the

truck beside him, driving around to where Old Man Red, their prize-winning Santa Gertrudis bull lived in air-conditioned luxury in his own barn.

Miranda had to stifle a gasp of pure pleasure when she saw the enormous animal. He had the most beautiful conformation she'd ever seen, and she'd seen plenty in her childhood and adolescence on her father's South Dakota ranch. She knew Old Man Red's name from the livestock sale papers, from the annual breeders' editions. He was a legend in cattle circles, and here he stood, close enough to touch. His progeny thrived not only in the United States, but in countries around the world.

"He's so big," she said, sighing with unconscious delight.

"Our pride and joy," Harden replied. He reached out and smoothed the animal's muzzle affectionately. "He's been cosseted so much that he's nothing but a big pet these days."

"An expensive one, I'll bet," she said, trying not to give away her own knowledge of his value.

"He is that." He looked down at her. "I thought you didn't like cattle, city girl," he murmured. "Your eyes sure sparkle when you look at him."

She reached up to his ear. "Roast beef," she whispered. "I'm drooling."

"You cannibal!" he burst out, and laughed.

The sound was new, and pleasant. Startled, she laughed, too. "I'm sorry. That was unforgivable, wasn't it?" she mused.

"I'd rather eat my older brother Evan than put a fork to Old Man Red!"

Her eyebrows went up. "Poor Evan!"

"No, poor me," he replied. "He'd probably take weeks of tenderizing just to be digestible."

She slid her fingers into his and followed him down the wide aisle of the barn, happier than she could ever remember being. "Did you grow up here?"

He nodded. "My brothers and I used to play cowboy and Indian."

"You always got to be the Indian," she imagined.

He frowned. "How did you know that?"

"You're stoic," she said simply. "Very dignified and aloof."

"So is Connal. You'll meet him tonight. He's bringing Pepi and the baby over." He hesitated, staring at her expression. "It's going to hurt, isn't it?"

She turned, looking up at him. "Not if you're with me."

His breath caught. She made him feel so necessary. He caught her by the arms and drew her slowly to him, enfolding her. He laid his cheek against her dark hair and the wind blew down the long aisle, bringing the scent of fresh hay and cattle with it.

"I suppose you played with dolls when you were a little girl," he murmured.

"Not really. I liked to—" She stopped dead, because she couldn't admit, just yet, that she was riding in rodeos when she was in grammar school. Winning trophies, too. Thank God Sam had kept those at his house, so Harden hadn't seen them when he came to her apartment.

"You liked to...?" he prompted.

"Play dress-up in mother's best clothes," she invented.

"Girl stuff," he murmured. "I liked Indian leg wrestling and chasing lizards and snakes."

"Yuuck!" she said eloquently.

"Snakes are beneficial," he replied. "They eat the mice that eat up our grain."

"If you say so."

He tilted her face up to his dancing eyes. "Tenderfoot," he accused, but he made it sound like a caress.

"You'd be happier with a country girl, wouldn't you?" she asked softly. "Someone who could ride and liked cattle."

He drew in a slow, even breath and let his eyes wander slowly over the gentle oval of her face. "We don't get to pick and choose the qualities and abilities that make up a person. Your inner qualities are much more important to me than any talent you might have had for horseback riding. You're loyal and honest and compassionate, and in my arms, you burn. That's enough." He scowled. "Am I enough for you, though?"

"What a question!" she exclaimed, touched by the way he'd described her.

"I'm hard and unsociable. I don't go to parties and I don't pull my punches with people. There are times when being alone is like a religion to me. I find it difficult to share things, feelings." His broad shoulders lifted and fell, and he looked briefly worried. "Added to that, I've been down on women for so many years it isn't even funny. You may find me tough going."

She searched his eyes quietly. "You didn't even like me when we first met, but you came after me when you thought I might be suicidal. You looked after me and you never asked for anything." She smiled gently. "Mr. Tremayne, I knew everything I needed to know about you after just twenty-four hours."

He bent and brushed his mouth over her eyelids with breathless tenderness. "What if I fail you?" he whispered.

"What if I fail you?" she replied. She savored the touch of his mouth on her face, keenly aware of the rising tide of heat in her blood as his hands began to move up her back. "I'm a city girl...."

His breath grew unsteady. "I don't care," he said roughly. His mouth began to search for hers, hard and insistent. His hands went to her hips and jerked them up into his. "My God, I don't care what you are!" His mouth crushed down against her parted lips, and his last sane thought was that she was every bit as wild for him as he was for her.

Heated seconds later, she felt his mouth lift and her eyes opened slowly, dazed.

"Harden," she breathed.

His teeth delicately caught her upper lip and traced it. "Did I hurt you?" he whispered.

"No." Her arms linked around his neck and she lay against him heavily, her heartbeat shaking her, her eyes closed.

"We can live in Houston," he said unsteadily. "Maybe someday you'll learn to like the ranch. If you don't, it doesn't matter."

Her mind registered what he was saying, but before she could respond to it, his mouth was on hers again, and she forgot everything....

CONNAL AND HIS WIFE, PEPI, came that night. They brought along their son, Jamie, who immediately became the center of attention.

Pepi didn't know about Miranda's lost baby, because nobody had told her. But she noticed a sad, wistful look on the other woman's face when she looked at the child.

"Something's wrong," she said softly, touching Miranda's thin hand while the men gathered to talk cattle and Theodora was helping Jeanie May in the kitchen. "What is it?"

Miranda told her, finding something gentle and very special in the other woman's brown eyes.

"I'm sorry," Pepi said afterward. "But you'll have other babies. I know you will."

"I hope so," Miranda replied, smiling. Involuntarily her eyes went to Harden.

"Connal says he's never brought a woman home before," Pepi said. "There was something about an engagement years ago, although I never found out exactly what. I know that Harden hates Theodora, and he's taken it out on every woman who came near him. Until now," she added, her big eyes searching Miranda's. "You must be very special to him."

"I hope I am," Miranda said earnestly. "I don't know. It's sort of like a trial period. We're getting to know each other before he decides when we'll get married."

"Oh. So it's like that," Pepi said, grinning.

"He's a bulldozer."

"All the Tremayne brothers are, even Donald, you just ask Jo Ann." Pepi laughed. "I used to be scared to death of Harden myself, but he set me right about Connal once and maybe saved my marriage."

"He can be so intimidating," Miranda agreed. "Evan's the only even-tempered one, from what I see."

"Get Harden to tell you about the time Evan threw one of the cowboys over a fence," Pepi chuckled. "It's an eye-opener. Evan's deep, and not quite what he seems."

"He's friendly, at least," Miranda said.

"If he likes you. I hear he can be very difficult if he doesn't. Don't you love Theodora?"

"Yes, I do," Miranda replied. "We got off to a rocky start. Harden brought me down without warning Theodora first, but she warmed up after we were properly introduced. I'm enjoying it, now."

Pepi frowned. "I thought you didn't like ranch life."

"I'm getting used to it, I think."

"You'll like it better when you learn to ride," the other woman promised. "I hear Harden's going to teach you how."

Miranda's silver eyes opened wide. "He is?" she asked with assumed innocence.

"Yes. You'll enjoy it, I know you will. Horses are terrific."

"So I hear."

"Just never let them know you're afraid of them, and you'll do fine." The baby cried suddenly, and Pepi smiled down at him, her eyes soft with love. "Hungry, little boy?" she asked tenderly. "Miranda, could you hold him while I dig out his bottle?"

"Oh, of course!" came the immediate reply.

Pepi went to heat the bottle, and Miranda sighed over

the tiny laughing face, her own mirroring her utter delight.

She wasn't aware of Harden's stare until he knelt beside her and touched a tiny little hand with one big finger.

"Isn't he beautiful?" Miranda asked, her eyes finding his.

He nodded. His eyes darkened, narrowed. His body burned with sudden need. "Do you want me to give you a child, Miranda?" he asked huskily.

Her face colored. Her lips parted. Her soft eyes searched his and linked with them in the silence that followed.

"Yes," she said unsteadily.

His eyes flashed, glittering down at her. "Then you'd better make up your mind to marry me, hadn't you?"

"Admiring your nephew?" Pepi asked as she joined them, breaking the spell.

"He's the image of Connal," Harden mused.

"Isn't he, though?" Pepi sighed, smiling toward her husband, who returned the look with breathless tenderness.

"Stop that," Harden muttered. "You people have been married over a year."

"It gets better every day," Pepi informed him. She grinned. "You ought to try it."

"I want to, if I could get my intended to agree," he murmured dryly, watching Miranda closely. "She's as slow as molasses about making up her mind."

"And you're impatient," she accused him.

"Can't help it," he replied. "It isn't every day that a

man runs across a girl like you. I don't want Evan to snap you up."

"Did you mention my name?" Evan asked, grinning as he towered over them. "Nice job, Pepi," he said. "Now, how about a niece?"

"Don't rush me," she said. "I'm just getting used to making formula."

"You're a natural. Look at the smile on that little face."

"Why don't you get married and have kids?" Connal asked the eldest Tremayne as he sauntered over to the small group.

Evan's expression closed up. "I told you once, they trample me trying to get to him." He stuck a finger toward Harden.

"They'll have to get past Miranda now, though," Connal replied. "Harden will go on the endangered species list."

"Evan has been on it for years," Harden chuckled. "Except that Anna can't convince him she's serious competition."

"I don't rob cradles," Evan said coldly. His dark eyes glittered, and his usual good nature went into eclipse, giving a glimpse of the formidable man behind the smiling mask.

"Your mother was nineteen when she married, wasn't she?" Pepi asked him.

"That was back in the dark ages."

"You might as well give up," Connal said, sliding a possessive arm around his wife as he smiled down at her. "He's worse than Harden was."

"Meaning that Harden is improving?" Evan asked,

forcing a smile. He studied Harden closely. "You know, he is. He's actually been pleasant since he's been home this time. A nice change," he told Miranda, "from his first few days home from Chicago, when he took rust off old nails with his tongue and caused two wranglers to quit on the spot."

"He was horrible," Connal agreed. "Mother asked if she could go and live with Donald and Jo Ann."

Evan chuckled. "Then she took back the offer because I threatened to load my gun. She's fonder of Harden than she is of the rest of us."

Harden's face went taut. "That's enough."

Evan shrugged. "It's no big family secret that you're her favorite," he reminded the other man. "It's your sweet nature that stole her heart."

Once, Harden would have swung on his brother for that remark. Now, he actually smiled. "She should have hit you harder while she had the chance."

"I grew too fast," Evan said imperturbably.

"Are you sure you've stopped yet?" Connal mused, looking up at the other man.

Evan didn't answer him. His size was his sore spot, and Connal had been away long enough to forget. He turned back to Harden. "Did you ever get in touch with Scarborough about that shipment that got held up in Fort Worth?"

"Yes, I did," Harden said. "It's all ironed out now."

"That's a relief."

The men drifted back to business talk, and Pepi and Miranda played with the baby until Theodora rejoined them. Dinner was on the table shortly, and all the solemnity died out of the occasion. Miranda couldn't remember when she'd enjoyed anything more.

Harden noticed how easily she fit in with his family, and it pleased him. She might not be the ideal ranch wife, but she was special, and he wanted her. They'd have a good marriage. They'd make it work. But one thing he did mean to do, and that was to show Miranda how to ride a horse. Tomorrow, he promised himself. Tomorrow, he was going to ease her onto a tame horse and coax her to ride with him. Once she learned how, she was going to love it. That would get one hurdle out of the way.

The rest would take care of themselves. He watched Miranda with an expression that would have knocked the breath out of her if she'd seen it. The flickering lights in his pale blue eyes were much more than infatuation or physical interest. They were the beginnings of something deep and poignant and real.

CHAPTER NINE

THE NEXT MORNING, Harden knocked on her door earlier than he had since they'd been at the ranch.

"Get up and put on some jeans and boots and a cotton shirt," he called. "If you don't have any, we'll borrow some of Jo Ann's for you—she's about your size."

"I've got some," she called back. "What are you up to?"

"I'm going to teach you to ride. Come on down to the stables when you finish breakfast. I've got to go and get the men started."

"Okay," she called with silent glee. "I'd just love to learn how to ride!"

"Good. Hurry up, honey."

His booted footsteps died away, and Miranda laughed delightedly as she dressed. Now that he was ready to accept the city girl he thought she was, it was time to let him in on the truth. It was, she anticipated, going to be delicious!

It was like going back in time for Miranda, who was right at home in jeans and boots and a red-checked cotton shirt. Harden met her at the stables, where he already had two horses saddled.

"You look cute," he said, grinning at the ponytail. "Almost like a cowgirl."

And you ain't seen nothin' yet, cowboy, she was thinking. "I'm glad I look the part," she said brightly. "What do we do first?"

"First, you learn how to mount. Now, there's nothing to be afraid of," he assured her. "This is the gentlest horse on the place. I'll lead you through the basics. Anyone can learn to ride. All you have to do is pay attention and do what I tell you."

He made it sound as if she'd never seen a horse. Of course, he knew nothing about her past, but still, her pride began to sting as he went through those basics in a faintly condescending tone.

"The hardest part is getting on the horse," he concluded. "But there's nothing to it, once you know how. It'll only take a minute to teach you the right way to do it."

"Oh, I'd love to learn the right way to get on a horse!" she exclaimed with mock enthusiasm. "Uh, would you hold the reins a minute?" she asked with twinkling eyes.

"Sure." He frowned as he took them. "What for?"

"You'll see." She walked away from him, trying not to double up with mischievous laughter as she thought about what she was going to do.

"Got him?" she called when she was several yards away.

"I've got him," he said impatiently. "What in hell do you want me to do with him?"

"Just hold him, while I show you how I've *been* getting on horses." She got her bearings and suddenly took off toward the horse at a dead run. She jumped, balanced briefly on her hands on the horse's rump, and vaulted into the saddle as cleanly and neatly as she'd done it in rodeos years ago.

The look on Harden's face was worth money. Evan had been standing nearby, and he saw it, too, but he didn't look as if he trusted his eyes.

Miranda shook back her ponytail and laughed delightedly. "Gosh, you look strange," she told Harden.

"You didn't tell me you could do that!" he burst out.

She shrugged. "Nothing to it. I took first prizes in barrel racing back in South Dakota, and Dad used to say I was the best horseman he had on the place."

"What place?" he asked explosively.

"His ranch," she replied. She grinned at his shell-shocked expression. "Well, you're the one who said I was a city girl, weren't you?"

Harden's face wavered and broke into the most beautiful smile she'd ever seen. His blue eyes beamed up at her with admiration and pride and something more, something soft and elusive.

"Full of surprises, aren't you?" he asked, laying a lean hand on her thigh.

"I reckon I am," she chuckled. "Got a hat I can borrow?"

"Here." Evan tossed her one, barely concealing a chuckle. "My, my, they must have lots of horses in Chicago. You sure do look experienced at getting on them."

"She's a South Dakota ranch girl," Harden told him dryly. "Nice of her to share that tidbit, wasn't it?"

"Nothing like the element of surprise," Miranda said smugly, putting the oversize hat on. She glowered at

Evan with it covering her ears. "If you'll get me a handle, I can use it for an umbrella."

Evan glared at her. "I do not have a big head."

"Oh, no, of course not," she agreed, flopping the hat back and forth on her head. She grinned at Evan.

"Okay," Evan said. "I'll relent enough to admit that you have a very small head."

"How long have you been riding?" Harden asked her.

"Since I was three," she confessed. "I still go riding in Chicago. I love horses."

"Can you cut cattle?" he persisted.

"If you put me on a trained quarter horse, you bet," she replied. "With all due respect, this rocking horse isn't going to be much good in a herd of cattle."

Harden chuckled. "No, he's not. I'll saddle Dusty for you. Then we'll go work for a while."

"Surprise, surprise," Evan murmured as he joined his brother.

"The biggest hurdle of all was her city upbringing," Harden said with pure glee. "And she turns out to be a cowgirl."

"That lady's one of a kind," Evan mused. "Don't lose her."

"No chance. Not if I have to tie her to the bedpost."

Evan gave him a dry look. "Kinky, are you?"

Harden glared at him and strode off into the barn.

FOR THE NEXT three days, Miranda discovered more in common with Harden than she'd ever imagined. But in the back of her mind, always, was the woman he'd loved and lost. He couldn't be over her if he still held such a bitter grudge against his mother. While his heart was tangled up, he couldn't love anyone else. And if he didn't love her, their marriage would have very little chance of success.

She watched Harden work on one of the purebred mares in foal, fascinated by the tenderness with which he helped the mare through her ordeal. For all his faults, when the chips were down, he was the coolest, most compassionate man she'd ever known. In an emergency, he'd be a good man to have around.

"One more week," he reminded her when he was through with the mare. "Then I'll take the decision right out of your hands."

"You can't force me to marry you," she said stubbornly.

His eyes ran down her body with possession and barely controlled desire. "Watch me."

"I'd have to be out of my mind to marry you," she exploded. "I couldn't call my soul my own!"

He lifted his head and smiled at her arrogantly, his pale eyes glittery. "I'll have you, all the same. And you'll like it."

"You arrogant, unprincipled, overbearing—"

"Save it up, honey," he interrupted, jerking his hat down over one eyebrow. "I've got a man waiting on a cattle deal."

He dropped a hard kiss on her open mouth and left her standing, fuming, behind him.

Harden had given her permission to ride any of his horses except an oversize, bad-tempered stallion named Rocket. Normally, she wouldn't have gone against him.

But he was acting like the Supreme Male, and she didn't like it. She saddled the stallion and took him out, riding hell for leather until she and the horse were too tired to go any farther.

She paused to water him at a small stream, talking to him gently. His reputation was largely undeserved, because he was a gentle horse as long as he had a firm hand. In many ways, he and she were kindred spirits. She'd left behind her unbridled youth, and Tim had made her uncomfortable with her femininity. She'd felt like a thing during most of her marriage, a toy that Tim took off the shelf when he was bored. But with Harden, she felt wild and rebellious. He brought all her buried passions to the surface, and some of them were uncomfortable.

When she glanced at her watch, she was surprised to find how much time had elapsed since she'd taken Rocket out of the barn. At a guess, she was going to be in a lot of trouble when she got back.

Sure enough, Harden was marching around the front of the barn, a cigarette in his hand, his normally lazy stride converted into a quick, impatient pacing. Even the set of his head was dangerous.

Miranda got out of the saddle and led Rocket the rest of the way. Her jeans were splattered with mud, like her boots, and her yellow cotton shirt wasn't much cleaner. Her hair, pinned up in a braid, was untidy. But her face was alive as never before, flushed with exhilaration, her gray eyes bright with challenge and excitement.

Harden turned and stiffened as she approached. Evan

was nearby, probably to save her from him, she thought mischievously.

"Here," she said, handing him the reins. She lifted her face, daring him. "Go ahead. Yell. Shout. Curse. Give me hell."

His face was hard and his eyes were glittery, but he did none of those things. Unexpectedly he jerked her into his arms and stood holding her, a faint tremor in his lean, fit body as he held hers against it.

The action shocked her out of all resistance, because it told her graphically how worried he'd been. The shock of it took the edge off her temper, made her relax against him with pure delight.

"I forgot the time," she said at his ear. "I didn't do it on purpose." She clung to him, her eyes closed. "I'm sorry you were worried."

"How do you know I was?" he asked curtly.

She smiled into his warm neck. "I don't know. But I do." Her arms tightened. "Going to kiss me?" she whispered.

"I'd kiss you blind if my brother wasn't standing ten feet away trying to look invisible. That being the case, it will have to wait." He lifted his head. His face was paler than usual. "Monday, we're getting married. I can't take any more. Either you marry me, or you get out of my life."

She searched his eyes. It would be taking a huge chance. But she'd learned that they were pretty compatible, and she knew he was beginning to feel something besides physical attraction for her. At least, she hoped he was. They got along well together. She knew and enjoyed ranch life, so there wouldn't be much adjustment in that quarter. Anyway, the alternative was going back to Chicago to live with her ghosts and try to live without Harden. She'd tried that once and failed. She wasn't strong enough to try it again. She smiled up at him softly. "Monday, then," she said quietly.

Harden hadn't realized that he'd been holding his breath. He let it out slowly, feeling as if he'd just been handed the key to the world. He looked down at her. "Good enough. But just for the record, honey, if you ever, ever, get on that horse again without permission," he said in a seething undertone, "I'll feed him to you, tail first!"

She lifted her eyebrows. "You and whose army, buster?"

He grinned. He chuckled. He wrapped her up and gave her a bear hug, the first really affectionate gesture of their turbulent relationship.

THEY WERE MARRIED the following Monday. Miranda's brother, Sam, gave her away, and Evan was best man.

Joan, Sam's wife, managed to get a radiant Miranda alone long enough to find out how happy she really was.

"No more looking back," Joan said softly. "Promise?"

"I promise," Miranda replied with a smile. "Thank you. Did I ever just say thank you for all you and Sam have done for me over the years?"

"Twice a week, at least." Joan laughed, and then she sobered. "He's a tiger, that man," she added, nodding toward Harden, who was standing with his brothers and Sam. "Are you sure?"

"I love him," Miranda said simply.

Joan nodded. "Then it will be all right."

But would it, Miranda wondered, when Harden didn't love her.

"What a bunch," Sam said with a grin as he joined them. He put an affectionate arm around his sister. "At least you're no stranger to horses and ranch life," he said. "You'll fit right in here. Happy, kitten?"

"So happy," she assured him with a hug.

"Well, Harden will take care of you," he said. "No doubt about that. But," he added with a level stare, "no more leaping on horses' backs. I'm not sure your new husband's nerves will take it!"

She laughed, delighted that Harden had shared that incident with Sam. It meant that he liked her, anyway. He wanted her, too, and she was nervous despite the intimacy they'd shared. She didn't know if she was going to be enough for him.

Evan added his congratulations, along with the rest of the family. Theodora hugged her warmly and then looked with bitter hopelessness at Harden, who'd hardly spoken to her.

"He'll get over it one day," Miranda said hesitantly.

"Over the facts of his birth, maybe. Over Anita? I don't think he ever will," she added absently, oblivious to the shaken, tragic look that flashed briefly over Miranda's features before she quickly composed them.

Suddenly aware of what she'd said, Theodora turned, flushing. "I can't ever seem to say the right thing, can I?" she asked miserably. "I'm sorry, Miranda, I didn't mean that the way it sounded."

"You don't need to apologize to me," she told the older woman quietly. "I know he doesn't love me. It's all right. I'll try to be a good wife, and there will be children."

Theodora grimaced. Harden joined them, gathering Miranda with easy possessiveness under his arm to kiss her warmly.

"Hello, Mrs. Tremayne," he said softly. "How goes it?"

"I'm fine. How about you?" she asked.

"I'll be better when we get the reception out of the way. I had no idea we were related to so many people," he chuckled. Then he glanced at Theodora, and the laughter faded. "Few of them are related to me, of course," he added cuttingly.

Theodora didn't react. Her sad eyes searched his. "Have a nice honeymoon, Harden. You, too, Miranda." She turned and walked away, ignoring her son's hostility.

Miranda looked up at him worriedly. "You can't keep this up. You're cutting her to pieces."

His eyes narrowed. "Don't interfere," he cautioned quietly. "Theodora is my business."

"I'm your wife," she began.

"Yes. But that doesn't make you my conscience. Let's get this over with." He took her arm and led her into the house, where the caterers were ready for the reception.

The reception was held at the ranch, but Theodora ran interference long enough for the newlyweds to get away.

Connal and Pepi showed up for the wedding, and Miranda found that she and Pepi were fast becoming friends. Connal reminded her a lot of Evan, except that he was leaner and younger. Pepi was an elf, a gentle creature with big eyes. She and Connal had little Jamie Ben Tremayne with them, and he warmed Miranda's heart as he had the night they'd had supper with the rest of the family. But he made her ache for the child she'd lost. That, along with Theodora's faux pas put the only dampers on the day for her, and she carried the faint sadness along on their honeymoon.

They'd decided that Cancun was the best place to go, because they both had a passion for archaeology, and some Mayan ruins were near the hotel they'd booked into. Now, as her memories came back to haunt her, she wished again that she'd waited just a little longer, that she hadn't let Harden coax her into marriage so quickly.

What was done was done, though, and she had to make the best of it.

Harden had watched the joy go out of Miranda at the wedding, and he guessed that it was because of Connal and Pepi's baby. He almost groaned out loud. He should have carried her off and eloped, as he'd threatened. Now it was too late, and she was buried in the grief of the past. As if to emphasize the somber mood that had invaded what should have been a happy time, it began to pour rain.

CHAPTER TEN

MIRANDA HESITATED IN the doorway of their hotel room. It really hadn't occurred to her that they'd be given anything except a room with double beds. But there, dominating the room with its ocean view, was a huge king-size bed.

"We're married," Harden said curtly.

"Yes, of course." She stood aside to let the bellboy bring the luggage in and waited while Harden tipped him and closed the door.

She walked out onto the balcony and looked out over the Gulf of Mexico, all too aware of Harden behind her. She remembered the night at the bridge, and the way he'd rushed to save her. Presumably her action— rather, what he perceived to be a suicide attempt—had brought back unbearable memories for him. Suicide was something he knew all too much about, because the love of his life had died that way. Was it all because of Anita? Was he reliving the affair in his mind, and substituting Miranda? Except this time there was no suicide, there was a marriage and a happy ending. She could have cried.

Harden misattributed her silent brooding to her own bitter memories, so he didn't say anything. He stood beside her, letting the sea air ruffle his hair while he watched people on the beach and sea gulls making dives out of the sky.

He was still wearing the gray suit he'd been married in, and Miranda was wearing a dressy, oyster-colored suit of her own with a pale blue blouse. Her hair, in a chignon, was elegant and sleek. She looked much more like a businesswoman than a bride, a fact that struck Harden forcibly.

"Want to change?" he asked. "We could go swimming or just lay on the beach."

"Yes," she replied. Without looking at him, she opened her suitcase on its rack and drew out a conservative blue one-piece bathing suit and a simple white cover-up.

"I'll change in the bathroom," he said tersely, carrying his white trunks in there and closing the door firmly behind him.

It wasn't, Miranda thought wistfully, the most idyllic start for a honeymoon. She couldn't help remembering that Tim had been wild to get her into bed, though, and how unpleasant and embarrassing it had been for her, in broad daylight. Tim had been selfish and quick, and her memories of her wedding day were bitter.

Harden came back in just as she was gathering up her suntan lotion and dark glasses. In swimming trunks, he was everything Tim hadn't been. She paused with her hand in her suitcase and just stared, taking in the powerful, hair-roughened length of his body, tapering from broad, bronzed shoulders down a heavily muscled chest and stomach to lean hips and long legs. A male model, she thought, should look half as good.

He lifted an eyebrow, trying not to look as self-conscious as that appraisal made him feel. Not that he minded the pure pleasure on her face as she studied him, but it was beginning to have a noticeable effect on his body.

He turned. "Ready to go?" He didn't dare look too long at her in that clingy suit.

She picked up the sunglasses she'd been reaching for. "Yes. Should we take a towel?"

"They'll have them on the beach. If they don't, we'll buy a couple in that drugstore next to the lobby."

She followed him out to the beach. There was a buggy with fresh towels in it, being handed out to hotel patrons as they headed for the small palm umbrellas that dotted the white sand beach.

"The water is the most gorgeous color," she sighed, stretching out on a convenient lounger with her towel under her.

"Part of the attraction," he agreed. He stretched lazily and closed his eyes. "God, I'm tired. Are you?"

"Just a little. Of course, I'm just a young thing myself. Old people like you probably feel the— Oh!"

She laughed as he tumbled her off the lounger onto the sand and pinned her there, his twinkling eyes just above her own. "Old, my foot," he murmured. His gaze fell to her mouth and lingered.

"You can't," she whispered. "It's a public beach."

"Yes, I can," he whispered back, and brought his mouth down over hers.

It was a long, sweet kiss. He drew back finally, his pale eyes quiet and curious on her relaxed face. "You were disturbed when we left the house. Did Theodora say something to you?"

She hesitated. Perhaps it would be as well to get it out into the open, she considered. "Harden," she began, her eyes hesitant as they met his, "Theodora told me about Anita."

His face froze. His eyes seemed to go blank. He lifted himself away from Miranda, and his expression gave away nothing of what he was feeling. Damn Theodora! Damn her for doing that to him, for stabbing him in the back! She had no right to drag up that tragedy on his wedding day. He'd spent years trying to forget; now Miranda was going to remind him of it and bring the anguish back.

He sat down on his lounger and lit a cigarette, leaning back to smoke it and watch the sea. "I suppose it's just as well that you know," he said finally. "But I won't talk about it. You understand?"

"Shutting me out again, Harden?" she asked sadly. "Is our marriage going to be like that, each of us with locked rooms in our hearts where the other can't come?"

"I won't talk about Anita, or about Theodora," he replied evenly. "Make what you like of it." He put on his own sunglasses and closed his eyes, effectively cutting off any further efforts at conversation.

Miranda was shattered. She knew then that she'd made another bad marriage, another big mistake, but it was too late to do anything about it. Now she had to live with it.

THEY HAD A quiet supper in the hotel restaurant much later. Harden was quiet, so was she. Conversation had been held to a minimum ever since they'd been on the beach, and Miranda's sad face was revealing her innermost thoughts.

When they got back to their room, Miranda turned and faced her husband with an expression that almost drove him to a furious outburst. It was so filled with bitter resignation, with determination to perform her wifely duties with stoic courage, that he could have turned the air blue.

"I want a drink," he said icily. "By the time I get back, you should be asleep and safe from any lecherous intentions I might have left. Good night, Mrs. Tremayne," he added contemptuously.

Miranda glared at him. "Thank you for a perfect day," she replied with equal contempt. "If I ever had any doubts about making our marriage work, you've sure set them to rest."

His eyes narrowed and glittered. "Is that a subtle hint that you want me, after all? In that case, let me oblige you."

He moved forward and picked her up unexpectedly, tossing her into the center of the huge bed. He followed her down, covering her with his own body, and unerringly finding her soft mouth with his own.

But she was too hurt to respond, too afraid of what he meant to do. It was like Tim…

She said Tim's name with real fear and Harden's head jerked up, his eyes glazing.

"You're just like him, really, aren't you?" she choked, her eyes filled with bitter tears. "What you want, when you want it, always your way, no matter what the cost to anyone else."

He scowled. She looked so wounded, so alone. He reached down and touched her face, lightly, tracing the hot tears.

"I wouldn't hurt you," he said hesitantly. "Not that way."

"Go ahead, if you want to," she said tiredly, closing her eyes. "I don't care. I know better than to expect love from a man who can't forgive his mother a twelve-year-old tragedy or even the circumstances of his birth. Your mother must have loved your father very much to have risked the shame and humiliation of being pregnant with another man's child at the same time she was married to your stepfather." She opened her eyes, staring up at him. "But you don't know how to love, do you, Harden? Not anymore. All you knew of love is buried with your Anita. There's nothing left in here." She put her hand against his broad chest, where his heart was beating hard and raggedly. "Nothing at all. Only hate."

He jerked back from her hand and got to his feet, glaring down at her.

"Why did you marry me?" she asked sadly, sitting up to stare at him. "Was it pity, or just desire?"

He couldn't answer her. In the beginning, it had been pity. Desire came quickly after that, until she obsessed him. But since she'd been at the ranch, he'd had other feelings, feelings he'd never experienced even with Anita. His hand went to his chest where she'd touched it, absently rubbing the place her hand had rested, as if he could feel the warm imprint.

"You love me, don't you?" he asked unexpectedly.

She flushed, averting her eyes. "Think what you like."

He didn't know what to say, what to do, anymore. It had all seemed so simple. They'd get married and he'd make love to her whenever he liked, and they'd have children. Now it was much more complicated. He remembered the day she'd gone riding, and how black his world had gone until she'd come back. He remembered the terror, the sick fear, and suddenly he knew why. Knew everything.

"Listen," he began quietly. "This has all gone wrong. I think it might be a good idea—"

"If we break it off now?" she concluded mistakenly, her gray eyes staring bravely into his. "Yes, I think you're right. Neither of us is really ready for this kind of commitment yet. You were right when you said it was too soon."

"It isn't that," he said heavily. "And we can't get a divorce on our wedding day."

She gnawed her lower lip. "No. I guess not."

"We'll stay for a couple of days, at least. When we're home...we'll make decisions." He turned, picked up his clothes, and went into the bathroom to dress.

She changed quickly into a simple long cotton gown and got under the covers. She closed her eyes, but she needn't have bothered, because he didn't even look at her as he went out the door.

THE REST OF their stay in Cancun went by quickly, with the two of them being polite to each other and not much more. They went on a day trip to the ruins at Chichen

Itza, wandering around the sprawling Maya ruins with scores of other tourists. The ruins covered four miles, with their widely spread buildings proving that it was a cult center and not just a conventional city. A huge plaza opened out to various religious buildings. The Mayan farmers would journey there for the year's great religious festivals; archaeologists also assumed that markets and council meetings drew the citizens to Chichen Itza.

The two most interesting aspects of the ancient city to Miranda were the observatory and the Sacred Cenote—or sacrificial well.

She stood at its edge and looked down past the underbrush into the murky water and shivered. It was nothing like the mental picture she had, of some small well-like structure. It was a cavernous opening that led down, down into the water, where over a period of many years, an estimated one hundred human beings were sacrificed to appease the gods in time of drought. The pool covered almost an acre, and it was sixty-five feet from its tree-lined edge down limestone cliffs to the water below.

"It gives me the screaming willies," a man beside Miranda remarked. "Imagine all those thousands of virgins being pushed off the cliff into that yucky water. Sacrificing people because of religion. Is that primitive, or what?"

"Ever hear of the Christians and the lions?" Harden drawled.

The man gave him a look and disappeared into the crowd.

If things had been less strained, Miranda might have

corrected that assumption about the numbers, and sex, of the sacrificed Mayans and reminded the tourist that fact and fiction blended in this ancient place. But Harden had inhibited her too much. Sharing her long-standing education in the past of Chichen Itza probably wouldn't have endeared her to the tourist, either. Historical fact had been submerged in favor of Hollywood fiction in so many of the world's places of interest.

Miranda wandered back onto the grassy plaza and stared at the observatory. She knew that despite their infrequent sacrificial urges, the Maya were an intelligent people who had an advanced concept of astronomy and mathematics, and a library that covered the entire history of the Maya. Sadly Spanish missionaries in 1545 burned the books that contained the Maya history. Only three survived to the present day.

Miranda wandered back to the bus. It was a sobering experience to look at the ruins and consider that in 500 B.C. this was a thriving city, where people lived and worshiped and probably never considered that their civilization would ever end. Just like us, she thought philosophically, and shivered. Just like my marriages, both in ruins, both like Chichen Itza.

She was somber back to the hotel, and for the rest of their stay in Cancun. She did things mechanically, and without any real enjoyment. Not that Harden was any more jovial than she was. Probably, she considered, he'd decided that there wasn't much to salvage from their brief relationship. And maybe it was just as well.

When they got back to Jacobsville, Theodora insisted that they stay with her until their own home was ready for occupancy—a matter of barely a week. Neither of them had the heart to announce that their honeymoon had resulted in a coming divorce.

Evan, however, sensed that something was wrong. Their first evening back, he steered Miranda onto the front porch with a determined expression on his swarthy face.

"Okay. What's wrong?" he asked abruptly.

She was taken aback at the sudden question. "W-what?"

"You heard me," he replied. "You both came home looking like death warmed over, and if anything except arguing took place during the whole trip, I'll eat my hat."

"The one that could double as an umbrella?" she asked with a feeble attempt at humor.

"Cut it out. I know Harden. What happened?"

Miranda sighed, giving in. "He's still in love with Anita, that's all, so we decided that we made a mistake and we're going to get it annulled."

He raised an eyebrow. "Annulled?" he emphasized.

She colored. "Yes, well, for a man who seemed to be bristling with desire, he sure changed."

"You do know that he's a virgin?" Evan asked.

She knew her jaw was gaping. She closed her mouth. "He's a what?"

"You didn't know," he murmured. "Well, he'd kill me for telling you, but it's been family gossip for years. He wanted to be a minister, and he's had nothing to do with women since Anita died. A ladies' man, he ain't."

Miranda knew that, but she'd assumed he had some experience. He acted as if he had.

"Are you sure?" she blurted out.

"Of course I'm sure. Look, he's backward and full of hang-ups. It's going to be up to you to make the first move, or you'll end up in divorce court before you know it."

"But, I can't," she groaned.

"Yes, you can. You're a woman. Get some sexy clothes and drive him nuts. Wear perfume, drop handkerchiefs, vamp him. Then get him behind a locked door and let nature take its course. For God's sake, woman, you can't give up on him less than a week after the wedding!"

"He doesn't love me!"

"Make him," he said, his eyes steely and level. "And don't tell me you can't. I saw him when you were late getting back on that killer stallion. I've never seen him so shaken. A man who can feel that kind of fear for a woman can love her."

She hesitated now, lured by the prospect of Harden falling in love with her. "Do you really think he could?"

He smiled. "He isn't as cold as he likes people to think he is. There's a soft core in that man that's been stomped on too many times."

"I guess I could try," she said slowly.

"I guess you could."

She smiled and went back inside, her mind whirling with possibilities.

THE NEXT DAY, Miranda asked Theodora to take her shopping, and she bought the kind of clothes she'd never worn in her life. She had her hair trimmed and styled, and she bought underwear that made her blush.

"Is this a campaign?" Theodora asked on the way home, her dark eyes twinkling.

"I guess it is," she sighed. "Right now, it looks as if he's ready to toss me back into the lake."

"I'm sorry that I mentioned Anita on your wedding day," the older woman said heavily. "I could see the light go out of you. Harden and I may never make our peace, Miranda, but I never meant to put you in the middle."

"I know that." She turned in the seat, readjusting her seat belt. "Does Harden know anything about his real father?"

Theodora smiled. "No. He's never wanted to."

"Would you tell me?"

The older woman's eyes grew misty with remembrance. "He was a captain in the Green Berets, actually," she said. "I met him at a Fourth of July parade, of all things, in Houston while my husband and I were temporarily separated. He was a farm boy from Tennessee, but he had a big heart and he was full of fun. We went everywhere together. He spoiled me, pampered me, fell in love with me. Before I knew it, I was in love with him, desperately in love with him!"

She turned onto the road that led to the ranch, frowning now while Miranda listened, entranced. "Neither of us wanted an affair, but what we felt was much too explosive to… Well, I guess you know about that," she added shyly. "People in love have a hard time controlling their passions. We were no different. He gave me a ring, a beautiful emerald-and-diamond ring that had been his mother's, and I filed for divorce. We were going to be married as soon as the divorce was final.

But he was sent to Vietnam and the first day there, the Viet Cong attacked and he was killed by mortar fire."

"And you discovered you were pregnant," Miranda prompted when the other woman hesitated, her eyes anguished.

"Yes." She shifted behind the wheel. "Abortion was out of the question. I loved Barry so much, more than my own life. I'd have risked anything to have his child. I didn't know what to do. I got sick and couldn't work, and I had nowhere to go when I was asked to leave my apartment for nonpayment of rent. About that time, Jesse, my own husband, came and asked me to come back to the ranch, to end the separation. Evan was very young, and he had a governess for him, but he missed me."

"Did your husband love you?" Miranda asked softly.

"Yes. That made it so much worse, you see, because he was jealous and overpossessive and overprotective—that's why I left him in the first place. But perhaps the experience taught him something, because he never threw the affair up to me. He brought me back home and after the first few weeks, he became involved with my pregnancy. He loved children, you know. It didn't even matter to him that Harden wasn't his own. He never let it matter to anyone else, either. We had a good life. I did my grieving for Barry in secret, and then I fell in love with my husband all over again. But Harden has made sure since Anita's death that I paid for all my old sins. Interesting, that the instrument of my punishment for an illicit affair and an illegitimate child is the child himself."

"I'm sorry," Miranda said. "It can't be easy for you."

"It isn't easy for Harden, either," came the surprising reply. Theodora smiled sadly as they reached the house. "That gets me through it." She looked at Miranda with dark, somber eyes. "He's the image of Barry."

"I wish you could make him listen."

"What's the old saying, 'if wishes were horses, beggars could ride'?" Theodora shook her head. "My dear, we're all walking these days."

Later, like a huntress waiting for her prey to appear, Miranda donned the sexy underwear and the incredibly see-through lemon-yellow gown she'd bought, sprayed herself with perfume, and exhibited herself in a seductive position on the bed in the bedroom they'd been sharing. Harden made sure he didn't come in until she was asleep, and he was gone before she woke in the morning. But tonight, she was waiting for him. If what Evan said, as incredible as it seemed, was true, and Harden was innocent, it was going to be delicious to seduce him. She had to make allowances for his pride, of course, so she couldn't admit that she knew. That made it all the more exciting.

It was a long time before the door swung open and her tired, dust-stained husband came in the door. He paused with his Stetson in his hand and gaped at her where she lay on the bed, on her side, one perfect small breast almost bare.

"Hi, cowboy," she said huskily, and smiled at him. "Long day?"

"What the hell are you dudded up for?" he asked curtly.

She eased off the bed and stood up, so that he could

get a good view of her creamy body under the gauzy fabric of her gown. She stretched, lifting her breasts so that the already hard tips were pushing against the bodice.

"I bought some new clothes, that's all," she murmured drowsily. "Going to have a shower?"

He muttered something under his breath about having one with ice cubes and slammed the bathroom door behind him.

Miranda laughed softly to herself when she heard the shower running. Now if only she could keep her nerve, if only she could dull his senses so that he couldn't resist her. She pulled the hem of the gown up to her thighs and the strap off one rounded shoulder and lay against the pillows, waiting.

He came out, eventually, with a dark green towel secured around his hips. She looked up at him, her eyes slitted, her lips parted invitingly while his eyes slid over her body with anything but a shy, innocent appraisal. The look was so hot, she writhed under it.

"Is this what it took for your late husband?" he asked, his own eyes narrow and almost insulting. "Did you have to dress up to get him interested?"

Her breath caught. She sat up, righting her gown. "Harden…" she began, ready to explain, despite her intention not to.

"Well, I don't need that kind of stimulation when I'm interested," he said, controlling a fiercely subdued rage over her behavior. She must think him impotent, at the least, to go so far to get him into bed. Which only made him more suspicious about her motives.

"You used to be interested," she stammered.

"So I did, before you decided that I needed reforming, before you started interfering in my life. I wanted you. But not anymore, honey, and all those cute tricks you're practicing don't do a damned thing for me."

He pulled her against him, "Can't you tell?"

His lack of interest was so blatant that she turned her eyes away, barely aware that he was pulling clothes out of drawers and closets. Tears blinded her. She hid under the covers and pulled them up to her blushing face, shivering with shame. This had been Tim's favorite weapon, making her feel inadequate, too little a woman to arouse him. Her pride lay on the floor at Harden's feet, and he didn't even care.

"For future reference, I'll do the chasing when I'm interested in sex," he said, glaring down at her white face. "I don't want it with you, not anymore. I told you it was over. You should have listened."

"Yes. I should have," she said hoarsely.

He felt wounded all over. She'd loved him, he knew she had, but she couldn't just be his wife, she had to be a reformer, to harp on his feud with Theodora, to make him seem cruel and selfish. He'd been stinging ever since Cancun, especially since some of those accusations were right on the money. But this was the last straw, this seductive act of hers. He'd had women come on to him all his adult life, their very aggressiveness turning him off. He hadn't expected his own wife to treat him like some casual stud to satisfy her passions. Was she really that desperate for sex?

He turned and went out of the room. It didn't help

that he could hear Miranda crying even through the closed door.

Evan heard it, too, and minutes later he confronted his brother in the barn, where Harden was checking on one of the mares in foal.

The bigger man was taking off his hat as he walked down the wide, wood-chip-shaving-filled aisle between the rows of stalls, his swarthy face set in hard lines, his mouth barely visible as his jaw clenched.

"That does it," he said, and kept coming. "That really does it. That poor woman's had enough from you!"

Harden threw off his own hat and stood, waiting. "Go ahead, throw a punch. You'll get it back, with interest," he replied, his tone lazy, his blue eyes bright with anger.

"She goes shopping and buys all sorts of sexy clothes to turn you on, and then you leave her in tears! Doesn't it matter to you that she was trying to make it easy for you?" he demanded.

Harden frowned. Something wasn't right here. "Easy for me?" he prompted.

Evan sighed angrily. "I wasn't going to tell you, but maybe I'd better. I told her the truth about you," he said shortly.

"About what?"

"You know about what!" Evan growled. "It was her right to know, after all, she's your wife."

"What did you tell her, for God's sake?" Harden raged, at the end of his patience.

"The truth." Evan squared his shoulders and waited for the explosion as he replied, "I told her you were a virgin."

CHAPTER ELEVEN

FOR A MINUTE Harden just stood staring at his brother, looking as if he hadn't heard a word. Then he began to laugh, softly at first, building into a roar of sound that echoed down the long aisle.

"It isn't funny." Evan glowered at him. "My God, it's nothing to be ashamed of. There are plenty of men who are celibate. Priests, for instance…"

Harden laughed louder.

Evan wiped his sleeve across his broad, damp forehead and sighed heavily. "What's so damned funny?"

Harden stopped to get his breath before he answered, and lit a cigarette. He took a deep draw, staring amusedly at his older brother.

"I never bothered to deny it, because it didn't matter. But I ought to deck you for passing that old gossip on to Miranda. I gave her hell upstairs for what she did. I had no idea she was supposed to be helping me through my first time!"

Evan cocked his head, narrowing one eye. "You aren't a virgin?"

Harden didn't answer him. He lifted the cigarette to his mouth. "Is that why she went on that spending spree in town, to buy sexy clothes to vamp me with?"

"Yes. I'm as much help as Mother, I guess," Evan said quietly. "I overheard her telling Miranda that you'd never get over Anita."

Harden frowned. "When?"

"At the reception, before you left on your honeymoon."

Harden groaned and closed his eyes. He turned to the barn wall and hit it soundly with his fist. "Damn the luck!"

"One misunderstanding after another, isn't it?" Evan leaned a broad shoulder against the wall. "Was she right? Are you still in love with Anita?"

"No. Maybe you were right about that. Maybe it was her time, and Mother was just a link in the chain of events."

"My God," Evan exclaimed reverently. "Is that really you talking, or do you just have a fever?" he asked dryly.

Harden glanced up at the lighted window of the room he shared with Miranda. "I've got a fever, all right. And I know just how to get it down."

He left Evan standing and went up to the bedroom, his eyes gleaming with mischief and anticipated pleasure.

But the sight that met him when he opened the door wasn't conducive to pleasure. Miranda was fully dressed in a pretty white silk dress that was even more seductive than the nightgown she'd discarded, and she was packing a suitcase.

She turned a tearstained face to his. "Don't worry, I'm going," she said shortly. "You don't have to throw me off the place."

He closed the door calmly, turned the lock, and tossed his hat onto a chair before he moved toward her.

"You can stop right there," she said warningly. "I'm going home!"

"You are home," he said evenly.

He swept the suitcase, clothes and all, off the bed onto the floor into a littered heap and bent to lift a startled Miranda in his hard arms.

"You put me down!" she raged.

"Anything to oblige, sweetheart." He threw her onto the bed. Her hair was a dark cloud around her flushed face as she stared up at him furiously, her silver eyes flashing at him.

"I've had enough of damned men!" she raged at him. "It was bad enough having Tim tell me I wasn't woman enough to hold a man without having you rub my face in it, too! I have my pride!"

"Pride, and a lot of other faults," he mused. "Bad temper, impatience, interfering in things that don't concern you…"

"What are you, Mr. Sweetness and Light, a pattern for perfect manhood?!"

"Not by a long shot," he said pleasantly, studying her face. "You're a wildcat, Miranda. Everything I ever wanted, even if it did take me a long time to realize it, and to admit it."

"You don't want me," she said, her voice breaking as she tried to speak bravely about it. "You showed me…!"

"I had a cold shower, remember," he whispered, smiling gently. "Here. Feel."

He moved slowly, sensuously, and something predictable and beautiful happened to him, something so blatant that she caught her breath.

"I want you," he said softly. "But it's much, much more than wanting. Do you like poetry, Miranda?" he breathed at her lips, brushing them with maddening leisure as he spoke. "'Shall I compare thee to a summer's day? Thou art more lovely, and more temperate…'" He kissed her slowly, nibbling at her lower lip while she trembled with pleasure. "Shakespeare couldn't have been talking about you, could he, sweetheart? You aren't temperate, even if you are every bit as lovely as a summer's day…!"

The kiss grew rough, and deep, and his lean hands found her hips, grinding them up against his fierce arousal.

"This is how much I want you," he bit off at her lips. "I hope you took vitamins, because you're going to need every bit of strength you've got."

She couldn't even speak. His hands were against her skin, and then his mouth was. She'd never in her wildest dreams imagined some of the ways he touched her, some of the things he whispered while he aroused her. He took her almost effortlessly to a fever pitch of passion and then calmed her and started all over again.

It was the sweetest kind of pleasure to feel him get the fabric away from her hot skin, and then to feel his own hair-roughened body intimately against her own. It was all of heaven to kiss and be kissed, to touch and be touched, to let him pleasure her until she was mindless with need.

"Evan said…you were…a virgin," she whispered, her

voice breaking as she looked, shocked, into the amused indulgence of his face when the tension was unbearable.

He laughed, the sound soft and predatory. "Am I?" he whispered, and pushed down, hard.

She couldn't believe what she was feeling. His face blurred and then vanished, and it was all feverish motion and frantic grasping and sharp, hot pleasure that brought convulsive satisfaction.

She lay in his arms afterward, tears running helplessly down her cheeks while he smoked a cigarette and absently smoothed her disheveled hair. She was still trembling in the aftermath.

"Are you all right, little one?" he asked gently.

"Yes." She laid her wet cheek against his shoulder. "I didn't know," she stammered.

"It's different, every time," he replied quietly. "But sometimes there's a level of pleasure that you can only experience with one certain person." His lips brushed her forehead with breathless tenderness. "It helps if you're in love with them."

"I suppose you couldn't help but know that," she said, her eyes faintly sad. "I always did wear my heart on my sleeve."

He nuzzled her face until she lifted it to his quiet, vivid blue eyes. "I love you," he said quietly. "Didn't you know?"

No, she didn't know. Her breath stopped in her throat and she felt the flush that even reddened her breasts.

"My God," he murmured, watching it spread. "I've never seen a woman blush here." He touched her breasts, very gently.

"Well, now you have, and you can stop throwing your conquests in my face— Oh!"

His mouth stopped the tirade, and he smiled against it. "They weren't conquests, they were educational experiences that made me the perfect specimen of male prowess you see before you."

"Of all the conceited people..." she began.

He touched her, and she gasped, clinging to him. "What was that bit, about being conceited?" he asked.

She moaned and curled into his body, shivering. "Harden!" she cried.

"I'll bet you didn't even know that only one man out of twenty is capable of this...."

The cigarette went into the ashtray and his body covered hers. And he gave her a long and unbearably sweet lesson in rare male endurance that lasted almost until morning.

WHEN SHE WOKE, he was dressed, whistling to himself as he whipped a belt around his lean hips and secured the big silver buckle.

"Awake?" he murmured dryly. He arched an eyebrow as she moved and groaned and winced. "I could stay home and we could make love some more."

She caught her breath, gaping at him. "And your brother thinks you're a virgin!" she burst out.

He shrugged. "We all make mistakes."

"Yes, well the people who write sex manuals could do two chapters on you!" she gasped.

He grinned. "I could return the compliment. Don't get up unless you want to. Having you take to your bed can only reflect favorably on my reputation in the household."

She burst out laughing at the expression on his face. She sat up, letting the covers fall below her bare breasts, and held out her arms.

He dropped into them, kissing her with lazy affection. "I love you," he whispered. "I'm sorry if I was a little too enthusiastic about showing it."

"No more enthusiastic than I was," she murmured softly. She reached up and kissed him back. "I wish you could stay home. I wish I wasn't so…incapacitated."

"Don't sound regretful," he chuckled. "Wasn't it fun getting you that way?"

She clung to him, sighing. "Oh, yes." Her eyes opened and she stared past him at the wall, almost purring as his hands found her silky breasts and caressed them softly. "Harden?"

"What, sweetheart?"

She closed her eyes. "Nothing. Just… I love you."

He smiled, and reached down to kiss her again.

When he went downstairs to have Jeanie May take a tray up to Miranda, Evan grinned like a Cheshire cat.

"Worn her out after only one day? You'd better put some vitamins on that tray and feed her up," he said.

Harden actually grinned back. "I'm working on that."

"I gather everything's going to be all right?"

"No thanks to you," Harden said meaningfully.

Evan's cheeks went ruddy. "I was only trying to help, and how was I to know the truth? My God, you never went around with women, you never brought anybody home… You *could* have been a virgin!"

Harden smiled secretly. "Yes, I could have."

The way he put it made Evan more suspicious than ever. "Are you?" he asked.

"Not anymore," came the dry reply. "Even if I was," he added to further confound the older man. The smile faded. "Where's Theodora?"

"Out feeding her chickens."

He nodded, and went out the back door. He'd said some hard things to Theodora over the years, and Miranda was right about his vendetta. It was time to run up the white flag.

Theodora saw him coming and grimaced, and when he saw that expression, something twisted in his heart.

"Good morning," he said, his hands stuffed into his pockets.

Theodora glanced at him warily. "Good morning," she replied, tossing corn to her small congregation of Rhode Island Reds.

"I thought we might have a talk."

"Why bother?" she asked quietly. "You and Miranda will be in your own place by next week. You won't have to come over here except at Christmas."

He took out a cigarette and lit it, trying to decide how to proceed. It wasn't going to be easy. In all fairness, it shouldn't be, he conceded.

"I...would like to know about my father," he said.

The bowl slid involuntarily from Theodora's hands and scattered the rest of the corn while she stared, white-faced, at Harden. "What?" she asked.

"I want to know about my father," he said tersely.

"Who he was, what he looked like." He hesitated. "How you...felt about him."

"I imagine you know that already," she replied proudly. "Don't you?"

He blew out a cloud of smoke. "Yes. I think I do, now," he agreed. "There's a big difference between love and infatuation. I didn't know, until I met Miranda."

"All the same, I'm sorry about Anita," she said tightly. "I've had to live with it, too, you know."

"Yes." He hesitated. "It...must have been hard for you. Having me, living here." He stared at her, searching for words. "If Miranda and I hadn't married, if I'd given her a child, I know she'd have had it. Cherished it. Loved it, because it would have been a part of me."

Theodora nodded.

"And all the shame, all the taunts and cutting remarks, would have passed right off her because we loved each other so much," he continued. "She'd have raised my child, and what she felt for him would have been...special, because a love like that only happens once for most people."

Theodora averted her eyes, blinded by tears. "If they're lucky," she said huskily.

"I didn't know," he said unsteadily, unconsciously repeating the very words Miranda had said to him the night before. "I never loved...until now."

Theodora couldn't find the words. She turned, finding an equal emotion in Harden's face. She stood there, small and defenseless, and something burst inside him.

He held out his arms. Theodora went into them, crying her heart out against his broad chest, washing away all the bitterness and pain and hurt. She felt something wet against her cheek, where his face rested, and around them the wind blew.

"Mother," he said huskily.

Her thin arms tightened, and she smiled, thanking God for miracles.

LATER, THEY SAT on the front porch and she told him about his father, bringing out a long-hidden album that contained the only precious photographs she had.

"He looks like me," Harden mused, seeing his own face reflected in what, in the photograph, was a much younger one.

"He was like you," she replied. "Brave and loyal and loving. He never shirked his duty, and I loved him with all my heart. I still do. I always will."

"Did your husband know how you felt?"

"Oh, yes," she said simply. "I was too honest to pretend. But he loved children, you see, and my pregnancy brought out all his protective instincts. He loved me the way I loved Barry," she added sadly. "I gave him all I could, and hoped that it would be enough." She brushed at a tear. "He loved you, you know. Even though you weren't blood kin to him, he was crazy about you from the day you were born."

He smiled. "Yes. I remember." He frowned as he looked at his mother. "I'm sorry. I'm so damned sorry."

"You had to find your way," she said. "It took a long time, and you had plenty of sorrow along the way. I knew what you were going through in school, with the other children throwing the facts of your birth up to you. But if I had interfered, I would have made it worse, don't you see? You had to learn to cope. Experience is always the best teacher."

"Even if it doesn't seem so at the time. Yes, I know that now."

"About Anita…"

He took her thin, wrinkled hand in his and held it tightly. "Anita's people would never have let us marry. But even now, I can't really be sure that it was me she wanted, or just someone her parents didn't approve of. She was very young, and high-strung, and her mother died in an asylum. Evan said that if God wants someone to live, they will, despite the odds. I don't know why I never realized that until now."

She smiled gently. "I think Miranda's opened your eyes to a lot of things."

He nodded. "She won't ever forget her husband, or the child she lost. That's a good thing. Our experiences make us the people we are. But the past is just that. She and I will make our own happiness. And there'll be other babies. A lot of them, I hope."

"Oh, that reminds me! Jo Ann's pregnant!"

"Maybe it's the water," Harden said, and smiled at her.

She laughed. The smile faded and her eyes were eloquent. "I love you very much."

"I…love you," he said stiffly. He'd said it more in two days than he'd said it in his life. Probably it would get easier as he went along. Theodora didn't seem to mind, though. She just beamed and after a minute, she turned the page in the old album and started relating other stories about Harden's father.

IT WAS LATE afternoon before Miranda came downstairs, and Evan was trying not to smile as she walked gingerly into the living room where he and Harden were discussing a new land purchase.

"Go ahead, laugh," she dared Evan. "It's all your fault!"

Evan did laugh. "I can't believe that's a complaint, judging by the disgustingly smug look on your husband's face," he mused.

She shook her head, as bright as a new penny as she went into Harden's arms and pressed close.

"No complaints at all," Harden said, sighing. He closed his eyes and laid his cheek against her dark hair. "I just hope I won't die of happiness."

"People have," Evan murmured. But his eyes were sad as he turned away from them. "Well, I'd better get busy. I should be back in time for supper, if this doesn't run late."

"Give Anna my love," Harden replied.

Evan grimaced. "Anna is precocious," he muttered. "Too forward and too outspoken by far for a nineteen-year-old."

"Most of my friends were married by that age," Miranda volunteered.

Evan looked uncomfortable and almost haunted for a minute. "She doesn't even need to be there," he said shortly. "Her mother and I can discuss a land deal without her."

"Is her mother pretty?" Miranda asked. "Maybe she's chaperoning you."

"Her mother is fifty and as thin as a rail," he replied. "Hardly my type."

"What does Anna look like?" Miranda asked, curious now.

"She's voluptuous, to coin a phrase," Harden answered for his taciturn brother. "Blonde and blue-eyed and tall. She's been swimming around Evan for four years, but he won't even give her a look. He's thirty-four, you know. Much too old for a mere child of nineteen."

"That's damned right," he told Harden forcibly. "A man doesn't rob cradles. My God, I've known her since she was a child." He frowned. "Which she still is, of course," he added quickly.

"Go ahead, convince yourself." Harden nodded.

"I don't have to do any convincing!"

"Have a good time."

"I'm going to be discussing land prices," he said, glaring at Harden.

"I used to enjoy that," Harden said, shrugging. "You might, too."

"That will be the day. I…"

"Harden, want a chocolate cake for supper?" Theodora called from the doorway, smiling.

Harden drew Miranda closer and smiled back. "Love one, if it's not too much trouble."

"No trouble at all," she said gently.

"Mother!" he called when she turned, and Evan's eyes popped.

"What?" Theodora asked pleasantly.

"Butter icing?"

She laughed. "That's just what I had in mind!"

Evan's jaw was even with his collar. "My God!" he exclaimed.

Harden looked at him. "Something wrong?"

"You called her Mother!"

"Of course I did, Evan, she's my mother," he replied.

"You've never called her anything except Theodora," Evan explained. "And you smiled at her. You even made sure she wouldn't be put to any extra work making you a cake." He looked at Miranda. "Maybe he's sick."

Miranda looked up at him shyly and blushed. "No, I don't think so."

"I'd have to be weak if I were sick," he explained to Evan, and Miranda made an embarrassed sound and hid her face against his shoulder.

Evan shook his head. "Miracles," he said absently. He shrugged, smiling, and turned toward the door, reaching for his hat as he walked through the hall. "I'll be back by supper."

"Anna's a great cook," Harden reminded him. "You might get invited for supper."

"I won't accept. I told you, damn it, she's too young for me!"

He went out, slamming the door behind him.

Harden led Miranda out the front door and onto the porch, to share the swing with him. "Anna wants to love him, but he won't let her," he explained.

"Why?"

"I'll tell you one dark night," he promised. "But for now, we've got other things to think about. Haven't we?" he added softly.

"Oh, yes." She caught her breath just before he took it away, and she smiled under his hungry kiss.

THE HARSH MEMORIES of the wreck that had almost destroyed Miranda's life faded day by wonderful day, as Miranda and Harden grew closer. Theodora was drawn into the circle of their happiness and the new relationship she enjoyed with Harden lasted even when the newlyweds moved into their own house.

But Miranda's joy was complete weeks later, when she fainted at a family gathering and a white-faced Harden carried her hotfoot to the doctor.

"Nothing to worry about," Dr. Barnes assured them with a grin, after a cursory examination and a few pointed questions. "Nothing at all. A small growth that will come out all by itself—in just about seven months."

They didn't understand at first. And when they did, Miranda could have sworn that Harden's eyes were watery as he hugged her half to death in the doctor's office.

For Miranda, the circle was complete. The old life was a sad memory, and now there was a future of brightness and warmth to look forward to in a family circle that closed around her like gentle arms. She had, she considered as she looked up at her handsome husband, the whole world right here beside her.

* * * * *

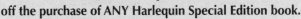

Get 3 FREE REWARDS!

We'll send you 2 FREE Books plus a FREE Mystery Gift.

FREE Value Over $20

Both the **Romance** and **Suspense** collections feature compelling novels written by many of today's bestselling authors.

HARLEQUIN
PLUS

Try the best multimedia
subscription service for romance
readers like you!

Read, Watch and Play.

Experience the easiest way to get
the romance content you crave.

Start your **FREE TRIAL** at
<u>www.harlequinplus.com/freetrial</u>.